the Rake

D1523104

To my brother, who will never read this.
I ran out of people to dedicate my books to, so here we are.

rake, *n.7* - A fashionable or stylish man of dissolute or promiscuous habits.

Author's Note

For the sake of this story, I took creative liberty in how property and holdings are handled by the British Monarchy.

It should be noted that Whitehall and Butchart are not current noble titles.

"Some of the most beautiful things worth having in your life come wrapped in a crown of thorns."

—**Shannon L. Alder**

Boston's most infamous femme fatale meets her match in a dangerously mild Englishman who has vowed to never marry.

Emmabelle Penrose has cruised through life never needing a man, a plan that has worked stunningly well until about five minutes ago, when she decided she must have a baby.

Devon Whitehall is 6'2" of premium DNA, financial security, and British royal titles. Best of all, he fears the one thing she dreads the most: getting hitched.

Emmabelle figures it's a no-brainer when Devon offers his services— sperm and involvement in her future child's life.

What begins as an innocent, modern-family arrangement, quickly erodes into a web of lies, dark pasts, and unfurled secrets.

Inside this chaos, Emmabelle and Devon are forced to face the awful truth—they are capable of love.

Even worse, they might feel it toward each other.

Trigger Warning: this story contains subject matters some may find triggering, including child abuse and grooming.
This book is not meant to make you feel comfortable and fuzzy inside.
Please take this into consideration before starting it.

Playlist

Empara Mi: "Alibi"

Purity Ring: "Obedear"

Rolling Stones: "Under My Thumb"

Young Fathers: "Toy"

Everybody Loves an Outlaw: "Red"

Prologue

Devon

I'D BEEN BETROTHED SHORTLY BEFORE I WAS CONCEIVED.

My future written, sealed, and agreed upon before my mother had her first ultrasound appointment.

Before I had a heart, a pulse, lungs, and a spine. Ideas, wishes, and preferences. When I was no more than an abstract idea.

A future plan.

A box to be ticked off.

Her name was Louisa Butchart.

Lou, really, to those who knew her.

Though I would not be aware of the arrangement until I turned fourteen. Told right before the traditional pre-Christmas hunting trip the Whitehalls had with the Butcharts.

There was nothing wrong with Louisa Butchart. Nothing that I could find, at any rate.

She was lovely, well-mannered, of excellent pedigree.

Nothing wrong with her at all, except for one thing—she wasn't *my* choice.

I suppose this was how it all started.

How I became who I am today.

A fun-loving, whiskey-drinking, fencing, skiing hedonist who answered to no one and tumbled into bed with everyone.

All the numbers and variables were there to create the perfect equation.

Great expectations.

Multiplied by crushing demands.

Morally divided by more money than I could ever burn.

I'd been blessed with the right physique, right bank account, right smirk, and right amount of charm. With only one invisible thing missing—a soul.

The thing about not having a soul was that I wasn't even aware of it.

It took someone special to show me what I'd been missing.

Someone like Emmabelle Penrose.

She cut me open and tar spilled out.

Sticky, dark, and never-ending.

This is the true royal rake's secret.

My blood never ran blue.

It was like my heart, pure black.

Fourteen Years Old.

We rode at sunset.

The hounds led the way. My father and his comrade, Byron Butchart Sr., followed closely. Their horses cantered in perfect rhythm. Byron Jr., Benedict, and I trailed behind.

They gave the young lads the mares. They were unruly and harder to break. Taming young, spirited females was an exercise men of my class had been given from a young age. After all, we were born into a life that required a well-trained wife, pudgy babies, croquet, and alluring mistresses.

Chin and heels down, back ramrod straight, I was the picture of a royal equestrian. Not that it helped me avoid being thrown into the sweat box, curling into myself like a snail.

Papa loved throwing me in there for the sake of watching me squirm, no matter how hard, how diligently, how *desperately* I tried to please him.

The sweat box, also known as the isolation bin, was a seventeenth-century dumbwaiter. It had a coffin-like shape and offered the same experience. Since I was notoriously claustrophobic, this was my father's go-to punishment whenever I misbehaved.

Misbehaving, however, wasn't something I did often, or even at all. That was the sad part. I wanted badly to be accepted. I was a straight A student and a gifted fencer. I'd even made it to the England Youth Championship in sabre, but was still thrown into the dumbwaiter when I lost to George Stanfield.

Perhaps my father always knew what I tried to keep concealed from view.

On the outside, I was perfect.

On the inside, however, I was rotten to the bone.

At fourteen, I'd already slept with two of the servants' daughters, managed to ride my father's favorite horse to its untimely death, and flirted with cocaine and Special K (*not* the cereal).

Now, we were going foxhunting.

I quite hated foxhunting. And by *quite*, I meant a bloody lot. I detested it as a sport, a concept, and a hobby. I drew no pleasure from killing helpless animals.

Father said blood sport was a great English tradition, much like cheese rolling and Morris dancing. Personally, I thought some traditions did not, in fact, age as well as others. Burning heretics at the stake was one example, foxhunting another.

Noteworthy to distinguish foxhunting was—or shall I say *is*—illegal in the United Kingdom. But men of power, I'd come to learn, had a complex and oftentimes tempestuous relationship with the law. They enforced and determined it, yet disregarded it almost completely. My father and Byron Sr. enjoyed foxhunting all the more because it was forbidden to the lower classes. It gave the sport an added shine. An eternal reminder that they were born different. *Better.*

We were heading into the woods, passing the cobbled path to the grand iron-wrought gate of Whitehall Court Castle, my family's estate in Kent. My stomach churned as I thought about what I was about to do. Kill innocent animals to mollify my father.

The soft tapping of Mary Janes clunked behind us, hitting the pebbles.

"Devvie, wait!"

The voice was breathless, needy.

I leaned back on Duchess, pushing my feet forward, pulling at the reins. The mare gaited back. Louisa appeared at my side, clutching something wrapped haphazardly. She was in her pink pajamas. Her teeth were covered in colorful, horrendous braces.

"I got you *thomthing.*" She slapped away pieces of the brown hair sticking to her forehead. Lou was two years my junior. I was at the unfortunate stage of adolescence where I found anything, including sharp objects and certain fruits, sexually appealing. But Lou was still a child. Loose-jointed and pocket-sized. Her eyes were big and inquisitive, drinking in the world in gulps. She was not exactly a looker, with her average features and boyish frame. And her braces gave her a speech impediment she was self-conscious about.

"Lou," I drawled, quirking a brow. "Your mum's going to have a fit if she finds you snuck out."

"Don't care." She rose on her toes, handing me something wrapped in one of her sensible cardigan sweaters. I tossed her jumper, delighted to find my father's engraved flask inside, heavy with bourbon.

"I know you dislike foxhunting, so I brought you thomthing to … how does Daddy say it? *Thake the edge off.*"

The others moved along, entering the thick, mossy woods

bracketing Whitehall Court Castle, either unaware or disinterested in my absence.

"You little nutter." I took a swig from the flask, feeling the sharp burn of the liquid rolling down my throat. "How'd you get your hands on this?"

Lou beamed with pride, cupping her mouth to cover all the metal. "I snuck into your papa's study. No one ever notices me, so I can get away with loads of stuff!" The despondence in her voice made me sad for her. Lou dreamed of going to Australia and becoming a wildlife rescuer, surrounded by kangaroos and koalas. I hoped for her sake that she would. Wild animals, no matter how aggressive, were still superior to humans.

"I notice you."

"Do you really?" Her eyes grew bigger, browner.

"Cross my heart." I scratched behind Duchess' ear. Females, I'd come to realize, were ridiculously easy to please. "You'll never get rid of me."

"I don't want to be rid of you!" she said hotly. "I'll do anything for you."

"Oh, anything, now?" I chuckled. Lou and I had the relationship of an older brother and younger sister. She did things to try and win my affection, and I, in return, assured her she was nice and caring.

She nodded eagerly. "I'll always have your back."

"Right then." I was ready to move along.

"Do you think you'll ever tell your parents you're vegetarian?" she blurted out. How did *she* know this?

"I noticed you shy away from meat and even fish when we dine." She buried one of her Mary Janes in the pebbles, digging her toes in, looking down in embarrassment.

"No." I shook my head, my tone cold. "There are some things my parents don't need to know."

And then, because we had nothing more to say, and maybe because I was afraid Papa would throw me in the dumbwaiter if he saw me loitering behind, I said, "Well, cheers for the drink."

I raised the flask in salute, squeezed Duchess' belly with my riding boots, and joined the others.

"Oh, look, if it isn't Posh Spice." Benedict, Lou's middle brother, poked a finger to loosen the strap of his helmet. "What was the holdback?"

"Lou gave us a good luck charm, Baby Spice." I tipped the flask in his direction. Unlike Louisa, who was a bit eager but overall agreeable, her brothers—for lack of better description—were complete and utter twats. Super-sized bullies who liked to pinch the maids on the arse and make an unnecessary mess just to watch others tidy after them.

"Bloody hell," Byron snorted. "She's pathetic."

"You mean considerate. Spending time with my father requires some level of intoxication," I drawled sarcastically.

"It's not about that. She's obsessed with your sorry arse," Benedict supplied.

"Don't be ridiculous," I growled.

"Don't be blind," Byron barked at me.

"Eh. She'll get over it. They all do." I took another swig, grateful that my father and Byron Sr. were so engrossed in discussing parliament-related matters, they did not see fit to turn their heads and check on us.

"I hope she doesn't," Benedict sneered. "If she is destined to marry your shite for brains, she should at the very least enjoy it."

"Did you say *marry*?" I lowered the flask. He might as well have said *bury*. "No offense to your sister, but if she is awaiting a proposal, she better get comfortable because one is not coming."

Byron and Benedict exchanged looks, grinning conspiratorially. They had the same coloring as Louisa. Fair as the fresh-fallen snow. Only they looked like I drew them with my left hand.

"Don't tell me you don't know." Byron cocked his head, a cruel smile spreading across his face. I never was fond of him. But I *especially* wasn't fond of him at that moment.

"Know what?" I gritted out, loathing that I had to play along to find out what they were talking about.

"You and Lou are going to tie the knot. It's all settled. There's even a ring."

I laughed metallically, kicking Duchess' right side to make her bump into Benedict's mare, throwing him off balance. What a load of rubbish. As I continued laughing, I noticed their smiles had vanished. They were no longer looking at me with playful mischief.

"You're taking the piss." My smile dropped. My throat felt like it was full of sand.

"No," Byron said, flat out.

"Ask your father," Benedict challenged. "It's been decided in our family for years. You're the eldest son of the Marquess of Fitzgrovia. Louisa is the daughter of the Duke of Salisbury. A lady. You will one day become a marquess yourself, and our parents want the royal blood to stay within the family. Keep the estates intact. Marrying a commoner would weaken the chain."

The Whitehalls were one of the last families in peerage people still gave half a fuck about. My great, great, great grandmother, Wilhelmina Whitehall, was the daughter of a king.

"I don't *want* to marry anyone," I said through gritted teeth. Duchess began picking up speed, entering the woods.

"Well, ob-*vi*-ously," Benedict made an unflattering *d'uh* face. "You're fourteen. All you want is to play videogames and fondle your meat to Christie Brinkley posters. Nonetheless, you're marrying our sister. Too much business between our fathers to let this opportunity go to waste."

"And don't forget the estates they'll both get to keep," Byron added helpfully, giving his mare a vicious kick to make her go faster. "I'll say, good luck giving her children. She looks like Ridley Scott's *Alien*."

"Children …?" The only thing preventing me from vomiting up my guts was the fact I did not want to waste the perfectly good brandy currently sloshing in my stomach.

"Lou says she wants five when she grows up," Byron cackled, enjoying himself. "I reckon she's going to keep you busy in the sack, mate."

"Not to mention exhausted," Benedict leered.

"Over my dead body."

My throat grew tight, my hands clammy. I felt like I was the butt of a terrible joke. Of course, I couldn't talk to my father about it. I couldn't stand up to him. Not when I knew I was always one wrong word away from the dumbwaiter.

All I could do was shoot helpless animals and be exactly who he wanted me to be.

His little well-oiled machine. Ready to kill, fuck, or marry as commanded.

Later that night, Byron, Benedict, and I sat in front of one of the dead foxes in the barn. The Pavlovian scent of death swathed around the room. My father and Byron Sr. had taken all their prized dead foxes to the taxidermist and left one for us to dispose.

"Burn it, play with it, leave it for the rats to eat for all I care," my father had spat before turning his back on the corpse.

It was a female. Small, malnourished, and dull-furred.

She had cubs. I could tell by the teats poking through her belly fur. I thought about them. How they were all alone, hungry and stranded in the dark, vast woods. I thought about how I shot her when Papa ordered me to. How I nailed a bullet straight between her eyes. How she stared at me with a mixture of amazement and terror.

And how I looked away because it had been Papa I wanted to shoot.

Benedict, Byron, and I were passing a bottle of champers back and forth, discussing the evening's events, with Frankenfox staring at me accusingly from across the barn. Benedict also obtained rolled-up cigarettes from one of the servants. We puffed on them heartily.

"Come on, mate, marrying our sister isn't the end of the world." Byron offered a Bond-villain laugh as he stood over the fox, one of his boots pressed against her back.

"She's a child," I spat. Strewn on a wooden stool, I felt like my bones were a century old.

"She's not going to be a child forever." Benedict poked the edge of his boot into the fox's gut.

"To me, she will be."

"She'll make you even richer," Byron added.

"No money can buy my freedom."

"None of us were born free!" Benedict thundered, stomping. "What's the incentive to stay alive, if not to gain more power?"

"I don't know what the meaning of life is, but I'm sure as fuck not going to take pointers from a pudgy rich kid who needs to pay the maids to cop a feel," I growled, flashing my teeth. "I'll choose my own bride, and it won't be your sister."

Frankly, I did not want to marry at *all*. For one thing, I was certain I'd be a terrible husband. Lazy, unfaithful, and in all probability obtuse. But I wanted to keep my options open. What if I *did* run into Christie Brinkley? I would marry the shite out of her if it meant getting into her knickers.

Byron and Benedict exchanged puzzled looks. I knew they had no loyalty to their younger sister. She was, after all, a girl. And girls were not as distinguished, not as *important* as boys in peerage society. They couldn't continue the family's name and, therefore, were treated as no more than a decoration you had to remember to include in Christmas card photos.

It was the same with my younger sister, Cecilia. My father largely ignored her existence. I always doted on her after he sent her to her room or tucked her away for being too round or too "dull" to parade around high society. I'd snuck cookies to her, told her bedtime stories, and took her to the woods, where we played.

"Get off your bloody high horse, Whitehall. You're not too good for our sister," Byron moaned.

"That may well be, but I'm not going to sleep with her."

"Why?" Byron demanded. "What's wrong with her?"

"Nothing. Everything." I poked hay around with the tip of my boot. I was fairly drunk by now.

"Would you rather kiss this fox's mouth or Lou's?" Benedict pressed, his eyes wandering around the barn, behind my shoulder, and beyond.

I gave him a wry look. "I'd rather kiss neither, you class-A minger."

"Well, you must choose one."

"Must I?" I hiccupped, picking up a stray horseshoe and throwing it at him. I missed by about a mile. "Why the bloody hell is that?"

"*Because*," Byron uttered slowly, "if you kiss the fox, I'll tell my dad that you're gay. That'd fix everything up. You'd be off the hook."

"Gay," I repeated numbly. "I could be gay."

Not technically, no. I loved women too much. In every shape, form, color, and hairstyle.

Byron laughed. "You sure are pretty enough."

"That's a stereotype," I said and immediately regretted it. I was in no state to explain the word stereotype to these two morons.

"Bleeding heart liberal," Byron cackled, elbowing his brother.

"Maybe he is gay," Benedict mused.

"Nah." Byron shook his head. "He's already shagged a couple birds I know."

"Well? Are you going to do it or not?" Benedict demanded.

I considered the proposal. Benedict and Byron were known for this kind of outrageous ploy. They spun lies around people, and others just bought it. I knew because I went to the same school with them. What was one silly kiss on a dead fox's mouth in the grand scheme of things?

This was my only hope. If I butted heads with my father, one of us would die. As it stood right now, that someone was going to be me.

"Fine." I pushed myself up from the stool, zigzagging my way to Frankenfox.

I bent down and pressed my lips to the fox's mouth. It was gummy and cold and smelled like used dental floss. Bile coated my throat.

"Mate, oh *gawd*. He is actually doing this." Benedict snorted behind my back.

"Why don't I have a camera?" Byron moaned. He was on the floor now, clutching his stomach he was laughing so hard.

I pulled back. My ears were ringing. My vision turned milky. I saw everything through a yellow haze. Someone behind me screamed. I swiveled back quickly, falling to my knees. Lou was there. At the open double doors of the barn, still in her pink pajamas. Her hand pressed against her mouth as she trembled like a leaf.

"You … you … you … *perv!*" she mewed.

"Lou," I grunted. "I'm sorry."

And I was, but not for not wanting to marry her. Only for how she found out about it.

Benedict and Byron were rolling on the hay, punching each other, laughing, and laughing, and laughing.

They'd set me up. They knew she was there, by the door, watching all along. I was never going to get out of this arrangement.

Lou whirled around and bolted. Her tears, like tiny diamonds, flew behind her shoulders.

The scream that tore from her mouth was feral. Like the one Frankenfox had made before I killed her.

I keeled over and threw up, collapsing into the remains of my dinner.

Darkness spun around me.

And I, in return, succumbed to it.

My father handed me a whiskey the morning after. We were in his big oak study with a golden bar trolley and burgundy drapes. One of the servants had hauled me into his office minutes earlier. No explanation was needed. He'd simply dragged me across the carpets and disposed of me at Papa's feet.

"Here. For your hangover."

Papa motioned for the tan leather recliner in front of his desk. I sat, accepting the drink.

"You're giving me *whiskey*?" I sniffed it, my lips curling in distaste.

"Hair of the dog." He sprawled in his executive chair, smoothing his moustache with his fingers. "Taking the hair of the dog that bit you eases up the withdrawal."

I took a swig of the poison, wincing as it scorched its way to my gut. I'd had a sleepless night on the hay in the barn. I kept waking up in a cold sweat, dreaming about tiny Louisa-like babies running after me. The taste of the dead fox's kiss didn't exactly soften the blow either.

The scent of black tea and fresh scones wafted through the hallways of Whitehall Court Castle. Breakfast wasn't quite over. My stomach roiled, reminding me that appetite was a luxury for men who weren't newly and unwittingly betrothed.

I drained my whiskey. "You wanted to see me?"

"I never *want* to see you. Unfortunately, it is a necessity that comes with siring you." Papa did not mince words. "Something quite disturbing was brought to my attention this morning. Lady Louisa told her parents what happened yesterday, and her father relayed to me the situation." My father—tall, lean, and striking with sandy-blond hair and a neatly pressed suit—drawled with accusation in his voice, inviting me to explain myself.

We both knew he disliked me on a personal level. That he would sire new successors, if it wasn't for the fact that I remained the eldest and therefore the heir to his title. I was too graceful, too much of a bookworm, too much like my mum. I'd allowed other boys to dominate me, to make me defile an animal.

"I don't want to marry her."

I expected a slap or a thrashing. Neither would come as a surprise. But what I got was a light chuckle and a shake of his head.

"I understand," he said.

"Do I not have to?" I perked up.

"Oh, you *will* marry the girl. Your wishes have no significance. Neither do your thoughts, for that matter. Marriages of love are for the great unwashed masses. People born to follow society's thankless rules. You shall not desire your wife, Devon. Her purpose is to serve you, sire children, and look lovely. Word to the wise—keep your desire for those of whom you can dispose. It's smarter and cleaner. Commoner rules do not apply to the upper class."

The need to violently smash his head against the wall was so urgent, my fingers twitched in my lap. When I remained silent for several minutes, he rolled his eyes, looking skyward, like I was the one being unreasonable.

"You think I wanted to marry your mother?"

"What's wrong with Mum?" She was pretty and reasonably nice.

"What's not?" He took a cigar out of a box and lit it up. "If she ran as much as her mouth, she'd be in good shape. She was a package deal, though. She had the money. I had the title. We made it work."

I stared into the bottom of my empty whiskey glass. That sounded like a tagline for the most depressing romantic comedy in the world. "We don't need more money, and I'll already have a title."

"It's not just the money, you eejit." He slammed his palm against his desk between us, roaring, "All that stands between us and the commoners that serve us is pedigree and power!"

"Power corrupts," I said curtly.

"The world is corrupt." His lip curled in disgust. I knew bloody well I was close to being thrown into the dumbwaiter. "I'm trying to explain to you in simple English that the matter of your nuptials to Miss Butchart is not up for debate. At any rate, it is hardly going to happen tomorrow."

"No. Not tomorrow and not at all," I heard myself say. "I won't marry her. Mum won't stand for it."

"Your mother has no say in things."

His azure eyes darkened into a marbled mirror. I could see myself in their reflection. I looked small and sunken. Not myself. Not the boy who rode horses with the wind dancing in his face. Who pushed his hand under a servant girl's dress and made her giggle breathlessly. The boy with the explosive speed and dazzling footwork who made some of Europe's best fencers weep. That boy could pierce his father's black heart with a pointy sword and eat his heart while it was still beating. This boy could not.

"You'll marry her, and you will give me a male grandchild, preferably one superior to yourself." My father finished his cigar, stubbing it in a nearby ashtray. "This matter is settled. Now go apologize to Louisa. You will marry her after you finish Oxford University—and not a moment later, or you will lose your entire inheritance, your family name, and the relatives who, for a reason unbeknownst to me, still tolerate you. Because make no mistake, Devon—when I tell your mother she is to disown you, she won't think twice before turning her back on her child. Am I understood?"

My cunningness overtook me just then, as it had the tendency to do, washing over my skin like acid. Making me turn inside out and become someone else. There was no point fighting him. I had no leverage. I could get thrashed, locked, mocked, and tortured … or I could play my cards right.

Do what he and Mr. Butchart did so often. Play the system.

"Yes, sir."

My father narrowed his eyes suspiciously. "I'm telling you to marry Louisa."

"Yes, sir."

"And apologize to her now."

"Certainly, sir." I bowed my head deeper, a ghost of a smile hovering over my lips.

"And *kiss* her. Show her you like her. No tongue or funny business. Just enough to prove you are true to your word."

Bile scorched its way up my throat. "I'll kiss her."

Astonishingly, he looked even less pleased, the tip of his upper lip twisting as he snarled. "What made you change your mind?"

My father was both mean and an idiot, a horrid combination. He had more temper than brains, which led him to make many business mistakes. At home, he reigned with an iron fist that, more often than not, landed on my face. The business mistakes were easier to deal with—my mother had taken over the books without his knowledge, and he was nearly always too drunk to realize. As for my abuse … she knew bloody well that if she tried to protect me, he'd take the belt to her too.

"Suppose you're right." I leaned back in my seat, crossing my legs casually. "What difference does it make who I marry, as long as I can sleep my way into the record books of history?"

He chuckled, the darkness in his eyes melting. This was more his speed. Having a heathen sinner of a son with a deficit of scruples and even fewer positive traits.

"Shagged anyone yet?"

"Yes, sir. At thirteen."

He brushed his thumb under his chin. "I first slept with a woman at twelve."

"Brilliant," I said. Though the idea of my father pounding into a woman from behind at twelve made me want to curl onto a therapist's sofa and not leave for a decade.

"Well then." He slapped his thigh. "Onward and upward, young lad. English aristocracy does not come cheap. One must preserve it in order to maintain it."

"Then I shall do my part, Papa." I stood up, shooting him a sly smirk.

That was the day I truly became a rake.

The day I turned into the crafty, soulless man I now saw when I looked in the mirror.

The day I indeed apologized to Louisa, even kissed her on the cheek, and told her not to worry. That I had been drunk, that it had been a mistake. That we would most *definitely* get married and that it would be a beautiful event. With flower girls and archbishops and a cake taller than a skyscraper.

I played my cards right for the next decade.

Sent her birthday presents, showered her with cards, and met her often during summer breaks. I tucked flowers in her hair and told her all the other girls I'd shagged were meaningless. I let her wait, and pine, and crochet a future for both of us in her head.

I even convinced my parents to fund my Harvard law degree across the pond and postpone the marriage for a couple years, explaining that I would be back as soon as I graduated to take Louisa as my wife.

But the truth was, the day I completed secondary education and was shipped to Boston was the last time I set foot on British soil.

The last time my father saw me.

It was the perfect betrayal, really.

I used his wealth and connections until I didn't need them anymore.

An advanced law degree from an Ivy League school was sufficient capital to bag a 400k a year partnership at one of the biggest law firms in Boston. By my third year, I tripled that amount including bonuses.

And now? Now I was a self-made millionaire.

My life was mine. To lead, to rule, and to cock up.

And the only dumbwaiter I was stuck in was deep in my head.

The voices from my past still echoed inside it, reminding me that love was nothing but a middle-class affliction.

One

Belle

Present Day.

"Uterine malformation," I repeated numbly, staring back at Doctor Bjorn.

I felt ridiculous. In my tight red leather pencil skirt and cropped white shirt, one leg flung over the other, my high-heeled Prada sandals dangling from my toes. Everything about me screamed woman. Everything other than the fact that, apparently, I couldn't have children.

"That's what the ultrasound indicated." My OB-GYN gave me a sympathetic look, somewhere between a flinch and a grimace. "We ordered the MRI to confirm the diagnosis."

It was peculiar that the thing I thought about in that moment wasn't the implication of my condition, but rather how profoundly and oddly hairy Doctor Bjorn was.

Like a Teacup Pomeranian, though not half as cute, he appeared to be in his early sixties, salt and pepper hair covering most of him. From his bushy eyebrows and wild mane to the fluffy tufts on his fingers. His chest hair curled out of his green scrubs, like he was hiding a chia pet.

"Explain to me what it means again. Uterine malformation." I cupped my knee, sending him a lip-glossed smile.

He shifted in his seat, clearing his throat.

"Well, your diagnosis is uterine septum, the most common form of uterine malformation. This is actually good news. We're familiar with it and can treat it in various ways. Your uterus is partially divided by a muscle wall, which puts you at a risk of infertility, repeated miscarriages, and premature birth. You can see it right here."

He pointed at the ultrasound photo between us. I wasn't in the mood to make direct eye contact with my failure of a uterus, but I looked anyway.

"Infertility?" I wasn't in the habit of parroting people's words, but … what the *shit*? *Infertility*! I was barely thirty. I had at least five more years to make gorgeous, memorable mistakes with random men before I needed to think about having babies.

"Correct." Doctor Bjorn nodded, still mesmerized by my lack of emotion. Didn't he know I had none? "Paired with your PCOS, it could be an issue. I am happy to discuss the next steps with you—"

"Wait." I raised a hand, waving my red-tipped French manicure back and forth. "Go back to that abbreviation. PC-what?"

"PCOS. Polycystic ovary syndrome. It says in your file that you were diagnosed at fifteen."

Right. Things were a bit hazy when I got to the hospital that time.

"I'm guessing it's not good either," I deadpanned.

He swiped a thumb on his phone—to me it was a low point in my life, but to him it was just another Wednesday. "It could cause more infertility issues."

Great. My womb gave Monica from *Friends* a run for her money. I wanted to pick a fight. I turned my wrath toward Doctor Bjorn.

"What does it even mean?" I huffed. "Isn't uterine malformation an issue that develops over the course of a pregnancy?"

With another apologetic smile, Doctor Bjorn turned to the screen in front of him and frowned, his bushy eyebrows high-fiving one another. He clicked his mouse to scroll through my medical history. Stupid mouse with stupid-sounding clicks.

"It *does* say here that you had a spontaneous abortion at the age of fifteen."

A *spontaneous abortion.*

Like I decided to go to coffee with a friend.

Doctor Bjorn looked so embarrassed that I was surprised he didn't dig a hole in the carpet and disappear to the bottom floor. His eyes asked me if it was true. His mouth did not. He knew the answer.

"Oops." I smiled grimly. "That's right. Must've forgotten. It was a busy year."

Doctor Bjorn stroked his furry arm. "Look, I know this is overwhelming—"

I let out a throaty laugh. "Please, doc. Spare me the we're-here-for-you leaflet speech and let's get down to business. What are my options?"

"You have plenty of options!" he announced, perking up. *This*, he could work with. Solutions. Facts. Science. "There are ways to ensure your future parenthood. If you are interested in becoming a mother, of course."

I was tempted to say no, I wasn't about the changing diapers or waxing poetic about stick figure drawings life. That motherhood was a force of disempowerment for women in a highly patriarchal society. To some extent, I even *believed* this post-feminist ideology. After all, I was a self-employed business owner whose life ambition was to piss people off. I would smash a pickle jar on the floor and eat it, glass and all, before I'd ask a man to open it for me.

But I couldn't get the words out of my mouth.

The truth was, I *did* want to become a mother. With every fiber of my being.

It wasn't sophisticated or ambitious or noteworthy, but it was true. Which was why a few weeks ago, I had paid my first visit to Doctor Bjorn to ensure my reproductive system was in pristine order and ready to go, whenever I decided to *go for it*. Needless to say, it wasn't.

"Yeah." I shrugged noncommittally. "I am, I guess."

Doctor Bjorn cocked his head and frowned. He tried to decipher why, exactly, I was behaving this way. Like he was trying to sell me solar panels and I was blowing him off. Was I not an environmentalist?

"In that case, the first stage is to freeze your eggs."

I shot him a sweet, impatient smile.

"Are you planning to carry your future children to term?" he asked.

"Can I evacuate them during the second trimester?" I yawned, checking my nails. "Don't babies need to be fully cooked?"

"What I mean is, your age should be one of your considerations. Each passing year, the risk of a miscarriage or a premature birth rises."

"What are you saying, exactly?" I pressed.

"You may want to consider surrogacy if you plan to have children later in life. Ideally, and considering the complications, if you're ready, you should try to get pregnant right away. But ultimately, I don't want you to feel rushed."

A little too late for that, boo. I went from having five years to being tossed onto the highway of motherhood the minute he said that. Because, again—what the shit? This wasn't my life. I was supposed to wait until thirty-five, choose a hunky sperm donor—I was even going to splurge and get the really expensive membership to the sperm bank so I could see pictures of these potential men—then pop out a couple kids and create my own mini family.

"Next month seems like a good time to get pregnant," I heard myself say. "Let me see if I can move my waxing appointment."

"Miss Penrose," Doctor Bjorn chided, standing up to pour me a glass of water. He handed it to me. I gulped it in one go. "I know it's not the news you wanted to hear. You don't have to be brave here. It is okay to be upset."

This, of course, was untrue. Breaking down was a privilege other people had. I was programmed to be fearless. Life threw curveballs at me left and right. I'd glided past them like a cartoon character with a smile on my face.

I picked up my Chanel tote from the floor. "If I need to get pregnant this year, I will. No man? No problem. I'll get a sperm donor. I hear they're tall, smart, and good with numbers. What more can you ask for in a baby daddy?" I let out a metallic laugh, standing up. The OB-GYN remained seated, still staring at me in complete shock.

Yeah, I know. I'm heartless. Emotionless. And, as of five minutes ago, clinically womb-less too.

"Don't you want to think about it?" he asked.

"There's nothing to think about. Time's working against me. I'll get a sperm donor and get it done."

I also didn't have the kind of money it took to use a surrogate. Plus, becoming pregnant was a part of the deal. In the past few years, I'd watched my friends and sister popping out kids like they were PEZ dispensers. Sporting round, beautiful bellies and eccentric cravings and giddy smiles as they mulled over the eternal question: pastel paint or wallpaper for the nurseries?

I wanted all those things.

Every single one of their mundane, trivial experiences.

Other than one.

The *husband.*

Getting married wasn't in my plans.

Men were volatile, untrustworthy, and above all … a danger to me.

"Well, in that case …" Doctor Bjorn reached his hand out for me to shake. "I'm prescribing you with 50 milligrams of Clomiphene. You should take it starting the second day of your menstrual cycle the month you intend to get pregnant. Five pills, one for every day, for five days. To be taken at the same hour. Stay hydrated and watch your cycle. Ovulation tests are going to be your new best friend. When you find your perfect donor, let me know. I want to read through their medical history to see if they're fit for you."

"Wonderful!" I turned around, swaggering my way out of the room, bolting before he managed to sneak in another grave diagnosis about my body.

I waved the receptionist goodbye and got out of the building without any memory of doing so. I guess I was having an out-of-body experience.

I advanced toward my sporty BMW, when my cell phone rang. I fished it out of my handbag. It was my sister, Persy.

"Hey, Pers." I greeted her warmly, no hint of distress in my voice. Pretending I had my shit together was an artform I'd perfected long ago.

"Hey, Belle. Where am I catching you?"

"Just got out of the OB-GYN."

"Nothing like having your insides poked by a complete stranger with a magnifying glass." She sighed with what I suspected was genuine longing. Dang, she and her husband Cillian were kinky. "Everything okay down there?"

I heard my nephew, Astor, making exploding sounds in the background. He loved imagining shit was blowing up when he was playing Legos. That kid was becoming ninety-nine percent tyrant, and I was here for it. Auntie needed brand new ice-breakers and having a dictator nephew was a great conversation topic.

"My vag is in immaculate condition, for someone who is overworked and underpaid." I slid my designer sunglasses up my nose, strutting along the street. "Ya need anything?"

My sister and I spoke at least four times a day, but she didn't normally ask me where I was. Maybe she wanted me to babysit Astor. Now that she had a newborn—baby Quinn, the most handsome little dude on planet Earth—she often needed a helping hand.

"Nope. Mom is coming over to take care of the kids. Cillian is taking me on a date. Our first since Quinn was born. I just had this weird urge to call you to make sure you're okay. I don't know what came over me," my sweet, intuitive baby sister lamented.

Persephone "Persy" Fitzpatrick was everything I wasn't—romantic, maternal, and a rule-follower.

Oh, and the wife of the richest man in America. *No big deal.*

I came to a halt, propping a hand against a red-bricked wall. Salem Street sprawled in front of me in all of its summer glory, sprinkled with bakeries, colorful cafes, and flowers spilling from hung baskets.

"No, Pers. You were exactly right. I needed to hear your voice."

Uneasy silence filled my ears. When Persy realized I wasn't going to elaborate on *why* I needed to hear her voice, she said, "Is there anything I can do for you, Belle? Anything at all?"

Can you have a baby for me?

Can you fix my uterus?

Can you erase my past, which screwed me up so thoroughly, so exhaustively, that I can no longer trust anything or anyone other than myself?

"Just hearing your voice is enough," I smiled.

"Love you, Belle."

"Right back at ya', Pers."

I slipped the phone back into my bag, smiling nonchalantly as though nothing was amiss.

And then … then I felt my cheeks wet with furious, unstoppable tears.

Was I full-blown crying in the middle of a busy main street? You bet your ass I was.

Bawling was more like it. Gasping for air worked too. My tears were bitter and hot, full of self-pity and fresh anger. The unfairness of my situation made my breath catch. Why was this happening? Why *me*? I wasn't a bad person.

Actually, I was a pretty kick-ass one.

I donated to charities and babysat my friends' kids and always bought Girl Scout cookies. Even the lemon-ups—which, let's admit it—were so bad they should have been illegal in all fifty states.

Why was having a child going to be more difficult for me—if it was even *possible*—when everyone around me fell pregnant whenever their husbands so much as asked them to pass the salt?

Dejected, anxious, and confused, I stumbled straight into the temple.

No, not the place where you pray. A place called Temple Bar.

Getting drunk in broad daylight might not be the smart thing to do, but it sure was comforting. Plus, I needed to pregame before going to a party tonight. And I was *definitely* partying tonight.

I pushed the door open, stomped to the bar, and ordered a tall glass of whatever the hell would get me drunk in record time.

"An After Shock and a glass of wine coming right up." The bartender saluted, slapping a polishing cloth over his shoulder and pulling a steam-filled glass from the dishwasher.

I slumped on a barstool, massaging my temples as I tried to process my new reality. It was either have a baby now or pretty much never.

Tourists and professionals lounged in green wooden booths, enjoying pints of Guinness, coddles, and Irish stews.

Irish folk songs belted from the speakers, jolly and full of mirth. Didn't the world know I was hurting?

The place looked like an authentic Irish pub, with ornate high ceilings and liquor-soaked walls.

The bartender came back with my drinks before I could burst into spontaneous tears. I hadn't cried since I was five, maybe six, and I wasn't going to start turning on the waterworks regularly now that I found out I had to get pregnant at thirty while financially insecure.

I downed the After Shock in one go, slamming the glass on the counter and moving straight to the wine.

A tall, dark, and handsome type appeared in my periphery. He propped an elbow against the bar, his body tilted in my direction.

"Aren't you Emmabelle Penrose?"

"Aren't you a middle-aged man with enough life experience to know better than interrupt people when they're trying to get drunk?" I snapped, ready for another round.

He chuckled. "Feisty, just like I thought you'd be. I wanted to say I appreciate your business model. And your ass. Both look great hanging from a billboard in front of my building." He leaned forward, about to whisper in my ear.

I swiveled on my stool, grabbing his wrist in a death grip and twisting it down, rotating his entire arm in the process, on the verge of breaking it. He let out a moan, squeezing his eyes shut.

"What the f—"

It was my turn to lean toward him. "The fuck is I'm trying to enjoy my drink here without getting sexually harassed. Think it'd be too much to ask? My being an owner of a burlesque club doesn't give you permission to try and feel me up. Just like if you were a dentist, it wouldn't give me the authority to lie on your dinner table at a restaurant and ask you to fill my cavity. Now beat it."

I pushed the guy, sending him careening across the bar, back to his stool, spitting out profanity in his wake. He grabbed his coat and stormed out of the bar.

"Whoa. Is your day as bad as the hangover you're going to have tomorrow morning?" The bartender grinned at me impishly. He looked to be in his mid-twenties, with ginger hair and a shamrock tattoo on his forearm.

"My day's worse than any alcohol poisoning recorded on planet Earth." I smacked my wine glass on the bar. "Trust me."

"Do *not* trust her. She's a flighty one." A posh English accent chuckled three stools down. The person it belonged to was shadowed in the depth of the bar, a stain of darkness concealing his elegant silhouette. I didn't have to squint to know who it was.

Only one man in Boston sounded like power, smoke, and an impending orgasm.

Say hello to Devon Whitehall.

Also known as The Bastard Who Broke My Strict One Night Only Rule.

He'd made it to a third hookup before I came to my senses and cut him loose. From the moment we jumped each other's bones about three years ago at my brother-in-law Cillian's cottage in the woods, I knew Devon Whitehall was different.

He was a dangerously mild creature, the scholar out of his group of friends. Manipulative, arrogant, and in a league of his own.

Other men around him had glaring shortcomings—Cillian, my brother-in-law, was a cold fish in a suit; Hunter, my best friend's husband, was loose-tongued and goofy; and Sam, my friend Aisling's husband, was … well, a *mass murderer*. But Devon had no giant neon sign warning you to stay away. He wasn't damaged, or broken, or angry. At least not outwardly. Still, he had that same untouchable quality that made you want to burn like a meteor, which would inevitably, reduce you to nothing but cinders.

He was everything a woman wanted, wrapped into one godlike package.

And that package had a state-of-the-art body, down to the corded, Michelangelo's Moses forearm muscles that made my IQ drop to room temperature whenever I touched them.

I had put a stop to our rendezvous after the third hookup, on the grounds that *I wasn't an idiot*. I always like to say that where there's a willy, there's a way. But in Devon's case, he looked like the kind of dude I could actually catch feelings for.

That hookup, after we had had animalistic sex, Devon turned around, dropped his head on the pillow next to me, and did something outrageous and vulgar. He fell asleep.

"Um, what do you think you're doing?" I'd asked, appalled.

What's next? Taking me to dinner? Matching Minnie and Mickey hoodies? Binge-watching Schitt's Creek together?

"Sleeping," he'd said in his patient, everyone-around-me-is-an-idiot tone. His eyes, blue and silvery like molten ice, blinked open. A devilish smirk formed on his lips. I sat upright, glaring.

"Go sleep in your own bed, bro."

"It's three o'clock in the morning. I have an early court day tomorrow. And please do not use the term 'bro'. Excessive use of common monikers is indicative of poor linguistic culture."

"Cool story, *bro*. Do you have a version of that sentence in English?" And then, because I really was tired, I said, "Never mind. Just get out of here."

"Are you taking the mick?" He wore a blank expression like it was a full-blown tux.

"*Out.*"

I had marched over to the door and tossed out his clothes and loafers. He stumbled out half-naked in my hallway, collecting the designer items from the floor. Truth be told, it wasn't my finest exhibition of character. I was overwhelmed with throat-clogging fear that I would get attached.

Now, Devon was in front of me, all tall and gorgeous and screwable. I caught his frame in the fringe of my sight, hands in pockets, square jaw as sharp as a blade.

"Calling me untrustworthy is libel, Mr. Hot Shot Lawyer." I puckered my lips, slipping into the role of the ball-busting siren. I wasn't in the mood to be quick-witted, eccentric Belle—but that was the only version of me people knew.

"Actually, it is slander. Libel is when the false accusation is written. I could text it to you, if you're so inclined." He turned to the bartender, tossing a black Amex card on the counter. "One Stinger for me, and a Tom Collins for the lady."

"W-why, yes, His Highness." The bartender flustered. "I mean, sir. I mean … what should I call you?"

Devon quirked an eyebrow. "I would honestly prefer if you didn't. You're here to serve me drinks, not hear my life story."

With that, the bartender was off to grab our drinks.

"I don't see a lady anywhere in this vicinity," I mumbled into my glass of chardonnay.

"There's one right behind you, and she is quite fit," he deadpanned, face stoic.

One of the good things about Devon Whitehall (and unfortunately, there were many) was that he never took himself seriously. After I had shamefully banished him from my bed, he had stopped calling me. The next time we'd met, however, at a Christmas party, he had hugged me warmly, asked how I was doing, and even showed interest in investing in my club.

He'd behaved as if nothing happened. And to him I guess nothing had. I didn't know why Devon had never married, but I suspected he suffered from the same relationship-phobia I was prone to. Over the years, I'd watched him parade one woman after another. They were all leggy, stylish, and held degrees in subjects I could hardly pronounce.

They also had the shelf life of an avocado.

Devon never tried to get with me again but remained wryly fond of me, the way you were fond of the childhood blanket you used to snuggle with but would not be caught dead in the same room with it anymore. These days, he made me feel chronically undesirable.

"What's got your knickers in such a twist?" he asked, running his fingers through his thick hair. Streaks of cool wheat and gold.

I wiped my eyes quickly. "Go away, Whitehall."

"Darling girl, your chances of evacuating an Englishman from a bar on a Friday afternoon are slim to none. Any requests I can actually fulfill?" The casual benevolence rolling off of him made me nauseous. No one was supposed to be *that* perfect.

"Die in hell?" I pressed my forehead to the cool bar.

I didn't mean it. Devon had only ever given me good conversation, compliments, and orgasms. But I was really upset.

He slipped onto the stool beside me, flicking his wrist to check his Rolex. I knew he wouldn't answer me. Sometimes, he treated me like an eight-year-old.

Our drinks arrived. He pushed the Tom Collins my way, handing my glass of chardonnay back to the bartender quietly.

"Here, now. This'll make you feel better. And then significantly worse. But since I won't be there to deal with the consequences…" He gave a careless shrug.

I took a sip and shook my head.

"I'm not good company right now. You'd have a better time striking up conversation with the bartender or one of the tourists."

"Darling, you're barely civilized, and still better company than any-one in this zip code." He gave my hand a quick but warm squeeze.

"Why are you nice to me?" I demanded.

"Why not?" Again, he sounded completely at ease.

"I've been nothing but horrible to you in the past."

I thought about the night I threw him out of my apartment, pan-icked that he'd somehow find a crack in my heart, pry it open, and sneak into it. The fact that he was here, pragmatic and unbothered, just proved that he had heartbreak written all over him.

"That's not how I remember our brief but joyous history." He sipped his Stinger.

"I kicked you out."

"My arse had suffered worse." He offered a dismissive flick of his wrist. He had nice hands. He had nice *everything*. "No need to take it personally."

"What *do* you take personally?"

"Not many things in life, to be honest." He frowned, giving it genuine thought. "Corporate taxes, perhaps? It's essentially double-taxation, an outrageous concept, you must admit."

I blinked slowly at him, wondering if I was beginning to see a hint of imperfection in the man everyone looked up to. Under the layers of manners and chiseled looks was, I suspected, a truly odd man.

"You care about taxes, but not that I humiliated you?" I challenged.

"Emmabelle, love." He gave me a smile that would make ice melt. "Humiliation is a feeling. One must submit to it in order to experience it. You've never humiliated me. Was I disappointed that our affair had run its course faster than I had wanted it to? Sure. But it was your right to end things at any given moment. Now tell me what happened," Devon coaxed.

His accent seemed to have a direct line to that place between my legs. He sounded like Benedict Cumberbatch reading an erotic audiobook.

"No."

He studied me coolly, waiting. It annoyed me. How confident he was. How little he spoke, and how much he conveyed with the few words he used.

"What do you want? We're complete strangers." My tone was matter-of-fact.

"I reject that framing." He slid a leaf of mint decorating his glass along his tongue. It disappeared in his mouth. "I know every inch and curve of your body."

"You only know me biblically."

"I'm fond of the Bible. It was quite a good read, don't you reckon? The passages about Sodom and Gomorrah were rather action-packed."

"I prefer fiction."

"Most people do. In fiction, people get what they deserve." He bit down on a smile. "Also, many would argue that the Bible *is* fiction."

"Do you think people get what they deserve in real life?" I asked dejectedly, thinking about Doctor Bjorn's diagnosis.

Devon rubbed a finger over his chin, frowning. "Not always."

He seemed so seasoned, so much older than me at forty-one. I usually went for men who were the complete opposite of Devon. Young, reckless, and unsettled. Guys I knew who wouldn't stick around and would not expect me to either.

Disposable.

Devon had the innate authority of a man who always had the upper hand, that royal male ethos.

"Why'd I even hook up with you?" I blurted out, knowing I was being bratty and taking my anger out on him and allowing myself to do so anyway.

Devon slid the pad of his finger over the rim of his glass. "Because I'm handsome, rich, divine in bed, and would never put a ring on your finger. Exactly what you're after."

It didn't surprise me that Devon had figured I had commitment issues, considering how we had parted ways.

"Also: arrogant, much older, and the designated creepy family friend." I made a cross with my fingers to keep him away, like he was a vampire.

Devon Whitehall was my brother-in-law Cillian's best friend and lawyer. I'd seen him at family functions at least three times a year. Sometimes more.

"I'm no psychologist, but if it smells like daddy issues and walks like daddy issues …" An ice cube slipped between his full lips when he took a sip of his cognac, and he crushed it between his straight white teeth, a smile lingering on his face.

"I don't have daddy issues," I snapped.

"Sure. Neither do I. Now tell me why you were crying."

"Why do you care?" I groaned.

"You're Cillian's sister-in-law. He's like a brother to me."

"If this is the part where you make us sound loosely related, I'm going to throw up in my mouth."

"You'll be doing that tonight, anyway, at the rate you're drinking. Well?"

He wasn't letting it go, was he?

"I'm not giving you an inch, Whitehall."

"Why not? I gave you nine."

Nine inches? Really? No wonder I still had vivid dreams about our hookups.

"For the last time, I'm not going to tell you."

"Very well." He leaned over the bar and plucked a cognac bottle and two clean glasses, slamming them between us. "I'll find out myself."

Two

Devon

An hour earlier.

I WAS SITTING IN WHITEHALL & BAKER LLP's CONFERENCE ROOM, discussing my favorite subject in the entire world, provisions (other P's, like pussy and poker, came at a close second), when my world exploded into miniscule particles.

"Mr. Whitehall? Sir?"

Joanne, my PA, burst through the door, her usually tamed gray curls wild, her reading glasses askew. I looked up from Cillian, Hunter, and the rest of the board of Royal Pipelines.

"As you can see, Jo, I'm in a meeting." Americans were a notoriously uncouth and unnecessarily dramatic bunch, but this was unbecoming.

"It's an emergency, sir."

That, of course, was impossible. Emergencies belonged to other people, with things to lose. I had very little family and a handful of friends. Most of them were currently in the room with me, and if I were honest, I wouldn't lose a limb to save one. Or even a night of full sleep, for that matter.

I lazed in my recliner, tossing my pen on the desk. "What's the matter?"

Panting, Joanne put a hand to her chest, shaking her head.

"It's a phone call," she wheezed. "Personal."

"Who from?"

"Your family."

"Don't have one. Try again."

"Your mother begs to differ."

Mum?

I spoke to my mother twice a week. Once on Saturday morning and then again on Tuesday. Our phone calls were planned by our respective PA's, and we hardly steered away from that arrangement. Naturally, my interest was piqued.

Cillian and Hunter, who sat on either side of me, flashed me curious looks. I'd never whispered a peep to them about my family life. Partly because said family life was a massive shite show. Not that the Fitzpatricks were at risk of winning any Brady Bunch awards, but privacy was crucial to me.

"Tell her I'll call her back." I impaled Cillian with a glare that said, *continue.*

Joanne didn't leave her spot by the door.

"Sorry, Mr. Whitehall, sir. I don't think you understand. You *need* to take this call."

Hunter cracked his neck loudly, rolling it left and right. "Just take the damn call so we can all move on with our daily plans. I have shit to do."

"Daily plans?" I marveled. The man was about as productive as a grave robber in a crematorium. "You can wank in the loo. I have a private one in my office." I frisbeed the key into his hands. The little prat was the best-looking man I'd ever seen outside of a Marvel movie. Fittingly, he also possessed the intellectual capabilities of a torn movie poster. Although it had to be said, marriage agreed with him. I still wouldn't put him in charge of any nuclear research facility, but at the very least, he wasn't a reckless sod anymore.

"Ha." Hunter threw the key back at me. "Go tend to your business before my fist tends to your face."

"I can't believe I'm saying this, but Hunter's right," Cillian drawled, dripping boredom. "Get it over with. Some of us have responsibilities that stretch beyond choosing who to sleep with tonight."

It was pointless to tell them I'd already chosen Allison Kosinki. She was expected at my flat at eight-thirty.

"*Go!*" they roared in unison.

With a healthy dose of irritation, I followed Joanne's hurried footsteps to my office.

"How're the kids, Jo?"

"Very well, thank you, Your Honor. I mean, Your Highness…" People always got flustered around a royal. Even if they worked with them on a daily basis. "Are you well?"

"Indeed I am."

"Good. Just remember we're here for you."

Uh-huh. No good news was ever received after "we're here for you."

Joanne opened the door for me then scurried back to her station, avoiding eye contact.

I glared at the switchboard for a beat.

Someone had better be terribly injured, or even better—dead.

I grabbed the receiver but didn't say anything. I waited for Mum to make the first move.

"Devvie? Are you there?"

"Mummy." The term of endearment wasn't my favorite—it made me sound like a four-year-old—but posh people, unfortunately, oftentimes spoke like they were still in diapers.

"Oh, Devvie. I am devastated! Are you sitting down?"

Still on my feet, I looked around my office, which was designed in an old-fashioned manner—coffered ceiling, built-in cabinetry, a large executive desk. "Yes."

"Papa passed away tonight."

I waited to feel something—*anything*—in light of the news that my father kicked the bucket. But for the life of me, I couldn't.

Edwin Whitehall had spent the majority of my childhood reminding me that I wasn't enough. He left me no choice but to run away from my homeland, my country, and denied me the most basic privilege of all—choosing my own wife.

No part of me mourned his death, and even if I'd kept a close relationship with Mum and Cecilia, he'd refused to see me until I married Louisa Butchart, to which I responded, *don't threaten me with a good time.*

I'd been having a ball since.

"That's terrible," I said flatly. "Are you okay?"

"I'm…" she sniffed "…f-f-fine."

She did not, in fact, sound fine.

"Was it sudden?" I leaned a hip against my desk, tucking a hand into the front pocket of my slacks. I knew it was. Mum made a point of telling me all about his golfing and hunting.

"Yes. Heart attack. I woke up this morning and he was next to me, unresponsive."

"Why, yes, but when did you find out that he was dead?" I murmured under my breath. Thankfully, she didn't hear me.

"I simply cannot wrap my head around it." She broke into another bout of tears. "Papa—gone!"

"Terrible," I repeated numbly, feeling quiet, unabashed glee. The world wasn't big enough for both me and Edwin.

"He wanted to see you badly," Mum whimpered. "Especially the last few years."

I knew that to be true. Not because he had missed me, god forbid, but because I was the de facto heir to the properties, monies, and his marquess title. Everything the Whitehalls valued and stood for lay at my feet, and he wanted to make sure I wouldn't kick it to the curb.

"My condolences, Mummy," I said now, with all the sincerity of a used car salesman.

"Will you be attending the funeral?"

"When is it?" I asked.

"Next week."

"Bloody hell." I pretended to sound devastated. "Not sure I can make it. I have merger meetings back-to-back. But I'm certainly going to come there and support you as soon as I can."

Mum and Cece had been visiting me twice a year since I'd moved to the States. I always showed them a good time, showered them with gifts, and made sure they were happy. But going back to England to show Edwin respect was one moral error I would not be able to live with.

"You'll have to come here at some point, Devon." Her tenor hardened. "Not only for the reading of the will, but as you well know, Whitehall Court Castle is now legally yours. Not to mention, now that Edwin is dead, you are officially a marquess. The most sought after bachelor in England."

Most sought after bachelor in England, my foot. Marrying into a royal family was only marginally worse than marrying into the mafia. At least Carmella Soprano didn't have to deal with The Daily Mail photographers taking pictures of her bin's content.

"I'll arrive to ensure the smooth transition of the estate and funds," I said. "And, of course, to be there for you and Cece. How's she handling it?"

"Not well."

My mother lived in the Whitehall Court Castle and so did my sister Cecilia and her husband, Drew. I intended to hand over the castle to them—I was never going to live in the bloody thing, anyway—and allot them a monthly allowance to keep them comfortable.

"I'll get there as soon as I can." Which, for the record, would still be too soon.

The last time I'd seen my mother was a year ago. I wondered what she looked like these days. Was she still tragically beautiful, draped head-to-toe in black silks? Did she maintain the habit of an afternoon cuppa with her lady friends, where she allowed herself half a shortbread cookie she'd later burn off on the treadmill?

"It's been over twenty years," she said.

"I can count, Mummy."

"And although we've seen each other often … it's not the same when you're not here."

"I know that too. And I'm sorry I had to go away." I wasn't. Boston suited me fine. It was culturally diverse, inherently rough, and drenched in history, much like London. But without the paparazzi chasing after me or upper-class aunties throwing their daughters at my doorstep hoping I'd make one of them my lawful wife.

"Are you seeing anyone?" Mum sounded like a crushed widow like I sounded like Celine Dion. It must be the shock, I thought.

"Some*ones*. Plural. I am, as you're well-informed by your friends across the pond, a well-established rake."

This part was true. I loved women. I loved them even more without their clothes. And I made it a point to go through them like they were the morning paper—one time was enough, and they needed to be exchanged daily.

"So was your father, until a certain point," Mum mused.

I picked up a wooden humidor, turning it in my hand. "That point was not after he'd gotten married, so don't mourn him too hard."

She whimpered in protest but changed the subject, knowing it was too late to convince me my father was anything but a monster. "Louisa is single again. You must've heard."

"I mustn't have." I put the humidor back on the desk, as the scent of aged tobacco leaves and amber musk filled my nostrils.

Louisa was my least favorite topic to talk about with Mum, even though she came up quite often. I was highly tempted to curl the cord of the switchboard around my neck and tug. "I don't keep tabs on anyone from home."

"The fact that you still call it home speaks volumes."

I chuckled softly. "Hope is like ice cream. The more you indulge in it, the more sickened you get."

"Well," she said brightly, refusing to admit defeat, "Louisa is, indeed, single. Lost her fiancé to a polo accident a year ago. It was quite dreadful. There were children watching the game."

"Goodness," I agreed. "Polo is boring for the average adult, let alone to children. How atrocious."

"Oh, Devvie!" Mum chided. "She was gutted when it happened, but now … well, I almost think it is fate, isn't it?" Mum sniffed.

Did this woman just find the silver lining in a man meeting his premature death in a violent, *public* accident? Ladies and gents, my mother, Ursula Whitehall.

"I'm glad you see the positive in the two deaths that'd bring Louisa and I back to the same post code," I said with a slight smile.

"She's been waiting for you, not so patiently."

"Color me skeptical."

"You can see for yourself when you get here. You owe her, at the very least, a proper apology."

This was one truth I couldn't escape. Before I got on a plane to Boston at eighteen, I had told Louisa I was coming back for her. That never happened, though she'd waited patiently the first four years, sending me print-outs of wedding gowns and customized rings. At some point, the poor lass realized our engagement would not be fulfilled and moved on. But it took her about a decade or two.

I owed her an apology, and was going to deliver one, but to think I owed her a whole entire marriage was preposterous.

"You know," my mother said, dropping her voice down an octave conspiratorially, "it was your father's last wish that you marry Louisa."

You know, I wanted to say, in the exact same tone, *I could not give one single toss.*

"While I sympathize with your pain, I find it extremely hard to make concessions for Edwin. Especially now, when he is not around to appreciate them," I said mildly.

"You need to settle down, my love. To have your own family."

"Not going to happen."

But Ursula Whitehall did not let a measly thing such as reality stand in her way of a good speech. I could practically envision her stepping onto the soapbox.

"I hear about you all the time from acquaintances on the East Coast.

They say you're sharp, astute, and never let a good opportunity go to waste.

"They *also* say that your personal life is in shambles. That you spend your nights gambling at that heathen Sam Brennan's joint, drinking, and keeping company with ditzy women half your age."

The first accusation was spot-on. The last one, however, was a plain lie. I had a strict five-year maximum in place. I'd take lovers five years younger or older. In fact, I had only broken the rule once, with the delightfully infuriating Emmabelle Penrose. For all my faults, I was not a sleazeball. There was nothing quite as pathetic as walking around with a woman who could be mistaken for your daughter. Thankfully, no one in their right mind would have thought I'd let my daughter dress like Emmabelle Penrose.

"I understand that you're upset, Mummy, but I am not going to be talked into marriage."

Through the vast glass door, I could see Cillian, Hunter, and the rest of Royal Pipelines' board trickling out of the conference room. Hunter flipped me the bird on his way out while Cillian offered me a curt, speak-later nod.

This phone call had put me an hour behind schedule. It was more time than I'd given my father in three decades. I was going to send him a hefty bill straight to hell. Meanwhile, Mum continued to drone on.

"…out of touch with your roots, with your lineage. I suspect a lot of things will resurface once you make it back home. I could send in the private jet if you like."

The private jet belonged to the Butcharts, not the Whitehalls, and I knew better than to take favors from people I had no intention of being indebted to.

"No need. I'll fly commercial, with the other peasants."

"First class is so common, unless it's Singapore Airlines." If there was something that could distract my mother from the fact she just became a widow, it was discussing wealth.

"I fly business," I said sardonically. "Brushing shoulders with honest-to-god average people."

I knew that for my mother, flying business class was akin to making the journey on a paper boat while surviving exclusively on raw ocean fish and sunrays.

"Oh, Devvie, I do hate that for you." I could practically envision her clutching her pearls. "When shall we expect you?"

"I'll be in touch in the next few days."

"Please hurry up. We miss you so."

"I miss you too."

When we hung up, it felt like my flesh had been ripped open.

I might have missed my mother and sister.

But I did not miss Whitehall Court Castle.

I took the rest of the day off. Contrary to general belief, I was not married to my work. In fact, I wasn't even engaged to it. I had a casual relationship with the firm I'd incorporated and used every chance I could to spend time out of the office.

Losing a father, even if I'd forgotten what he looked like, was a brilliant excuse to take time off.

Clouds glided lazily overhead, curiously watching to see what my next move would be. Not one to keep nature waiting, I wandered into Temple Bar, an Irish pub down the street from my office. I was sitting at the bar when Emmabelle Penrose burst through the sticky wooden doors, tears streaming down her face, looking like a train wreck seconds after a colossal explosion.

Emmabelle was the most beautiful woman on planet Earth. It was not an exaggeration, but a plain fact. Her hair, long and luscious, looked like it drank in every sunray it had been exposed to, falling in strings of different shades of blond. Her feline eyes, the color of a blueberry slushie, were perpetually hooded. Her lips were bee-stung, puffy like she'd just been kissed savagely.

And that was without even talking about her body, which I was inclined to suspect might cause a Third World War one day.

She was young. Eleven years younger than me. The first time I'd seen her, three years ago, when I'd gone to serve her younger sister, Persy, with Cillian's prenup papers, I caught a glimpse of her asleep and spent the next month fantasizing about conquering the fair-haired nymph's bed.

What made Belle even more enticing was the fact that she, like me, rejected marriage as an institution and treated her romantic affairs with the same practicality she would her finances. I found her fire, intellect, and nonconformist ways refreshing. What I did *not* find refreshing was the way she'd kicked me out of her apartment in the middle of the night shortly after we started sleeping together.

Miss Penrose could be Aphrodite herself, rising from seafoam on the Cypress shore, but I was still a man of self-respect and social standing.

I forgave, but I did not forget.

Though now that I took a good long look at her, she looked a bit … *frayed*?

Like she was on the verge of bawling into her glass of chardonnay.

A man came on to her not even a second after she walked into the bar, and I sat in the corner, watching her nearly snap his arm in two, chuckling to myself.

But with the amusement came a rather exasperating sense of responsibility gnawing at my gut. No matter how unappealing I found the idea of helping out this bratty vixen, I knew Cillian's wife and Belle's sister, Persy, would put me through all of Dante's nine circles of hell if she found out I'd simply ignored her.

Plus, Emmabelle was not the type to self-indulge in a full-fledged mental breakdown over a broken fingernail. As a lawyer, I'd always been anthropologically curious. What could make this tough-as-nails woman crumble?

I approached her, showered her with compliments and reassurance, and tried coaxing the information out of her. Belle refused to cooperate, like I knew she would. The girl was thornier than a rose garden—and just as beautiful.

I decided to loosen Belle's tongue through the international, unofficial truth serum. Alcohol.

It was after the third cognac that she turned to look at me, her big turquoise eyes aglow, and said, "I have to get pregnant immediately if I want to have a biological child."

"You're thirty," I said, still sipping the same Stinger I started the evening with. "You have plenty of time."

"No." Belle shook her head furiously, hiccupping. I suppose today was the day of hysterical females. I couldn't seem to escape them. "I have a … medical condition. It needs to happen sooner rather than later. But I don't have anyone to have it with. *Or the financial stability."*

A practical, albeit sick idea began forming in my mind. A two-birds-one-stone situation.

"The father part is not a big deal." Belle snuffled, about to take another sip of her drink. I pried it out of her hand and placed a tall glass of water there instead. If she had fertility issues, becoming an alcoholic was not a step in the right direction. "I could always get a sperm donor. But Madame Mayhem is just now starting to turn in a substantial profit after months of breaking even. I shouldn't have bought out the other partners."

Belle was the sole owner of a burlesque club downtown. From what her brother-in-law had explained to me, she was a shrewd businesswoman with killer instincts on the fast track to turn a seven-figure profit. Buying out the two other partners of the club put a dent in her bank account.

"Babies cost money," I *tsked* regretfully, setting the groundwork for what I was about to propose.

"*Oof.*" She sipped on the water reluctantly, throwing her arms on the bar. "No wonder people usually stop at two."

"Not to mention, you'll need to go back to work at some point. You work nights, don't you? Someone'll have to take care of the babe. Either a costly babysitter or the father."

I was going to hell, but at least I was going to head there in style.

"A father?" She looked at me incredulously, as though I suggested she leave it with a street gang. "I already said I'm going to use a sperm donor."

Was she now?

Impregnating Emmabelle Penrose was the perfect solution for all my pressing problems.

I would not propose to her—no. Neither of us wanted a marriage, and I suspected Belle was harder to tame than a honey badger on crack. But I would come to an arrangement with her of sorts. I would provide for her. She, in return, would be my mark of Cain. My ticket out of royalty.

My mother would be off my case, Louisa would want nothing to do with me, and other women would have no false illusions about making me settle down. Not to mention, I genuinely *wanted* an heir. I did not want the marquess title to die along with me. Recently, the British Parliament, in an effort to be more progressive, introduced a bill to say that children born out of wedlock were now legitimate heirs. It was like the universe was sending me a message.

Emmabelle was a flawless candidate for my plan.

Detached. Ruthlessly protective of her independence. Owner of a womb.

Plus, it needed to be said—impregnating the woman wasn't going to be the hardest chore I'd ever been tasked with.

As my mind began drafting the fine print of such agreement, Belle was four steps behind me, still mourning her insufficient bank account.

"...probably need to get a loan from my sister. I mean, do I want to? No. But I can't operate from a place of pride here. I've never not paid a loan, Devon. It's hard to sleep at night when you know you owe people money. Even if it's your sister—"

I cut her off, swiveling on my stool to face her. "I'll have a baby with you."

The woman was so drunk, her initial response was squinting at me slowly, like she'd just realized I was there in the first place.

"You, um, what?"

"I'll give you what you want. A child. Financial security. The whole nine yards. You need a baby, money, and a co-parent. I can give you all of those things, if you give me an heir."

She coiled away from me.

"I don't want to marry, Devon. I know it worked for Persephone, but the whole monogamy thing ain't my jam."

Ain't. She said ain't. Pick up your things and leave.

My cock compelled me to stay.

I picked up the glass of water in front of her and guided it to her lips.

"I'm not offering you marriage, darling. Unlike Cillian, I have no interest in conveying to the world that I've been tamed and declawed. All I want is someone to have a child with. Separate households. Separate lives. Think about it."

"You must be high." Rich, coming from a woman who currently could not count the number of fingers on her right hand.

"Your child may be His or Her Highness, if you say yes," I hissed.

There was not one sodding soul in Boston who wasn't aware of my royal titles. People treated me like I was next in line to the throne, when in practice, about thirty people in the monarchy would have to find their untimely—and unlikely—death before I'd be made king.

I put my glass down, flagging the bartender and ordering her something greasy in a bun to help with her impending hangover. Outside the pub, night descended on the streets of Boston. The clock was ticking. I knew Emmabelle spent her nights either working at Madame Mayhem or clubbing.

"And that child would be a marquess?" She chewed on a lock of her yellow hair, more amused than contemplative.

"Or a marchioness."

"Would they be invited to royal functions in England? A baby christening? Would I have to wear silly hats and curtsy?"

"Perhaps, if you fancy punishing yourself by RSVPing."

"I don't own any funny hats." She scrunched her nose.

"I'd gift you one if we reproduce," I said roughly, growing more and more enamored with the idea each passing second. She was perfect. And by perfect, I meant a mess. No one would touch me with a ten-foot pole if I got her pregnant. Least of all Louisa Butchart. "Look, we've already had sex, so we know the conception part would be dynamite. I'm rich, local, and of good health and IQ. I would pay child support, put you in a nice place, and help raise the child. We could go the joint custody route, or you could let me have visitation over the weekends and holidays. Either way, I'd insist on spending regular time with the babe, since I'd leave it an astronomical inheritance and royal title."

She slanted her head to the side, studying me as though I was the one being unreasonable between us two.

"Think about it. That way you get all the things you need—more than a sperm donor, a father to the child, and cash for your trouble—without all the things you don't want, namely a husband, someone to tie you down, and a person to answer to."

"Are you insane?" she rubbed her forehead. I gave it some genuine thought, in case we'd skipped into the DNA ancestry part without my notice.

"It's a possibility, but mustn't be hereditary."

"I can't do this with you!" She flung her arms skyward.

"Why not?"

"For one thing, I'm not a gold digger."

"You're not," I agreed as the bartender slid a plate with a cheeseburger and crisps Belle's way. "Which is a shame. Gold diggers are underrated. They're go-getters with a plan."

"Our families would go nuts," she said around a healthy bite full of relish, beef, and ketchup, licking her fingers. There was nothing sexier than Belle Penrose enjoying meat. Other than, perhaps, Belle Penrose enjoying *my* meat.

It was going to be a pleasure to put a baby inside this woman.

"Not sure about yours, but mine is already not exactly sane," I said impassively, removing lint from my peacoat. "Jokes aside, I'm in my early forties. You're in your thirties. We're both the most independently accomplished individuals out of our group of friends. Everyone else around us has inherited or married into their positions. No one could look down on this arrangement."

"*I'd* look down on it." Belle popped a crisp into her mouth and chewed on it thoughtfully. "It'd complicate things for me. A sperm donor would have no claim over my child. I wouldn't have to ask them permission to do anything. What school to send them to, how to raise them, how to dress them. The control would be all mine. I don't like relinquishing power."

"Sweets." I pulled out a rollie from the tin box in my pocket and pushed it between my lips, lighting it up. "Very little in your life is in your power. Pretending otherwise sets yourself up for heartbreak. If you truly don't want to play by mortals' rules, tie your destiny to mine."

"You're not supposed to smoke in here, ass face." She dropped the half-eaten burger on her plate, turning to watch the bartender intently to see what he'd do.

"Reality dictates otherwise." I could take a shite right there on the bar and no one would bat an eyelash. I turned to look at the bartender, puffing a plume of smoke directly in his face.

"Isn't that right, Brian?" I hissed.

"Ay, my lord, and it's Ryland." He bowed his head.

Belle cocked her head, regarding me skeptically. "What's the trick here?"

"There's no trick. Respect is given to those born into it."

"Is this your selling point, Einstein? Because no part of me wants a spawn as condescending and spoiled as you."

Smirking cordially—we both saw past this rubbish—I said, "Name your price."

"Stop calling her 'it' for starters."

"How do you know you'd be having a girl?" I was highly amused. I did not think of Emmabelle as an emotional, dream-filled female. You live, you learn.

"I just do."

"Well?" I asked curtly. "Are we going to make the most genetically gifted person on planet Earth or what?"

Belle stood up, grabbed her secondhand designer bag, and flipped me the bird. "*Or what*. Find another woman to be your womb for hire.

I'm going out to drink until this conversation erases itself from my conscience. No way it deserves any room in my gray matter."

She departed, leaving me with the bill, an idea I was becoming enamored with, and a cell phone with a dozen missed calls from England and one frustrated Allison Kosinki who'd been waiting outside my apartment for the better half of the evening in high heels, a coat, and nothing else … waiting to get fucked.

Bugger.

Three

Belle

Fourteen Years Old.

F IRST CRUSH.

That's what they call it.

Now I'm starting to understand why.

It feels like I'm crashing into the ocean.

Not cannonballing either. More like slamming into it horizontally. You know, when breaking the surface feels like hitting concrete.

It hurts like a bitch.

Hurts to look at his brown eyes. The way they zing when our stares meet across the hallway or in class.

Hurts when he lets out a laugh, and I feel it rattling my bones, and then I feel his happiness spreading in my body, warm and sticky, like it's honey.

Hurts when I see other girls talk to him, and I just want to grab them by the shoulders and SCREAM that he is mine. Because he is. That's why he saves those smiles and looks and cocked eyebrows just for me.

I don't know if it's normal to feel this way. Like this one guy holds the key to my moods.

The weird part is ... this is so not me. I'm not boy crazy. I'm more like ... I don't know, a crazy boy.

A tomboy. A scallywag. Always up to no good. Pulling pranks, climbing trees, begging Mom to let me stay out and play a few more minutes before dinner. This is my first encounter with feelings that have nothing to do with my family.

I've never had a crush before. So I can't tell if it's okay to feel this way. Like he is carrying my heart in his pocket.

One thing is for sure.

Ninth grade is going to be a long year.

Because the person I'm crushing on?

Well, it's Mr. Locken, my coach.

Four

Belle

ALITTLE OVER A DECADE AGO, MY SISTER PERSY, MY BEST friend Sailor, Aisling, and I were at a charity ball, hosted by the Fitzpatricks.

As we watched one of our high school friends being paraded around like a prized horse by one of the older men, we made a pact there and then. We promised each other to only marry out of love.

Not because of money, not because of circumstances, or any other ulterior motive.

Not all of us fulfilled that promise with equal success.

Sailor, forever the overachiever, had kept her word. Hers was a love match by the book, full of heart emojis and chubby-cheeked babies, and a reformed manwhore of a husband who kissed the ground she walked upon.

Persy married Cillian Fitzpatrick, Hunter's brother. Those two were what I called a hot mess express. They'd started as strictly business. But I knew my sister had always loved the eldest Fitzpatrick brother. He, in return, fell in love with her the way you fall into an abyss. Hard and fast, with nothing to grasp on your way down.

Aisling was caught in the poisonous claws of Boston's favorite monster, only to find it was lethal to everyone but her. Sam Brennan had no fear of God, but touch a hair on his wife's head and he would tear the city apart.

And then there was *me*.

I knew I'd never marry, yet I'd still participated in the pact. Not because I believed I'd change my mind, but because I understood my sister, Aisling, and Sailor needed that reassurance.

The reassurance that I was okay. That nothing was broken. That I was capable of falling in love, even though I wasn't.

Or maybe I was. I wouldn't know, because I'd never been at risk of facing such a travesty.

"Ma'am? Mistress of the manor? Are you even with us?" Sailor snapped her fingers in front of my face, trying to pull me out of my reverie. We were all flung over the couch in my apartment, enjoying our weekly takeout meal. Peruvian, this time. Me, Sailor, Persy, and Aisling, Cillian and Hunter's baby sister.

"Her brain short-circuited." Aisling swept her raven-black hair off her face, snatching my phone from between my fingers while munching on seafood paella. "She must be overwhelmed. Pass me the wine, please. I'll take over."

Aisling was tucked next to me. Persy, with her golden hair fanned over my shoulder in silky ribbons, sat on my other side, peeking over my head to watch the screen as Aisling scrolled through my phone. Perched on the coffee table, Sailor—redheaded, freckled, and youthful—refilled all of our wine glasses and wolfed down ceviche.

I'd designed my apartment to express my personality. And my personality, according to the tiny place I occupied, was schizophrenic, fun, and in desperate need of a good scrub.

With palm tree wallpaper, a deep green ceiling, and bright orange couch, you couldn't accuse me of having conservative taste. I had pop art paintings, a collection of vases from all around the world, and prints of feminist quotes I found particularly compelling.

Oh, and massive promotional posters of me wearing nothing but a thong and a smile, enjoying a champagne bath in a huge glass. Those were plastered all over Boston's billboards too.

Madame Mayhem: Where Your Morals Go to Die

"I can't believe you two are drinking." Sailor peered at Persy and Aisling, both of them mothers to breastfed babies. Aisling, especially, was the kind of woman who couldn't even jaywalk without breaking into hives. Ambrose, her son, was still tiny.

"I cannot believe you never pumped and dumped." Aisling "Ash" Fitzpatrick shrugged, taking another sip of her wine. "And people think *I'm* the nerdy one."

"You are!" we all said in unison.

Ash had been late to the Boston Belles party. Persy and I knew Sailor through school, but Aisling became part of the gang only after Sailor had met Hunter. She was the goodie two-shoes out of us four. The doctor. The pedigreed, well-heeled daughter of an oil family who went and married Boston's most brutal and forbidding mafia prince.

"I know they call breastmilk liquid gold. But this?" Persy lifted her glass, clucking her tongue. "This is priceless. I have to enjoy it while I can."

"Why's that?" Sailor frowned.

Persy's soot-black eyelashes concealed her eyes as she looked down, grinning.

"Cillian and I will be trying for a third one in a few months."

"You guys are like rabbits." I gagged.

"You know how it is when you want a little one," Persy said defensively.

A stab of agony cut through my insides. I'd been going out and getting trashed every night since Doctor Bjorn informed me my uterus was more useless than the G in Lasagna. I'd been trying to drink and party away the pain. I couldn't believe how, overnight, I went from hell on heels to a pile of hormones. I couldn't reconcile my old self with the new one. Why did I want a child? They were messy and expensive and messed with your sleep.

But they were yours. Your family. Your constant. Your compass.

I was surprised with how my friends and sister had taken the news that I was in a race against the clock to get knocked up. They were so supportive, so *excited*, it made me feel a little less sorry for myself.

Persy volunteered to babysit for me as much as I wanted ("I already have two at home, what's one more?"), Ash offered to take night duties ("I'm a doctor, pulling all-nighters is no skin off my back"), and Sailor said she'd give me *all* of her baby supplies and furniture ("My way of telling Hunter there's no way in hell we're having a third one").

Now there was just the measly, small business of, you know, *getting* pregnant.

Taking Devon Whitehall up on his offer was a no-go. I had zero desire to force my child into an outdated institution of stuffy, inbred white people.

Which was why we were now scrolling through sperm donor profiles to see if there was someone who tickled my fancy. Which was depressing, because the meaningful qualities in humans weren't something you could find on a supermarket list. You had to *experience* a person to appreciate them fully. That was why online dating almost always sucked.

Blond and Bashful, AKA donor number 4322, born 1998, whose favorite animal was a dolphin might be genetically great, but what if he was a terrible human?

"What about this one?" Ash shoved the phone screen in my face. There was no picture of the guy—just another gray, faceless avatar—but a highly detailed description of him, and a profile name he chose for himself.

"*Grill Master*? For real?" I drawled. "If the one thing he chooses to highlight about himself is his talent for flipping burgers, I'm going to have to pass. If I'm paying for jizz, I want to get my money's worth."

And the jizz didn't come cheap. I promised myself I'd go for the premium. The one that cost four-figures. My child deserved the very best.

"The man is 6'3" with dimples. In the staff notes, they said he looks like young Sean Connery," Persy exclaimed.

"What about this one?" Sailor pointed at another profile. "Multiethnic. Tall. Athletic. Crazy high IQ. Best friends with his mom."

I grabbed the phone from her, frowning. "Yeah. His blood type is AB negative, which means if god forbid something happens, it'd be a bitch to find blood donations for my child. He also calls himself Come Together. I mean, can it be any more ironic? Literally, *he* was the only bastard that came when creating our hypothetical baby."

"All right, Grumpy Pants. Someone walked into this whole experience with some prejudice." Sailor curved an eyebrow.

"Oh, you'll find him, Belly-Belle. I promise." Persy brushed my hair lovingly while Ash shook her head, still scrolling on my phone.

We went through profiles for about forty more minutes before we found the perfect match. He called himself Friendly Front Runner, was 6'1", East Asian, with a master's degree in political science and public policy. His dream lunch would be with Nikola Tesla, and his profile seemed engaging, fun, and intelligent without sounding like he was trying too hard.

"The guy's perfect." Sailor smacked her hand on the coffee table she was sitting on. "Honestly, I'd get knocked up by him if I had the chance."

"Whatever happened to not wanting another child?" Persy teased, braiding my hair.

Sailor held her hands up. "I'm just trying to get our girl here to agree on a donor before all of our eggs die of old age."

"There's a limited number of vials for this guy, so you need to be quick about it," Ash warned, flipping through his entire history on my phone.

I knew she was right. I also knew that Friendly Front Runner was probably the best option out there. He seemed genuinely funny and engaging. Down to earth and bright. And yet … I couldn't get excited about choosing him as the father of my child.

I mean, what did I really know about this guy, other than his credentials and the things he would probably tell me on a first date?

Was he kind to strangers?

Did he chew super loudly?

Did he think pineapple pizza was an acceptable dish in civilized society?

There were so many makes-or-breaks that would remain a mystery to me.

And there was something else. Something I couldn't stop thinking about, even though I knew it was a recipe for disaster.

Devon Whitehall's suggestion.

"*Oh-oh*. We're losing her again. I feel like I'm in a bad episode of *Grey's Anatomy*." Sailor threw a tempura shrimp into her mouth.

"They were all bad, and highly inaccurate, medically speaking," Aisling chimed in.

"Belle." Persy propped her chin on my shoulder, her baby blues shining full of concern. "Is everything okay?"

I put my wine glass down. "I forgot to mention there's another option."

Aisling slanted her head to the side. "You know God is not going to do you the same solid he did the Virgin Mary, right?"

"Duh. I've been such a bad Christian, I've got a better chance of banging a stork." I rolled my eyes.

"What do you mean, then?" Sailor sat straighter, using the pad of her finger to swipe the remainder of her food from the container, putting it to her lips.

I toyed with a lock of my braided hair. I was in a pink satin pajama set that said *You Look Like I Need a Drink*.

"Devon Whitehall offered his services—and dick. He basically said he'd love to have an heir, but doesn't want to get married. In return, he'd help me out financially and co-parent. That's so cringe, right?"

"Holy shit." Sailor slapped a hand over her mouth. "Isn't he, like, a duke?"

"A marquess," I corrected, as if I had any idea what *that* meant. "I don't think he is. Not yet, anyway."

"What he is *is* a millionaire, smart, and a study in hotness. What are you doing sifting through college students' profiles when an offer like that is on the table?" Aisling demanded. "It's unlike you, Belle. You're usually the street smart one."

True, I wanted to say. *And because I'm smart, I know better than to give a man like Devon the keys to my life.*

"Plus, you have a real chance here to give your baby a father figure," Persy added.

"It's not that simple." I scowled, dropping my takeout box on the coffee table by Sailor. "The whole exercise of having a kid on my own is to ensure no one will butt into my business and tell me how to raise my child."

"Would a second opinion about things every now and then really be so horrible?" Aisling asked quietly. "Children are hard work. You'll be needing all the help you can get."

"And anyway," Persy swooped in, "parenthood is like an office job. Those who've been in it for longer are now your superiors. You're going to be given unsolicited opinions whether you want them or not. I mean, Mom didn't let me take Astor out for a walk in the park the entire winter because she thought he'd get pneumonia."

"It's easy for you to say." I took another sip of my wine. "You're all in relationships with men who are certifiable when it comes to you. Of course for you, it was an easy decision to pop a few kids out. I don't know Devon, Devon doesn't know me, and I'm not hot on the idea of a stranger with money and a questionable rep calling the shots when it comes to my future child."

But inside, I was already seeing dollar signs and posh private schools for my kid. I'd sworn off men for a good reason. But I could still ride Devon's dick—and credit card—while keeping him at arm's length.

"Sorry, Belle, did you start talking out of your ass?" Sailor pretended to lean down to my behind, as if to check her theory. "What shots? Don't pretend you'll be into homeschooling or raising your child vegan or pagan. You're going to raise this child like any other ordinary kid in America. Only with more money and a daddy whose accent makes women weak in the knees."

"What if we have a falling out?" I challenged.

"Gimmie a break." Sailor snorted, picking up the empty takeout containers and taking them to the kitchenette. "The man made a fortune making people like him while simultaneously screwing them over. He is a seasoned diplomat. Why would you have a falling out?"

"But I'll be breaking the pact," I said finally.

Sailor dropped the takeout containers into my trash can while Aisling rinsed the wine glasses in the sink. Persy stayed by my side.

My sister murmured into my ear. "Love stories are not like musicals. You don't need to have a perfectly constructed beginning, middle, and end to make them work. Sometimes love starts off from the middle. Sometimes it even starts from the end."

"I'm not like you." I turned to look at her, dropping my voice so no one would hear us. "Listen, Pers, I—"

I was going to say I was never going to get married, fall in love, live the uninspiring, white picket fence dream, when my sister pressed a finger to my lips, shaking her head solemnly.

"Don't say what you're about to say. You can, and you will. Nothing is stronger than love. Not even hate. Not even *death*."

My sister was wrong, but I didn't tell her that.

Death was stronger than anything.

It had been my path to deliverance, and rebirth.

My soul had been its price.

That, and any hope of love.

Later that evening, while in bed, I got bored and texted Devon. I still had his phone number from three years ago, when I rode his face on my way to Orgasmville before kicking him out.

Belle: why do you want a child anyway?

He answered after twenty minutes. Probably busy entertaining one of his toothpick-legged, PhD-holding female friends.

Devon: is this the national census?

Bastard either deleted my number or never saved it in the first place. That definitely brought me down a couple notches ego-wise.

Belle: it's Belle. Answer the question.

Devon: why must there be a devious reason behind my desire for an heir?

Belle: because you're smart, and I don't trust smart people.

Devon: putting your trust in stupid people is worse. Smart people are, at the very least, highly predictable.

Belle: all I know about you is that you are a royal. And rich.

Devon: that's enough for most women to offer their complete submission to me.

Belle: I'm not most women, Devon. Even your closest friends don't know shit about your ass. If we do this, and I'm not saying we will, I don't want to be in the dark.

He kept me waiting for a few minutes. I wondered if it was because he wanted to make a point—that he wasn't dropping whatever he was doing tonight to converse with me—or because he really was with another woman. I didn't care if he was currently having sex with the entire team of the Miami Heat Dancers. Or if he was at Sam Brennan's joint, drinking and smoking himself to an early grave and questionable sperm count.

Devon: you won't be in the dark. I'd ravish you in full daylight.

I flipped over to my belly on the mattress. My fingers flew over my screen.

Devon: who wouldn't want this? <image attached>

I thought, for sure, the stuffy stuck up sent me a dick pic. But when I opened the image, it was a picture of a baby with a shock of white-blond hair and piercing blue eyes in a full sailor's costume. The outfit looked like a dress, and the baby was so cherubic, I wanted to bite his soft thigh rolls.

Belle: SHUT THE FUCK UP.

There was no reply. Dammit, he was so literal.

Belle: is that you?

Devon: it's me.

He was the cutest baby in the world, that was for damn sure. But for some reason, my mentally challenged self couldn't pay him this simple compliment.

Belle: blue and white are not your colors, bro. And that dress makes your ankles look huge.

I knew he was laughing, just as I knew he wasn't going to write LOL. Devon was above abbreviations and acronyms. He once threw a bar of soap at Hunter when he used the word "rando" to refer to a stranger, and insisted he scrub his mouth with it, since he sullied up the Queen's English.

Devon: I've refreshed my cardio schedule since. Fencing, mainly.

Belle: why do you want to have a child? I insisted, asking again.

Devon: I need someone to inherit all I'll leave behind.

Belle: ever heard of charity?

Devon: sounds like a stripper.

Belle: ha ha. For real now.

Devon: charity begins at home. Ask Dickens.

Belle: pretty sure he's a little too dead to answer. Is that what it's all about? The money?

I had no idea at what point I grew a conscience, but there we were. What right did I have to judge him when I was (maybe) entering this arrangement for his dough and to be invited to royal weddings?

Devon: no. In addition, I rather enjoy children. I think they're

entertaining, insightful, and generally more cultured than most grown-ups.

Belle: if we do this (and again, I'M NOT SAYING WE WILL), I'd never sleep with you after we conceive. I'd never date you, never marry you, never give you all the things men want from the mothers of their children.

I was getting kind of into the idea of doing this with him. The money was a huge factor, but I also liked that he was not a gray avatar in a sea of sperm bank donors. I had points of reference I could later compare to my future baby. I knew he was a gifted fencer, that he found money talk tacky, and was a grammar Nazi. I knew he was appalled by American football and smitten with world history. That he was a skier and owned an Aga and old Barbour jackets. I knew how he smelled after sex. The sweaty masculinity, the expensive leather and sandalwood of him.

And I knew he owed me exactly nothing and could have a child with any other woman on the East Coast. Most would fall at his feet just for a chance.

Devon: understood and underrated. Having sex with the same person for longer than five months is daunting to all parties involved.

Who talked like that? Like, *who*?

Belle: you're really old.

Devon: you're filibustering.

Belle: people would think you're a creep if you get me pregnant.

Devon: perhaps, but I wouldn't be the creepiest royal, so they'd get over it quickly.

Belle: so how do you see this going down?

Belle: (IF WE DO THIS, AND I'M NOT SAYING WE WILL).

Devon: we could start this month. I have some business to conduct in England, but I should be free going forward. Just call when it's time.

Belle: I'll need to see an STD test to know you're clean.

Devon: I'll fax it over.

Fax. The man still used a fax machine. He was so ancient, I was surprised he didn't send me the results via carrier pigeon.

Devon: I'll draft a contract in which we settle things such as custody, financials, and so forth. I'd require a certain amount of involvement to ensure the contract is satisfactory to both parties.

Belle: we're really doing this, aren't we?

Devon: why not?

Belle: well, let's see …

Belle: BECAUSE IT'S CRAZY?

Devon: not half as crazy as getting pregnant by a faceless stranger, and yet people do that all the time. Evolution, darling. At the end of the day, we're nothing but glorified monkeys trying to ensure our footprint in this world is not forgotten.

Belle: did you just call me a monkey? Strong romance game, Whitehall.

He didn't reply. Maybe Devon wasn't so old as much as I felt so young in comparison to him.

Belle: one more question.

Devon: yes?

Belle: what's your favorite animal?

I thought he would for sure say a dolphin or a lion. Something corny and predictable.

Devon: pink handfish.

Oh, awesome. More weird shit.

Belle: why?

Devon: they look like drunk football hooligans trying to pick a fight at a bar. And their hands are eerie. Their flaws demand compassion.

Belle: you're weird.

Devon: true, but you are interested, darling.

Five

Belle

THE NEXT DAY, I STOPPED AT WALGREENS ON MY WAY TO WORK and got an ovulation kit and chewable prenatal vitamins. Passing by a billboard sign of myself naked, I popped four into my mouth and read the instructions on the kit. I pushed the door open to the back office of Madame Mayhem.

Madame Mayhem was a stone's throw from Chinatown Gate in downtown Boston. It was tucked between two brownstones, a travel agency, and a produce shop. The price was dirt cheap when I bought it with two other partners and turned it from a failing restaurant into a trendy bar. Two years ago, the guy who owned the launderette next to us went bankrupt, and I convinced him to sell us the lot at a reduced rate. I'd run back and forth to city hall, trying to get approval to knock down the dividing walls between the two properties. By the end of the process, the new and improved Madame Mayhem had been invented—big, bold, and risqué.

Just like me.

Now, I was the proud owner of one of the most infamous establishments in the city. The place wasn't just a trendy nightclub with an obscenely expensive cocktail menu, but also offered burlesque shows, complete with 50's-style recreations of New Orleans entertainment, women and men in fine lingerie, as well as an amateur night every Thursday, in which exhibitionists in the making had a chance to flaunt their goods.

On paper, I made a great profit. But since I'd bought out the other two partners, and refurbished the place completely, my personal income was modest. Not too bad, but bad enough that having a baby would put a serious dent in my savings.

Still, I was a hard worker, undeterred by hiccups. I worked in the back office during the day and helped my bartenders by night.

"Belly-Belle," Ross greeted me as soon as I slipped into my gray shoebox of an office. He slid a coffee cup along my desk and took a seat on the edge of it. My best friend from school had grown up to be my chief bartender and staff manager at Madame Mayhem. He *also* grew up to be a total hottie. "Boston is not used to seeing you with clothes on. How are you feeling?"

"High on life and low on cash. What's shaking?" I took a sip of my coffee, my purse still slung on my forearm. I needed to pee on one of the ovulation sticks before I got to work.

Ross hitched a shoulder up. "Just wanted to make sure you were okay after last week's shit show."

"There was a shit show last week?" I was kind of busy drinking my own body weight and trying to forget about the news Doctor Bjorn gave me, so my memory was blurry.

"Frank," he clarified.

"Who the hell is Frank?" I blinked.

Ross gave me a you've-got-to-be-kidding me glare.

"*Riiiight*, that bag of bullshit." Frank was a former bartender. Last week, I'd caught him sexually harassing one of the burlesque girls in the backroom. I fired him on the spot. Frank had agreed to walk away, but not before giving me a piece of his own mind about what a train wreck of a drunk bitch I was. Luckily for me, I was always ready for a fight, especially with a man. So when he screamed at me, I screamed louder. And when he tried to throw a lamp at me … well, I threw a chair at *him,* then deducted the cost to replace the broken chair from his last paycheck.

"There you go, you oxygen-wasting piece of crap. Now make sure you skip town, because this town sure is going to skip you after I fill in all my club-owner friends about what you did!"

I didn't stop there. I also sent his employee picture to local newspapers and told them what he did.

Too harsh? Too bad. Next time, he shouldn't get handsy with the staff.

"It's all forgotten now." I waved my hand in the air dismissively. I didn't have time to talk about Frank. I needed to check and see if my eggs were doing their goddamn job.

"We'll need to fill his spot." Ross was still perched on my desk. I resumed my stride toward the bathroom.

"Yeah, well, just make sure they're fully vetted."

I got into the bathroom, crouched down, and peed on the ovulation stick. Rather than put it aside and wait for the results like an actual adult, I glowered at the stick, praying to see two strong pink lines rather than one dull one.

When two lines indeed appeared on the stick, I snapped a picture of it with my phone and sent it to Devon with the caption: **it's a go.**

I went outside, sat at my desk, and tried concentrating on the Excel sheets in front of me. My eyes kept darting sideways, to my phone, waiting for Devon to reply. When he didn't send anything back for an entire hour, I flipped the phone over so the screen wasn't visible.

Time to calm your tits, I scolded myself internally. The man had a career. Every hour of his working day was billable. Of course he couldn't just drop everything and run to Madame Mayhem to put a baby in me.

About two hours after I sent the text message, Ross strode into my office again. He slammed an expensive-looking bottle of champagne on my desk. It had a little golden card dangling from its neck.

"Dom Perignon?" I raised a skeptic eyebrow. This specific edition went for about a grand a pop. "We don't carry it here. Where'd you get it?"

"Ah, that's the question of the hour. Open the damn envelope and we'll find out." Ross jerked his chin toward the card, which, upon a second examination, looked like a miniature envelope. Dread filled my guts. This looked a lot like romance, and I didn't do romance. I liked it better when Devon was comparing us to monkeys.

"How do you know it's for me?" I eyed him suspiciously.

"Bitch, please. The only drink my dates buy for me is a fountain soda. Go on. Who's it from?"

My fingers worked quickly to unwrap the mysterious envelope. Two tickets spilled out of its mouth. I picked one up, noticing my fingers were trembling.

"Tickets to the opera?" Ross's voice asked in wonder. "What kind of lies are you feeding these poor men on Tinder? This dude obviously doesn't know you."

This is taunting my ass. He knows damn well I don't do dates.

"I said I loved Oprah, not opera. He obviously misheard." I let a provocative yawn loose. There was no way I was telling Ross about Devon. It was soul-crushing enough to admit my infertility to my girlfriends. I was a woman of great pride.

"How come men never take me anywhere nice?" Ross pouted.

"You give away the goods too quickly," I murmured, still staring at the ticket in my hand like it was a dead body I needed to get rid of.

"You do too. And you don't even one-date them."

"You can have my ticket, if you want it."

I was not going to watch an opera today. I had work to do. We were one bartender short.

I reminded myself that Devon did this for the same reason he did everything else—to manipulate, play, and throw people off-kilter. He probably thought it was hilarious to make me feel like we were dating. I had to set the record straight.

Belle: hello, you snail-eating, gilet-wearing, regatta-attending posh bloke, you. I won't be able to join you at the opera today,

but you may stop at my apartment any time after midnight and I promise to hit those high notes. – B.

That message, too, remained unanswered.

I worked into the evening, manning the bar along with six more bartenders, clad in a ruffled lace overbust corset dress. The scent of my own sweat had become so familiar to me over the years I'd built my career, I relished it.

I served drinks, cut limes, and hurried to the storage room to fetch more cocktail umbrellas. I danced on the bar, flirted with men and women, and rang the bell several times, signaling a tip-a-thon.

The burgundy curtain had ascended over the front stage, revealing a live band in tuxes. Their jazzy tune soaked into the tall walls. The burlesque dancers prowled slowly across the stage in high heels and sage-colored sequined dresses. People hooted, clapped, and whistled. I stopped, a crate of cocktail umbrellas in my arms, sweat dripping from my forehead, and watched them with a grin.

My decision to buy Madame Mayhem wasn't accidental or offhanded. It stemmed from my wanting to promote the idea that being a sexual creature wasn't sinful. Sex didn't mean dirt. It could be casual and *still* be beautiful. My dancers weren't strippers. You couldn't touch them—you couldn't even *breathe* in their direction without getting kicked out of the venue—but they took control of their sexuality and did whatever they goddamn pleased.

This, in my opinion, was true strength.

When I got back behind the bar, it was almost eleven. I knew I needed to wrap things up soon if I wanted to make it back home before midnight, with sufficient time to take a shower, shave my legs, and look the part of Devon Whitehall's sexual partner.

"Ross," I roared over the music, gliding across the sticky floor behind the bar and aiming a soda gun into a glass, making a vodka diet coke for a gentleman in a suit. "I'm off in ten."

Ross's thumb rose up in the air to signal he'd heard me. His other hand plucked a fifty-dollar bill from a woman leaning against the bar, her breasts spilling out of a neon-yellow sports bra.

I was about to take an order from a bunch of women wearing bachelorette party sashes (*Maid of Dishonor, Bad Influence*, and *Designated Drunk*). When I propped forward to do so, a hand shot toward me from the dark, gripping my forearm and giving it a painful squeeze.

I spun my head in the hand's direction and was about to yank my arm away when I noticed the person attached to said hand was staring at me with death in his eyes.

His face was so scarred that I couldn't guess his age even if I'd wanted to. A large portion of it was tattooed. He was swathed head-to-toe in black and looked nothing like the usual clientele we had here.

He gave me Lucifer vibes … and he wasn't letting go of me.

"I suggest you remove your hand from my arm right now, unless you're not feeling particularly attached to it," I hissed out through gritted teeth, my blood boiling over.

The man smiled an awful, rotten smile. It wasn't that his teeth were bad. On the contrary, they were big, white, and shiny, like he'd recently had dental work. It was what was behind him that made me uneasy.

"I have a message to deliver to you."

"If it's from Satan, tell him to come to me personally if he's got the balls," I spat out, yanking my arm away with force. His hand dropped, and I used every ounce of my self-control not to stick the lemon knife in it.

"I suggest you listen carefully, Emmabelle, unless you want very bad things to happen to you."

"Says *who*?" I chuckled.

"If you don't—"

Just as he began to speak, a tall, elegant form materialized from the shadows of the club, tossing the man away like he weighed no more than a straw. My scarred offender collapsed on the floor. Devon appeared in my line of vision, clad in a full-blown designer tux, his hair gelled back, his cheekbones as sharp as blades. He stepped onto the man—deliberately—scowling down at his loafers like he needed to clean dirt off of them.

"I was in the middle of something." I flashed him my teeth.

"Allow me not to sympathize."

"Are you capable of sympathy?"

"Generally? Yes. With women who leave me waiting? Not so much."

Devon leaned over the bar in one swift movement and hurled me across his shoulder, turning away and marching toward the entrance doors. I looked up, catching Ross's deer-in-the-headlights expression, frozen with a bottle of beer in one hand and a bottle opener in the other.

"Should I call security? The police? Sam Brennan?" Ross crowed from the depths of the bar, over the music. Devon didn't slow down.

"No, it's okay, I'll kill him myself. But get this creeper's details." I was about to point at Scarface where I last saw him on the floor, only to find him gone.

I didn't fight Devon. Being carried after working on one's feet for six hours straight wasn't the worst punishment in the world. Instead, I launched a verbal attack on him. "Why are you dressed up like a fancy waiter?"

"It's called a suit. It's an appropriate form of dress. Though, I gather the men you enjoy often sport orange jumpsuits."

"Who told you? Persy?" I shrieked. "I only slept with *one* ex-con. And it was for a Ponzi scheme. It's pretty much like screwing a politician."

"I waited for you," he said flatly, his voice turning icy.

"Why?" I huffed, resisting the urge to pinch his butt. "I already told you I'm not going to the opera."

"No, you did not," he said dryly, his fingers curling deeper to the curve of my ass. "My champagne and tickets arrived safe and sound, and since I hadn't heard back from you, I assumed the plan was to meet tonight."

That was impossible. I sent him a message.

Oh. *Oh.* The message must've not gone through. My cellular company had very poor reception. Especially when I was in the underground bunker called my office.

"I sent you a message. It didn't go through. You think this whole alpha-male charade turns me on or something?" I let out a snort. Because, let me tell you, it *absolutely* did. Not that I would ever admit it out loud.

But holy hell. It had been a hot minute since I'd been handled with such brash confidence.

"Not all of us engage in theatrics to survive, my dear Emmabelle. What you think of me is absolutely none of my business." Devon burst out of my club into the cool, crisp night, striding toward his car. "You say you want a child, but you also go prancing around, drinking and working yourself to the bone. One of us knows how to get you pregnant, and I'm afraid that person is not you."

The nerve of this asshole. He was mansplaining sex to me. I could stab him if I wasn't, indeed, a little drunk and a lot exhausted from the day's work.

Devon threw open the passenger door to his dark green Bentley, tucking me inside and buckling me up. "Now tell me who that man was. The one who held your arm."

He shut the door and rounded the car before I could answer then slipped beside me. A waft of his irresistible, rich scent drifted into me.

"I have no idea. I was about to find out when you thundered in, giving me your best *Straight Outta' Savior Complex* impression."

"Is it an ordinary occurrence? Men grabbing you at work?" He started the car, zipping through the ice-crusted streets toward my apartment. My heart had no business skipping a beat because he remembered my address. What was happening in my chest better be a goddamn heart murmur.

"What do you think?" I sassed.

"I think certain men feel they can touch you because of your line of work," he answered honestly.

It happened often, actually. Especially when I danced on the bar or got onstage with my dancers. But I knew how to set boundaries and put people in their place.

"It's true." I grinned. "I constantly need to fight men off. How do you think I developed these babies?" I kissed my biceps.

When he said nothing, I opened his glove compartment and began sifting through his shit. I often did things like that. Goaded people into a reaction. You could learn a lot about humans by the way they carried themselves when angry. I found a small engraved fossil and pulled it out.

"I'm not impressed with what I've seen tonight." Devon, as calm as the Dalai Lama jerked the fossil from my hands and dumped it between us.

"My goodness, you're not!" I slapped a hand over my cleavage, exhibiting my best fake British accent. "Heavens above. I must quit right this minute and become a governess or a nun. Whatever suits your taste, *milord*."

"You're infuriating." He scrubbed at his perfect cheekbone, exasperated.

"And you were in my way," I concluded, taking the small fossil again and messing with it. "I can fight my own battles, Devon."

"You're barely capable of keeping yourself alive." His glacial expression told me he wasn't being funny. He truly thought that.

At my building, Devon took the flight of stairs to my apartment, rather than use the elevator, still carrying me in his arms. *More* weirdness. How come none of his super-fans in this city ever picked on how odd he was?

"There's an elevator *right* here. Put me down, Mr. Caveman."

"I don't do those." His voice was clipped.

"You don't do elevators?" I asked, relishing the feeling of his abs and pecs against my body.

"Correct. Or any sort of confined space I can't get out of with ease."

"What about cars? Planes?" There went my mile-high dream with a royal. It was good while it lasted. Also: very specific.

"Logic dictates I use both, but I try to stay away from them whenever possible."

"Why?" I was baffled. It seemed like such an irrational fear for a man who was pure rationalism.

His chest quaked with a chuckle. He looked down at me, amused. "That's none of your business, darling."

When we arrived at my apartment, I was surprised to find Devon was in no hurry to peel my clothes off and have wild, unbridled sex with me. Instead, he produced a batch of documents from a stylish leather briefcase and set it on the coffee table, taking a seat. I sprawled on a colorful recliner, glaring at him.

"What are you doing?" I asked, even though it was pretty obvious he was removing enough paper documents to papier-mâché the Statue of Liberty, setting them on the table.

Devon didn't bother to lift his eyes from the files. "Attending to our legally-binding contract. In the meantime, feel free to catch up on the opera you've missed tonight. *La bohème.*"

He offered me his phone, on which a recording was already playing.

"How'd you get in? You sent me two tickets."

"I wanted to make sure you had a spare in case one got lost, so I purchased the entire row."

Motherfucker. That was swoony as all hell, but in a jerk sort of way, because he still worked under the assumption I was not going to have my shit together.

I snatched the phone from his hands. "How do you know I won't go through your messages?"

"How do you know it's my personal phone rather than the one I use for work?" he clapped back.

I shot him a *whatever* look. Because, apparently, the current age gap between us wasn't enough. I just had to act like a teenager.

"Watch it." He jerked his chin to the phone, unbothered by my evil looks.

"You recorded the whole thing?"

Not very many people had the ability or talent to shock me, but this did. I was usually the one raising a scandal.

Devon picked up a red Sharpie, reading through the material in front of him, still not sparing me any attention. "Correct."

"But why? I screwed you over."

"And I'm about to screw you senseless. Your point?" His impalpable face did not waiver. "Now, please watch the opera while I read through the contract one more time."

For the next forty minutes, I did just that. Watched the opera as he worked. The first ten minutes, I stole glances at him. It was nice, knowing I was about to be under this potent, sophisticated male.

But ten minutes into the opera, something weird happened. I started … well, kind of getting into it. *La bohème* was a story about a poor seamstress and her artist friends. The whole thing was in Italian, and even though I didn't know one word of the language, I *felt* everything the heroine was feeling. There was power in it. The way the music tugged at my emotions like I was a marionette on a string.

At some point, Devon slid his phone from my hand and tucked it back into his pocket. He was sitting closer to me now.

"Hey!" I sent him a dirty glare. "I was in the middle of something. Mimi and Rodolfo decided to stay together until springtime."

"The ending is exquisite," he assured me, sliding an expensive-looking pen out of his briefcase. "You'd have loved it, had you joined me at the opera."

"I want to see the ending."

"Play your cards right, and you will. Let's go over the contract together."

"And then?" I raised an eyebrow, folding my arms across my chest.

"And then, my dear Emmabelle," he smiled devilishly. "I'm going to fuck your brains out."

One hour and twenty-three minutes.

That was how long it took Devon and I to go over all of the provisions in the contract he'd drafted for us.

He then proceeded to show me his STD test—the man was as clean as a whistle—and proceeded to let me know that he agreed to waive my own test on the grounds of trying to create a respectable and trustful working environment.

I liked that he referred to the arrangement as work. It felt clinical, detached.

Problem was, by the time we were done going over legal documents, it was the middle of the night, and I was curled on the couch next to him, yawning into a throw pillow. I was still in the same corseted dress I wore for work and looked like a medieval prostitute who was about to corrupt the king's first son.

"Is this your secret weapon? Exhausting people into submission?" I purred into the pillow, fighting the unbearable weight of my eyelids.

I heard Devon putting the signed contracts back into his leather briefcase and zipping it shut.

"Among others." His jaw ticked, and I thought I saw something cold and emotionless pass across his face.

I let my eyes rest for a few seconds.

"Hmm," I replied, hugging the pillow I was resting against, curling around it like a cat. "I believe you've just met your match. I never bow to anyone."

"Have you ever had a boyfriend?" he asked.

"Nope."

"That's what I thought."

"And you?" I was already half-asleep when I asked it.

"No to a boyfriend. I've had a few girlfriends. None of them survived the six-month mark, though."

"That's *whaddathought*," I slurred, letting out a soft snore. At this point, I was snoring into my own armpit, in an exhibition of bursting allure and delicate femininity.

"*Sweden*." His low voice rolled like a dark cloud above my head. "Up you go."

"You going to Sweden?" I was drooling over my throw now. The cold, sticky saliva gluing my cheek against it.

He chuckled. "Not Sweden, *Sweven*."

"Oh." A pause. I was still asleep, but still somehow talking to him. "What's that?"

"A dream, a vision. Something that comes to you in your sleep. You're a fantasy, Emmabelle. Too good to be true. Too bad to be experienced."

"Whoopy me," I groaned. I hoped he wasn't going to ask me to marry him. I was exhausted and sleep-deprived enough to consider it.

"Time to take a shower."

"Tomorrow," I garbled.

"It *is* tomorrow," he argued. "And Google told me your ovulation window is only twelve to twenty-four hours. Get into the shower so we can fulfill our contract."

Swiftly, and without making a sound, Devon picked me up honeymoon-style and carried me along my apartment. *Finally*, I thought, my eyes still closed. The bastard was taking me to my bed. We'd do it tomorrow, or the next day, or …

What the hell?

My eyes snapped open when I was met with icy needles of frozen water. Disoriented, I found myself lying on the floor of my shower. Both showerheads were spitting at me. I looked around frantically, spotting Devon standing on the other side of the glass door, his narrow hip leaning against the wall, his shirtsleeves rolled up to his elbows, exposing mouthwatering, veiny forearms.

The devil's smirk was smeared across his face.

I scrambled out of my already ruined dress, which became heavy with liquid, dumping it with a slap on the floor beside me.

"I'm going to kill you!" I clawed at the door like a wet feline, fully awake—and *naked*—now. I was about to pry it open and pounce on him. He moved over to the other side of the glass door, pulling the handle and keeping it shut.

"Kill me later. First, I need you clean and alert."

"The only touching we'll be doing when I get out of here is me stabbing you in the face." I bared my teeth through the glass.

I didn't remember him half as exasperating when we had casual sex. Did he have a shitty personality transplant or something?

"Angry sex is the best sex." Devon brushed his thumb over his lower lip, throwing me over the edge of my sanity.

"I'll freeze to death!" I was trying to bargain now.

"I'll write you a lovely obituary."

"You can't be that heartless!" I banged on the glass door with my fist.

"Of course I can." He smiled cordially, like a host in a Michelin-star restaurant. "Besides, diamonds are made under pressure."

"Let go of the handle."

"Wash first."

"*Or* what?" I felt crazy with the need to retaliate for what he was doing to me. My mind began working overtime. I wasn't going to let him get away with that. No way.

"*Or* this will be the only way you'll get wet tonight. And threats aside, we both know you've been dreaming about this since the night you threw me out all those years ago."

His words made me glance down to his slacks. To the impressive tent that awaited my attention. My eyes snapped back up to him. "Sorry, pal. My time with you didn't chart in the first twenty memorable fucks I've had."

Devon grinned, little crinkles of happiness decorating his jewel-colored eyes. "*Liar.*"

He turned around and strolled out of the bathroom, all confidence and suaveness. I seized the opportunity and launched out of the shower, jumping in front of him, and blocking his way. I pushed him back toward the bathroom, my body soaking his tux with water.

"Not so fast, Duke of Cuntington. I believe it's your tur—"

Before I could finish the sentence, he pushed me against the wall, and covered my mouth in a punishing, bruising kiss.

His hands roamed my back, running down to my ass and cupping it with strong fingers. He pushed me against his erection through his pants. The air around us buzzed with rage and frustration and darkness. We were both starved.

He tore his mouth from mine, rolling his thumb over my lips, erotically prying them open.

"Now, now, Sweven. Don't be so upset. I knew I needed to wake you up to be inside you, and touching you before I boarded a plane to England was of paramount importance."

"When are you leaving?" I darted my tongue out to swirl it over his thumb. His lips parted, a half-drunk look forming on his Adonis face.

My fingers unbuttoned his slacks. My body lit up like a live wire.

"Tomorrow."

"Why?"

"Business." His mouth dipped between us, to my breasts, and he took one of my nipples between his teeth, gazing up and smiling at me before it disappeared inside his mouth when he sucked.

"But what if we miss my ovulation window?" I let my head roll backward, a low moan escaping me. I threaded my fingers through his hair, the intense pleasure of being in his arms coming back to me in full force.

Devon's lips quirked. "Then I'm afraid we'll have to go through another month of fucking one another. Remember, you have five months before I discard your lovely arse."

His cock sprang free from his slacks as his knuckles brushed my slit. I knew he wasn't going to finger me. It wasn't Devon's style. There was something outrageously proper about the way he fucked. He screwed you in a way that felt both clean and dirty. It was why I was so obsessed with him—in bed—in the first place. My body trembled with anticipation the way it had all those years ago, when he cornered me in Cillian Fitzpatrick's cabin and dared me to let him make me come five times in one night. He'd delivered on that promise. In spades.

Devon fisted his thick, engorged cock, rolling it along my slit, slapping my clit with it. We both watched intently, our hot breaths mixing together.

He pushed his tip inside me to find that I was completely soaked. His eyes traveled up. We both grinned at each other. I nodded once, giving him permission.

He slid his entire cock inside me, grabbed the back of my thighs, and began fucking me against the wall. The cold surface behind me dug between my shoulder blades.

And yet I didn't care.

Didn't care Devon was still fully clothed.

Didn't care it was the middle of the night and I was moaning loud enough to wake up people in Wisconsin.

Did. Not. Care. About anything other than the moment we were sharing.

The intense pleasure of having him inside me again was gratifying, but it was the possibility of creating another life that made me feel frenzied.

We came together, wave after wave of pleasure crashing through me. It was different from the times before. The orgasm was great, but when he started to come and I felt the hot, sticky liquid spilling inside me, we both held each other's gazes, quivering in each other's arms, smiling. The fact that he was so present exhilarated me.

He lowered me down to the floor carefully, taking a step back. I read somewhere in one of my internet hunts that it was a good idea to lie on the bed with my legs up to increase my chances of conceiving. Suddenly, I was slammed with a hurry to do just that.

"Well." I swayed my hips as I plucked a robe from a hanger, wrapping it around me, feeling less dignified than I looked as traces of his cum slithered down my inner thigh. "Thank you for your services. Now if you could kindly get the fuck out of my apartment, I would appreciate it greatly."

Again, I used the same fake British accent I hoped was going to make him dislike me.

His pants—or trousers, if to go by what he called them—were down to his knees. He re-tucked his shirt into them, taking his time to make himself presentable.

"I'll be off to England for the remainder of the week, as I mentioned—" he began, but now it was *my* turn to catch him off guard.

"Dude. I'm not going to need you until next month, if at all. Share your schedule with someone who cares."

I shoved him toward my front door. Normally, moving a tall, built man of his size wasn't that easy. But since his pants were still half-done, he lost his footing and stumbled backward a little.

"You're as refined as an alley cat," he said with great satisfaction.

"I'm not the one who threw a half-asleep person into a cold shower." I gave him another shove.

He made a show of pretending to bite my hand as I pushed him. "I regret nothing, Sweven. It was a pleasure to fuck you."

"And a one-off," I reminded him, opening the door behind him and giving him a final thrust. "Also, don't try to make Sweven happen. We're not those people."

Outside, in the communal hallway, half dressed and laughing gruffly, still hopping from side to side as he pulled his pants on, he gave me the most devastating smirk I'd ever seen. I had to remind myself that he was a flirt and a rake. A man who, despite his beautiful face, had an ugly rap sheet with the ladies.

"You don't know what kind of person I am. But you're about to find out."

Six

Devon

THE BAD NEWS WAS THAT I'D ACCIDENTALLY MADE IT TO MY father's funeral.

The good news was that I was so happy to spot Mum and Cece, not even the fact I was there honoring my father managed to put a damper on my mood.

The original plan was to arrive a day after the funeral. They must've conducted the funeral a day early, seeing as they did not need to accommodate my schedule any longer. I showed up during the last act, when the casket was lowered into the ground.

My father was buried in the back of Whitehall Court Castle, by a deserted church, where his ancestors had been buried. Where, presumably, I would one day rest for eternity too.

My childhood home was a grand fortress. With medieval-style turrets, Gothic Revival architecture, granite and marble, and an unholy amount of arched windows. The castle was surrounded by a horseshoe-shaped garden at the front, and an out-of-service old church around the back. There were two barns, four servant cottages, and a manicured walkway leading to a wild forest.

On a clear day, you could see the French coast from Whitehall Court

Castle's rooftop. Memories of my younger self, lean and bronzed, daring the sun to burn me alive and melt me into the stone I'd lain upon, chased one another in my head.

I strode toward the thick cluster of people in black, mentally ticking off the attendance list in my head.

Mum was there, dainty and dignified as ever, patting her nose with a wad of tissues.

My sister, Cecilia, was there with her husband Drew Hasting, whom I'd met multiple times when they visited me in the States. Though I skipped their wedding in Kent, I made sure to gift the couple a lovely studio apartment in Manhattan so they could visit me regularly.

Cecilia and Drew were both plump and tall. I suppose to the naked eye, they looked like twins. They stood shoulder-to-shoulder but did not acknowledge one another. Though I had tried very hard to like Hasting for the sake of my sister, I couldn't ignore how staggeringly unimpressive his entire being was.

While he did come from good pedigree and a highly connected family, he had been known around gentlemen clubs in England as a rather dull, dim-witted man who couldn't hold on to a job if one chained itself to his leg.

Byron and Benedict were standing on the far end of the throng. They were in their mid forties, both looking bloated and wrinkled. It was as though they had spent every waking moment since I'd left drinking and smoking themselves into their current state.

And then there was Louisa Butchart.

At thirty-nine, Louisa had managed to become agreeable to the eye. She had hair as dark as my soul, short and shiny, scarlet lips, and a fine and graceful bone structure. Her trim figure was clad in a double-breasted black coat.

A woman any respectable man of my position and title would want on his arm.

I had to admit if it wasn't for the fact I needed to reject her on principle, Louisa was sure to make a man like me very happy one day.

I tucked a rollie into the side of my mouth and lit it up as I made my way to the gaping hole in the lush green grass. I stopped when my chest bumped into Cecilia's back. I leaned forward, my lips finding her ear.

"'ello, Sis."

Cecilia turned to me, her blue eyes swimming with shock. I kept my gaze on the coffin as little by little, piles of dirt concealed it from view. For a moment, I was acutely aware of the fact that everyone's attention had drifted from the casket and focused on me. I couldn't blame them. They probably thought I was a hologram.

"Devvie!" Cecilia threw her arms over my shoulders, burying her face in my neck. "How we've missed you! Mummy said you wouldn't be here until tomorrow."

I wrapped my arms around her, kissing the top of her head. "Lovely girl, I will always be here for you."

Even if I have to honor the wanker who gave me life.

"My goodness. I almost had a heart attack!" Mother cried out. She hobbled toward me, her heels sinking into the muddy ground. The air smelled like English rain. Like home. I collected her in my arms and squeezed, kissing her cheek.

"Mummy."

Mourners began huddling toward us, curious glances on their faces. It made me pettily content, knowing I'd yet again stolen the limelight from Edwin, even on his last journey.

Mum reared her head back, placing her frozen palms on my cheeks, tears making her eyes glitter. "You're so handsome. So … so *tall*! I keep forgetting your face if I don't see you over a few months."

Despite myself, something between a grumble and a laugh escaped me.

I'd been so adamant not to return to England as long as my father was alive, I almost forgot how much I had missed Mother and Cecilia.

"You managed to make it, ay? Good on you, mate." Drew clapped my back.

Still hugging my mother, I felt a hesitant hand on my arm. When I swiveled my head, I caught Cecilia smiling shyly, her skin pink, fragile as lightbulb glass.

"I've missed you, Brother," she said quietly.

"Cece," I growled, almost in pain. I stepped out of the embrace with my mother and gathered my sister into my arms. Her yellow curls tickled my nose. I was surprised to discover she still smelled of green apples, winter, and the woods. Of a childhood with too many rules and too little laughs.

Regret ripped me open.

I'd all but deserted my younger sister. Left her to fend for herself when she was a teenager.

Mum was right. Coming back to England *did* resurface old memories and unsolved issues.

"Will you be staying for a while?" Cece pleaded.

"I'm staying for a few days." I stroked her hair, glancing over the top of her head and making eye contact with Drew, who shifted from foot to foot, looking anything but happy to have another male in the house. "*At least*," I added meaningfully.

She quivered in my arms, and suddenly, I became furious with myself for not being more involved in her life. Growing up, she'd always needed me, and I was always there. Yet somehow my hatred toward my father made me miss her wedding three years ago.

"Are you happy with him?" I mouthed into her hair so only she could hear me.

"I—" she started.

"Well, well," Benedict said, with Byron on his heels. He squeezed my shoulder. "I thought I'd see pigs fly before I caught sight of Devon Whitehall back on British soil."

I disconnected from Cecilia, shaking his and his brother's hands.

"My apologies, but the only pigs I know are right here on earth, and looking like they could use a trip to rehab."

Benedict's smile collapsed. "Very funny." He grit his teeth. "I have thyroid issues, for your information."

"And you, Byron?" I turned to his brother. "What issues are preventing you from looking like a sober, functioning member of society?"

"Not all of us are so vain as to mind their appearance as much. I hear you're a self-made millionaire now." Byron smoothed his suit with his hand.

I finished off my fag and flicked the bud toward the grave. "I get by."

"Being known for your accomplishments is such hard work. Better to be known by your last name and inheritance." Benedict cackled. "Either way, it's good to have you back."

Thing was, I wasn't back. I was just a visitor. A bystander in a life that was no longer mine.

I'd built a life elsewhere. It was tied to the Fitzpatrick family, who took me under their wing. With my law firm, and my fencing, and the women I wooed. With a new twist in my story, Emmabelle Penrose, a girl who had more demons than gowns in her closet.

As people engulfed me from all directions, demanding to hear about my life in America—my mates, my partners, my clients, my conquests—I noticed only one person stayed away, on the other side of the dirt-filled shallow grave.

Louisa Butchart studied me from a safe distance under her lashes. Her mouth was curled in a slight pucker, her back arched, as if flaunting her new assets.

"Come now." Mother laced my arm in hers, tugging me toward the sprawling manor. "You'll have plenty of time to talk to Lou. I cannot wait to show you off to all the servants."

But there was nothing to discuss.

I owed Louisa Butchart an apology.

And nothing more.

An hour later, I sat at a grand table in one of the two dining rooms of Whitehall Court Castle. I was at the head of the table. My family and childhood friends surrounded me.

It astonished me how nothing had changed in the years I was gone. Down to the plaid carpeting, carved wooden furniture, candelabras, and floral wallpaper. The walls were sodden with memories.

Eat your greens or end up in the dumbwaiter.

But, Papa—

No Papa. No son of mine will grow up to be pudgy and soft like Butcharts' kids. Eat all your greens now, or you're spending the night in the box.

I'll throw up if I do!

Just as well. Vomiting would do your portly figure good.

As I looked around me, I couldn't help but feel sorry for Cece and Mother—even more than I was for myself. At least I went and built myself another life. They stayed here, burdened by my father's godawful temper and never-ending demands.

"So, Devon, do tell us all about your life in Boston. Is it as dreadful and gray as they say?" Byron demanded, chewing loudly on shepherd's pie and meatloaf. "I've heard it isn't much different from Birmingham."

"I suppose the person who told you that has never been to either," I said, swallowing a chunk of shepherd's pie without tasting it. "I rather enjoy the four seasons of the city as well the cultural establishments." The cultural establishments being Sam's gentleman club, in which I gambled, fenced, and smoked myself to death.

"And what of the women?" Benedict probed, well into his fifth glass of wine. "How do they chart in comparison to England?"

My eyes met Louisa's from across the table. She didn't shy away from my gaze but didn't offer any type of emotion either.

"Women are women. They are fun, necessary, and an overall bad financial investment," I drawled. I was hoping to convey I was still the same, no-good tomcat who'd run away from England to avoid marriage.

Benedict laughed. "Well, if no one's going to address the elephant in the room, I might as well do so myself. Devon, don't you have anything to say to our dear sister after leaving her high and dry? Four years, she waited for you."

"Benedict, *enough*," Louisa snapped, tilting her chin up demurely. "Where are your manners?"

"Where are *his*?" he crooned. "Someone has to call him out on this, since Mum and Dad can't."

"Where's the Duke of Salisbury and his wife?" I asked, realizing for the first time they hadn't attended the funeral.

There was a beat of silence before my mother cleared her throat. "They passed away, I'm afraid. A car accident."

Christ. Why hadn't she told me?

"My condolences," I said, looking at Louisa rather than her brothers, whom I still hadn't considered to be on the same evolutionary scale as me.

"These things happen." Byron waved a dismissive hand. Clearly, he was too enamored with being a duke these days to care about the price of his new title.

There was another short-lived silence before Benedict spoke again.

"She'd told all of her friends you were coming back to her, you know. Louisa. Poor bird went to see venues for engagement parties all across London."

Louisa gnawed on her inner cheek, swirling her glass of wine and looking into it without drinking. I wanted to drag her somewhere secluded and private. To apologize for the mess I'd created in her life. To assure her I fucked myself over just as much as I fucked her over.

"*Gawd*, do you remember?" Byron cackled, slapping his brother's back. "She even chose an engagement ring and everything. Got our father to pay for it because she didn't want you to think she was too demanding. You properly mugged her off, mate."

"That was not my intention," I said through gritted teeth, finding no appetite for my dish nor the company. "We were both children."

"I do believe this is something Devon and Louisa shall address privately." My mother tapped the corners of her mouth with a napkin, although there was no trace of food on her face. "It is inappropriate to broach this matter in company, not to mention at my husband's funeral dinner."

"Besides, there's so much more to talk about," Drew, Cece's husband, exclaimed with faux excitement, grinning at me. "Devon, I'd been meaning to ask—what are your thoughts about Britain's mortgage boom? The inflation risk is quite high, don't you reckon?"

I opened my mouth to answer, when Byron cut into the conversation, raising his wine glass in the air like a tyrannical emperor.

"Please, no one cares about the housing market. You're talking to people who don't even know how to spell the word mortgage, let alone ever had to pay one." He slammed the wine glass on the table, its carmine-red contents spilling over on the white tablecloth. "Instead, why don't we talk about all the promises Devon Whitehall hasn't kept throughout the years? To our sister. To his family. How reality has finally caught up with Lord Handsome, and he now needs to make some serious concessions if he wants to keep whatever's left of his previous life."

Louisa stood up and slapped her napkin over her still full plate.

"If you will excuse me." Her voice trembled, but her composure remained perfect. "The meal was fantastic, Mrs. Whitehall, but I am afraid my brothers' company was not. I'm terribly sorry for your loss."

She turned around and stalked off.

My mother and I exchanged looks.

I knew I needed to rectify the situation, even though I wasn't the one to create it.

But first, I had to deal with the two clowns occupying my dinner table.

I speared Benedict and Byron with a glare.

"While I'm sympathetic to your recent loss of your parents, this is the last time you speak to me this way. Like it or not, I'm the lord of the manor. I choose whom to entertain, and more importantly, whom *not* to entertain. You've crossed the line and made your sister and my mother upset. Next time you do this, you'll be met with a bullet to the arse. I may be a rake of few scruples, but as we all know, I am a damn good shot, and your arses are an easy target."

Byron and Benedict's smug smiles evaporated into thin air, replaced with scowls.

I stood up and stormed in the direction in which Louisa went. Behind my back, I heard the Butchart brothers droning a half-hearted apology about their behavior, blaming the wine for their poor manners.

I found Louisa in my old conservatory room, surrounded by exotic plants, big windows, and mint-colored wood. Her fingertips moved over an assortment of colorful roses in an expensive vase. A gift from a French viscount, which dated all the way to the nineteenth century.

Rather than touch the velvety petals, Louisa played with the thorns. I stood on the threshold in awe. She reminded me of Emmabelle. A woman who was more charmed by the pain of a beautiful thing than the pleasure it offered.

Louisa prickled the tip of her index finger. She withdrew from the thorn unhurriedly, sucking the blood, showing no signs of distress.

I closed the door behind me. "Louisa."

She didn't look up, her neck turned downward like a graceful swan. "Devon."

"I believe an apology is in order." I rolled a finger along a wood panel, finding it to be layered with a thick blanket of dust. Jesus Christ. Whitehall Court Castle was usually flawless. Did my mother and Cece have money issues?

"To me or to your family?" Louisa returned to caressing the thorns, and I found myself unable to look away from her.

She seemed so calm. So accepting, even after all these years.

I strode deeper into the room, the overwhelming humidity and heavy sweetness of blossoms suffocating me. "Both, I suppose."

"Well, consider yourself forgiven by me. I'm not one to hold a grudge. Though I'm not too sure the same could be said about Cece and Ursula."

"We get along fine," I clipped out curtly.

"That may be so, but they've been very lonely and sad since you left."

My throat clogged with self-loathing.

"What's the situation with my sister and mother?" I asked, taking a seat in front of her on the armrest of a green upholstered couch. "Whenever I see them, they look happy and content with their lives."

Then again, I made a habit of housing them in the best apartments, taking them to the best restaurants, and treating them to the most lavish shopping sprees whenever they came for a visit.

"Mr. Hasting is positively skint. He hasn't a dime to his name and hasn't been pulling his weight in this household, which, now that your father's money is held up in the will, might pose an issue." Louisa furrowed her delicate eyebrows, grazing a thorn with her stung finger. "Cece is quite miserable with him, but she feels she is too old and not pretty or accomplished enough to divorce him and look for someone else. Your mum and Edwin had a less than ideal marriage, and I suspect she's been very lonely, especially in the last decade."

I stood up, ambling over to the glass and propping an elbow against it. A flock of ducks waddled across the lawn. "Does Mum have any support?"

How did I not know the answer to my own question?

"She's stopped taking social calls in recent years. It seems pointless. With her younger daughter married to a fool, and her older son being the most infamous rake Britain has produced, she never has any good news to share. Though I try to visit her whenever I'm in Kent."

Even as she said this, Louisa didn't sound particularly accusing or antagonistic. She was the exact opposite of Emmabelle Penrose. Soft and pliant.

"Cece never had any children," I mused.

"No." Louisa came to stand in front of me, her modest cleavage pressing against my chest. I noticed her fingers were full of broken flesh, bruised by thorns. "I doubt Hasting has a taste for more than gambling and hunting. Children are not high on his to-do list."

Her body pressed harder against mine. The game had changed between us, and Louisa was no longer the timid little girl who'd begged me to throw crumbs of attention her way.

Run away again, her eyes said, *if you dare*.

No part of me wanted to move. She was attractive, attentive, and interested. But I couldn't take my mind off Sweven. The woman who snuck into my dreams like a thief, flooding them with desire and need.

"And what about you, Lou?" I curled my fingers around the back of her neck and drew her an inch away from me. Her skin pricked with goose bumps under my touch. "I heard you lost your fiancé. I'm sorry."

"Yes, well." Louisa licked her lips, smoothing my suit with a dark chuckle. "I suppose you could say I've never had the best of luck when it comes to men."

"What happened to us had nothing to do with luck. I was a selfish wanker who ran away from responsibility. You were always collateral, never the main objective."

"I never held a grudge, you know," she murmured, her voice calm, collected. It surprised me. I imagined heads would roll if I were in her position. "Anger just seems like such a wasteful feeling. Nothing good ever comes of it."

"That's a lovely way of looking at things." I smiled gravely, thinking, *If people let go of their anger, us solicitors would be left with no job.*

"You're back now." Her dark eyes met mine, daring me again.

I took her hand, which was on my chest, near my heart, and pressed her cold knuckles to my warm lips. "Not for good." I shook my head, my gaze holding hers. "Never for good."

"Never say never, Devon."

After stuffing drunken Benedict and Byron into their Range Rovers and instructing their drivers not to stop until they were on the other side of the island, I kissed Louisa farewell. I promised to call her next time I was in England, a promise I had every intention of fulfilling.

When our guests were gone, I snuck into the garden and smoked three rollies in a row, checking if I had any text messages or phone calls from the States. Specifically, from a certain American vixen. I did not.

She is too bloody broken, and you aren't in any danger of winning any sanity awards anytime soon either. I trudged back into the sprawling, dark mansion through the back kitchen, passing Drew snoring in front of the telly in one of the drawing rooms and Cece sitting at the grand piano, staring at it silently without playing.

Fuck her, impregnate her, and forget about her.

Things were looking dire on all fronts.

I headed to what used to be my father's office. My mother was there.

She looked to be in her natural habitat behind his Victorian desk, scribbling in the margins of some documents while typing numbers on a calculator next to her. It reminded me what I knew to be the truth for years—that my mother was indeed the operating force behind the Whitehall empire. My father was a rake with a title, while Ursula was her father's smart and resourceful daughter. Tony Dodkin might've been a common earl, but he was a math genius and a real estate mogul who knew his way around a good deal. Mum took after him. She was extremely capable.

Which begged the question, how had she not known that he was abusing me? But opening that old wound wasn't going to do much help.

"Devvie, my love." She let out a little sigh, putting her pen down and tilting her head up with a smile, like a flower stretching and opening for the sun. "Do sit down."

I took a seat in front of her, gazing at the portrait behind her: Papa and myself, when I was a boy of maybe four or five. We both looked so utterly miserable and out of place, the only thing connecting us was DNA. Our sharp Nordic features and glacial eyes.

"The conservatory is dusty," I drawled.

"Is it, now?" She licked her finger before flipping a page on the document in front of her. "Well, I must tell the cleaners to pay extra attention to the room tomorrow."

"Are you having financial issues?"

She was still frowning at the number splayed on the paper. "Oh, Devvie. Must we talk about finances? It's so very common. You just got here. I want us to brunch and to catch up properly. Maybe catch a horse race."

"We'll do all of that, Mummy. But I need to know that you're taken care of."

"We'll survive." She looked up, offering me a wobbly smile.

"When's the reading of the will exactly? Tomorrow or the next day?"

"Actually…" she finished writing a sentence on a document, setting her pen down "…the reading of the will, will be severely delayed, I'm afraid."

"Severely?" I arched an eyebrow. "Why?"

"Mr. Tindall is currently abroad."

Harry Tindall was my late father's trusted solicitor.

"And you failed to mention that before I boarded a plane?"

She smiled thoughtfully, staring at my hair like she wanted to swipe her motherly fingers across it lovingly. "I guess you could say the opportunity to see you presented itself, and the human that I was, I yielded to temptation. I'm sorry." Her eyes shone with unshed tears. "Terribly so."

That soothed my anger. "Shush, Mum. I'm here for you."

I reached across the desk and grabbed her hand. She was frail under my touch.

"I'll wire you money to tide you over until the reading of the will," I heard myself say.

"No, darling, we couldn't possibly …"

"Of course you could. You're my mother. It's the least I can do for you."

For a moment, all we did was stare at each other, drinking every new line and wrinkle we'd accumulated in the last year.

"I hear Drew leaves much to be desired in the making Cecilia happy department." I sprawled in my seat, crossing my ankles over the desk.

My mother picked up her pen again and scribbled on the edges of the file, gnawing on her lower lip, as she did whenever my father was up to no good and she knew she was about to clean up his mess. "Quite."

"What can I do to help?"

"There's nothing you can do, really. That is for your sister to handle."

"Cece is not used to taking care of such things." Understatement of the fucking century. When we were kids, I got into hot water on a daily basis to save my sister's arse.

Mum tugged at her lower lip, mulling this over. "All the same, it is time for her to start learning how to hold her own. The only thing you can do for me now is refrain from providing us with any scandalous headlines. We certainly don't need those."

In that moment, my mother looked so broken, so tired, so weathered by the tragedies life had thrown at her, I couldn't crush her completely. Not when there was so little hope left for her.

Which was why I couldn't tell her I was planning to impregnate a ditzy burlesque club owner out of wedlock, who, by the way, was sprawled on billboards all over the East Coast positively naked.

But Belle wasn't even pregnant. What was the point of telling my mother about this? This situation could be revisited in three, four, or five months, when the dust on my father's grave had settled.

No need to give my mother more bad news.

"No scandalous headlines …" I grinned back at her. "Promise."

Seven
Devon

Devon: still ovulating?

Belle: six days later? Do I look like an African driver ant?

I had to Google the reference to learn that the average African driver ant produced three to four million eggs each month and was considered to be the most fertile animal on planet Earth.

Devon: not from this angle. Get on your knees with your bum up and hold a crumb of bread just so I can be sure.

Belle: why are you asking anyway?

Devon: trying to conceive tonight couldn't hurt our chances, correct?

Belle: technically not, but said chances would be slim.

Devon: slim, but in existence.

Belle: are you waiting for an invitation?

Devon: from your ill-mannered arse? No. I'm already on my way.

Belle: this is going to stop as soon as I'm pregnant.

Devon: absolutely.

Belle: I mean it. I already feel personally attacked by your presence in my life.

Devon: no point asking why you hate men so much, I suppose?

Belle: none, if you want a straight, honest answer.

Devon: understood. Consider yourself rid of me as soon as you're with child.

Belle: WITH CHILD.

Belle: you embarrass my soul.

Belle: I'm waiting at Madame Mayhem.

Devon: I'm pulling over. Do not wear knickers.

I didn't even bother getting into the shower after landing at Boston Logan International Airport.

I cabbed it straight to Madame Mayhem, relying on my good friends, mint gum and deodorant.

The entire journey from England to America, all I could think about was burying myself inside the voluptuous, hotheaded woman. I was not completely sure where my fascination with Emmabelle stemmed from, but if I were to take a wild guess, I'd say it was because she was genuinely independent. She did not rely on a wealthy man—unlike her sister and friends—and seemed completely unfazed to be the only single person in the room, other than myself, even when things got awkward.

She was outspoken, fierce, and confident.

She was also a stunner.

In the cab on my way to Belle, I wired my mother a handsome amount of money. Just as I was about to tuck the device back to my pocket, a message popped on the screen:

Unknown Number: are you still home? Lou. x

Louisa and I had exchanged phone numbers before she left Whitehall Court Castle after my father's funeral. Since I didn't want to repeat my ghosting mistake twice, I added her to my contacts and answered her.

Devon: back in Boston, but I'll be headed to Britain for the reading of the will. Lunch?

Louisa: and drinks.

Devon: I never say no to those.

Louisa: good. Then I'll make sure to crack open that Remy Martin cognac.

When I got to Madame Mayhem, I cut the four-hundred-yard line, slapped a few Benjamins on one of the bouncer's chest and sauntered in, leaving a trail of disgruntled people behind me.

I found Belle manning the bar again, serving beers and flinging her blond hair behind her shoulder. She was clad in a top that looked like crème, ripped bodice, and cherry-red leather pants I was soon going to destroy with my teeth.

Goodbye to my promise of no scandals. It was good while it lasted … a couple days and some change.

Zeroing in on her, I made my way across the club, shouldering past people dancing and drunkenly laughing into each other's ears.

Belle was so wrapped up in serving her customers, she didn't even glance my way when she asked. "What can I get for you, honey?"

Honey.

The woman was a national embarrassment. What on earth propelled me to put a baby in her?

"Bend over, on all fours, while wearing nothing but a sultry expression, while begging me to fuck you."

Her head twisted as shock flashed across her beautiful face. Her glare melted into an amused smile.

"I have twenty more minutes here." Her hands moved quickly behind the bar. She seemed in no hurry to cater to me, the exact opposite of Louisa.

"No, you don't. You'll be waiting for me in your office in no more than ten minutes, buck naked and in the position I want you in."

"*Or?*" She snorted, angling the soda gun in my direction threateningly.

"Or…" I grabbed the soda gun from across the bar and shoved it into her cleavage, right between her tits, lowering my voice an octave, my lips hovering over the shell of her ear "…I will see to it that you spend the night with your good friend, Magic Wand."

"At least the magic wand doesn't make idle promises," she whispered back.

I pushed the button and sprayed cold diet coke between her breasts. Bubbles spilled over from her push-up bra. She let out a squeak, pushing me away.

"What do you think you're doing, asshole?"

"Standing up to you, unlike all the other poor sods you pick as your lovers," I said dryly.

"Withholding sex from me as punishment is your idea of standing up to me?" She let out a wild laugh, leaning down to grab a cloth and patting her chest dry. "Dude, you're high. I can get it anytime I want it, anywhere I want it."

"No arguments there. But it's not sex you are after, Sweven. It is a child, and I know I'm the only one who'll do." I took a step back, glancing at my watch. "I have a conference call with Tokyo. I'll see you in ten."

"You're going to pay for that little stunt," she warned, slapping the cloth against the bar.

She threw more threats into the air, but I was already gone, accepting the call Joanne connected me to.

The call did not take more than four minutes. While Emmabelle wrapped things up, I wrote an email to my late father's solicitor, Mr.

Tindall, to see when the reading of the will would happen. Worry gnawed at my gut. Mum and Cece were in trouble.

I was careful to let Emmabelle wait an extra eight minutes before I pushed open the door to her office. She was waiting for me on her desk, which was littered with paperwork, envelopes, and a laptop, exactly as I requested. Naked and on all fours. She faced the wall, not the door, her yellow hair spilling in sheets across her back.

At the sound of the door clicking open, she whipped her head around. I *tsked*. "Arse up and eyes on the wall."

"I've heard better dirty talk from decorative houseplants, but I'm having too much fun to kick you out." She turned back toward the wall.

I locked the door and strode into the room unhurriedly. Her pert arse was high in the air, the center of her pink and already glistening. She was ready for me, and I was going to take my sweet time enjoying her.

I stopped in front of her, silently admiring every perfect curve of her. Emmabelle Penrose was exquisite to a point she needn't work a day in her life if she wished to. She could marry into fortune. Yet, she hadn't.

"You still there?" she groaned. Secretly, her deliberately bad grammar amused me, even though the same trait grated on my nerves on anyone else.

"Patience." I rolled my knuckles over the side of her arse, the touch so brief, so fleeting, her entire body flushed and her back arched as if I'd stuffed my cock into her.

"You're such a tease," she moaned. "Knock me up already."

"With pleasure." I bit the side of her bum softly, my teeth sinking into her derriere like it was a juicy peach.

I pried the lips of her pussy open with my thumbs from behind, and licked her slit, using the tip of my tongue to drive her mad.

"Arghhhhhhhh," she drowsed, letting her head drop as her arms began to shake.

Plastering a hand over the small of her back to lower her upper body, I pushed her open even wider, licking in long, deep strokes. I drank her sweetness, watching as she thrashed her head, stifling her little grunts of pleasure just to spite me. Her knees were shaking. She was liquid fire, every inch of her body scorching with arousal.

"Oh. Oh. Shit. Shit. Fuck," she murmured. The future mother of my child, ladies and gentlemen.

"My lady," I drawled sarcastically, my fingers wrapping around the flesh of her arse tighter, licking her more fervently. She came so violently she fell flat on her stomach across the desk.

"Damn." She plastered her sweaty forehead to the desk. "That's never happened to me before. That was *fast*."

"Better you than me." I gave her rear a patronizing little pat.

"Holy crap, dude. Did you use some kind of trick? That was *intense*."

Rather than answer her observation, I flipped her on her back and grabbed the back of her knees, dragging her across the desk until her bum was perched on its edge, wrapping her bare legs around my waist.

She unbuckled me. The glee in which her hands moved told me she was more than glad I was back on American soil.

"Are you ever going to be fully naked when we have sex?" she teased, her tongue circling patterns along my neck.

"You're the one who wants to keep it detached." My bored tone did not match the monstrous erection the woman in front of me had just freed out of my trousers. Or the rush of erotic excitement coursing through me.

"Fair point," she laughed.

I tormented her a few minutes before pressing home.

She *ohhhhhed*.

Being with her again felt better than the last time, and all the times before it. That was the issue with Emmabelle Penrose. She tasted like the greatest sin, and I was a well-known transgressor whenever temptation came knocking on my door.

She came again before I spilled my seed inside her. I collapsed on top of her, spent, the jet lag catching up with me all at once.

"Bro," Belle said after a few seconds of my panting atop of her. "Heavy much? Get off of me."

I peeled away and took a seat on the chair in front of her desk, this time refusing to evacuate myself like a common prostitute. I had to establish some sort of authority with this wild child.

I made a show of propping my legs on her messy desk and lighting myself a rollie, sinking idly in my seat.

"Aren't you going to ask how my England trip went?" I sent a plume of smoke skyward, watching as it ribboned around itself.

She hopped off the table and got dressed under the lamp, unbothered by the stark, unflattering light. "No. I don't give two shits what or who you do when I'm not around."

"My father died." I ignored her sheer vulgarity.

That made her stop. She made a show of pressing a fist against her lips, as if stuffing her words back inside. "That was a foot-in-mouth moment for me. I'm really sorry, Dev."

"I'm not," I said flatly. "But thank you."

"How're you … er, handling things?" She shoved a leg into her leather pants.

"Quite well, considering I loathed him with every atom in my body."

"I'm surprised Cillian and Sam didn't say anything." Belle watched me carefully for a reaction. Smart lass. We both knew I hadn't shared anything about my personal life with my mates. She must've wondered what business I had confiding in her of all people. I happened to wonder the same bloody thing. As far as sympathetic audiences went, she was a tad cooler than Antarctica.

"I keep my private life private." I exhaled rings of smoke, sending arrows into them.

"Still…" Belle flipped her hair out of the back of her top and swaggered over to me, slinging herself against the desk "…losing a parent is always hard. Even if—and sometimes especially—you don't get along with them. It reminds you of your own mortality. Living is a messy business."

"So is your desk," I commented, ready to change the topic. "Why does it look like an Office Depot branch exploded all over it?"

She let out a laugh. "I'm a messy person, Devon. Welcome to my life."

"That's not true." I swung forward, removing my loafers from her desk and sifting through the wrinkled and stained envelopes on it. "You are highly calculated and driven. You have a fourteen-foot-high bill-board of yourself bathing in a massive champagne glass and a business you could sell tomorrow and live comfortably. Yet there are piles upon piles of unopened letters here. Walk me through your logic."

To reinforce my statement, I lifted a batch of a dozen or so envelopes in the air. They all looked handwritten and addressed to her person-ally. Sweven snatched them from my hand and dropped them into the bin beneath us. A witchy smile marred her face. I knew I'd hit a nerve.

"Why should I? They're not bills; unlike some fax-using dinosaurs, I pay mine online. And they're not from friends, because they would pick up the phone and call me. Ninety-nine percent of these letters are written by ultra-conservative lunatics who want to inform me that I'm going to burn in hell for running a burlesque club. Now why would I put myself through that?"

"Is that all these letters are?" I pressed. "Hate mail?"

"Every single one of them." She picked up another batch, sliding one of the papers from an envelope. She cleared her throat theatrically and began reading:

"*Dear Ms. Penrose,*

My name is Howard Garrett, and I'm a sixty-two-year-old mechanic from Telegraph Hill. I am writing to you today in hopes you would change your ways and see the light, as I find you solely responsible for the corrup-tion and veenality—he spelled venality wrong—*of our youth.*

My granddaughter visited your establishment the other day after seeing an ad with naked women about it in a local magazine. Three days later, she arrived at my house to inform me that she was now gay. A co-incidence? I don't think so. Queerness is, in case you are unaware, an act of war against God … should I continue…" she perched her chin on her knuckles, a faux-angelic look on her face "…or did your brain short-circuit?"

"He sounds like he's from the Stone Age."

"Maybe you're neighbors," she smirked.

"There are dozens of letters here. Are all of them from religious old sods complaining about sex?" I pressed.

Belle was a basket full of complications. Her job, her personality, her attitude. And yet I couldn't find it in me to back out of our arrangement.

"Yes, I'm sure." Belle scowled, plucking the cigarette from between my fingers and giving it a puff and returning it back to me. "I'm a big girl. I can take care of myself."

"Being taken care of is not a sin."

"I know." She grinned devilishly at me with a wink. "If it was, I would be all over it."

"Did you know there's a bird called a shoebill that looks uncannily like Severus Snape?"

"Did you know Chinese water deer look like Bambi after he got himself a brand-new moustache?" She grinned back at me, and just like that, the tension between us was over.

Belle's phone began dancing on the desk, flashing green with an incoming call. She craned her neck to see the name on the screen, let out a sigh, and picked it up. "Hey."

She hopped down from the desk and scampered as far away from me as possible in the tiny office. I could tell she didn't want me to stay during this conversation, which naturally made me find an even more comfortable spot so I could listen carefully.

"Yes. I'm doing good, thank you. And yourself?" she asked curtly.

I was surprised with how pliant and polite she sounded. How completely not herself. There was no hint of the fireball who teased me a second ago.

She stopped in front of a batch of pictures pinned to a corkboard by her window, fingering the colorful pins absently. It looked to be her family members, though I couldn't see from afar.

"Now's a good time. Why? Did something happen?" she asked.

There was a pause while she listened to the person on the other line then answered with an uncomfortable laugh. "Yes, well, tell her I accept her invitation. What wine should I bring?"

Pause.

"Yes, I'm sure everything is fine. I'm just at work."

Pause.

"Busy."

Pause.

"I bought you all the fishing supplies. No, you don't have to pay me back. We're family. I'll bring them when I come."

Something about her exchange with the mysterious person made my blood turn into ice. She sounded foreign, far away. She shed her personality like a snake before picking up the call.

She finally hung up, rearranging her hair distractedly.

"Who was that?"

"My dad." She made her way to the door, flinging it open. She tilted her head in its direction. "Out."

"Are your parents still together?" I asked, in no hurry to vacate my spot behind her desk. I'd met them at a few family functions, such as Cillian and Persy's wedding and the christenings of their sons, but I never paid close attention to either one of them. They were, indeed, as dull as their daughter was extraordinary.

"Happily." She tapped her foot impatiently. "But that's another story, to be told to someone I'm actually, you know, friends with. We're done now, Devon. Get out."

I took my sweet time standing up just to spite her, asking myself for the millionth time why I was doing this. Yes, she was stunning, intelligent, and strong-willed. But she was also utterly horrible to me and any other man I'd ever come across. There was no thawing her. Even when we were physically together, she was so far away she might as well have been on the moon.

"His marriage might be happy, but his daughter isn't whenever he calls her," I said, strolling toward the door.

Belle pounced over to the threshold, blocking my way out. A venomous, pained smile touched her lips.

"Aw, Devvie. I forgot to say no family talk."

Grinning—she really shouldn't have pushed me—I turned around and walked over to the pinboard, squinting to take a better look at it. Digging into people's Achilles heels until they screamed the truth was my specialty. I didn't want to do that to her—she was not a client—but

Belle was also a woman who knew how to push all my buttons. And there weren't many.

My suspicion proved to be right.

Emmabelle had pictures of all of her family members: her mother, her sister, her nephews, and even some photos of that redheaded banshee she called a friend—Sailor.

But not one of her father.

"The daddy issue theory is getting warmer, Sweven," I said on my way to the door.

"Yeah, well, maybe I'm not the only one with daddy issues. You seem a little too glad your father passed."

"Party's tomorrow night. Wear something fun," I quipped back.

"Wowza. I'm no fortune teller, but I see a lot of therapy in your future, dude."

"I'm perfectly fine with how I turned out. You, however, have a big, fat secret, Emmabelle, and make no mistakes. I'm going to uncover it."

As always, she slammed the door the minute I was out of it.

As always, I laughed.

It was only when I got back home that I noticed Belle's payback for my stuffing her cleavage with a cold drink.

All in all, it was a lovely little surprise.

A used pair of lady knickers stuffed in the front pocket of my slacks.

Sitting at my study, I tugged it out, grinning at the pink lacey fabric. I leaned back in my recliner, throwing my head back, giving it a hearty sniff. I draped the undies over my head and groaned with pleasure, getting a stiffy, when a note fell from them.

I picked it up.

Hey Dev,

You just sniffed my best friend, Ross' balls.

Hope you enjoyed.

—Sweven

Eight

Belle

Fourteen Years Old.

"GROSS."

I announce to the universe, because honestly, it is. Watching your parents making out in the front seat of their Honda Accord Wagon like two teenagers is next level cringe.

Persy doesn't seem to share the sentiment, sighing romantically beside me in the back seat. "Let them be."

"Nah, your sister's right. There's a time and a place for everything, and this ain't it." Dad pulls away from Mom, dropping one last kiss on her shoulder before putting his hands where I can see them—on the steering wheel.

To make matters worse (and you have to admit, shit's already pretty dire if I have to watch my parents exchanging saliva with nowhere to run), we're in the drive-thru line, about to pick up our burgers and milkshakes. Like I have an appetite after that make out sesh.

Burgers and shakes are a Sunday night staple and a decade-long Penrose tradition. Each week, we grab the food, drive to Piers Park, and *annihilate greasy french fries and shakes while watching Boston's dancing lights.*

I've already decided that when I get married, a trillion years from now, I'm going to keep this tradition with my husband and kids.

The car before us slides away from the drive-thru, and it's our turn. Dad rolls down his window and plucks a wad of cash out of his tattered wallet, waving it at the uniformed teenager in the window.

"There ya' go, sweetheart. And I'll pay for the person behind us too."

He does that every week.

Pays for the person behind us.

Sometimes it's a single mom in a beat-up car.

Sometimes, like today, it's a group of rowdy college kids. Their windows are open and a thick cloud of weed smoke curls up from their Buick LeSabre.

"That's very nice of you, sir," the cashier says, leaning forward to hand him the brown paper bags with our food and our drinks.

Mom lets out a breathless giggle.

"A little kindness goes a long way." Dad drapes his arm along Mom's passenger seat. He beams at her like they're on their first date and he wants to make an impression. I wish Coach Locken would beam at me like that.

I think he came close. Once.

Locken is my track and cross-country coach. And I just happen to be the star of his mediocre team. A team I didn't even think about trying out for before he walked into my class on the first week of ninth grade and pleaded with us to try out for it.

It's been a few weeks now, and I think I'm putting a real dent in getting him to notice me. That almost-beam is my breakthrough.

It happened in the cafeteria last week. He was on lunch duty that day. He looked rad in his blue windbreaker—our school logo emblazoned on it—khaki pants, and trendy sneakers. He was way taller than all the other boys, even the seniors, and had stubble and dimples in his cheeks.

"Stop looking at him," Ross, my best guy-friend, chided, ducking his head down at our lunch table. "He is a grown-ass man."

"Like it ever stopped you before." I threw a french fry at him. Ross had just come out to me two weeks ago. Shocking, it was not. I noticed how we both shared the same appreciation of Channing Tatum while watching Magic Mike.

"I only look, I don't touch." Ross dodged the french fry like it was a bullet. I think he's been watching his weight since preschool.

"I don't touch Mr. Locken." I pointed at him with a baby carrot.

"Not yet." He leaned forward and snatched the carrot between his teeth, chewing. "You always get what you want. It's actually kind of scary."

I snuck another glance at Coach Locken, and lo and behold, he smiled at me.

Not just smiled … beamed.

I was about to stand up and walk over to him. But then the rest of the cross-country team huddled in the cafeteria. All dudes. There was a cross-country team for girls too, but I was so ridiculously better that Coach decided to let me practice with the guys. I wiped the floor with their asses too, but at least they came somewhat close.

Planting my butt on the bench, I cursed them inwardly. I couldn't be seen striking up conversation with Steve Locken now. People'd think I was pulling strings, cutting corners.

"You need Jesus." Ross shook his head when he saw the longing in my face.

There's only one problem with Steve Locken.

Well, two, if you count the fact that he is twenty-nine and my teacher.

He is also married.

"Belly-Belle? Time to get out." Dad twists in his seat and pats my knee now. I jump, startled. Oh shit. Right. I'm with my family on a Sunday outing. I look out the window. We're at Piers Park.

Tomorrow is Monday, which means early track practice in the woods.

Which means more Coach Locken time.

Which means bliss.

"Ah, look at the dreamy smile on her face. I miss those days when I was young," Dad comments, pulling me out of my reverie. "What are you thinking about, sunshine?"

"Nothing." *I unsnap my seat belt.*

Everything, *I think as I make my way out of the car.*

Nine

Belle

TURNED OUT THE OVULATION KIT I'D SHELLED OUT GOOD money for at Walgreens was as necessary as sunscreen when taking a lengthy summer vacation on the sun.

Because that month, after Devon had come back from England, we had sex every single day. You know, *just in case.*

Actually, we sometimes had sex twice a day, which was totally unnecessary and yet too much fun. I knew this wasn't something I'd revisit after I got pregnant, so I figured why not?

(Apparently, the answer to the question *why not?* could be found on medical sites. It explains that sperm count—and quality—decreases if couples do it every day. Joke's on them, because Devon and I weren't a couple).

We'd meet in the mornings, after he got back from his fencing sessions and before he went to work. Or during his lunch breaks. Or whenever I happened to get in my ten thousand steps per day by his office and decided to stop by to say hello.

Then again at night, after I was done with work.

We screwed in every position, every hour of the day.

Devon was always charming, cordial, and aloof. He accepted all my quirks and flaws, even when I was being deliberately unbearable to remind him that I was not marriable. At the same time, his detachment scared the bejesus out of me. I'd never seen a guy so out of touch with his feelings.

I figured from his phone calls whenever we were together that he was waiting for an important message from England. Something about his inheritance. He spoke to his mom on the phone. *A lot.* Cooing and doting on her in a way that made me happy he was going to be the father of my child.

Even when he spoke to his sister, he always used a calm, sweet tone that made my bones turn to mush. In a way, it was really cruel of him to be so kind. A girl could forget to keep her guard up with such a perfect guy. That girl, fortunately, wasn't going to be me.

Nice men are still men. Don't get close.

Though I tried really hard to keep Devon at arm's length, I knew he was getting intimate glimpses into my life. Into my family. Into my story.

I didn't like it.

Which was why when our arrangement hit the four-week mark, and I looked at the calendar and realized my period was a day late, I was filled with elation tinged with mortification.

There was a chance I was pregnant.

With a marquess's heir.

I held off the pregnancy test for two more days, which took herculean effort.

Mainly, I was scared. Scared of a negative result—what if the hormones didn't work—and scared of a positive result—a baby! I can't take care of a whole freaking baby! I can barely take care of a chia pet. In fact, I did *not* take care of my last chia pet. Aisling took it from me at some point and tried to save it, but it was too far gone.

Finally, on the third day, I bit the bullet, marched into Walgreens, and purchased a pregnancy test. I treated myself to the bougie-ass one. The 99.99% fancy test, where it spells out the result for you. It dawned on me, on the way to checkout, that nothing was quite as frightening as a pregnancy test. Each woman who bought one had very strong feelings about what she wanted to see. Pregnancy was not like whole-wheat bread. You couldn't be indifferent about it.

Either you *really* wanted to get pregnant.

Or you really *didn't* want to get pregnant.

There was no middle ground.

When the cashier slipped the test through her scanner, I noticed her glancing at my bare wedding finger. She curved a judgmental brow.

Yeah, well, my kid is about to become English royalty, Karen.

Smiling extra wide, I said, "Isn't that scary?"

"Depends on your situation," she answered briskly.

"Yeah. Mine is not that bad. I only have to figure out who the father is."

She paled. I laughed. I grabbed the plastic bag and darted to work. I locked myself in the restroom, trying not to remember all the times Devon had devoured me on my desk, my chair, and on my floor during the weeks we were trying for a baby.

Squatting over the toilet to pee on a stick, I decided to occupy myself by getting into my group chat with the girls while my pee worked its way along the pregnancy test.

The group was always super active, so all I really needed to do was jump in.

Sailor: Hunter wants to go to Cancun for the summer. Are y'all game?

Persy: sure. Just give me the dates and I'll tell Cillian to block them off in his schedule.

Aisling: dunno about me and Sam. We want to visit Switzerland for a few weeks. I have to visit the clinic.

Persy: oh yeah. Cillian mentioned joining you guys in Zurich. Something about meeting with his bankers?

Look at these bougie ass bitches, making plans for the summer like it wasn't still wintertime.

Sailor: what about you, Belle? Up for margaritas poolside with the Fitzpatricks?

Belle: as much as I want to feel like a third wheel in this basic bitch couple-a-thon, some of us have actual businesses to run.

Sailor: aunt flow's in town, I see. Tuck your attitude back in, Belle. It's showing.

She was so off base it was comical. At least, I *hoped* she was.

Persy: come on @BellePenrose. You work so hard. Our treat.

I didn't want to be treated to things. I wanted to be independent enough to never rely on other people's good graces. It was something my sister, who had always been a romantic, couldn't fully understand. She was fine letting people take care of her because it was in her nature to take care of *them*. Even when she married Cillian, it wasn't for his money. Not really.

Belle: that's sweet of you, Pers, but I really do have a lot of work.

Persy: don't say I didn't try.

Sailor: don't worry, Pers. We'll tag team her when we see her.

Belle: ah, just like in college. Only you're not the entire baseball team.

Aisling: have you ever had a threesome, Belle?

Aisling: (and before you ask, yes, I'm blushing).

Belle: more like reverse harem.

I checked the timestamp on the beginning of the conversation and realized six minutes had passed. Taking a deep breath, I picked up the pregnancy test from the vanity in the restroom and closed my eyes.

It's going to be okay.

You'll get pregnant.

You're doing this with a man who would move mountains to get what he wants, and he wants an heir.

I flipped the pregnancy test over and popped my eyes open.

Pregnant.

The gasp that tore out of my throat rattled the walls. I was sure of it. There was joy and fear and delight in it.

I was pregnant.

I was going to become a mother.

This was happening.

Maybe. The trouble wasn't just conceiving, but keeping the baby, remember? a voice inside me cautioned.

For a few moments, I didn't know what to do with myself. I paced around the small restroom, stopped by the mirror over the sink, and pinched my cheeks, screaming silently a-la Macaulay Culkin in *Home Alone.*

A mother.

Me.

There was no one else I was going to need.

No one but my baby. We were going to be there for each other. Finally, I would have someone else to take care of, someone who would look after me the way Persy and I did before she married Cillian and started her own, tight-knit family.

After pulling myself together, I snapped a picture of the pregnancy test and sent it to Devon. No caption was needed. I wanted to see his reaction.

The two blue V's signaling Devon had received and opened the message appeared on the screen.

Then … nothing.

Ten seconds.

Twenty seconds.

After the thirty second mark, I began feeling uneasy. Almost defensive.

What the hell was his problem?

I began typing a scathing message, with plenty of profanity and a good dose of accusations, when a call appeared on my screen.

Devon Whitehall

I cleared my throat, adopting his bland, annoying tone.

"*Whaddup?*"

"We make a good team, Sweven." Devon's laugh echoed from the other side of the line, reaching the pit of my stomach. It made a stopover in my heart, making my pulse stutter unevenly.

I wasn't expecting the joy in his voice. I wasn't expecting any kind of feeling from this Adonis statue of a man.

"I mean, we *did* work super hard and long on this," I sassed.

"Don't forget thick." I heard him lighting up a cigarette.

"I could never forget the thick part. It is the thing I'll remember you by when I'm old and wrinkly and you're long dead and buried next to your beloved fax machine."

"The fax machine gets cremated. She wants her ashes to be spread in the ocean, and you know I can't refuse her." Dammit, he was funny, in an odd kind of way.

"A baby," I whispered again, shaking my head. "Can you believe it?"

"Still digesting," he chuckled. But he didn't sound as overwhelmed as I was, for better or worse. "Well, it was indeed a pleasure to do business with you." I heard the hustle and bustle of his office in the background. "I will, of course, begin wiring you an amount of twenty thousand dollars a month. We'll discuss your accommodations and furnishings for the babe's rooms in our respective places during the second trimester. Though, of course, as per our contract, I shall expect weekly updates from you."

Um, okay.

Technically, Devon didn't say anything bad. On the contrary. I told him I wanted nothing to do with his ass after I got pregnant, and he was just sticking to the script. To what we signed off on that night I stood him up at the opera. But I couldn't shake this weird feeling that I'd been discarded like an old sock.

You wanted to be discarded like an old sock. In fact, you threw your-self headfirst into the laundry basket.

"Duh." I yawned audibly, pretending to be undeterred by his businesslike manner. "Is email okay for the updates? I would fax them, but I'm under seventy-five."

"Email is great. We should also schedule a weekly call."

Now *that* sounded more personal.

"I'm down," I said, a little too quickly.

What was wrong with me? Hormones, I decided. Also, I was going to celebrate by consuming my body weight in cake. I was now eating for two, even if the other person inside me was currently smaller than a grain of rice.

"I'll have my secretary, Joanne, contact you about times and dates that suit both of us."

All right, scratch that. Totally not personal.

"I'll probably have to see my doctor every week because my uterus is hostile and my ovaries are polycystic."

I made a note to add this to my Tinder profile whenever I got back to the one-night stand pool. It made me sound like a real catch. *Not.*

"Sweven …" Devon said. It felt like honey had been poured inside my guts when he called me by that stupid nickname. "I promise to be the father this child deserves. A better father than we both had."

His comment was like a bucket of ice poured over my fuzzy feeling. I never told him anything bad about my dad. He just made that assumption from the two-minute phone call. But that was bullshit. My dad and I were perfectly fine.

Great even.

I would totally shed a tear or two when he died, unlike cold and uncaring Devon, who looked practically relieved when his dad kicked the bucket.

Not wanting to display any more emotion than I already had, I laughed throatily.

"Speak for yourself, Devon. My dad is the bomb dot com."

"I may be seventy-five, but at least you'd never catch me saying what you just said."

"What was that?" I challenged.

He chuckled. "Nice try."

"How about a moment of zen?" I offered. "Let's talk about weird-ass animals. Have you ever seen a lowland streaked tenrec?"

"Can't say I have."

"They look like bleached skunks who just woke up after a night of partying and MDMA and need to get their roots done."

"What about markhors?" he asked. "They look like women in BabyLiss commercials. Have a great day, Sweven. Thank you for the good news."

After we hung up, I shot Doctor Bjorn an email informing him of the development and asking him if I needed to do anything other than eat well, sleep well, rest, and all the other mumbo-jumbo I'd already read about in the dozens of pregnancy articles I consumed on a daily basis.

I reopened the chat with the girls, my fingers shaking with excitement. It was too soon. I knew that. And totally irresponsible considering it was a high-risk pregnancy. But I was never really good at delaying gratification.

Belle: I have news to share. Meet tomorrow at Boston Common?

Aisling: absolutely.

Persy: I think I know what it is and I'm excited.

Sailor: see you there.

I didn't need Devon.

I had the Boston Belles.

Ten

Belle

Fourteen Years Old.

T HE FIRST TIME IS INNOCENT.

I don't even think you can call it a first time.

We're deep into ninth grade now—exams, homework, girl cliques. I stay away from the white noise and stick to the goal: running the fastest, making sure my baby sister Persephone and her friend Sailor are not getting picked on at school, and fantasizing about kissing Coach Locken.

During one of our grueling track practices, I feel a sharp pain in my knee.

I keep running—I'm no quitter. But when Locken blows the whistle that's eternally tucked inside his mouth, I stop, limping my way back to him with the rest of the harriers. I try to cover up my limp, because I'm starting to understand something about human nature. When people smell weakness, that's when they pounce.

"Shit, dude. That looks rough." Adam Handler makes a face, jerking his chin in the direction of my knee. I look down, still wobbling over to Coach. Shit indeed. My knee is swollen and red.

"It's fine," I snap defensively. "I can barely feel it."

"What's happening here, Penrose?" Mr. Locken parks his fists on his waist. His voice is tender, softer than the tone he uses with the boys. No one ever calls him out on it. Why would they? I'm the only girl on the team, so people just figure, you know, it's about trying to make me feel welcome.

Only I know the truth.

The truth is that he's been beaming at me more and more lately.

And that I've been beaming right back.

I know it's wrong. I know he's married. That his wife is pregnant. I'm not dumb. But I'm not planning to take this anywhere. I just want to enjoy his attention. That's all. In a way (a truly screwed-up, roundabout way), I even think I'm doing his wife a favor. As long as he keeps his eyes on me, he is in no danger of acting on his urges. At least he won't cheat on her.

Anyway, it's dumb. I don't know her, and I don't owe her anything. And also, maybe it's just in my weird head. Maybe he is not looking at me after all.

"All good, Coach." I smile through the pain, showing him I'm a trooper.

"Doesn't look good to me. C'mere."

I do. All the other boys surround me, toothpick legs and overgrown ears poking from their bodies. They all wince and point at my knee.

Here comes trouble, as Dad loves to say.

Coach Locken bends on one knee and frowns at my leg. I can feel his breath scraping my skin. It's hot and moist. Excited tingles chase one another down my spine.

"I'll get you an ice pack. Wait in my office."

"No, really, I'm good," my dumb mouth protests, even though my brain tells it to shut up and take advantage. I've never had one-on-one time with Coach Locken.

"Nothing will be good when you're benched all season because of a runner's knee and I lose my cross-country star and you lose your scholarship." Locken already has his back to me as he herds the rest of the boys to the locker room.

I limp my way to his office, which is tucked at the end of the hallway. The door is open. I take a seat in front of his desk and let out a whimper, because hot damn, it does hurt. *Looking for a distraction, I peer around me. There's a crap load of books about running on his shelves, a few trophies, and framed pictures of him hugging famous athletes. On his blond wooden desk is his engagement picture with his wife. They're in some kind of a hay field, kissing, and her hand is tilted to the camera to catch the diamond ring. She looks small and is a brunette and … I don't know … good. She looks like a nice person, not like all the things I hoped she'd be. I'm slammed with terrible, disgusting guilt for constantly fantasizing about him kissing me.*

This is stupid. I should get up and leave.

Quit cross-country while I'm at it. Volleyball sounds more like my jam.

I'm bracing the armrests, about to stand up when he walks into his office and closes the door. He is bigger than I remembered. Taller. He fills up the room. It reminds me of my dad, and I'm crazy about my dad. But Mr. Locken also still looks boyish enough that, unlike my dad, it's not creepy to think about kissing him.

I lean back in my chair. Business as usual.

Coach Locken lifts an ice pack in the air then tosses it over to me. "Press."

I do as I'm told. The cold feels nice against my knee. I groan. "I better get a scholarship. I don't even like running."

He laughs and to my surprise drags his chair and positions it in front of mine. My heart beats a thousand miles a minute.

"How's it feeling now?" he asks. His timbre is low, gruff.

"Yeah. Fine." I feel so dumb, so young, so juvenile. I wish I had something sophisticated to say. Something to blow him out of the water. To make sure he knows I'm more than just a kid.

"Let me have a look." He pats his knee in invitation.

I swing my gaze to him, uncertain what he's asking me for. Surely, he's not suggesting …

"Put your foot in my lap. I wanna see what's the damage."

I do as I'm told, my chest swelling with pride. I'm pretty sure he'd never offer this to any of the other boys on my team.

His lap is taut with muscle. Hard as a rock. My leg is long and skinny and if you look closely, there's a dusting of blond hair covering it. He leans forward, removing the ice pack I'm pressing against my knee. He frowns.

"Doesn't look any better."

"It feels okay," I lie.

"Try rotating your leg."

I try. Fail. I mean, I can do it. It just hurts like a mothertrucker.

Coach Locken releases a resigned sigh.

"It'll help if we encourage some blood circulation. May I?" He lifts his hands—nice hands, I note—and keeps them in the air, looking at me questioningly.

He wants to touch me? Really?

"Just to get the blood flow back to the knee," he explains.

Duh. Of course. I have to get my mind out of the gutter. This is so embarrassing.

I gulp, looking into those brown eyes.

He kind of looks like Matthew Broderick in Ferris Bueller's Day Off. *Dorky-hot. The kind of hot you can trust because the world still has expectations of him to behave.*

Honestly, I'm not even sure why I'm being weird about it. It's not like he's sexually harassing me. He is literally asking me if it's okay. A rapist would just jump on me without permission. I'm reading way too much into this.

I nod, watching him through inquisitive eyes as he begins massaging my knee. It feels innocent. I'm at a stage where I'm curious about kissing and fondling and stuff, but penises are still a major turnoff. They're just so … extra. Like, sit down. You don't have to stand there like a stripper pole every time someone takes their bra off.

He pushes his thumbs toward my knee to help the circulation. The once sharp pain becomes mild now. I feel the muscles unknotting under his fingers.

"Better?" Locken asks.

I nod again. Swallow. Stare at his fingers. At his wedding ring. At the way his hands curl and massage the back of my knee now, the sensitive spot, and I giggle and squirm despite myself.

"Your muscles are really tight." His frown deepens. That damn wedding ring feels like fire every time it touches my skin. Why does it have to be there? He could've waited until I graduated—what's four years in comparison to a lifetime—and we could be together.

"You need to work on your stretches, Penrose. Your muscles are shortening. Probably genetic."

"Probably from my mom's side," I agree. Count on Mom to pass down short muscles to me.

His fingers hike up to my thigh. Now it doesn't feel all that innocent anymore. My body tingles. But there's also something else. A ball of anxiety in my throat.

"Y-yeah," I stammer, filling the silence, which has now become uncomfortable. "I should stretch more. I'll add it to my nightly routine."

"It's important."

My leg feels loose and pliant under his touch. I don't even mind that he can see I haven't shaved.

"God, this is so good." I throw my head back and groan.

He chuckles. "You're lucky you're so talented, Penrose. Not everyone gets special treatment."

But is it my talent that makes him do this for me?

His index finger flicks the edge of my track shorts once, close to my groin. I'm about to jerk back, but he pulls away completely, standing up. His smile is shy but calm. He looks me straight in the eye.

"All better?"

Flustered, I grab the ice pack next to me and dart up. "All better."

"Let me know if you need help again. Anytime. Sometimes diamonds need a little rub to shine."

The same day, I raid my dad's bathroom, find a razor, and shave my legs all the way up to my groin area.

I would go to him to massage my knee—my thigh—for the next two months.

Telling myself it's all for the scholarship.

Eleven

Belle

I MET AISLING, SAILOR, AND PERSY AT BOSTON COMMON THE following day.

All three young mothers arrived with their strollers, babies, and two cents to weigh in on my situation.

They were a reminder that soon I was going to have to transport myself from a world of thongs and nightclubs to the wonders of bamboo breast pads, burp cloths, and swaddles.

My friends' strollers matched their personalities.

Sailor pushed a city jogger. Sporty, efficient, and all black. "A customer favorite," she boasted to me once when I was in a great mood and pretended to care.

Persephone had the double Bugaboo for both Astor and Quinn, off-white and trimmed, although she strapped Astor to a dog-like leash and let him roam the park like a drunken Chihuahua.

Then there was Aisling, who had the silver cross Balmoral stroller. It looked classy, expensive, prim and proper—just like the woman it belonged to. Ambrose looked right at home inside it.

We were all bundled up in our coats, striding through the tree-lined common, passing by the Freedom Trail and the soldiers' and sailors' monuments.

The sky was a curtain of ice, clouds moving across in navy blue like the morning throng of downtown professionals.

"Did you know that in the seventeenth century, a woman named Ann Hibbins was executed in the Boston Common on charges of witchcraft?" Sailor asked as she pushed the stroller with Xander. "They hanged her for all to see."

"Christ, Sailor." Aisling did a sign of the cross, side-eyeing our friend. "What a fun-fact to start the day with."

Persy laughed. A stab of melancholy pierced through me. Devon would have appreciated that jab. But I couldn't just text him willy-nilly. We weren't supposed to talk about non-baby related stuff. My rule, which I stood behind. It just sucked.

"Anyway!" Persephone exclaimed. "As much as I'd love to hear about women being hung for witchcraft, Belle has something to tell us."

"Thanks for the subtle transition, Sis."

Since I was the only one who didn't have a stroller to push, I held Rooney, Sailor's toddler daughter, on one of those leashes while she tried chasing pigeons off the paved walkway. She looked like a tiny drunk man trying to pick a fight. I was here for it.

"It's still early, but I wanted to let you know that there's a bun in this oven." I pointed at my stomach.

The girls stopped pushing their strollers and jumped on me with hugs and squeals of delight. Rooney and Astor, who had no idea what was going on but sensed the excitement, pushed between our legs and hugged me too, squealing, "Auntie Belle! Auntie Belle!"

I gathered everyone into my arms and laughed, a little embarrassed. I was going to tell my parents on the phone later this evening. They weren't going to be super happy about my having a child out of wedlock, but I knew they'd come to expect nothing better from me. They knew I wasn't the marrying kind. They had no illusions about me following in my younger sister's footsteps.

"Did you and Devon basically lock yourselves in the bedroom for an entire month? That was fast!" Sailor reached back for her stroller, mirth still dancing in her green eyes.

"Not sure I want to have this conversation when the average age of this group is about two and a half." I waved a hand toward the strollers and kids.

"The kids have no idea what we're talking about," Aisling said primly. "To be honest, mine is still color-blind, he's so young."

"There's Rooney and Astor," Persy reminded her with a smile. "Let's save it for our weekly takeout night."

"In which Belle won't be drinking any wine." Sailor beamed triumphantly. "More for us."

"She won't be going clubbing anytime soon either." Persy seemed particularly happy by that turn of events. "Which means no one can slip anything into her drink."

Not that it ever happened, but my sister was a worrier.

"Anyway, I hope you know we're here for you. Whatever you need, just say the word. Although I think Devon wants to play a huge part in the pregnancy." Persephone tilted her chin downward, inspecting me.

"Devon can screw right off. He knew the score. Wait …" I said as we resumed our walk. "How do you know that?"

"Devon couldn't help himself. He called Cillian last night to break the good news." Persy's face almost splits from her huge grin. "Cillian told me."

I made a mental note to maim Devon with the pregnancy test for his lack of discretion.

"That's total bull. Isn't there some lawyer code or whatever?" I complained, even though it didn't feel half bad knowing Devon was informing the Western world he was going to be a great dad. Especially after his frigid reaction when I told him I was knocked up.

"He's not *your* lawyer, dum dum." Sailor pretended to knock on my temple. "Although, I'm pretty sure he'll have to be at some point with the shenanigans you get yourself into."

"Besides, he probably told Cillian not to tell, and Cillian just couldn't help himself. My brother would give away national secrets and the state of Texas without blinking to meet his wife's approval." Aisling swung her gaze at Persephone with a smile.

Persy's cheeks colored. She ducked her head. Aisling had a point. Cillian was defenseless against his wife. Hunter and Sam weren't too good about saying no to their respective wives either.

I shook my head. "It doesn't matter. I'm just glad it didn't take a bunch of time. I mean, the real risk is to keep the pregnancy. Getting pregnant was the easy part. But still."

"Hmm, guys? I don't mean to be a party pooper, but is it just me or is there a dude with a black coat following us?" Sailor raised an eyebrow.

"Where?" Aisling looked left and right, confused.

"Three o'clock."

Aisling and Persephone immediately froze, subtly trying to sneak a few glances. I had less finesse than that. I turned my head sharply, narrowing my eyes at a man who was tucked behind a tree a few dozen feet from us. He was tall and broad. He wore a hat and was clad in all black from head to toe, so I couldn't see what he looked like.

"Is this something you should tell Sam about?" Persy asked Aisling.

Aisling frowned, her eyebrows drawing together. "I don't think so. He has no open beefs with anyone right now. Ever since he dismantled the Russians, things have been quiet. Maybe even too quiet for his taste. If he thought I was in any kind of danger, he wouldn't let me out the door without at least two of his soldiers."

It was true. Sam would recruit an entire army to keep Aisling safe. If she didn't have bodyguards, that meant Sam was having a peaceful year.

"What about you?" Sailor spun to Persephone. Even though my sister's husband was clean as a whistle in his business, there was no denying kidnapping his family was a lucrative idea.

Persy shook her head. "The Fitzpatrick clan works with a security company. All former secret service agents. We always know what level of threat we're facing for every scenario, including kidnapping. Right now it's low because Royal Pipeline's stock is tanking on Wall Street."

"Poor you," I purred. "However will you pay your next month's mortgage?"

All eyes drifted toward me. I looked over my shoulder again. The man was gone now, but I bet he just found another tree to hide behind.

"What?" I huffed. "Who could be going after *me*?"

There was one person I could think of, actually, but they were very dead.

"Maybe one of the nutcases who writes you letters?" Sailor suggested. "You're one of the most notorious women in Boston, Belle."

"No freaking way. Those guys can barely operate a landline, let alone plot a well-executed murder." But I tugged redheaded Rooney closer to me, just in case. "I bet it's just a creep who's going to rub one off after we're gone."

"Mommy, what's to rub one off?" Rooney clucked at Sailor, who shot me an *are-you-happy-now* look. My expression told her, *yes, very*.

"Well … I can see him again now, and he is looking at you, Belle." Persephone's voice was a sharp blade rolling against my skin.

The small hairs on the back of my neck pricked. My palms became sweaty. Mentally, I sifted through all the issues I had with people throughout the years, but nothing seemed big enough to warrant … *this*.

Logic dictated that Aisling, with her mafia prince husband, and Persy, who was married to one of the richest (and cruelest) men on planet Earth, were the prime targets. But they were both right—precisely *because* their husbands knew their situations, they made security arrangements to make it impossible for them to get hurt.

"Is there anything you're not telling us?" Aisling crooned, using her best peacemaker tone. "You can tell us. You know we're on your side. Always."

But I couldn't.

Because there was *nothing* to tell.

"Everything's fine." I tried to catch another glimpse behind my back.

A trail of a black peacoat disappeared behind a statue.

Oh fuck that.

"Hold this please." I gave Sailor Rooney's leash and started after the man. I ran toward the statue, fury burning like acid in my bloodstream. No matter who this man was after, he had a lot to answer for.

I bolted behind the statue to find him leaning against it, scrolling through pictures on his phone. Pictures of *my* back, I realized, when I caught a glimpse of my red peacoat on his screen.

"Cute number, huh? You should see the front." I swung my fist backward, about to punch him square in the face. His eyes snapped up. He let out a groan, and took off. My fist slung across the air, hitting nothing.

I began chasing him. Persy was at my feet.

"Belle!" she exclaimed, frantic and breathless. "Come back. You can't do this!"

Of course I could do this.

It was my *duty* to do this.

I vowed long ago to never let men hurt women just because they could. Because they were physically stronger.

I picked up my pace while my sister ran behind me. The man was gaining speed. Meanwhile, Persy had decided to show her athletic side for the first time since she was born and managed to catch up with me, tugging me back to the others by my coat collar.

"Leave me alone, Pers!" I roared. "Asshole had the guts to take pictures of me, now I want to know why." I shook her off, pushing through my bad knee and running faster. Persy was persistent. Where did all this new strength come from?

"You can't!" She jumped in front of me, serving as a barrier between me and the man, who was now too far away for me to be able to chase him.

This man could have been the same guy who approached me at Madame Mayhem a little over a month ago. *Dammit.*

Persy grabbed my shoulders, her eyes wild in their sockets. "Listen to me now. I know you're brave, and I know you're a ballbuster, but you *have* to understand, it's not just you anymore. There's someone inside you, and you need to think about them. Understand?"

Flashes of my conversation with Doctor Bjorn came back to me.

High-risk.

Miscarriage danger.

We'll have to monitor you closely.

I nodded grimly. I knew she was right. What the hell was I think-ing, taking off like that?

"Fine," I said surly. "*Fine*. But I can't just let this shit slide."

"I'm not asking you to," Persephone stressed. "I'll talk to Cillian. We'll see what we can do."

But I wasn't going to let a man, not even my brother-in-law, play babysitter to me. I was going to handle my own business.

"No, I'll take care of it."

"Not by approaching him on your own," Persy said.

I nodded in agreement but refrained from using my words. God was in the fine print.

Persy gathered me into a hug. "Now, that's my favorite sister."

"You mean your *only* sister," I groaned, my cheek squashed against her insanely swollen, milk-filled bosom.

She patted my head. "That too."

Twelve

Devon

THREE DAYS AFTER EMMABELLE ANNOUNCED HER PREGNANCY, I got on the phone with Mother for our weekly chat. She sounded breathless and delighted. Not for long, I thought. The mirth train would stop as soon as I told her about my pending fatherhood.

While I was delighted at becoming a parent, I was surly about disappointing my mother. Even worse, now that Sweven was pregnant, I was no longer allowed into her messy, in-need-of-a-good-wash bed.

It was like I was being punished for my good behavior.

"Hello, darling Devvie. If this is about Harry Tindall, then I regret to inform you he is still in Cayman Islands, but I got word he'll be returning fairly soon."

"Thank you, Mum. But there's something else we need to talk about." I strode the length of my apartment—a loft in the Back Bay—wearing nothing but a towel on my waist after a grueling workout.

"There is?" Mum asked. "What's on your mind, sweets?"

I stopped in front of the fireplace in my living room and flicked the electronic switch on.

"Are you sitting down?" I gave her the same treatment she gave me when my father died. I could hear her sinking into a leather seat.

"I am now," she sounded strained. "Has something bad happened?"

"*Breathe.*"

"Breathing is overrated. Just tell me, please."

"I'm about to become a father."

"I … uh … what now?" She sounded genuinely surprised.

"A dad," I cemented. "I'm going to have a baby with someone."

I heard a sharp thud—she probably dropped her phone—followed by her scrambling to pick up the receiver. The next time she spoke into my ear, her breathing was rough and labored. "You mean to tell me you're about to father a *bastard*?"

"Or a bastardess," I said easily. "Probably a bastardess. The mother of the child told me she thinks it'll be a girl, and she's not usually wrong."

"But … but … how? Where? When?"

Was the where really necessary? I had no idea if it happened when I drove into Belle while she was sprawled on her office desk, or when I plowed into her in her shower.

I made my way into the kitchen of my four thousand square foot apartment. I'd never seen something so big and lavish in a building, especially in Back Bay. It was designed with the same meticulous care and old-fashioned nature as my office. Loads of carved oak, expensive fabrics, bronze plinths, and a crimson painted frieze.

Most importantly—it was a vast, open space with very few walls. Exactly as I wished, suffering from raging claustrophobia.

"Her name is Emmabelle. Our liaison was of a casual nature. We were never officially together. She is going to keep the child."

When the silence on the other line told me my mother needed substantially more information, I added carefully, "Emmabelle is in the burlesque business. You could find a picture of her online. She wrote some articles about sexual liberation as a contributing columnist and posed for an erotic calendar. I believe you two would get along swimmingly."

I believed no such thing, of course, but disappointing her so close to my father's death didn't feel quite right.

"Why would I ever meet her?" Mother retorted.

"Because she is going to be the mother of your precious grand-child," I said easily.

"I do not consider whatever is going to come out of her a grand-child." She was so angry her voice shook.

Though I did not expect Mother to throw me a party, I did not ex-pect her to be quite so hostile about the matter either. After all, I had kept my alliance with her and Cecilia and helped them financially. My only expectation was for her to accept the way I lived my life.

And my way did not include locking nonconsenting women in cel-lars and eating their skin. Having children out of wedlock was common practice in this day and age.

I threw the fridge open, starting to fix myself a turkey sandwich. "Don't see your grandchild, then. Your loss."

"I might change my mind with time," she explained, her tone soft-ening. "I just don't want one illegitimate child to ruin your entire bright future. This is the twenty-first century. We are perfectly capable of keep-ing this silent and under control."

"*Why* would I want to keep it silent and under control?"

"Because you might want to get married."

I vowed to never get married, but I didn't think Mum could take any more bad news in one call.

"In that unlikely event, I'd be upfront with my wife."

"Not every wife would be happy about it."

"How about we stop beating around the bush? Say what you want to say."

"*Louisa,* Devvie."

Her name rang in my ear. A throwback to my father making me kiss her made my jaw clench.

"What about her?" I kicked the fridge door shut and slapped tur-key over wheat bread, scantily covered in light mayo and some mus-tard. "Think she is going to accept my arrangement with the burlesque nymph I knocked up?"

"You mean a *stripper*?" My mother gasped, scandalized. "This is what you call a stripper these days, don't you?"

"Sure." I yawned sardonically. "Call her whatever you want."

My insides turned to lava, sizzling with heat. That was a lie. One Sweven wasn't going to appreciate. So it was a good thing Mum didn't want to see her grandchild. Because if she ever tried to look down on Belle in front of her face … God help her, she would have no face to look down from anymore.

"Yes, well, there are ways to work around anything, Devvie. Rakes were not extinguished from the world with modern civilization. We high society women just learned new tricks to keep your discretions discreet."

"I cannot marry Louisa." I smacked a slice of cheese on my sandwich with ferocity that implied it was personally responsible for my current distress. "Where is this coming from? You've never pushed me on the matter. Only Papa ever did, and he paid for it by losing his only son. Not only can I not marry Louisa, I can't even be *seen* with her again. The media in Britain would have a field day if they found out I'm about to father a child out of wedlock with a ditzy American while mooning after a duke's daughter."

The Daily Londoner had an entire team of journalists dedicated to following every royal's move. There was no way this would be kept a secret.

"It's not the end of this discussion," my mother informed me, businesslike. "When is this thing due?"

"I believe she is about six or seven weeks along, so *this thing* will not be here for a while."

"That's very early to know you are pregnant. Almost like she planned the whole thing," my mother mused.

I did not tell her that Emmabelle and I had both agreed to have this child. Though I loved my mother, it was none of her business.

"Not everyone is as cunning as the Whitehalls, Mother."

I hung up the phone. Taking a bite of my sandwich, I chewed without tasting it.

Whatever my mother's next move was, I knew I would meet it head-on.

"Are you going to murder me?" My fencing partner, Bruno, asked the next day while I nearly pierced his brain through his mask. A *corps-a-corps*, bodily contact between two fencers, was illegal in fencing. It was the third time I did it. "What's bothering you?" Bruno asked through his stainless-steel mask.

Not gracing his question with an answer, I went on the attack again, thinking about my conversation with my mother, about the radio silence coming from Belle.

Fencing was physical chess. It required a level of intellectuality, not just quick limbs and fast instincts. That's why it was my favorite sport. I lunged forward, while Bruno became more guarded, backing away from the strip.

"Devon." He stumbled out of the mat, ripping the mask from his head. His face was sweaty, his eyes wide. "Devon, *stop*!"

It was only after he begged me to stop that I realized I had almost killed him. That he was small and scared, tucked into a corner of the room, his sabre sword down, his body shaking.

"You're going through something, man. You need to get your shit together."

With that, he stormed off. I peeled my mask off, frowning.

My shite was never together, you fool.

From there, I went to Sam's club.

Not to be confused with the retail warehouse chain store. My mate Sam Brennan's establishment, Badlands, was home to the best gambling tables, whiskey, and cocaine.

The club itself wasn't underground but instead open to the general public. The poker rooms in the back, however, were carefully curated.

I frequented those rooms as much as I could. At least three times a week. Sometimes more.

Tucked into one of the snug gambling rooms, Sam, Hunter, Cillian, and I played a game of cards around a table covered with green felt. A cloud of cigar smoke hovered over our heads. An assortment of half-empty glasses of brandy and whiskey bracketed our elbows.

"Congrats on knocking up the ultimate femme fatale." Hunter flashed me his Colgate smile behind his hand of cards. We were playing Rummy, which did nothing to help my already growing suspicion I was, indeed, an old fart in Sweven's eyes.

A sardonic smirk found my lips. "It was no trouble at all."

"Trouble? No. Weird? Yes. I didn't think y'all were still bumping uglies," Hunter mused.

I had no interest whatsoever in discussing Emmabelle Penrose. Not with Cillian and Hunter—two people whom I still considered clients—and Sam Brennan, whom despite his persistent pleas, I did *not* agree to take as a client.

"Was it accidental?" Cillian probed, sucking on his cigar and sending me a chillingly hostile gaze. Not because something happened. That was simply his usual expression. The only time he looked remotely content was when he was with his wife and children. Any other time, you could mistake him for a serial killer in the mood to practice his favorite hobby.

"That's none of your business," I said cheerfully, sliding a new card off the pile in the middle of the table.

"I'm sure it was an accident. No one is dumb enough to willingly tie their future to that she-wolf." Sam took a pull of his Guinness, scanning the room with boredom.

"Last I checked, your wife married a man with enough blood on his hands to fill the Mystic River. What does it say about *her* IQ?" I quirked an eyebrow.

"It means her IQ is divine, like the rest of her. Yours, however, is questionable at best. Knocking my wife to my face is a great way to find yourself six feet under."

"Control those feelings, son. They could be a tremendous liability." I patted his hand patronizingly, my tone as blank as my expression.

He kept forgetting I wasn't one of his fanboys. All eyes turned to me curiously.

"Do you have a crush on that wild child?" Hunter gave me a pitiful look. "Damn, Dev. You never defend *anyone* unless there's a 100k retainer involved."

Cillian smirked. "He had a good run."

"A short one too, if he continues talking to me like that." Sam chewed on his electric cigarette dispassionately.

This, despite what an outsider might think, was an agreeable evening in our universe.

"I don't know if I could do it though, man." Hunter shook his head. The good-looking bastard was cleaner than the pope's STD results. He hadn't had a stiff drink in years, not since he got together with his wife.

"I did her quite happily and find it hard to believe any red-blooded man wouldn't." I studied my cards, drumming my fingers over the table. Suddenly, the prospect of spending the entire night here wasn't so appealing.

I wanted to pick up the phone and call Belle, listen to her laugh, to her sharp, witty whips. I knew it wasn't an option.

"Not being able to be next to the woman who carries your child seems insane. There are so many things you're not going to experience. The kicks, the little flips the baby does when they change positions. Seeing them for the first time in an ultrasound. I swear to God, the first time I saw Rooney on that black and white screen I almost pissed my pants. She gave me the finger and had her legs wide open." Hunter let out a proud laugh, like he'd just announced his daughter was nominated for the Nobel Prize.

"The kicking is the good part," Sam agreed gruffly, drawing another card from the center of the table. "Aisling used to wait up for me after work with a tall glass of cold water and drink it so I could feel Ambrose kick."

"Since when did you all turn into a bunch of old maids?" I rolled up my sleeves. It was becoming increasingly hot in here, or maybe they were just getting on my nerves.

I wasn't at all sure that being spared the pregnancy was a good thing. But I didn't have a choice. I looked over to Cillian, who stayed silent the entire time. Out of all the men at the table, he was the closest to me in character—sans the fact that I actually possessed some kind of heart and a wonky, though still working, moral compass.

"It's all rubbish, isn't it?" I huffed at him. "Pregnant women are hormonal, demanding, and out of their bloody minds. My father sent my mother to live with her parents each time she got pregnant just so he wouldn't have to deal with her."

All eyes darted to me. I realized I'd finally said something personal about my family, after years—decades—of keeping mum about them.

Cillian was the first one to recover.

"It's true. A pregnant woman can be all of those things." He shrugged. "And she is also the person who is carrying the most important human in the world to you. The truth is, you fall in love with a woman twice. Once, so that you want her to give you a child. And a second time, when she does and you realize you cannot live without her."

Later that night, I stumbled my way out of Badlands and found myself walking toward Madame Mayhem. The two establishments weren't too far apart, and I could use the fresh winter air.

I gave it some thought during the card game and realized I wanted to take an active role in Emmabelle's pregnancy. Didn't Sweven say hers was a high-risk pregnancy? It was important I stayed in the loop in case she needed anything.

Plus, I wanted all the things my mates had.

Flipping babies.

Unborn children giving them the finger during ultrasounds.

Tall glasses of cold water (granted, I forgot the context in which this had been mentioned).

When I got to Madame Mayhem, I remembered how aptly named it was. Chaos teemed between the blood-red walls. There were three people behind the bar. One of them was Emmabelle, her hair sticking to her temples as she ran from one point to the other. The place was overflowing with people. There was no bloody way they adhered to the maximum capacity it could host. Customers were piling on top of each other trying to get to the bar. The supply and demand ratio was askew. Things were getting out of hand. The daft cow had more than enough to take an early leave and monitor her pregnancy, but she wasn't a fan of yielding control. Well, that made two of us.

Onstage, the burlesque dancers were getting all their moves wrong, too distracted by the commotion. The band played out of tune.

I hopped behind the bar without thinking much of it, took off my tweed jacket, rolled up my sleeves, and began serving people.

"Where's the beer fridge?" I hollered over the music, using my arse to push the mother of my unborn baby aside. "And the clean glasses."

"What are you doing here?" Sweven yelled back, dripping sweat. It was worth noting she didn't look half pleased to be rescued by me.

"Saving you from collapsing." I took a few orders at once and began popping beer bottles open and doing my best following cocktail recipes from what I remembered in my head.

"I don't need—" she started with her usual I'm-an-independent-woman-hear-me-roar spiel. I turned toward her abruptly, placing a finger over her lips.

"Help. I know. I don't doubt that for one second, or I wouldn't have put a baby inside you. I find neediness quite off-putting, to be honest. But you are also the mother of my future child, and I'm not going to see you work yourself to death. Understood?"

She glared.

"Am. I. Understood?"

"Yes," she glowered, taken aback.

For the next hour and a half, I served fruity cocktails, refilled wasabi peas bowls, overcharged people for cans of organic soda, and even got tipped an amount akin to what I make the first fifteen seconds of a consultation meeting.

Afterward, when things calmed down, I grabbed Belle by the arm and dragged her into her office. When she was safely inside, I closed the door, walked over to a mini fridge, took out two bottles of water, and unscrewed one, handing it to her.

I hated her office. It was small and confined enough to make my head swim, bringing back bad memories.

"I'm not thirsty," she sassed.

"Drink this water," I said through gritted teeth, "or I will tell your sister how little you're doing to protect this pregnancy."

"You'll rat me out?" Her eyes narrowed.

"In a heartbeat, darling."

Hesitantly, she began sipping the water.

"Why're you here, Devon?" She leaned against her desk, which, incredibly, was even messier than I remembered.

Did she need an intervention? Was this a treatable condition?

"I had an interesting conversation with the lads tonight. After which I came to the decision that I want to be present during your pregnancy, not just after the delivery. The first trimester is the most crucial one, yes? I can't have you running around doing five people's jobs. I want to help take care of you, and the first thing I intend to do is hire two or three more bartenders. You're awfully short on staff."

"Don't you think I know that?" she asked, chugging down the rest of her water and wiping her brow.

I was surprised she didn't fight me on that point. Then again, she looked particularly greenish and not at all her usual nymph self.

"The problem is, I have insane standards and no one Ross and I have interviewed so far seems good enough. I have to make sure I hire people who would be good with my dancers and with the other bartenders."

"You can't work yourself to the bone."

"Can't I?" Her head lolled from side to side, like it wasn't entirely connected to her neck. I was becoming increasingly worried this woman was going to kill herself just to prove a point. "I've done a good job so far, haven't I?"

"At what price?" I stepped in her direction, using every ounce of my self-control not to touch her. It seemed unnatural not to put my hands on her when we were together, but it was something I had to get used to. I needed to respect our agreement. "And why would you want to anyway? Hasn't this experience taught you anything? There's more to life than work."

A mocking laugh rolled out of her. "Easy for you to say, you're a damn royal, bruh. You were born into money."

There was no point telling her that I hadn't had access to a penny of my family's fortune since the age of twenty-one, or that *bruh* was not, in fact, a word, but rather a spit in the face to the English language.

"You're not fooling me or yourself, Sweven. We all make decisions emotionally then tag rational reasoning to them. Whatever you're selling, I'm not buying. You must concentrate on what's important. Let me deal with finding you new employees. I will speak to this Ross bloke. I already feel quite close to him, seeing as I sniffed his bullocks a few weeks ago."

She let out a faint laugh, slumping into herself like a collapsed blanket fort, looking tired and young. *Too* young all of a sudden.

"All right?" I tilted my chin down.

She nodded. "Whatever. But that doesn't mean you get to act like you're running this show. It's a one-off, okay?"

"A one-off," I agreed, when in my heart I knew it was going to be one of many.

And that I was not done screwing her either.

Thirteen

Belle

T HE NEXT MORNING, I RAN TO THE TOILET AND THREW UP whatever little was in my stomach.

I'd been having issues with morning sickness since the beginning of the week.

The problem was that I could only keep down three things without getting up close and intimate with the toilet bowl: rice cakes, ginger candy, and diet coke.

Now, I was no nutritionist, but I was pretty sure those three things did not make for a balanced diet rich in vitamins and minerals for me or my baby.

They did, however, make for a lovely dieting plan that would result in my losing the extra five pounds I'd been struggling with for three years.

I plastered my forehead to the toilet seat, pathetically enjoying its coolness against my burning brow. I was sweaty and exhausted. My hair was stuck to my neck and hung in wet strands.

I blinked, white spots dancing across my vision as I tried to focus on the lime-green floor in my bathroom.

THE *Rake*

"Please, Baby Whitehall, let me eat a piece of toast with some cheese today. You need the protein and I need the variety. I get that morning sickness is nature's way to tell women to stay the fuck away from all the bad stuff, but I promise, I'm not getting near coffee, alcohol, raw meat, or sashimi for the next nine months. Hell, I'll throw in pickles and hard candy if you give me a break."

Baby Whitehall, which according to a chart I found on the internet, was currently the size of a kidney bean and didn't find my plea compelling. Sure enough, another bout of puking began.

With my last strength, I picked up the phone and texted Devon.

Belle: I know you said you want to be more involved. I'm thinking of booking an appointment with my OB-GYN.

Devon: ?

Belle: I can't be farther than two feet from the bathroom at all times.

Devon: number 1 or 2?

Belle: three.

Belle: (puking).

Devon: I'll have Joanne book an appointment and send a cab for you.

Ah, his trusted secretary. Because when he said he wanted to get involved, what he really meant was he wanted to control me until I produced him a healthy, chubby baby.

Belle: it's fine. I can do it myself.

Devon: keep me posted.

Belle: screw you.

But I didn't actually send that last message. It reeked of emotions, and I didn't do those.

Simmering in a pool of self-pity, I dragged my feet across my shoe-box apartment, glancing dejectedly at the place and wondering where in the world I was going to fit an entire baby. The baby itself wouldn't take too much space, but her stuff would need a room.

And babies this day and age had all sorts of stuff.

My sister and all my friends had kids, and their toys and furniture needed acres of land. Cribs, changing tables, dressers, highchairs, bassinets, toys. The list was never-ending, and I was currently struggling to find a place for my coffee cups.

Too exhausted to figure out the accommodations, I spent the first half of the day binge-watching true crime documentaries on Netflix (because nothing screams a nurturing mother-to-be like following the chronicles of a serial killer). A knock on the door jolted me.

I groaned, flinging my feet off the couch. I threw my door open, only realizing I should've asked who it was when the memory of my trip to the Boston Common and my stalker resurfaced.

Well, crap in a basket.

I'd been meaning to call Sam Brennan and ask him what he charges these days for a bodyguard to protect a bitch, but my pregnancy brain fog took over my life. Besides, things had been calm the last few days.

"Sweven?" A pimply guy in an upscale chain store uniform smiled at me, holding approximately a gazillion brown bags.

Phew. Not a serial killer.

"I seem to be answering to that nickname recently, yeah." I looked left and right to make sure he was alone and didn't happen to have a serial killer with him.

"I have a delivery for you. Clean juices, exotic fruit baskets, and ready-made meals for a week by OrganicU. Where should I put this?"

I motioned with my head toward the kitchen, leading the way.

My baby daddy was a prick, but at least he was a considerate one.

I got to work looking like I'd been dragged there by an angry beaver.

Bloodshot eyes, knotty hair haphazardly gathered in a bun, and a dress I lovingly referred to as The Period Dress. *For a reason.*

Ambling into the club, I noticed Ross was standing with three people I did not recognize. My heart immediately jerked in my chest. I wasn't a fan of strangers, in general, but especially after the incidents with the strange man at my club and the other man who'd chased me in the Common.

"Oh good. Sleeping beauty's here." Ross turned to beam at me, handing me my coffee. I placed it on the bar, the mere scent of it making me want to throw up every slice of pizza I'd ever consumed in my lifetime.

"I'm only three minutes late." I dropped my clutch on the counter and not so gracefully plopped into a seat. "No offense, but, um, who the hell are these people?"

"Your new employees, hired by a third party. Charming, right?"

That third party, I guessed, was Devon Whitehall. The man who managed to be a helicopter parent before the baby was actually born.

The first employee was Morgan, a vertically-challenged spitfire with pixie hair, a nose ring, and enough attitude to light up Vegas. She introduced herself as a certified mixologist with five years' experience at Troy and Sparrow Brennan's Michelin-starred restaurant and explained to me assertively that she was specifically hired to work double shifts.

The second was Alice, a forty-something-year-old with twenty years of experience running a bar in New York. Alice's rough hands implied she was well-versed in throwing creepers and troublemakers out of bars if need be.

The third employee was a man named Simon Diamond (stage name, anyone?), who was approximately the size of a RAM truck. Simon eyed me the entire time like I was a prisoner he needed to keep from running away. When I asked about his work background, he offered a half-baked explanation. "Was a bouncer for a decade."

"Oh. We don't need any more bouncers." I smiled politely, already planning to have Ross and Morgan teach him how to make cocktails.

Simon returned a smile—only it made my bones snap in fear. "I'm not here to be a bouncer."

"What are you here for?" I took a sip of my coffee then immediately dribbled it back into the cup. Bad idea. Bad, bad idea. Baby Whitehall wasn't impressed with my unkept promise not to touch caffeine.

"This and that. Everything, really."

"Jack of all trades, huh? Well, that won't be necessary."

"I've already been paid for the next nine months, ma'am. You won't be able to get rid of me."

I didn't know what I found more disconcerting. The fact that he forced his presence on me or the fact that he called me ma'am.

I *also* had no idea how Devon convinced these people to work for me. They were obviously overqualified. I was pretty sure he paid through the nose to compensate for the fact they were going to serve a lot of gin and tonics to middle-aged men coming to get an eyeful of the burlesque dancers.

"Belle, honey, a little more appreciation and a little less bitchiness would be great." Ross materialized from the back office and strolled toward the bar, looking grim and a little put off. I didn't even notice he was gone. "Devon brought me up to speed about the fact you're eating for two."

He put a hand on my shoulder and peered down at me. "Why on earth didn't you tell me? I thought I was one of your best friends."

"You are." I licked my lips, not used to being called out, but appreciating it anyway because Ross had every right to be hurt. "I'm sorry, Ross. It's just because … general health stuff. This is a high-risk pregnancy, so I didn't want to announce it too early."

"Oh." I could feel him defrosting, but he still wasn't happy that I'd kept it from him.

"Devon needs to be gagged. I'm surprised he didn't commission a Times Square banner." I looked around me dispassionately. Speaking of banners and billboards, my days posing naked were over. Baby Whitehall was going to have enough material for her future therapist without my nudity adding to the mix.

"Give him time. He might do that too."

I flipped Ross the finger. He curled my middle finger back into my fist, but there was no anger in his voice. "I'll let this one slide, because it seems like you've experienced many changes in the past few weeks."

I gnawed at my lower lip, deciding to drop the ball-busting charade for a second. I mean, this was *Ross*. My Ross. "Thank you."

"You're welcome."

"So … you've met him." I didn't put a question mark at the end of the sentence. My insides liquefied.

"I have." Ross nodded cryptically while Morgan, Alice, and Simon pretended to look around the place and talk to each other.

"And … what did you think?"

"I think…" he flipped my hair, playing with it lovingly, "…he is hotter than the devil's dick, talks like a Netflix duke, and is crazy about you. I approve of the arrangement."

"Thanks for giving me the blessing I didn't ask for."

"You're welcome. And while we're on the topic—I know you're going to manage to screw it up somehow, because you're allergic to relationships, but please, Belly-Belle, *puh-lease*, can we keep him for just a little longer?" He clapped his hands together and gave me puppy eyes, like a child who came across a stray cat he wanted to adopt.

"No." I produced a small mirror from my clutch and checked my red lipstick, using my pinky to wipe the lines. "His job is done."

"You should tell him that. He threatened that if I let you work the bar tonight, he'd personally kick my ass. So I'm going to go ahead and send you to work in the office until no later than six o'clock, after which you'll go back home."

"Six o'clock?" I roared. "It's four o'clock right now!"

"Four twenty. Don't forget you were late." Ross grabbed the small mirror, checking his own reflection. He raised his eyebrows to check his Botox situation. In my opinion, he had at least three more months in him before he needed to visit his dermatologist.

"You can't kick me out of my own workplace." I snatched the mirror and shoved it into my clutch.

"Wanna bet? Mr. Whitehall asked me to refer you to clause 12.5 of your contract—by the way, *so* hot that you have one—in which, if you endanger your unborn child, he may have grounds to sue you."

Holy crappers. Why couldn't I get knocked up by the Friendly Front Runner? He wouldn't give two shits if I drank myself to death under a bridge.

There was no point arguing with Ross or Devon. Not because I was one to pass up a chance to quarrel, but because I could actually use a few hours of sleep. I was exhausted. As much as I hated to admit it, Devon was right—I *needed* rest.

Begrudgingly, I retreated to my office. Powering up my MacBook, I noticed a pile of envelopes sitting on the edge of my desk. I remembered what Devon had said about opening them to ensure they weren't only just hate mail.

Maybe I won the lottery?

Maybe there's some fan mail in there, telling me how awesome I was for celebrating the extravagant, fun, and sexually liberal wonders of burlesque?

I jerked the stack my way and began sieving through them.

A bunch of bills I'd already paid, two angry letters about my substantial role in corrupting the youth of Boston, and one thank you letter from a woman who came to see a show a few months ago and was inspired to quit her job as a marine biologist and join the burlesque cast of *A Midsummer Night's Dream*.

I picked up another letter, this one printed.

To: Emmabelle Penrose.

I tore it open.

The letter was short and contained a return address for a PO Box in Maryland.

Emmabelle,

Are you worried for your life yet?

You should be.

If you only paid more attention to what was going on around you, you'd have noticed that I've been watching you for a long time now.

Planning my revenge.

I know where you live, where you work, and who you hang out with.

That's the part where you get scared. You'd be right to. I'm not going to rest until you're dead.

No one can help you.

Not your best friend's husband, Sam Brennan.

Not your idiotic sister, Persephone, or her billionaire husband.

Not even that fancy man you've been hanging out with recently.

Once I made up my mind, your destiny was sealed.

You can take this letter to the police. In fact, I encourage you to. It'll just give you more shit to worry about and disrupt your already messed up life.

I'm going to kill you for what you did to me.

And I'm not even going to be sorry about it.

Never yours,
The person you took everything from.

My stomach twisted, clenching around the stupid clean juice I drank for breakfast.

So that man in the Boston Common *was* there for me.

Was he the same person who thought I'd wronged him, or was he there just to spy?

Either way, someone was after me.

After my *life.*

An invisible enemy.

A noose formed around my neck.

Who could it be?

Taking inventory, I had to admit, I was far from being the nicest person on planet Earth, but I by no means had arch-enemies. I'd hurt no one, no one that I could think of. Certainly not to a point of such rage.

There was *one* incident long ago. But the only person affected was no longer alive.

Good thing I had a gun, which I was going to take with me everywhere from now on just in case, Krav Maga skills, and the badass bitch attitude with which to strangle this person with my own hands if they came anywhere near me.

Plus, I couldn't exactly advertise what was happening to me. Telling Devon and my closest friends about this letter would only create more chaos.

As it was, my baby daddy was trying to take control of my life, and I didn't want to give him more leeway than he already had to make decisions on my behalf.

No, this was another challenge I would have to meet head-on.

There was someone else I needed to take care of, and I was going to kill for her if need be.

My baby.

Fourteen

Belle

THE OB-GYN CHECKUP CAME JUST IN TIME. I WAS EAGER TO hear about Baby Whitehall's life inside my hostile womb and also to get approximately five thousand prescription drugs for my morning sickness, which now had me dropping six pounds—involuntarily, of course.

Joanne, Devon's secretary, called me in the morning to let me know she'd sent a cab for me. She sounded like the sweetest person on planet Earth, Jennifer Aniston included.

"Now, I'm not saying I know what it's about, but I sure hope our friend Lord Whitehall is treating you well," she clucked on the other line.

"Ma'am, he is treating me *too* well."

"There's no such thing!" she bellowed. I could practically hear her contemplating her next words before she said, "Again, I have no idea what I'm booking this for, but … I do hope this is going to stick. He's a fantastic man. Strong, confident, sturdy, razor sharp. He deserves a good woman."

He does, I thought bitterly. *Too bad I'm incapable of being that for him.*

When I slid into the cab an hour later, clad in oversized sunglasses and a faux fur coat, I was surprised to see Devon sitting on the other end of the passenger seat, dressed in a dashing suit and a peacoat, typing emails on his phone.

"Sweven." He pocketed the phone as he turned to me, drawling in his signature Hugh Grant accent. Fuck me.

"Asshole," I volleyed back, still surly about the fact he'd shoved himself into my business, figuratively and literally. "You're here. Yay me. Should've known you'd try and take control of this situation too."

"Enjoying your new employees?" He ignored my barb. All of them, actually. Why wasn't he backing away? Why wasn't he giving up on me, just like every other man I exhausted into submission?

"Ask me in a week."

"I'll set a reminder." I couldn't tell if he was sarcastic or not.

"I'm going to pay you back for them, you know." I rested my head against the cool seat and closed my eyes to ease the sickness.

"You look terrible, darling."

"Thanks, boo." Wasn't I just a bundle of joy?

"By that I mean you look exhausted. How can I help?"

"You can get out of my hair."

"Sorry, it smells too good."

I let out a tired smile. "I'm not going to turn you off with this attitude, am I?"

He shrugged, throwing me a lopsided grin that made my heart slow almost to a complete stop. "Exquisite things often have thorns. It's to keep away unwanted attention."

"You really think you're going to screw me again, huh?" I blinked.

"Positive," he confirmed.

When we arrived at Doctor Bjorn's office, my OB-GYN was under the bizarre impression Devon was an ex-boyfriend of mine and that we rekindled our romance. No reason for him to think that, of course. He just did.

"There's nothing I like to see more than old flames spark anew due to baby-making." He ushered both of us to a checkup room, clapping his hands excitedly.

"The only blaze analogy I'd use for this man would be my setting him on fire," I assured the happy doctor.

Devon chuckled darkly, rubbing my back in comforting circles. We made our way through the hallway littered with pictures of sleeping babies in baskets. When you thought about it, babies and kittens had a lot in common in terms of appropriation.

"As you can tell, her hormones are already all over the place." Devon was being deliberately chauvinistic to grind my gears.

I wasn't going to let him know he was ruffling my feathers, though.

"Don't expect wedding bells, Doctor Bjorn," I said. I needed to ensure that Devon knew I was not up for the taking. I was already straddling the edge of an anxiety attack just from hanging out with him.

Some girls didn't want to be touched after a traumatic experience.

But me? My body was very receptive to male attention. It was my brain, heart, and soul that rejected the idea of them completely.

We entered a small room with wooden cabinets, an examination table, and more charts about babies and STDs.

"Duly noted, Ms. Penrose. So, Mr. Whitehall, would you like to join us for the vaginal ultrasound exam?" My OB-GYN asked Devon, not me. These two were really hitting it off.

Also—shouldn't I be the one to decide such thing?

"He wouldn't," I said at the same time Devon exclaimed, "I'd be delighted to."

Doctor Bjorn looked between us. "My apologies. Usually when a man arrives with his partner for an ultrasound, I draw a certain conclusion. I'm sorry if I overstepped. I'll leave you to decide and come back in a few minutes. Please ensure that you're in your robe and undressed from the waist down on the examination table, Ms. Penrose."

Devon and I engaged in a stare-off for a few seconds before he drawled, "And your problem is?"

"It's a vaginal exam."

"So? I've seen yours before from all angles. Fucked it, licked it, fingered it, and played with it."

"This is a pivotal moment in my life, you caveman," I barked.

"Intimate for both of us. It's *my* child in there." He pointed at my stomach.

"And *my* vagina," I reminded him.

"My god, you are childish." Finally—*finally*—he was over my behavior. But it didn't feel half as satisfying as I thought it would.

"Well, I *am* over a decade younger than you."

"Look," he sighed, shaking his head like I was an unruly child. "I promise not to look anywhere … sensitive. I just want to see the baby. *My* baby."

"There's nothing to see." I threw my hands in the air. "At this point, it's as big as a bean."

"*Our* bean," he corrected.

He had a point, and I hated that he had a point. I also hated that I couldn't say no to him. Not about the employees or joining me at the doctor's or anything else. Because the truth was … doing shit with someone else around didn't feel so bad after all.

"Fine. But if you peek at my muffin, I swear to god I'm going to destroy your baked goods."

He frowned at me. "You need to work on your analogies."

"I meant I'd punch your junk."

"Subtle."

The vaginal ultrasound went as well as a vaginal ultrasound could go. Devon and I saw the little dot in my uterus, static and proud. Both of us stared at it with awe and amazement.

"The little bean is looking good. Make sure you are rested and keep your stress levels low." That was Doctor Bjorn speaking. To Devon, naturally.

"Roger that, Doc."

"All right, hop off and meet me in my office."

This was when I glared at Devon. "Do you mind?"

I caught him staring at me like I'd just performed a magic trick he hadn't seen before. Big azure eyes swimming with emotion and pride. And it killed me. It killed me that I couldn't wrap my arms around him and kiss him and tell him that I felt the same.

All of it. The shock. The excitement. The awe.

Instead, I raised my eyebrows, as if to say *well?*

"Right. Of course." Devon stood up, looking around him, like he had another reason to stay. "I'll just … well, yes. Yes. See you at the doctor's office when you're done dressing."

Doctor Bjorn prescribed me with some pills to ease the morning sickness and told us we were doing a good job. I wasn't sure Devon would have agreed with the assessment had he known about the Glock nestled in my clutch, and that I was ready to get into a physical fight with a stalker at any given moment.

We swung out of the office, and I called the elevator while Devon took the stairs. I didn't try to convince him to go down the elevator with me. I knew damn well *I* didn't like it when people pushed me out of my comfort zone or minimalized my triggers, so I tried to accommodate his preferences.

We met again at the ground floor and stood in front of each other on the street, bracketed by skyscrapers and pedestrians.

Suddenly, I had a sweven of my own. A vision of us holding hands. Smiling at each other. Enjoying this moment, like an ordinary couple.

Devon cleared his throat and looked away. "I better head to work."

"Right." I rearranged my ponytail. "Me too. I have employees to train."

"That must be a pain," he offered politely.

"Necessary evil," I concluded.

Stop me. Tell me not to go. Let's stay a little longer.

Whoa. I had no idea where those thoughts came from.

"Well, catch you later." I took a step back and started for the street.

I began walking in the opposite direction when his voice pierced the air.

"Perhaps …"

I froze in my spot, my soul in my throat. *Yes?*

"You'd like some brunch? You heard what the doctor said. You need to keep your energy levels up. I can pick up your pills while you wait for our order. There's a café down the street—"

"Yes." I turned sharply. My entire body shook. With excitement. Dread. Fear. "Yes. I need to eat."

"Yeah. Okay. All right."

Neither of us moved. *Again.* A few weeks ago we were fucking each other like the world was ending, and *now* we were being awkward? How was this my life?

"Anytime would be good now." I folded my arms over my chest, jutting one hip out with a grin. "Today, tomorrow. The day after it."

He let out a chuckle and rushed toward me. He pressed his hand against the small of my back, and I swear, a jolt of electricity ran through his fingers and exploded right between my legs.

What the fuck.

What the fuck.

What the fuck.

"Bean looks very cute, huh?" I asked when we walked to the nearest café. People were doing a double take when they saw me—probably recognizing me from billboards—but they also stared at *him*. Everyone knew there was a British royal living in Boston.

"Dashing," he agreed. "I've yet to see a better looking bean."

"I'm not even into legumes very much." Oh my God, what was I saying?

Devon laughed. "You little nutter."

"Dev?"

"Hmm?"

"Now's a good time to tell me why you're a raging claustrophobe."

"Ask me again later."

"How much later?"

"When I trust you."

"That may never happen," I pointed out.

"Exactly."

We arrived at a quaint café with bay windows and potted flowers on the tables. When the hostess showed us to our table, running her gaze along Devon's body appreciatively, I internally groaned.

I wondered if that would have happened if I were showing.

Then I reminded myself that it didn't matter because we weren't a couple.

"Aren't you a lord? I mean, a duke?" The waitress fawned over him.

Devon shot her a polite yet short smile. "Marquess," he corrected.

After pulling my chair out for me to sit, my baby daddy proceeded to order the entire menu without even looking at it.

"We have twenty-seven items on the menu," the waitress warned, batting her eyelashes at him. Was I invisible next to this bastard?

"Good. My date likes variety," Dev said. I had a feeling he was referring to my sexual conquests.

"Any particular order you want the food to come out?" The waitress was now half leaning against him, and again, I wanted to pick up the fork from the table and stick it between her eyes.

"Ask my date. While you're at it, could you kindly keep an eye on her? She is very good at making me worry."

He took my prescription and driver's license and dashed across the street to the pharmacy to grab my morning sickness pills.

When he returned, I noticed the bag he was carrying was far larger than it should have been.

"Did you buy out the entire place?" I raised an eyebrow, sipping a terribly green and offensively healthy juice.

This baby better come out ready for a triathlon because I was doing *everything* right.

Devon turned the bag upside down and poured its contents on the table.

"Did you know there's an entire aisle dedicated to pregnant women?"

"Yes," I said matter-of-factly.

"Well, I didn't. So I decided to buy whatever they had to offer. We have things for heartburn, dietary supplements, morning sickness, constipation, and vaginal imbalance."

"You mean pH imbalance. If my vag was imbalanced, I'd send her to a pussy shrink."

Devon sputtered the sip of coffee he took while sitting down. He was laughing hard. I felt his laughter bubbling in my own chest.

"My mother is going to love you," he deadpanned.

Surprisingly, I found myself cackling out loud despite my best efforts not to. Not only because the idea of my ever meeting his mother was deranged, but also because he was right. His family would probably have a collective heart attack if they ever met me.

"Did you tell her about your new status?" I asked.

"Yes."

"And?"

"She wasn't impressed," he admitted.

"And …?" I probed, my heart sinking a little.

"I'm in my forties and in a position to do whatever the hell I please. And what I wanted to do was *you*. Case closed."

There was so much more I wanted to ask—to know—but I had no right to probe. Not after I drew a thick glaring line between us.

"So tell me a little about your fear of elevators, cars, planes, etc," I said as I tore into some eggs Benedict.

He grinned. "Nice try. You didn't gain my trust in the last half hour. And, to be frank, I don't think you ever will."

"Why not?"

"Trust cannot be placed in the hands of someone who does not trust themselves. I'm not against telling you my story, Emmabelle, but weaknesses should be exchanged in the same way countries exchange war hostages. It's a rather bloody and bleak thing, isn't it? Our insecurities. One should not relinquish information without gaining some."

"Ha." I smiled, buttering a piece of carrot cake, even though it made no sense. "So you're not, in fact, perfect?"

"Not even close. Not even in the realm." His smile was contagious.

I ducked my head down and tried to concentrate on the food.

"Well, I'm not ready to put my trust in you yet either," I admitted.

"Would it be so bad?" he asked kindly. "To have some faith in another person?"

I gave it some thought then nodded slowly. "Yes. I think it would."

He held my gaze. I had a feeling I was making a terrible mistake, and yet I couldn't stop it.

"Am I waiting for you, Emmabelle?" he asked quietly. "Is there even a reason for me to wait for you?"

Say yes, you idiot. Give him something to hold on to, so you'll have something to hold on to.

But the word slipped out of my mouth anyway. Harsh and blunt, like a stone. "No."

For the next hour and a half, we talked about everything that *wasn't* our respective phobias of confined places and relationships.

We talked about our mutual friends, our childhoods, politics, global warming, and our pet peeves—his included when people said 'literally' when what they meant was not, in fact, literal; mine consisted of using the same knife for the peanut butter *and* jelly, and when people told me I was not going to believe something, when I absolutely was going to believe it.

"Humans are just deplorable!" I threw my hands in the air, summing up our brunch. Devon paid the bill and, if my sneak-peek wasn't mistaken, was also leaving one heck of a tip.

"Inexcusable," he cemented. I was glad he was okay with our conversation after I told him not to wait for me. "But one must deal with them anyway."

"Thanks for not being completely horrible, boo." I pressed my fist to his bicep in a friendly manner. Bad call. I was met with his bulging muscles through his clothes and immediately wanted to jump his bones.

Devon looked up from the bill and rolled his thumb against my brow. "Darling, do you have a fever? I do believe you just paid me a compliment."

"Well, you just paid for one hell of a meal. I didn't mean it or anything," I huffed. Way to go, Belle. Channeling your inner five-year-old.

"You're thawing." He grinned.

I made a gagging sound and scooped my clutch. "Not in this lifetime. As I said, don't wait up for me to change my mind about us."

He escorted me to a cab to take me to Madame Mayhem then waited with me when the driver went in circles for ten minutes trying to find us and apologized profusely, saying he'd just moved to Boston from New York.

The driver parked in front of us, and Devon did the duck-head-into-window shtick and told him to drive extra slow because his wife was pregnant and nauseous, which made me want to vomit from excitement and dread at the same time.

Devon erected back to his full height, rubbing my jaw tenderly. The gesture was so gentle, so soft, a shiver rolled along my spine, making my skin tingle. He leaned forward, and I caught a waft of his scent. Spicy and dusky. A scent I'd grown to chase each time he left my office or my bed.

I found myself admiring the planes of his face. My fingertips itched to touch him. Knowing I was carrying his DNA inside me gave me a thrill I'd never had in my thirty years of clubbing.

He tilted his face to one side, and for a moment, I thought he was going to kiss me. Drawn to him like a moth to a flame, I rose on my tiptoes, my mouth falling open. His body moved forward, engulfing me. My heart began to hammer.

It was happening.

We were breaking the rules.

When Devon was a few inches behind me, he reached his arm past my shoulder and opened the car's door, stepping aside to give me some room to enter.

Holy embarrassing shitballs.

I almost devoured his face when all he wanted to do was help me into a taxi.

"Have a good day, Emmabelle." He took another step back, looking casual and dry as fuck.

"Yeah!" My voice broke. Hello, thirteen-year-old-boy Belle. "You too."

The entire taxi ride to work, I reminded myself that this was all my doing. I wanted to keep him away. Hanky Panky with an older man had its price tag, and I'd once paid for it dearly.

This is how it starts, I chided the seeds of hope that had taken root inside me. *Sweet and unassuming. It's all fun and games until he destroys your life.*

But no one was going to destroy me anymore.

Then I remembered one of the quotes hanging on the wall in my apartment.

It's okay.

You just forgot who you are.

Welcome back.

Fifteen

Devon

I ARRIVED ON ENGLISH SOIL APPROXIMATELY TWENTY MINUTES after my father's solicitor, Harry Tindall, returned from his exotic vacation.

I left Sweven with a heavy heart. Not because I was going to miss her (although, pathetically, I suspected that was going to be the case), but also because she seemed an expert at landing herself in hot water.

I took comfort in the fact I'd made some arrangements to ensure her safety. As well as one could, anyway.

Besides, I did not expect to be in England for more than a few hours.

The reading of the will took place in Tindall's office in Knightsbridge. An official matter that should've been done the week my father had passed away. Better late than never, I suppose.

It surprised me that my mother and Cecilia, who were assumingly strapped for cash, did not seem hostile to the idea of waiting for Harry to return from his vacation. Then again, I did send them money and called Mum every other day to ensure she was doing all right.

I arrived at Harry's office still wearing my work clothes. Ursula, Cece, and Drew were already there, seated in front of Tindall's desk.

"He should only be a few minutes," his secretary said. The

Joanne-like woman in a full tweed suit brought refreshments inside. Drew attacked the pastry platter and fresh coffee before it was even set on the massive boardroom stand.

My mother hugged me tightly. "Good to see you, Devvie."

"Same, Mummy."

"How is that woman doing?"

That woman was Emmabelle Penrose, and as much as I resented her for not wanting to ride me like an unbroken horse, I couldn't deny the delight I'd felt whenever we spent time together.

"Belle is doing quite well, thank you."

"I can't believe you're going to be a father." Cecilia flung her arms at me, going for a bear hug.

"I can. It is time I produce an heir. If Edwin's death reminded us of something, it was that having someone to leave your legacy to is important."

But that wasn't the reason I was excited to become a father. I wanted all the things I saw my friends do with *their* kids. The T-ball games and ice-skating outings and sun-drenched summers on the Cape and stealing a quickie in the shower when the kids were watching Bluey in the other room.

I wanted domestic bliss. To pass down not only my fortune and title, but also my life experience, my morals, and my affections.

Mr. Tindall walked in looking tan and well-rested.

After a round of handshakes, half-arsed condolences, and a terribly boring monologue about Mr. Tindall's island vacation, he finally opened the file containing my father's will.

I took Mum's hand and squeezed it reassuringly. I found it clammy and cold.

Prefacing the reading of the will, Tindall cleared his throat, his chin flapping about. He was a very large man, with the tendency to turn fuchsia pink whenever he was rattled. Not what you'd call a grade-A looker.

"I would like to preface this by saying that this will is certainly unconventional, but it was written in accordance with Edwin's desire to preserve the values and principles of the Whitehall family. That being said, I do hope that everyone will remain respectful and sensible, since, as you all know, it is irrevocable."

Mum, Cecilia, and Drew all squirmed in their seats, a dead give-away that they had a fair idea of what could be in the will. I, on the other hand, did not particularly care. I had my own fortune, and I did not rely on anyone else's.

But as Harry Tindall began reading the will, I got increasingly confused.

"Whitehall Court Castle goes to Devon, the first son…"

The estate went to me, the son he rejected and positively loathed and had not seen in two decades.

"The investment portfolio of two point three million pounds goes to Devon …"

So did all of his funds.

"The car collection goes to Devon …"

In short, everything now belonged to me. I was bracing myself for the punchline. I was listed as the sole inheritor of the estates and monies, but there was no way this would be unconditioned. The more Tindall spoke, the more my mother shrunk into her seat. Cecilia looked the other way, fat tears rolling from her cheeks, and Drew closed his eyes and dropped his head backward, like he didn't want to be there.

And then, I found it. The fine print. The violent dare.

Mr. Tindall raised his voice when he got to the last sentence.

"All properties and funds will be released upon Devon Whitehall, The Marquess of Fitzgrovia, on the day of his wedding to Lady Louisa Butchart. Until then, they will be held and maintained by Tindall, Davidson and Co. In the event of Mr. Whitehall's refusal of the ar-rangement, and/or failure to marry Miss Butchart for a period exceed-ing twelve calendar months from the date of the reading of the will, the abovementioned properties and funds shall be released and trans-ferred to the multiple charities Edwin Whitehall has aforementioned." Tindall looked up and arched an eyebrow. "From here on out is a list of The Masters of Foxhounds, dedicating to protecting the sport, and other questionable charities. In case Devon and Louisa do not marry. But, of course, I am sure we will not get to that point."

Bloody hell.

Edwin Whitehall had left nothing to his wife, daughter, or son-in-law. Even from his grave, he tried to bully me into marrying Louisa, and now, he'd dragged the remainder of my family into that mess.

A distant memory of my conversation with Edwin when I was fourteen years of age resurfaced.

"Now be a good boy and go apologize to Louisa. This matter is settled. You will marry her after you finish Oxford University, and not a moment later, or you will lose your entire inheritance and your family. Am I understood?"

Only I never ended up going to Oxford. I went to Harvard instead.

He said it loud and clear decades ago. It was his way or the highway.

Now he had created the perfect storm. My mother knew if I didn't marry Lou, she'd be stripped of everything she had—and she was already struggling financially. This was why she was clammy and cagey today. This was why the news of Emmabelle's pregnancy nearly destroyed her.

"Outrageous," I commented in my mildest tone, taking a sip of my coffee.

"Quite," Drew whined. "My darling Cece and I haven't inherited bloody used toilet paper!" He squashed a cookie to dust in his fist.

"Oh, zip it, would you?" Mother barked impatiently. It was the first time I saw her address her son-in-law directly, and it was fair to say she thought more fondly of war criminals than the latest addition to the family. "Cecilia will be taken care of. I'd never let my daughter go without."

"Cecilia?" Drew whined, darting up from his seat—but not man enough to actually storm out. "And what about me?"

"I can't take this will seriously." I picked an apple from the assortment of refreshments and sprawled in my seat, eyeing Tindall as I rubbed the red fruit clean against my Armani suit.

He gave me the nasty smile of a man who knew I could and indeed should.

"I'm sorry, Devon. You should know better than anyone that law and justice have nothing to do with one another. The will is irreversible, as unreasonable as it may seem to you. Edwin was lucid and present when he wrote it. I have three witnesses to attest to that."

"He's breaking hundreds of years of tradition," I noted. I would be the first son since the seventeenth century to be given an empty treasure chest. "Then again, tradition is just peer pressure from dead people."

"Whatever tradition is, it is here to stay," Tindall scoffed.

"There is another way." Mum approached gently, putting her hand on my arm. "You *could* get to know Louisa …"

"I'm going to become a father." I turned in her direction, frowning.

My mother hitched one delicate shoulder. "There are modern families everywhere these days. Ever watched Jeremy Kyle? A man can father children with more than one woman. Sometimes even more than three."

"Are you getting life lessons from Jeremy Kyle now?" I drawled.

"Devvie, I'm sorry, but you have more than just yourself to think about. There's me and Cece."

"And me," Drew butted in. Like I cared if he keeled over right here and now and was dragged into hell by the ear by Satan himself.

"The answer is no." The ice in my voice offered no room for argument.

I had avoided my father all those years, partly because he couldn't accept my decision regarding Louisa, and now I was at risk of losing Mum and Cecilia over it. Because no matter how rich I was, how capable I was of taking care of them on my own—I was robbing them of millions in estate and fortune by not marrying Lou.

"Devon, please—"

I stood up and stormed out of the office—out of the *building*—lighting a hand-rolled cigarette and pacing across the pebbled road. Darkness descended on the streets of London. Harrods was awash with bright golden lights.

It reminded me of the famous history nugget. Harrods had sold kits with syringes and tubes of cocaine and heroin during the First World War, mainly for wounded soldiers who were either nursed back to health or were dying a painful death.

I remembered those stories both well and fondly. Mum's family was one of the merchants who sold the product to the posh department store. That was how they became so filthy rich.

Mum's family had an abundance of poppy fields, a flower known to symbolize the remembrance of those who lost their lives during WWI, for its ability to blossom anywhere, even during distress.

I quite fancied Emmabelle Penrose to be like that flower.

Sweet but vicious. Multifaceted.

"My goodness, you've let your emotions get the best of you. That exhibition inside was pure Yankee behavior. Your father must be rolling in his grave." Mum poured herself into the freezing cold of London's winter, bundling up in a checkered white and black peacoat.

I sucked hard on my rollie, releasing a train of smoke skyward. "I hope he rolls himself all the way to hell, if he isn't there already."

"Devvie, for goodness' sake," Mum chided, making a show of fixing my jacket collar. "I'm sorry you're in this position, darling."

"No need to be. I hadn't played into Edwin's hands when he was alive, and I'm not going to do it now."

"You will. In a few days, perhaps weeks, after you calm down, you'll realize that marrying Louisa is best for everyone. You, Cece, the Butcharts—"

"And, of course, you." I smirked darkly.

She blinked at the ancient buildings in front of us, looking dejected and glum. "Is it so wrong that I think I should be entitled to some of my own fortune?"

"No." I flicked my cigarette, watching as it tumbled down the sewer. "But you should've talked him out of amending the will."

"I had no idea," she murmured, staring hard at what Belle would call "fresh-ass nails." The mother of my future baby was quite fond of attaching the word ass almost to anything.

"Is that so?" I watched her carefully.

"It is."

Something occurred to me then. I swiveled in her direction, narrowing my eyes. "Wait a minute. Now I understand."

"Understand what?"

"Why Byron and Benedict goaded me about Louisa the entire dinner when I showed up at Edwin's funeral."

"Devvie, I do wish you'd call him Pap—"

"Why she was there. Why she was forgiving, and sympathetic, and pliant. You all knew I was going to be pushed into a corner to marry her, and you played your cards."

"Oh, of course I knew." Mum sighed tiredly, slackening against the building and closing her eyes. She looked ancient all of a sudden. Not the same, glamorous woman I grew up with. "Edwin told me about the will after executing it. There was nothing I could do about it. Our mutual funds had dwindled over the course of the last decade, and everything we had left—his car collection and properties—he bequeathed to you. I am essentially poor. You cannot do this to me. You cannot *not* marry Louisa."

And then she did something terrible.

Something I couldn't stomach.

She lowered herself to her knees, right there on the street, her eyes twinkling like diamonds in the night.

She looked up at me, her face defiant, her shoulders shaking.

I wanted to lower myself to her level, to be right there with her, to shake her and explain that I couldn't do it. Couldn't be what my father had wanted me to be. I never could.

"I'm sorry, Mum," I said, then walked away.

Two nights later, Sam and Cillian dropped in for a visit.

I didn't entertain a lot because A: there was nothing entertaining about these two dreadful cunts. And B: the longer I was around people, the more I felt pressured into behaving the way normal people did, hiding my flare, my strange musings, and claustrophobia.

For instance, I always used the elevators whenever I visited Royal Pipelines. I had to take half a valium beforehand for courage, but I did it.

Or when we were at Badlands, I had to think before I spoke, no matter what the subject matter was, reminding myself that I had a persona to uphold. That I was a womanizer, a rake, a man of certain tastes and standards.

I could never truly be myself with my mates, which was why even though I liked them on a personal level, I never truly opened up to them about my family.

"The will is iron-clad. I reread it enough times to make my eyes bleed." I growled into my stiff drink, perched in my study, in front of the only two men I knew who could weasel themselves out of serious trouble, albeit in very different ways.

Now I *had* to talk to them about my family, even if I only gave them the CliffsNotes version.

"Suddenly the fact that you've never told us about your family makes sense." Cillian stood in front of my floor-to-ceiling window, overlooking the scenic view of the Charles River and Boston's skyline. "Your parents sound worse than mine."

"I wouldn't go that far." Sam took a sip of his own drink, sitting in front of me on a designer recliner. "And what happens if the charities, say, decide to skip on the fat donations?"

"The money and estate will go to various relatives, none of whom are my immediate family. Quite frankly, every Whitehall man I've ever come across is either a drunk, a brute, or both."

Not to mention, I didn't want to be indebted to Sam Brennan in any way or form. He had yet to succeed in luring me into business with him, and I wanted to keep it that way.

"Aren't there primogenitures about shit like that?" Sam asked. "The Crown itself should grant you the lands. Even my simpleton ass knows that."

"Loopholes," I explained bitterly. "I'm not an immediate royal relative, so not all rules apply to me."

Only the ones that were to my father's liking.

"Remind me why you're opposed to marrying this Lilian chick?" Cillian brooded.

"Louisa," I corrected, rolling some ciggies to keep my hands busy. "Because I won't cower to my father's demands, not in life and definitely not from beyond the grave. Not to mention, there's a pre-written pre-nup my father had put in place to ensure that if we ever got a divorce, she would get everything."

"Even if you concede to his demand, he'd never know," Sam growled into his whiskey. "He is, for all intents and purposes, dead."

"*I* would know."

"Marriage takes different faces and forms." Cillian strode from the window toward the liquor cabinet, sifting through my drinks. "You could marry her and still see other people."

"And make her miserable?" I chuckled gravelly.

Sam shrugged. "That's none of your business."

"I am incapable of making someone suffer unnecessarily." I scooped up an ice cube, rolling it absentmindedly over the rim of my glass.

"Not incapable, just reluctant," Cillian drawled. "We're all capable of whatever it is we need to do to survive."

"The thing is, I don't need to survive this. My mother and sister do." I let the cube drop into my glass. "Would you marry someone for money?"

Sam laughed sardonically, his gray eyes gleaming wickedly. "I would've married someone for a piece of toast if I needed to, back in the day. But the universe provided, and I chose my bride because I wanted her, not because I needed her."

Cillian made a face. "That's my sister we're talking about."

"Don't remind me." Sam drained his whiskey. "The fact that Ambrose shares a genetic pool with your ass without my throwing chlorine into it still gives me hives."

"Peculiar." Cillian *tsked*. "I don't remember you coming from generations upon generations of neurosurgeons and army pilots."

I didn't have to ask if Cillian was willing to marry someone he didn't love. He did exactly that a few years ago and ended up falling for the woman.

I rubbed my knuckles along my jawline. I thought about how

Emmabelle would react if I told her I was getting married and realized she would probably laugh it off and ask if she needed to wear a fancy hat for the wedding.

Don't wait for me.

"Well, my mother does need the money direly. And Cece would like to divorce her husband and start fresh, I suspect. Plus, I want the estate to stay in my immediate family."

"Then what's there to think about?" Cillian plucked a brandy bottle from an impressive row and poured himself two fingers. "Marry the woman. Make an escape plan afterward."

"It's complicated," I growled, thinking about the pre-written prenup.

"Dumb it down for us, Einstein," Cillian coaxed.

"I want the inheritance, not the woman." Actually, I wanted neither, but Mum and Cecilia needed to be provided for.

"As established, you don't *have* to spoon with her for the rest of your fucking life." Sam knocked down his drink and stood up, done with the conversation. "Just put a ring on her damn finger. Bonus points if you can knock her up so you'll have someone to leave the inheritance to."

"I do have someone to leave it to. My child with Emmabelle."

Cillian threw a pitying look behind his shoulder from across the room. "Leaving a title to a bastard? Really?"

I shot up to my feet, my legs carrying me toward him before I even knew what was happening. I grabbed him by the collar and slammed him against the liquor cabinet, snarling in his face.

"Call my unborn child a bastard one more time and I'll make certain you will need all your fucking teeth replaced."

Brennan jumped up. He put his body between us, pushing us away to the opposite corners of the room.

"Easy there. Cillian has a point. Maybe the reason why you're so adamant not to marry Laura is because you have a boner for your baby momma."

"*Louisa*," I gritted.

"No, Belle. Even I know that. Get some gingko, man." Sam shook his head.

"The other woman's name is Louisa."

Cillian sipped his whiskey, looking casual, while Sam took a step back, confident we wouldn't try to kill each other again.

Both of them were staring at me.

"What?" I asked, my eyes narrowing to slits. "What the fuck are you looking at?"

Cillian smirked. "This is how it starts."

"How *what* starts?"

He and Sam exchanged amused looks.

"He's already gone," Sam observed.

"Never stood a chance," Cillian said, inclining his head.

"Poor Livia," Sam chuckled.

This time, I didn't correct them.

Sixteen

Belle

Fourteen Years Old.

"**S**CUMBAG," DAD SPITS ON THE FLOOR.
Oh boy. Mom's gonna smack him in the head for that.
He's lying on his incliner, catatonic, in front of the TV after a long workday.

Mom is somewhere in the house, having a breakdown. Not a huge one, just a mini meltdown. She's been a mess for … how long now? Since Auntie Tilda died, over a year ago. Auntie Tilda raised her. They had a ten-year gap between them. Auntie helped raise us too, so of course I'm bummed. But Mom … sometimes it's like she's on another planet.

"Daddy, language." Persephone gasps from her spot on the carpet, working on her two-thousand-piece puzzle, her tight braid swung over one of her shoulders. She looks so wholesome. I wish I could be her.

"Sorry, sweetheart. I get riled up when I see stuff like this."

I look up from my homework, which I'm doing on the sofa. It's the local news channel, and they're talking about a geography teacher who was caught having an affair with a junior at the local high school he worked for. They show his mugshot. He can't be under fifty-five.

"People like him should rot in hell." Dad stands up, starts stomping around the living room.

I tell myself that it's no big deal.

That it has nothing to do with me and Coach Locken.

Besides, what the hell am I even thinking? Coach and I haven't kissed, hugged, or touched in any way that's inappropriate. He helps me with my bad knee and short thigh muscles. It's not his fault that I'm broken.

And let's get real here, it's not like Dad's mood is all because of this news article. He's been worried sick about Mom, trying to convince her to go to therapy. But Mom says everyone is fed, clean, and that the house is in top condition. Which is all true. She's a great mom, even when she is sad.

"I hope you girls know you should tell Daddy if something like that ever happens." Dad points at the TV.

"Yes, Daddy," Persy and I say in unison.

Later that evening, I get a text message from Coach Locken. It's not out of the ordinary to get texts from him. Sometimes practice needs to be rescheduled or moved around because of the weather.

Only for the first time, the text is not dropped in the cross-country group with all the other runners. It is sent directly to me.

Coach Locken: morning practice time change. Meet at the entrance to Castle Rock Reservation at seven. Don't be late.

Seventeen

Belle

WEEKS CHASED ONE ANOTHER LIKE PAGES IN A GOOD book.

The only outward signs I was pregnant were the violent bouts of morning sickness I woke up to each day, paired with weekly visits to Doctor Bjorn, in which we watched Baby Whitehall (or Mr. Bean, as Devon liked to call her) growing nicely in my weirdly-shaped, polycystic womb, giving zero damns about the hostile environment she was in.

Atta girl.

Devon accompanied me to all of my appointments without fail. He always brought along something for me. A freshly baked pastry and a bottled water, vitamin gummy bears or ginger candy. He never missed our weekly calls, in which we made plans about what was going to happen after we have the baby.

"I want her to have a big room," I told him once.

"Your entire apartment doesn't qualify as a midsized room," he said, cerebral as always. "You could move into my building."

I cringed. Not because I didn't want to be close to him, but because

I could already see myself punching my way through all of my walls whenever I caught him sneaking home with one of his hookups. "Nah, I'll find somewhere else."

"Sweven?"

"Yes?"

"Tell me about a weird animal."

We did that a lot lately. Talked about strange shit. It was tragic that on top of being viciously handsome Devon was also quirky and adorably awkward. He wasn't at all the stuck-up ass I pegged him to be when we first hooked up.

I had slumped against my pillow, tucking my hand under my head and staring at the ceiling, smiling. "Ever seen a Southern Cassowary?"

"Negatory." I could hear the smile on his face. It made my chest hurt.

I had closed my eyes, swallowing hard.

"It's an Australian bird. It looks like a Karen who is asking to talk to the supervisor after discovering her fat-free latte had two pumps of regular vanilla syrup instead of the sugarless."

He spluttered, delighted. "I'm Googling it right now. Oh God. You aren't wrong. That face …"

"Your turn."

He thought about it, then said, "I always thought naked mole rats looked like shriveled-up penises. Of the ill-equipped, might I add."

I laughed so hard that I peed my underwear a little.

There was silence afterward.

"Should I still not wait for you, Belle?"

My body felt heavy and full of pain, but I didn't cry. I never cried over a man. "No," I had said quietly.

And that was that.

As time passed, so did my fear that I was going to be brutally murdered by my stalker/s. I hadn't heard from them (him?) in weeks, even though I checked my letters, looked around me, and took my gun everywhere.

Plus, Simon, whom I referred to as Si just to rile him up, had taken it upon himself to shadow me everywhere I went, specifically whenever I was in Madame Mayhem. I read between the lines that his job wasn't to help with the club, but to help keep me alive. Surprisingly, I wasn't overtly upset about it. I was an independent woman, yes, but I was also not a complete moron. I appreciated any help I could get keeping myself safe until I found out more about who was after me.

Devon was supportive in more ways than one. He went along with all of my whims and requests.

When I told him I didn't want to know the gender of our baby, he didn't protest even once, although I knew he was the kind of man who liked to know everything about everything.

Until one day, when he came to pick me up for our weekly OB-GYN meeting and ran three minutes late. This was new. He was usually the one I kept waiting for a minute or two while I got my shit together upstairs.

I got into the cab and smiled at him. He smiled back, looking a little … off. Like a layer of ice had blanketed his face.

"I thought about another weird animal yesterday, after we talked," I said, buckling up.

"Do share." He sat back, quirking an interested eyebrow.

"Marabou stork. They look like they have a soggy ball sack under their beaks."

He chuckled, and that was when I noticed them.

The faint pink scratches on his neck.

My insides flipped. Weakness made my knees buck. I had to breathe through my nose and lean against the door.

"I see you've been busy." I narrowed my eyes at his neck.

"I'm always busy, darling. It's called being a grown-up. You should try it sometime." But he had the nerve—the audacity, actually—to turn a little pink.

"Good thing one of us is getting some, even if it isn't me."

I needed to shut up. I had absolutely no right to do this to him, after preaching to him about how much we were *not* a couple.

He rearranged his collar, looking uncomfortable, which made

things worse. He wasn't even an asshole about it, so I couldn't throw a proper fit.

"Tell me all about it," I demanded.

"No," he drawled, narrowing his eyes at me.

"Do it now, Devon. I want to hear." I crossed my arms over my chest, unsure why I was doing this to him. To myself. But the answer was clear—I wanted it to hurt. Wanted to punish myself for giving a shit in the first place. His mouth flattened into a grim line before he spoke.

"I had an unexpected two-hour window yesterday. An old friend was in Boston for a medical conference. We went to dinner in her hotel—"

"Let me guess, and you ended up staying for dessert?" I smiled viciously.

His face was blank. Unresponsive. I was going to burst in tears. Or maybe just burst period. Maybe my skin would rip apart. Maybe green, jealous goo would pour out. Maybe I would finally remember what I seemed to forget recently—that men are horrible creatures designed to hurt you.

"You slept with her." I said it as a statement, hoping he would deny it or he'd say that he kissed her and it didn't feel right so he left. Or promise it would never happen again, because he didn't even enjoy it—that it was me he had thought about the whole time.

But he simply said, "Yes."

The cab driver shifted in his seat uncomfortably, uncomfortable with the prospect of his car becoming a crime scene when I murdered Devon. Poor thing. I was going to tip him double.

"Did she suck you off?" I asked in a businesslike tone.

The cab driver choked on his saliva.

Devon picked at invisible lint on his sharp suit, looking bored and closed-off. "Sweven—"

"Don't call me that, you asshole. Don't you even dare use my nickname right now."

"I've a suspicion you will come back from the jealous haze you're wrapped in right now in a few moments and regret this. Let's change the subject," Devon said confidently. He wasn't wrong. Which drove me even more crazy.

"Not until you answer me. Did. She. Suck. You. Off?"

His pale eyes met mine soberly. "Yes."

"And did you enjoy it?"

"Yes."

I laughed throatily. The world spun out of balance around me. I was going to be sick.

"You said not to wait for you. Twice, in fact. Logic dictates you have no authority nor claim on my affections."

His *affections*. My ass just had to go and mess with the only dipshit in Boston who talked like a Jane Austen novel dropout.

"Fuck your logic," I said.

"Gladly. But it's not going to be the only thing I'll be fucking."

"Your phone's ringing," I said dryly.

He pulled his phone out, frowning at the screen.

Tiffany.

He sent the call to voicemail.

Tiffany called again. He pressed his lips into a thin line, sending her to voicemail—*again*.

The cab pulled up at my OB-GYN's clinic. I tipped the guy fifty bucks and dashed out, Devon at my heel. His phone flashed in his hand again. This time the screen said it was Tracey calling.

I started taking the stairs to the third-floor clinic without even realizing what I was doing, knowing Devon didn't do elevators and not wanting to part ways.

"Do you only fuck women whose first names start with a T?" I asked cordially.

"Tracy is a partner at the firm."

"I bet you screwed her too."

"She is sixty."

"So are you." Seriously? I had the mental maturity of a cupcake.

He gave me another pitiful look before we reached the door to the clinic.

This, I reminded myself, was a valuable lesson. A *good* thing. If anything, the last half hour was proof I was right, as per usual.

That Devon was still a man, still incapable of keeping his junk in his pants, and still a great danger to me.

Sure, he was nice—more civilized than the men I'd encountered over the years—and polished to a fault. But a man nonetheless.

Devon grabbed my arm, spinning me around and pushing me against the door, crowding me. I looked at him, feeling his body everywhere and craving it and hating it and loving it. All at the same time.

"Leave me alone!" I growled.

"Not in a thousand years, darling. Now tell me—have you not been with anyone since we started hooking up again?"

I hadn't. Before I got pregnant, I wanted to limit my sexual encounters to Devon in order to ensure he'd be the father of my child. And after, I just couldn't see myself jumping into bed with some rando when I had a child inside me.

I thought about telling him I had sex all the time. It was the obvious Belle thing to do.

But when my mouth opened, I just couldn't do it.

He had a way of getting the truth out of me, even when the truth sucked.

"No," I admitted. Then added louder, "I haven't been with anyone since you."

A grunt left his beautiful lips, and he closed his eyes briefly. When he opened them again, there was fire behind him. "I could kiss you, Emmabelle Penrose."

I forced myself to smile, pushing the door open, just as Tiffany called him again.

"*Don't,* Devon Whitehall."

One day, while I was cradling my flat, three-month-pregnant belly, eyeballing rows of diaper bags and infant car seats at *buybuy Baby* while slurping on a deplorable green juice, I noticed a distressed-looking, heavily pregnant woman breaking down at the register.

She folded in two, hands flat on the conveyor belt, a mountain of essential baby supplies in front of her. A diaper bag, burp cloths, and bibs. Things any new mother needed to survive the crazy journey called motherhood. At first I thought she was going into labor. *Oh shit. I'm going to stop leaving the house as soon as I hit week thirty-eight,* I thought. With my luck, my water was going to break in an elevator full of people. And then we'd somehow get stuck there.

The woman's stomach had reached a tipping point, where her bellybutton was almost facing down and poking through the fabric of her shirt. Tears ran down her face, weighed down by clumps of mascara.

"I'm sorry. I'm sorry. I don't know what came over me." She used the back of her sleeve to wipe snot off her face. "I'll take some of it back. Just give me a second."

"Take your time, honey." The cashier looked like she was ready to bury herself under the tiles, she was so uncomfortable.

"Well … I guess I could really do without burp cloths. Old shirts will do just as well, right?"

I put the nipple ointment I was checking out back on the shelf and rushed over to the cashier, yanking my credit card out of my wallet and slapping it on the counter. "No. Don't put anything back. I'll pay."

The pregnant lady eyed me miserably. She rubbed her belly, as if comforting her unborn baby. Now that I took a closer look at her, she couldn't be older than nineteen. Fresh faced and rosy cheeked. I wanted to cry right along with her. What a situation to be in.

"I don't even know why I came here," she said, her chin wobbling.

"You came here to get things for your baby." My fingertips touched the back of her arm gently. "As you should. Don't worry about it. You're getting out of here with all of the supplies you need."

"Are you … are you sure?" She winced.

"Positive, dude."

A sheepish smile spread across her lips. She wore holed leggings and a shirt that clung to her belly like plastic wrap. I wished I could give her some of the maternity dresses I'd purchased with the outrageous budget Devon had poured into my account each month. I didn't need mine yet. My stomach was flat but hard.

"Thanks." She sniffed. "My boyfriend got laid off a few months ago, and he still hasn't found a job. Really screwed us over."

"Shit, I'm sorry." I plucked a gift card from the rack by the cashier and pointed at it. "What kind of employer does that to someone? Please put two thousand dollars on this."

I needed to know this girl had a constant stream of diapers and baby clothes until her beau found a new job. Otherwise, I wasn't going to sleep at night.

She cried even harder as a reaction, this time with relief. Then she spoke, her speech littered with hiccups and sniffles. "Yeah. It's been a shit show. We were counting on this gig. It really changed him … getting fired. Lately, he's been losing his temper. He's nervous about the hospital bill, but what am I supposed to do? Have the baby in the bathroom?" Her brows knitted together in anger. "He's the one who said we were being careful enough. Which, of course, was bullshit. If we were careful, we wouldn't be pregnant."

"It takes two to tango." *And three to create a soap opera*, I thought bitterly, remembering Tiffany.

"Right?" Her eyes widened. "At least I found a job at the local thrift shop. *He* barely gets out of the house these days. Just drinks and watches TV and … shit, I'm sorry." Her cheeks turned crimson. She ducked her head, shaking it. "It's not your problem, obviously. You're too kind."

"Dude, I spill my guts to anyone who's willing to listen, so don't even think twice about it. My insurance broker knows my blood test results, and the lady at the grocery store across from my apartment is my reluctant therapist." I handed her the bags full of the things she needed, along with my business card. "Call if you need anything—if it's something for the baby or just a shoulder to cry on."

She took everything gratefully, her eyes clinging to me.

"This must be a sign that things are getting better. You know, half an hour ago, my boyfriend asked me out of the blue if I wanted to come here. He never takes me anywhere. This is *so* fate."

"Fate is like a stalker. It has its ways of finding you." I winked at her.

Twenty minutes and five dubious purchases later (did I really need a baby body mop and a booty fan?), I made my way from *buybuy Baby* to my car, swinging the bags in my hands, contemplating how many scoops of ice cream I was going to treat myself and Baby Whitehall to.

Three, I decided. One for me, one for her, and then another one for me, because Momma hadn't had sex in a long-ass time and needed a mood boost.

When I popped open the trunk—featuring my novelty license plate BURSQGRL—to discard the bags, I realized that my car looked … *different*. I looked down and let out a little gasp, stumbling back.

All four of my tires had been slashed.

I slammed the trunk closed, looking around manically, trying to see who else was in the parking lot. It was possible the asshole who did this was still around to ravish in my misery.

A car honked in the distance of the parking lot. Heart pounding, I swiveled my head in its direction. A beat-up 1996 red Camaro rolled past, the windows down, the driver's arm propped out. I recognized the woman in the passenger seat immediately—it was the distressed girl I helped thirty minutes ago at the cashier. She stared at her lap, fresh tears rolling down her cheeks.

But the man in the driver's seat was the one who took my breath away …

Frank.

As in the man I'd fired months ago.

The bitter, violent, sexual harassing asshole I came to blows with.

A piece of the puzzle clicked together.

Frank.

He was the son of a gun who went after me.

He *also* had a pregnant girlfriend I didn't know about when I fired him.

It went without saying that when I caught him with his hand

between the burlesque dancer's legs, the first thing that popped into my head wasn't, *I bet this guy is a great family man who is on the cusp of becoming a father.*

Now? Now he was broke and in big trouble.

But so was I.

Because he wanted me dead.

Frank shot me a sneer, flipping me the bird as he sped out of the parking lot.

I thought about chasing him, but I didn't want to put myself or his girlfriend in danger. I was going to deal with this, though. Now that I knew who he was.

I pried my phone out of my bag and called Devon. My hands felt cold and shaky, and it took me several attempts to find his name in my contacts.

It was the first time I'd called him for something that wasn't our scheduled weekly meeting. A breach of contract, if you would.

It was also the first time I called him voluntarily since I found out he was bumping uglies with *Tiffany*. And yes, italics were necessary.

He answered on the first ring.

"Is the baby okay?"

I gulped air, my oxygen supply dwindling as the implication of what I'd just discovered slammed into me. Shit, shit, shit. Frank had been the one to send me a string of clues and threats, and this one was the latest. Did I even know where he lived? No, I didn't. After I sent him the last check, it was returned to Madame Mayhem. He must've moved after I sent the reporters to hound him.

"The baby's fine." *I think.*

"What's going on?" Devon sounded sincerely alarmed.

"I ... someone slashed my tires. I need a ride."

And a drink.

And a shoulder to cry on.

A graceful, elegant, infuriatingly gorgeous almost-prince to make it all better.

Not necessarily in that order.

"Why would anyone do that?" he demanded.

I wasn't telling him what was going on with me. Screw that. He would lock me in a tower and never let me see the light of day.

"I don't know, punks?"

"Where are you?"

"*buybuy Baby*."

"The place is known for high crime activity around it," he drawled impatiently, yet again exceling at making me feel like a kid. "Send me the address. I'm on my way."

"Uh, hmm …" I was showing off my magnificent eloquence.

"What?" he asked, sensing there was more.

I looked around me again. No one promised me Frank wasn't going to return after dropping his girlfriend off to put a bullet in my head.

"Can we … uh, talk on the phone until you get here?"

"Sweven," he sighed, his icy demeanor melting a little, "of course."

I was so happy to hear my nickname, I could cry.

He stayed on the phone with me. Asking me about my purchases (he wasn't impressed with the mop bodysuit) and what burlesque show was featured in Madame Mayhem these days (Suicide Girls Blackheart), trying to get my mind off what'd happened to me.

To Devon's credit, he dropped everything and showed up fifteen minutes later, double-parking his Bentley and slamming it shut as he pounced on me.

"Are you all right?" He scooped me into his arms and buried my head in his shoulder, engulfing me in a bone-crushing hug. For a reason unbeknownst to me, I immediately began bawling into his Tom Ford suit, smearing my foundation and colorful eyeshadow onto it. I hadn't cried in so long. This was unlike me.

Devon massaged my neck in circles, dropping feathery kisses on the crown of my head.

"Why would anyone do something like this, Belle?"

"I … I … I don't know," I hiccupped.

But I did know.

Even worse, I wasn't going to call the police on Frank. Even if he was responsible for the letter and for the man who stalked me all those months ago, which I had evidence was the case. The two other men looked different, and neither of them appeared to be connected to Frank.

Truth of the matter was, Frank had been radio silent for months. Now I knew he was behind all those things. Surely, he wasn't stupid enough to continue. Maybe it was his last hurrah before he let it go. Plus, he had enough problems on his hands. He needed to find another job and provide for his growing family. Hopefully one where he stayed far away from women.

"I thought something was wrong with you. Physically." I heard Devon's voice through the cloud of self-pity and adrenaline surrounding me. He guided me gently into his passenger seat and closed the door.

I buckled up and stared out the window, locking my jaw so my chin wouldn't tremble.

"I'm glad you called," Devon added.

About that …

Why *did* I call him and not Persy, or Sailor, or Aisling, or *Ross*? Even my parents would have made the journey into the city to pick me up. Among the list of people who could come and help me, Devon was the busiest and the person I was least close to.

Yet I chose him to save me.

"Where should I take you?" Devon asked.

"My apartment."

"Not Persy's?"

"No."

I was too wounded, too raw to watch Pers parading her perfect family with a perfect husband who adored her and her perfect kids who stared at her with wonder and awe.

Devon hit the gas, sensing that I wasn't super talkative.

"I'm sure it was some dumb kid," I told him, realizing how it must've looked from his point of view.

"Like the dumb kid who followed you in Boston Common?" Devon choked up on the steering wheel to the point of white knuckles.

"Who told you?" I whipped my head around to look at him.

"Someone who cares about your safety."

"A snitch," I contradicted.

"You can call them whatever you like. You still haven't answered my question."

"My answer is that it's the 21ˢᵗ century, and women can fend for themselves. We can take care of our own well-being, even—try not to be scandalized—vote!"

"If you choose to ignore a stalker, maybe you, specifically, shouldn't have the right to vote."

Technically *three* different men. But now wasn't the time to bring that up.

"I carry a gun with me everywhere."

"That's supposed to make me feel *better*?" Devon asked slowly, sarcastically, to highlight how dumb I sounded. "This isn't the Wild West, Emmabelle. You can't shoot people willy-nilly on the street if you think they're stalking you. You need to go to the police."

It was the first time I'd seen him even remotely angry, and it was so fascinating. For a second there, I forgot about my problems.

I slanted my head, watching him intently. "I have a secret," I stage-whispered. "I don't work at making you happy, Devon."

He gave me a look that made my soul shrivel into itself. The look that told me he was growing seriously tired of me, and I couldn't blame him. I was horrible to him. I was so tragically afraid of him that I constantly pushed him away.

"All I'm saying is that I've got this," I mumbled, examining my colorful, pointy fingernails.

"Is that why you called me?" he bit out. "Because you've *got this*?"

Our first fight. Awesome. How could I explain to him that I didn't like people butting into my business? Into my life? That I couldn't rely on others?

"My bad. Next time, I'll call someone else."

"No, you won't. I'm the only person capable of dealing with your brand of bullshit for longer than an evening."

He parked in front of my apartment building, got out, rounded the car, and opened the door for me, doing it all with a face that hinted he was going to chop me into shrimp-sized pieces and feed me to the sharks.

"Thanks for the ride. You've been a lovely companion." I slipped out of the car and proceeded to my entrance, feeling very much like a misbehaving child tossed into their room for a timeout.

He followed me wordlessly. I knew better than to send him away. First of all, I didn't want to be alone right now. And second, I was the one who called him.

When we got to my apartment (stairs again, whoopy-woo), Devon disappeared into my bedroom to talk to Joanne on the phone. He asked her to arrange for my car to be towed. He also asked her to put Simon on the phone for him. Ah, good ole Si, the bodyguard who pretended to do shit no one needed done in the club, like filing or sorting boxes into the different recycling bin.

The fact he once jumped on top of me to defend me when Ross accidentally dropped a beer crate was a dead giveaway.

"…is not why I bloody pay you. Step up, or I will ensure your next job is a McJob."

There was a brief silence.

"Then do better!" Devon roared.

When he returned to the living room, his eyes landed on me. He looked like an eagle zeroing in on his prey. "You're shaking and sweating."

"No, I'm not." The fact that my teeth chattered as I said it didn't help my case. Goddammit. It was only Frank. I could take him down if I needed to, right?

Wrong. You need to stop being a pussy and go to the police. So what if his girlfriend is pregnant? You aren't the one who knocked her up.

"Come. I'll draw you a bath." He walked over and offered me his hand. The easy laughter and polite manner that usually oozed from him was gone, though. Now that I thought about it, it had been gone the entire day, from the moment he answered the phone and then when he picked me up.

Horrifyingly, I realized Devon had stopped flirting with me.

He had given up on me. On *us*.

Well, good. That was exactly what I wanted. I was happy he was done making shit awkward.

When I remained planted on the couch, he scooped me up and carried me to my bathroom.

"I hate it when you're being perfect," I moaned.

"Ditto, darling. Especially when it's wasted on you."

He sat me on the closed toilet seat and drew me a hot bath, rolling his sleeves up to his elbow and exposing his Michelangelo's Moses forearms.

Oof. I missed sex.

My insides twisted hotly, tension building inside me.

What was life without sex? Just work and taxes and a good dose of dish-washing.

It was so unfair that I didn't want to have sex with anyone who wasn't the father of my child for the duration of my pregnancy.

I couldn't even rationalize this decision. Maybe I *did* have some leftover traditionalism in my body, residue from sharing a roof with Persy for most of my life.

My eyes followed every movement of his corded arms as he dropped a bath bomb into the tub.

"So, have you been sleeping with anyone interesting lately?" I shifted on the toilet seat, eyeing his strong, long fingers.

Was I … getting turned on right now? The friction from the surface beneath me made my nipples pucker. I removed my clothes, item by item, while Devon twisted his face like something smelled horrible in the room.

"I thought you were done torturing yourself."

"Come on," I laughed, boomeranging my blouse to the floor. Though I wasn't showing yet, my breasts were already heavy and veiny. Much bigger than he remembered. "I know you're still having sex with other people. Let me live vicariously through you. I forgot what it feels like."

Dryly, he said, "You have enough experience for the entire

East Coast, darling. Grab some gingko and use the power of your imagination."

"Remind me, what do you do once the two of you are in bed? I forgot," I purred, ignoring his annoyance.

He looked at me like I was crazy. And in that moment I was.

"You haven't been drinking, have you?" he asked worriedly.

I laughed. "No. I'm just … tender around the edges."

"Sounds like code for unhinged."

"Come on…" I smiled, "…I'm trying to be cordial."

"I noticed. We've been in the same room for close to eight minutes and you still haven't tried to stab me."

He turned off the faucet and stood up, stepping aside. "Let me help you in."

"You can join me too, if you feel so inclined." I tried my hand at a half-hearted seduction, too horny to afford my pride.

He completely ignored me, ushering me by the small of my back to the bathtub.

I rolled my eyes. "Is that a no?"

"You told me specifically—and repeatedly—to stop trying with you," he reminded me dryly.

"Well, maybe I've changed my mind!"

Jesus, couldn't a girl make a definitive statement then change her mind due to horniness? And they said America was the freest country in the world.

"Why don't you get in and we'll discuss it after you've calmed down?" Devon suggested.

"I *am* calmed down!" I protested with a screech, slapping my own thighs like a toddler.

"Evidently," he deadpanned.

Finally, I stepped into the bath and lowered my body into it. Closing my eyes, I felt the warmth of the water and the tingling of the soap clinging to my body.

The scent of strawberry and citrus was heightened by the humidity in the room. Behind me, Devon took a seat on the edge of the bathtub and began massaging my shoulders.

"You're aroused," he stated. His fingers tickled the flyaways escaping from my high bun. They slid lower, toward my breasts, avoiding the sensitive territory but skating closer.

"*Aroused*," I repeated with a chuckle. "You're so old."

"You're so pregnant."

"What's that supposed to mean?"

"You have cravings. Needs," Devon explained.

"Yeah," I admitted with a sigh, momentarily disarmed by the massage and the bubble bath and the knowledge I was safe with him.

"What stops you from sleeping around?" he asked, lethally blasé.

"Uh, the fact that I'm knocked up?"

"It's not going to hurt the baby. Doctor Bjorn told us that himself."

Yeah, Doctor Bjorn, who was shipping Bellon (Belle + Devon), constantly reminded us we could and indeed should pork.

"I don't want to share my body with anyone else."

"Not anyone?" he asked with mock innocence, his confident fingers rolling lower toward my heavy, sensitive breasts.

"You've already made your mark on me for the next few months." I flicked pearls of soap at his face teasingly. "It wouldn't feel as outrageous if we got in bed together."

Devon's fingers slid to the back of my neck, digging in delicious, slow circles. "Let's make a deal—you'll answer a few questions, and if I'm satisfied with your answers, I'll bring you to release."

"Nice grandiose ego you've got yourself there. I still own vibrators, you know," I groaned.

But he was right. My whole body was aflame. I wanted to grab his collar and pull him down with me.

"It's okay to need someone sometimes," Devon whispered, the warm air from his mouth skating over the shell of my ear. He was so close that I could feel the heat of his body against mine. Every hair on my body stood on end. My nipples ached, and my thighs rubbed together underwater.

I was minutes away from slipping a hand between them and doing the job myself.

I turned to face him, our eyes meeting. Blue on blue. His, crystal clear as the morning sky. Mine, a much darker shade, dotted with purple around the irises.

"It's never okay to need anyone," I croaked.

"That's a terrible way to exist, Sweven. I'll always be there for you. Rain or shine."

"How many questions?" I sniffed.

"That wholly depends on your answers."

I nodded my approval.

"Question number one. Why didn't you tell me a man stalked you in Boston Common all those months ago?" Devon cupped my breasts, his thumbs rolling around my nipples, making my whole body quake.

My breath hitched. "I didn't want you to interfere with my life more than you already had."

"Second question—have there been any more signs since that someone is after you?"

I didn't want to admit that there were. Didn't want him to put more Simons on me. Anyway, I truly did believe Frank was probably done. The parking lot thing was a one-off. Why else would he make himself known?

When Devon noticed my hesitation, one of his hands slipped from my breasts, sliding down my stomach, his pinky flicking my groin with just the faintest touch. I gasped and writhed shamelessly. How was I supposed to conduct a conversation like this?

"This is blackmail," I said hotly.

"I never pretended to be fair. Now answer the question." He bit the shell of my ear softly.

"Yes. A letter arrived shortly after Boston Common. Threatening to kill me. That's when I started carrying my gun everywhere."

"Why didn't you go to the police at that point?"

"I didn't want the bad press to stick to Madame Mayhem or have you and my family on my case. I get hate mail on a daily basis. And look, months have passed with no more signs."

"Do you know who it might be?"

His hand cupped my pussy, but there was no penetration. Just the delicious pressure of him holding me there while I helplessly tried to arch myself into his touch.

"Y-yes," I stuttered, closer to the edge than I should be when he'd barely even touched me.

"Who?" Devon pressed.

"A man named Frank. A former bartender of mine. I fired him a few months ago for grabbing a burlesque girl. I saw him in the parking lot today."

"Why aren't you sitting at a police station right *now*?"

"He is just a kid, and his girlfriend is pregnant. They have no money. He just wanted to let off some steam. Probably sent a friend of his to scare me in the Common." Although that still couldn't explain the man at Madame Mayhem the day Devon had taken me home. "I don't think I'll hear from him again."

"You're crazy, and you're carrying my baby," he said matter-of-factly, more to himself than to me.

He didn't move his hand from my mound, but he didn't give me the release I craved either. Why did he withhold my orgasm like that? Wasn't this a crime against humanity?

"I'll be fine," I bit out. "I've taken care of myself for a long-ass time now. Never had any problems."

"A few little rules, and then you can go back to entertaining me in my bed," Devon clarified, letting me know I was not off the hook yet.

I didn't answer, because I wanted to get it over with and for him to just touch me there. It was pathetic, but desperate times called for desperate measures. I *needed* to take my mind off things. This was a coping mechanism, okay?

"Rule number one—you never leave Simon's side when you're at work."

"Bodyguard Si?" I laughed throatily. "Whatever."

"No. Not whatever. You're not a teenager, Emmabelle. Give me a yes or no answer."

Sheesh.

"Fine! Yes."

"Rule number two …" I felt his pinky grazing my opening. My whole body awakened with excitement. I eagerly opened my legs for him. Finally, I was getting some action that didn't require any batteries.

"Don't go out alone. Always have someone accompany you. It could be your mates, your parents, Simon, or even me."

A bold-ass request, but again, I didn't *have* to do anything I didn't want to. He was hardly here twenty-four-seven to watch me.

"Sure." Then, when he didn't move his hand again, I groaned. "Oh, right. Yes or no. *Yes.*"

"Last condition …" Devon's fingers probed my opening, closer than ever. It only took one push for him to fill me completely. His other hand kept working on my breasts. "Move in with me. Just for the time being. I could protect you. We can look for an apartment for you in my building while you're there. It has top-notch security, so I never have to worry about you."

My eyes popped open and alarm bells began blaring in my head.

"Move in with you?" I repeated slowly.

I felt his nose nuzzling the crook of my neck.

"Come now, Sweven. You're brave enough to shoot someone in the face if they come after you. Surely, you can tolerate a few months rooming with the father of your child."

It was a dare. His index finger slipped into me, and I gasped, arching my back, my nipples resurfacing from the waterline. Devon bent down and captured one of them in his mouth, sucking fervently.

"So sweet. So, bloody sweet." His straight, white teeth grazed the sensitive peaks. "I'll make it worth your while," he murmured, swirling his tongue around the tip of my nipple before nibbling on it. At the same time, he mercilessly fucked me with his finger under the water.

I pushed my groin toward his hand, chasing my release, knowing it was close.

"You'll never be able to tame me," I warned.

"I have no desire to." He licked his way up my neck, sealing my mouth with a red-hot kiss. With all the tongue and droplets of water and so much desire, I thought I was going to combust. "I like you just the way you are. Unlikely, I know, considering your mule of a personality, but true."

"I'm a mess," I panted.

"Be *my* mess."

It was more tempting than I could admit. Alluring like a beacon of light in a sea of darkness.

I came undone, climaxing on his fingers. I clenched around them so hard he laughed into our kiss, the spasms making my muscles tighten.

After a few seconds, he pulled away, quirking an eyebrow.

"Just for a few months," I lamented—more to myself than to him.

It wasn't like I had anywhere to put a baby in my current apartment anyway.

"Just for a few months," he repeated, biting my lower lip playfully.

The glint in his eyes said it all.

I'd agreed to be his, even for a little while.

Giving up the thing I held most dear.

Complete freedom.

Eighteen

Belle

FOUR DAYS LATER, I MOVED INTO DEVON'S LOFT.
It was the first time I'd visited his apartment. Throughout our long and chaotic relationship, I was the one calling the shots, so I always demanded he come to see me.

Oh, how the mighty have fallen.

I had no idea what to expect, but somehow, the place fit into my perception of him perfectly.

An extensive chunk of open space with furnishings and colors I would imagine Queen Elizabeth herself favored. The lack of walls and vast hallways surprised me. The place looked like a repurposed warehouse. I'd always imagined Devon in a sprawling, dark manor—cluttered with family portraits and expensive yet stunningly ugly antiques. Then I remembered he didn't like closed spaces. He was somewhat of a claustrophobic.

It was a real upgrade from my tiny apartment.

I was feeling particularly nice toward Devon that day. He'd made sure to come to my apartment every day since Frankgate and ensured that *I* came.

On his dick, on his tongue, on his fingers.

You name it, he shoved it in me.

I hadn't broached the subject of exclusivity, but I made a mental note to let him know that I was not down with him dipping his sausage in every sauce available in the all-you-can-eat Boston dating scene buffet.

I spent the four days leading up to the move trying to convince Persy, Aisling, Sailor, and Ross that I was definitely, *definitely* not in a relationship with Devon.

Luckily, the Frank story made it easy to explain how we'd become roommates.

Everyone thought Devon was a dreamboat for providing me shelter, and that I was a complete and utter moron not to kiss his feet and beg him to wed me.

Things looked like they were finally settling down.

I would even go as far as to say I was getting comfortable in one of Devon's spare rooms.

He sneaked into my bedroom every night since I'd moved in, but I always kicked him out to the master bedroom afterward, citing that I would never be able to sleep with a man next to me.

During my time here, I caught glimpses of conversations between him and his mother. She called him frequently, sometimes a few times a day. He always seemed polite and reserved, friendly—even though, it had to be said, Ursula Whitehall sounded like a giant pain in the ass.

"No, Mum, I haven't changed my mind."

"No, I don't know when I'll come to England next. Is the money I've sent you not enough?"

"No. I've no desire to speak to her. I've apologized. That should be enough."

This last tidbit made me want to ask questions, but then I reminded myself it was none of my business.

Three days after I moved in with Devon, he went to work and I stayed behind.

I was sitting in front of the alabaster marble nook, enjoying an assortment of exotic fruit and grains—fine, it was Froot Loops. I was eating Froot Loops—minding my own business. I wore nothing but an oversized shirt (*Snaccidents Happen*). Thank you, Etsy, for providing me with a wealth of inspiration and life mantras and my brazen attitude. The doorbell chimed. I went to open it without thinking much of it. I mean, his casa was mi casa now, right?

Besides, what if it were a delivery person bearing more yummy shit? Dudebro had five hundred fancy food box subscriptions.

In front of me stood a tall, stork-like woman with dark locks and a Kate Middleton outfit. She had stilettos, a face full of tasteful makeup, and an irritated look on her face. She smelled like an upscale mall.

And she stared at me like I'd stolen her husband or something.

"Hullo."

British accent. She must've been Devon's sister. Or maybe his mother with a very (*very*) good facelift.

"Heya." I propped my elbow against the doorjamb, thinking to myself, *if this is Tiffany, I'm going to give her a five-step head start before I bitch slap her.*

"I suppose you're the stripper he knocked up accidentally who is now standing in his way of his family fortune?"

Hmm ... what?

"That's exactly who I am!" Recovering from the blow, I exclaimed cheerfully, refusing to show an iota of weakness, "And you are ...?"

"His *fiancée*."

Nineteen

Devon

THAT DAY, WORK HAD BEEN GLOSSED OVER.

Coming back home and burying myself in Emmabelle seemed more important than helping my clients get out of whatever trouble they'd gotten themselves into.

I knew what we had was temporary. Women like Sweven hardly made for domestic goddesses. But like all mere mortals, I was fond of playing with deities, even though I knew all about how these stories end.

Also, I really needed to ensure she was safe until my baby was out of her body.

Also, Mum was getting on my last nerve, begging me to come to England and meet Louisa for a cuppa, which meant I needed to head back to Britain soon and explain to my family that I wasn't going to marry someone just because my dead sperm-donor strong-armed me.

I took the stairs up to my loft two at a time.

I keyed in the code, flung the door open, and sing-songed, "Honey, I'm home!"

And stopped dead in my tracks.

Belle was sitting at my breakfast nook, still wearing the same ridiculous oversized shirt she sported before I'd gone to work.

She wasn't alone.

"Hello, *Devvie*." Sweven's smile was saccharine, but her eyes darted poisonous daggers at me. "*Busted*."

Across from her sat Louisa, sipping green tea.

Shite.

Louisa stood up, dangling her hips seductively while she made her way over to me. She placed a lingering kiss on my cheek, her whole body angled toward mine.

"Darling, you've been missed. Your mother gave me your address. She is awfully distraught. She asked that I come speak to you personally."

Brazen move. Even—dare I say—deranged? But there were several million dollars on the line in properties and heirlooms, and Mum had no liquid assets and no other income sources.

As for Louisa, I was the one who got away. The prized match.

"You could've called." I smiled enchantingly, bowing my head to kiss her knuckles easily.

"I could say the same," Louisa remarked smartly, not looking half-bothered by my icy welcome. She was sharp, but not—I noticed—hostile, like Belle was. "When's a good time to talk?"

"Now," Belle interrupted from her place at the breakfast nook, reaching into a cereal box and withdrawing one Froot Loop, popping it into her mouth. "Now's a bomb-ass time to tell me what the shit is going on. Spare no detail, boos."

"She does have a way with words." Louisa swung her gaze to me, arching an eyebrow.

"You should see me with my fists," Belle said sunnily.

I choked on my saliva.

Louisa blinked slowly, calm and collected. "Don't let my exterior fool you. I'm not afraid to get my hands dirty."

If I had to put my bet on either of these women, I'd say Louisa better run, because Emmabelle Penrose could probably turn her into dust.

Still, Lou had definitely grown up, and I couldn't help but appreciate this newly improved version of her.

Sensing a looming catfight, I sauntered toward Belle, sitting next to her. I took her hand, kissing the back of it gently. She withdrew immediately, like I'd bit her.

It was time to face the music, even if it was a terrible, sugary pop song that made my ears bleed. I turned to Belle.

"As you know, my father passed away not long ago. When I went back for the reading of the will, I discovered that he left everything to me, but on the condition that I marry Louisa. I rejected the idea immediately. My apologies for keeping you in the dark. The only reason I did so was because your shite plate seemed full enough. It was—*is*," I corrected, "as far as I'm concerned, subject closed."

"How much did he leave you?" Belle asked, businesslike.

"Thirty million pounds in estates and heirlooms," Lou intervened from beside us. "Although Whitehall Court Castle is priceless. And by priceless, I mean, the next in line to inherit the castle is England. It'll get turned into a museum. It is prominent in British history."

"That's a crap ton of dough." Belle popped another lone Froot Loop between her luscious lips, nodding thoughtfully. No trace of emotion on her face or posture, I noticed.

Louisa turned to me. "*Now I am* absolutely *not saying she's a gold-digger …*" She sang in a perfect, American accent, quoting the Kanye West song.

"But I ain't messin' with no broke." Belle laughed. "Damn straight."

"This discussion is futile." I rubbed at my forehead.

Internally, however, I was beginning to question my own statement. What stopped me from marrying Louisa? She was gorgeous, well-bred, well-read, and well-mannered. She was smart and still fond of me. I would get richer, sort all my family's problems, and have a marriage on my terms. Most of all I'd be able to marry, something I prevented myself from doing thus far.

"It shouldn't be." Louisa played with the teabag poking from her green tea. "There's much to discuss, and time is running out."

"I don't understand. We've already agreed we're not exclusive." Belle scrunched her nose. "What's stopping you from marrying this obnoxious, pompous, stylish woman?" She pointed at Louisa like she was a statue. "No offense."

"From you, none taken," Louisa huffed.

"Everybody wins," Belle added.

Not everyone, I thought. *Not me.*

Belle flashed me a smile I'd never seen on her face before. It looked wounded. Almost ugly. She stood up, surveying Louisa head to toe with a look that would make most humans die from the frostbite.

"I think you two have a lot to sort out, and honestly, if I wanted to see a bunch of Brits squirming around the subject of sex and relationships, I'd watch *Sex Education*. At least I'd get a few laughs out of it."

With that, she grabbed the cereal box from the nook and made her way to her room, slamming the door behind her.

Louisa turned to me. "Darling, that woman is not fully cultured. How could you possibly find her attractive? How old is she? Twenty-four? Twenty-five? She's hardly even a woman."

"She is the most maddening, infuriating, annoying woman I've ever come across, but a woman nonetheless," I replied. Taking out my tin of rollies, then thinking better of it, I set it down on the nook.

Now that Sweven lived here, I couldn't smoke indoors. I had her and the baby to think about.

Louisa stood up and waltzed over to me, lacing her arms around my shoulders.

It felt good to be embraced by a woman who wasn't constantly on the brink of busting my balls for breathing in her vicinity.

"Lou," I said softly, moving my hand across her back. "I appreciate the last-ditch effort, but it isn't going to work."

"Why?" she asked, her dark, deep eyes dancing in their sockets. "You've always been such a cunning, smart man. Practical and pragmatic. Why not marry into a world of wealth and titles? Even your little girlfriend thinks it's a bad idea to pass this chance up."

I grabbed her arms and lowered them gently. "I wish I could give you what you want."

"Why can't you?" Her voice cracked.

"Edwin," I answered simply. I was never going to let him win.

"He's not going to know." Her eyes filled with tears. "And he cannot hurt you anymore. Look, I know you don't want to play into his hands. But he is not here to see this. He died knowing you defied him."

I smiled sadly. "You know me too well."

Even after all these years, it was true. Louisa knew what made me tick. What my walls were built of.

She looked down, drawing a deep breath. "Cecilia is on suicide watch."

"No. That's not true." I reared my head back.

Lou nodded.

"Can you blame her? Her life is practically over. She doesn't want to stay with Drew, but you took away her options when you said you wouldn't marry me. Ursula and her were going to convince you to sell the Battersea complex building and live off the money after Edwin blew through their savings and investment portfolio."

The news hit exactly where it was supposed to. Right in my heart.

"Your mother is in a deep depression. There's no one to pay the hefty bills. I know you cannot take care of them, Devon. You're doing very well for yourself, but you have your own life to sustain. Tying the knot could make all of this go away. I'm willing to overlook your little mistake with this … *Belle* girl." She shuddered when she said her name. "Make an honest woman out of me. It'll make everyone happy. Including, by the way, your stripper. I just spent a few hours with her. She doesn't care for you at all, Devvie. The entire time, she couldn't stop telling me how much she was looking forward to getting out of here. To start *dating* again."

Sweven missed dating, did she?

My senses became oversaturated with fresh white anger.

The only reason why she was here, in my apartment, was because she had a literal death threat hanging over her head and sexual needs she wanted me to take care of.

She was a selfish, uncaring woman, and she would be the first one to admit it.

I was categorically idiotic, refusing to even entertain the idea of marrying Louisa simply because it would have delighted my father, who by now was nothing more than a bag of bones in a suit.

"I'll give it some thought." I rubbed at my jaw.

Louisa took a step back. I scanned her body. She was, indeed, a delightful creature. Not as wildly exotic and exciting as Belle, but satisfying nonetheless.

It was good to remember that Louisa would never put herself in a position of getting death threats, would never opt out of contacting the police, nor would she carry a gun or eat Froot Loops for breakfast, lunch, and dinner.

"Can I stay here in the meantime? I gave myself a tour and noticed you have a couple of guestrooms," Lou murmured.

The idea of sharing a roof with both Emmabelle *and* Louisa was about as appealing as castration by a blind man. This could easily end in a double murder. Frankly, I didn't want the mother of my child to give birth in prison.

"Get a hotel." I took a step forward, brushing my thumb along her cheek. "I'll pay."

"No, thank you. I have my own money." She smiled politely, but I could tell by her face that she was wounded. "Dinner tomorrow? Show me Boston?"

"Sure," I groaned. "Just let me check my calendar."

She immediately melted into my body, smiling up to me, her eyes shining with the same intensity they had when we were kids.

Louisa.

She'd never cheat.

Never show a hint of disloyalty.

Would be so easily trained.

"I'll stay local." She caught my wrist between her fingers, pushing her cheek into my palm like a spoiled kitten.

"I'll stay in touch."

"God, Devvie, I'm so glad we had this conversation. Your mother will be delighted."

Apparently, Belle would be too.

I escorted Louisa to the door, kissed her cheek goodbye, and closed it after her.

Maybe it was time to let one door close and another one open.

Belle

She was gone.

But not before he rubbed his thumb across her cheek.

Not before he looked down at her with the same aloof amusement he looked at me.

I spied on them through the crack of the slightly ajar door of the guestroom.

I had spent the entire day telling Louisa how much I didn't care for Devon, how I was eager to get back to my normal life. All in order to save face.

But none of it was true.

Admit it. You have feelings for the father of your child, and you're in over your head.

I clutched my belly, flinging myself on a bed that smelled like him.

Betrayal was betrayal. And this felt reminiscent of my past. That same helpless feeling of putting your heart in the hands of a man and watching as he crushed it into shards of nothing.

I curled into myself over the linen of the queen-sized bed and seethed.

I needed to get out of here. To move back to my apartment.

Thank *fuck* I hadn't stopped paying rent.

I wanted to give it a few weeks, just to see if Devon and I would get along. Turned out we did.

Only one thing was standing in our way—his *fiancée*.

Or maybe she wasn't his fiancée right now, but she was right in what she told me this afternoon, when he wasn't here.

"Devon always does the right thing, and the right thing is to marry me. Bow down, Emmabelle. It's game over for you. He doesn't have a choice."

A soft knock on the door sounded behind my back. I made no move or sound.

"May I?" Devon asked gruffly from the other end.

He didn't sound apologetic at all. More like he was looking for a fight. Well, this was his lucky day.

"It *is* your apartment."

He'd told her I was a stripper. Otherwise she wouldn't have said it. He probably bragged about my being a burlesque club owner. Many men found my occupation sordid and attractive. Not a marry-her-one-day attractive. More like, look-at-the-freak-show-I'm-fucking attractive.

I felt the edge of the mattress dipping behind me. His impressive frame filled the bed, and there was nothing I could do about it.

"I would like to stress to you, again, that Louisa and I are not currently together nor are we engaged. I never would have bedded you had I been with someone else."

I snorted out a laugh, refusing to face him. "Please. You admitted to me yourself that you were fucking around after I conceived."

"Fucking around is not the same as having a partner."

"Well, go tell all your other hookups that you finally found a keeper."

"I don't have any other hookups," he said irritably, like I was the one who was being unreasonable. Was I? "The day your tires got slashed was the day I stopped taking other women's calls. What do you take me for?"

"Oh, you really don't want me to answer *that* question."

Silence descended over the room. I could hear the birds chirping and cars honking outside. Middle of the day, ordinary noises sounded so depressing when your entire world was crumbling.

"Go marry her, Devon."

After all, it was going to be the perfect proof that he was like all the other men in my life. Disloyal and unreliable.

"Do you want me to?" He reframed it as a question. A tricky one at that.

Did he want my blessing? To feel good about himself?

The man was going to destroy me. But I'd learned long ago that destruction had its flip side.

It set the ground for rebuilding.

"Yes," I heard myself say. "Nothing would make me happier than seeing your ass married to someone else. Maybe that way you'll finally stop chasing after me. It's getting a little desperate, you know. A man of your age."

"You're not as young as you think you are," he said pitifully.

"You're considering it," I said accusingly.

Fuck, I didn't know what I was thinking. What I was saying.

Why was I pushing him like that?

"Yes," he said quietly.

I broke into a thousand pieces inside.

This is what you get by opening up, even an inch.

"Well …" I smiled, hoping he couldn't see the tears that began streaming down my face, "…don't let me stand in your way."

I felt the edge of the bed rise as he stood up and walked to the door.

"Roger that, Sweven."

For the next two weeks, I was irritated and combative.

I put my anger into everything I did. I banged on the keyboard in my office while working the spreadsheets. Yelled at Ross for the dumbest reasons when he dared talk to me about anything that wasn't work.

When my mother came over for a visit from the suburbs bearing little yellow baby clothes, I roared at her that shopping for the baby before she was born was bad luck.

And I was pretty sure I jogged everywhere instead of walked, just because of the adrenaline running through my veins.

I hadn't seen Louisa since that day, but I could only guess Devon was seeing her.

He stopped coming home every day at six o'clock sharp as he used to.

In fact, I hardly ever saw him at all. When we did cross paths, usually early in the morning, when I woke up on the hunt for a snack and he came back from his fencing matches, he nodded at me curtly but didn't stick around for the daily verbal abuse I treated him to.

More than anything, I felt a sharp, awful loss. I mourned all the times I treated him terribly, knowing I brought it on myself. From day one, I'd been impossible. And now, when I wanted to be possible for him, it was too late.

I was sure Louisa was still in Boston, loitering with the sole purpose of making him hers.

He was out of the apartment all hours of the day and night, probably getting to know her, reconnecting, and planning their new life together.

One morning, in the kitchen, I couldn't take it anymore.

When he made himself a protein shake and I poured myself a tall glass of matcha juice, I turned to him and asked, "How's Louisa doing, anyway?"

"Quite well," he said stonily.

This was the part where I would normally insert a barb, an insult of sorts, but I was so exhausted, so depressed, so angry at myself, I asked, "Are you guys …?"

He curved one eyebrow up, waiting for the rest.

Long gone were the days when he made things easier for me.

"Are you together?" I spat the rest of the question out.

"Uncertain. Ask again in a couple weeks."

I wanted to throw up, and I didn't even have morning sickness anymore.

"Devon, I'm sorry."

Sorry for the way I had treated him.

Sorry for not going to the police even though I knew it was the smart thing to do.

Sorry I was so screwed up I couldn't keep a good thing when it was handed to me.

"Why, darling, we did both agree fucking the same person for a period exceeding five months is outrageously boring." He reached over to caress my face with his sardonic smirk. "Time's up."

The night that changed our new status quo happened on an unassuming Friday.

I was just getting ready to leave Madame Mayhem and go back to Devon's apartment.

Prior to Louisa's arrival in Boston, I'd tried to cut down on hours at the club. This time I stayed late, knowing that in all probability Devon wasn't going to be home.

I had been good with hanging out with Si as much as I could and making sure Persy, Ash, and Sailor were always with me when I went out in town, so I let my guard down a little.

It was almost eleven at night when I locked the back office. I strolled through the alleyway toward my car, clutching my bag to my chest, my gun inside it.

Though it wasn't loaded for obvious reasons, it still made me feel significantly safer.

My car's lights flashed when I unlocked it with the key fob.

I took a few more steps, stopping between the industrial trash cans, hating that I told Simon to leave early today.

I felt a terrible weight launch itself at me from behind.

I stumbled forward, fumbling for the gun in my bag, but the person who tackled me was faster.

They grabbed me by the arm and slammed my back against my car in the darkness. I gasped for air.

"Let go!" I growled, coming face to face with a man wearing a black balaclava.

It couldn't be Frank because he was taller and leaner than my former employee.

But it could be the man from the Common. The one I hadn't heard from in months.

"I don't think so, honey. We're going to have a long productive talk about how you need to leave this city."

Leave the city? What happened to killing me? Had I been demoted to banishment only?

He reached out with his gloved hands, trying to pin me to a nearby wall. I took the chance to kick him in the balls. My knee crashed right between them.

He folded in two. I kicked him in the chest, and he fell to the ground. Leaning down, I pulled the balaclava from his head.

It *was* the man from the Common.

What the fuck?

"Did Frank send you?" I pushed my stiletto heel against his throat, threatening to crush it if he made a wrong move.

"Who the fuck is Frank?" He looked at me absurdly.

The plot thickened. How many people did I piss off this year? This was getting ridiculous.

"Who *are* you?"

"You need to leave Boston."

"Tell me who sent you." I pressed my heel harder to his neck.

"Your water broke," he said.

What? How did he even know I was pregnant? I wasn't showing.

I looked down. He took advantage of it. He twisted around, rolling on the ground, jumping to his feet with ease.

I ran for shelter, opening my passenger door, shutting it behind me and locking all four doors automatically, panting hysterically.

His hands slapped my window with force as he tried to get to me again.

"Bitch!"

"Who are you?" I turned the ignition on with shaking fingers. "What do you want?"

"Leave Boston!" He kicked at my car. "Start driving and don't look back!"

I floored the accelerator, knocking over one of the trash cans while rounding my way to Main Street. I drove past Madame Mayhem's entrance, Chinatown, and the hustle and bustle of downtown Boston toward Back Bay, my heart beating wildly in my chest.

I thought about calling Pers, or Sailor, or Aisling but ultimately didn't want the questions and probing. The only person I really wanted to speak to was Devon, but I forfeited all of that the night I told him to marry Louisa. Maybe if he were home, we could talk.

I could tell him what happened, and we could have a conversation.

Or maybe you could do the right thing and take matters into your own hands.

That was how I found myself stopping in front of a police station. I knew this was what Devon would want. And I finally acknowledged that I had to learn to take care of myself before I gave birth.

I heaved in the driver's seat for a few minutes, trying to regulate my breaths and give my body a chance to stop sweating buckets. This elevated heart rate couldn't be healthy for Baby Whitehall.

"It's okay, we're okay." I patted my stomach, hoping she believed me.

Sliding out of the car, I walked into the police station and stood in front of the desk clerk who, I swear to God, wad doodling on the book in front of him, yawning and giving me a view of the gum inside his mouth.

"I'd like to file a complaint."

Or was it a report? I'd never done this before. I only knew police stations from movies and TV shows.

"What's it about?" He popped his gum in my face. Nice. Professional.

"Stalkers."

"Plural?" He raised an eyebrow.

"Unfortunately."

"Take a seat. Someone'll be with you in a second."

But someone wasn't. In fact, I waited thirty minutes before a police-woman came to file my complaint. She seemed extremely uninterested in my story, about the man at the club, and the Common, and Frank, and what happened tonight.

"Call me if you have any new information." She passed me her card, also yawning before bidding me farewell.

Okay then. Color me underwhelmed.

"That's it?" I asked, blinking.

She shrugged. "Did you expect fireworks and bodyguards?"

I expected your ass to be competent. But saying that would only land me in trouble with the law, and already, Devon thought I was incapable of making myself an omelet without burning down his "flat."

The entire journey back, I had to talk myself into not going back to the station and giving the officer a piece of my mind.

I parked in the underground lot of Devon's building. He had two parking spots and used none of them. He opted to park outside, in the open air, even when it was freezing cold.

Taking the elevator up, I got out on his floor and stepped into the hallway of his loft, when I heard the sound of utensils clinking coming from behind the door. I checked my watch. It was nearly one AM. Homeboy sure didn't adhere to the *no food after six* rule.

My heart immediately somersaulted, this time with hope.

This is good. He's home.

This time yesterday, he was out. Probably at Badlands or with Louisa—or both.

I punched in the code to the door and pushed it open, butterflies swarming inside my chest.

This time, I was going to take an honest stab at not being a raging asshole. Whatever happened between Devon and Louisa, he was still the father of my child, and we still needed to get along.

I found Devon sitting at the dining table across from Louisa, grinning at her while she pressed a cool glass of wine to her cheek as she laughed like a vixen.

No. No, no, no, no, no.

For the first few seconds, I stood frozen to my spot at the door, watching them.

The pain in my chest was excruciating. They looked close. Intimate. Like a couple. They made *sense* together. No matter how I spun it, Devon and I looked like an unlikely couple. The Prince and the Prostitute.

"Oh, look, it's your little friend," Louisa exclaimed with fake sympathy, like she'd learned to like me in a span of two weeks.

Devon didn't even turn his head to look at me.

His eyes remained focused on his food.

"Night, Emmabelle."

Emmabelle. Not Sweven.

"Thanks, Dev. I can look out the fucking window."

"Delightful," Louisa muttered. "How're you feeling, Emmabelle? You should come home earlier. Give the baby some rest."

"I hadn't realized you were a doctor," I said cordially.

"Oh, I'm not," Louisa smiled.

I smiled right back, in a way that said, *so why don't you shut up?*

"Just trying to be helpful!" She leaned her shoulder against Devon's. I noticed that he didn't push her away or even look mildly uncomfortable.

God, this was awful. I was going to die of jealousy, wasn't I? The first person in the world to be deceased from the feeling.

"We have some asparagus and steak left. I made you a plate. It's in the fridge," Louisa noted.

Wow. Her *Understanding Trophy Wife* game was strong. Not only had she cooked for him, she also somehow managed to make me the side piece in a few easy steps.

"Fantastic. Well, don't mind me on your way to negotiating the whitest marriage in the history of the world, complete with likely-inbred kids and definite infidelities down the road," I chirped, making my way to my guestroom. "Enjoy the rest of your night!"

When I flung myself on the bed, I took out the card the officer gave me and blinked at it in fury.

The police weren't going to help me.

My story didn't even make any sense.

I tore the card to pieces.

I'd be my own protector.

Twenty

Belle

Fourteen Years Old.

D
AWN BREAKS ACROSS THE SKY IN BRILLIANT PINKS AND
blues.
Coach Locken and I are the only people in Castle Rock
reservoir.

"Thought you'd work on your times without the other harriers. I've
been weeding out the good track and field camps for you for the summer,"
he says.

I feel myself turn a brilliant shade of pink, at least five times darker
than the dawn above our heads.

Coach Locken looks particularly good this morning. Clean-shaven
with gray sweatpants that highlight his strong legs and a blue hoodie that
clings to his muscles. I saw that creepy geography teacher on TV, and I'm
sorry, but you just can't compare them. I can think of at least fifty girls
at school who would disappear with Coach Locken in the wrestling room
and open their legs for him. That other teacher was old and gross.

"Not gonna let you down, Coach."

Then I'm off.

Running in the woods is my favorite. I like the cool temperature, the fresh air. The unfamiliar sounds.

I run a two-thousand-meter loop. Three rounds. Coach starts his stopwatch. He is standing on the edge of the loop, and when I look back before I disappear into the thick blanket of trees, I notice his eyes linger on my legs.

I'm not going to lie, I'm wearing super short shorts. It's not accidental. Lately, my daydreams about kissing Coach Locken leak into the nights. I always wake up sweaty and damp between my legs. I try calming myself down with cold showers and watching movies with other hot guys, but it's not working. He's the only boy (well, man, really), I truly like.

All my other friends are already kissing and making out. I'm the only one who hasn't yet. But even if I did want to get a boyfriend to kiss, I know it's not going to feel as nice, as good as Coach's fingers on my knees and thighs, so what's the point?

It's just a fixation, *I tell myself as I round the first loop and see him in the distance.* Once you kiss him, you're not going to be obsessed anymore.

And then I start making excuses for myself again. So what if he's married? That his wife is pregnant? What she doesn't know won't be able to hurt her.

One kiss is not going to mean anything. He is probably going to do me a favor and never think about it again. And I'll be able to move on and meet someone my age.

But then I think about what my dad said about that geography teacher, and my stomach knots so many times over it becomes heavy with dread. I think about Dad kissing another woman who is not Mom, and I want to throw up. It's wrong.

I don't want to be that person, the person who makes someone's life … wrong.

But if Coach Locken decides to cheat on his wife, then things between them are not that good. You can't destroy a good relationship, can you?

The second loop is a breeze. I'm so deep inside my head, on autopilot, my legs carry me at the speed of light. I don't even have to regulate my breathing. It's on the third loop that my knee starts giving in. It's more than a dull, persistent pain. This time there's a sharp zing in my foot too. The cramp is unbearable. I limp the rest of the way to him.

"What happened?" *I hear Coach Locken before I see him as I descend the hilly loop.* "You were about to break your record before that last loop."

"My foot is cramping," *I shout back.*

"All right. Let's see."

He offers me his arm when I get to him, and I lean against it as we scurry toward his car. It's the only car parked on the edge of the reservoir. Dad drops me off for practice before he goes to work—not before making sure other kids and Coach are there—and I normally get a ride back to school with one of the harrier's parents.

It's a big, silver Suburban. He pops the trunk open and it's the size of my room. There's sports equipment strewn everywhere.

"Hop in." *He jerks his chin. But I can't. My foot is down for the count. With an understanding smile, Coach Locken reaches for me.* "May I?"

I nod. He hoists me up by the back of my thighs to sit on the edge of his open trunk. He takes my injured foot, slips my running shoe and sock off, and starts massaging, really digging his thumbs as he arches my foot, rotating it here and there.

"Holy crappers," *I moan, plastering myself horizontally across his trunk, so I'm lying down.* "This feels like giving birth."

It also makes me think about his pregnant wife and douses the excitement of being touched by him.

"Watch that language, young lady." *But he sounds more like a friend than a teacher.*

"Sorry, but it hurts like a mofo."

Does he even know what this slang means?

"Perfection costs."

"I better get that scholarship."

"Chances are good. Would you wanna stay local or go somewhere else for college?" *he asks.*

"West Coast, maybe." *I blink back at the ceiling of his SUV.* "California."

Golden beaches and blistering sun sound like my vibe. I bet Santa Barbara and I are going to get along swimmingly.

"Really? Growing up, I lived in Fresno for a while. If you move, I'll give you my aunt's number. You know, so you wouldn't feel so alone. What does your boyfriend think about it?" he hums. "You wanting to move all the way to the other side of the country."

"I don't have a boyfriend," I supply, a little too breathlessly, a little too fast.

"Ross Kendrick is not your boyfriend?" Locken asks innocently, rolling up his sleeves.

Oh. Come on. Ross Kendrick doesn't like girls, and isn't shy about it either. Coach is in no risk of winning any Oscar prizes for his acting.

"How's your wife?" I change the subject. It's one thing skating over the forbidden and another walking right into it. "Are you having a boy or a girl?"

"A boy." He doesn't sound too hot about answering the question, his tone turning sour. "She went to live with her mom. It's complicated."

"Okay."

We hear a pop a few seconds later, coming from my foot.

"Ahh. You broke me," I laugh.

"Not yet," he mutters under his breath, but I hear it. I hear it, and suddenly I'm filled with fresh desperation to be touched by him.

"Roll your ankle. Stretch your heel."

I bring my knee to my chest and do as I'm told. I know what view he's getting now, when I'm in this position. My running shorts ride up and he can see my panties. White cotton.

"Feels much better. Thank you."

"A massage for those short muscles?" he offers, his voice comically thick now. "We still have twenty minutes before school starts."

"Sure."

This time, he gathers my heels together, pulling my knees as far apart as he can. I'm wide open in front of him as his fingers start traveling my inner thighs. It's a brutal stretch, but I need it.

Even so, I know he is not supposed to touch me that way at all, and that we've crossed a line. The invisible, red string that separates us from casually inappropriate to doing something that could land him in jail and me in therapy for a lifetime.

"Thanks," I groan. *It feels so good. The stretch. His hands. Everything. I'm going to hell.*

"Yup."

His thumbs touch the hem of my shorts as he draws circles on my skin. One time. Two times. On the third, I know it's not accidental. I know we're on the brink of something. I know this is not supposed to happen.

He picks up my foot and stretches my hamstring, pinning my foot next to my head. When he leans into me, I feel his penis pressed against my groin through our clothes. It feels like it's pulsating. My mouth goes dry.

"So your wife lives with her mom now?" *I ask loudly. I don't know why. Maybe to distract him. Maybe to distract myself. Maybe to remind both of us that she exists.*

"Yeah. We're not on the best of terms. It's not … we're not really together."

He releases me from the hamstring stretch. The tips of his thumbs are touching the hem of my panties under my shorts now. He stills. I swallow hard. Close my eyes.

"Emmabelle."

It's the first time he doesn't call me Penrose. I don't answer. I don't breathe. I hate that a part of me wants this. I hate that my panties are damp again.

"I can make this really good for you, sweetie. But you can't tell anyone, okay?"

My words are gone. Shriveled inside my throat. I know I should say no. I want to say no. But somehow I hear myself saying yes. I want to please him.

"I'll get into a lot of trouble if people find out. But I know you want to. And … well, I've been wanting to for a while."

A beat passes without either of us saying or doing anything. His thumbs on the sides of my panties feel weird. Foreign. But also … thrilling.

Just when I think he is going to pull my shorts down and remove my

*panties and enter me—the way I saw in a porn movie once—he tugs both
to the side. A cool breeze passes over my vagina, letting me know that it
is completely exposed to him.*

I pop one eye open and watch him watching me, licking his lips.

"Fuck," he says.

"I … I'm a virgin."

*But what I'm really trying to say is that I want to keep it that way. I'm
not like Persy. I don't wanna wait until marriage before I lose my virginity,
but I want it to mean something. Not to think back in a few years and remember I gave it to someone who was expecting a child with someone else.*

"Yeah, I know. I'll never hurt you, sweetie."

*And then before I know it, he is crouched down, in front of his open
truck, sucking my vagina into his mouth. I'm mortified. It feels so awkward. I want to push him away, but I also don't want to look like a cry-
baby, especially after how good he's been to me. How he always pays me
extra attention, massages my legs, works on my knee.*

I squeeze my eyes shut and remind myself that no one is going to know.

*Not Persy. Not my parents. Not Ross and Sailor, my best friends.
Definitely not the other harriers. If a tree falls in the middle of the woods
and no one hears it … did it actually happen?*

This will be our little secret.

The thing I take with me to the grave.

*Everything feels wet between my legs. I don't know if I like it or not.
I mean, I like the attention, but … I don't know. Not necessarily everything else.*

*After what feels like forever but is probably only ten minutes, he stops,
turns around from me, and I see his arms flexing through his hoodie. He
is rubbing one out. He finishes. I don't see any of it, as his back is to me.
He cleans himself off with baby wipes then returns to the trunk. By then,
I'm sitting down on the edge again, legs dangling from it, like nothing
happened.*

*We're cool. Everything's fine. He is not really with his wife, and this
is consensual. It's not like that news article at all. Besides, if it's so bad,
why does it feel so good?*

"Hey." He grins.

"Hi."

Then he kisses me, tongue and all, and I taste the muskiness and earthiness of myself and his saliva—a mixture of things I've never tasted before.

That's when I decide sin doesn't taste so bad.

Twenty-One

Devon

SECONDS AFTER SWEVEN SLAMMED THE DOOR TO HER ROOM with a loud bang, Louisa turned to me and said, "I'm not stupid, you know."

"Never thought you were," I said easily, taking a sip of my wine.

"You still haven't touched me. Not even a kiss."

It had been six dates. They were good dates too, although I was careful to be Respectable Devon around her. We did not discuss weird animals, and she did not tease me about my age or my language or my accent—and, come to think about it, my existence.

"I pride myself on my good behavior," I said idly.

"You're the biggest sinner of them all, and we both know that." She offered me an impatient smile. "If you wanted me, you would've taken me by now."

I leaned back in my seat, scanning her face pensively.

Louisa was on the cusp of looking her age, her skin had become thinner, clinging to her bones delicately, giving her an elegant, slightly malnourished look. She was a far cry from the plump-cheeked Sweven, with the dusting of freckles and flushed, healthy skin.

Louisa's beauty had history, and wrinkles, and stories.

She was lovely in a way that was far more interesting than a bomb-shell who looked photoshopped within an inch of her life.

"I fancy you," I admitted to Louisa.

"Not enough to make a move, apparently," she said easily.

Everything was easy with her, and therein lied the temptation of yielding to my mother's request.

"Then why are you here?" I asked.

"I still have hope. Is it foolish?" She twisted the wineglass here and there on the table, holding it by the stem.

"Foolish? No. Unlikely? Always."

"I reckon I might be able to break you," Louisa mused, sipping her red wine. Candlelight danced across the planes of her face, making her smile appear softer. "If I told you a year ago that we'd be sitting together, discussing a potential affair, you wouldn't have believed me."

"No, I wouldn't," I admitted.

"Yet, here we are."

"Here we are."

I stole another glance at Sweven's door.

This time, she didn't eavesdrop or peek.

At the end of that week was a gala.

The seventy-eighth annual Boston Ball, a fundraiser for the Gerald Fitzpatrick Foundation, a 501c3 tax-exempt non-profit organization that symbolized to many the official arrival of spring.

Proceeds of the ball, which usually sat at around three million dollars, went to various local establishments I didn't care for nor wanted to know about.

But it was an excellent write-off for my firm, not to mention a terrific excuse to wear my Ermenegildo Zegna suit.

Attending the Boston Ball was also a business move.

I'd be hard-pressed to find a better place which gathered all of

Boston's Private Island Owners' Club, most of which were existing or potential clients.

As I stood there, at the O'Donnell Ballroom, scanning the place, I couldn't help but feel a tinge of pride.

I'd become the polar opposite of my father.

A hardworking, law-respecting man who did not let himself be swayed by women or booze.

The O'Donnell Ballroom was a five thousand square foot venue on Boylston Street, with grand windows, elegant Tudor architectural details, black wooden beams, ecru chandeliers, and champagne-silk draperies.

Waiters floated across the room, bypassing women in ball gowns and men in dashing suits. I stood in a cluster of people, including Cillian, Hunter, Sam, and Sam's stepfather, Troy, while keeping an eye out for Emmabelle.

I knew she was going to be here. Her sister helped organize the event, and Sweven celebrated every one of her sister's mundane accomplishments.

"…said him starting a private bank is as laughable an idea as my starting a Christian crusade to save hairy frogs. I'd never buy into his ventures," I heard Cillian explain to Troy.

If Cillian was here, his wife was nearby. And if Persephone was on the premises, Belle couldn't me more than a few feet away.

"I've only put two mil into it," Hunter cried out defensively. "So I could be on the board and gain some experience. If it bombs, it bombs. It's no skin off my back."

"Devon? What do you think about James Davidson's new bank?" Sam pulled me into the conversation, the devious smirk on his face telling me he knew I didn't listen to a word they said.

I tapped my index finger over the glass of champagne I held.

I tried to think *what* I thought. I'd been more focused on trying to find my roommate than the conversation. "I think Davidson is rubbish at everything he does, and I said so to Hunter when he came to me with the proposition. Luckily, Hunter needs his money like I need another hormonal female to handle, so as he said, no worries."

"How is Emmabelle doing anyway?" Hunter asked. "Is she starting to show?"

I thought she was, last time I saw her, a couple of days ago. When she'd passed me in the kitchen, I thought I caught a glimpse of a rounded stomach. I couldn't tell for sure. But since I kept my cards close to my chest when it came to my personal life, they had no idea I was not on speaking terms with her.

"Moderately."

"Are you taking advantage of the pregnancy cravings?" Sam elevated an eyebrow.

I raised my champagne in the air in salute. "Same answer."

"Well…" Cillian took pleasure in directing his pinky beyond my shoulder, pointing at something "…then you may want to ensure you're the only one enjoying those cravings, because Davidson seems to be working on his next private venture."

I followed his line of vision, turning around to see Emmabelle standing in the corner of the room, wearing a light blue silk Cinderella gown, her sandy hair in an elegant do.

She was laughing at something James Davidson was saying, her fingers fluttering over her necklace.

The same Davidson who wouldn't know a rotten deal from a good one if it chopped off his leg without anesthesia.

He was objectively handsome in a white bread sort of way, with brown, thick hair, big white teeth, and the languid, lazy manners of a man who never had to work for what he owned.

And he was completely enchanted with the lurid, shockingly vivid woman in front of him.

I squinted, focusing on her midriff. To my disappointment, her dress hid her belly quite well. It didn't even matter. If Belle wanted to sleep with Davidson tonight, nothing was going to stop her.

"Isn't James Davidson married?" I was surprised to hear my question sound more like a moan.

"Newly divorced," Hunter corrected, off to my right. He bumped his shoulder against mine as we both looked on at Belle laughing throatily at something Davidson said.

What could have possibly made her laugh? The guy was dryer than a rice cake.

"His ex just bought a new Cadillac and a pair of tits to taunt him, but I hear he's moving onto nicer and better pastures."

"That pasture isn't going to be Emmabelle."

Cillian *tsked*. "Doubt she got that memo."

"She is just being polite," I lamented.

"Yes, your baby momma is known for her manners." Sam chuckled.

"Also, polite people don't touch other people's chests." Hunter laughed.

Buggers. She *was* touching his chest.

I wasn't a violent man, but I was quite sure I was well on the way to doing something that would land me in state prison.

"What do you think?" I asked Sam.

Across the room, Emmabelle shook her head when a server approached her with a tray of champagne while James leaned closer to her, whispering something in her ear.

"I think if I were in your shoes, James would have had six teeth missing and a punctured lung by now," Sam said indolently.

That was all the assurance I needed that I wasn't overacting. Even though I *was* overacting, because I was currently dating another woman, even if technically, I did not touch her.

I moved quickly, brushing shoulders, crossing the vast room, my fingers pressing hard against the thin champagne glass.

I wanted to kill James, and lock Emmabelle in an ivory tower. Though really, could I blame her? She thought I was about to get engaged to someone else in a few short weeks, maybe even days.

What kind of claim did I have over this woman? None at all.

I stopped in front of them, smiling like all was well in the world.

"Belle, darling, I've been looking for you." I made of show of kissing her cheeks, but ignored it when James reached for a handshake.

Politeness went out the window when his eyes landed on what was mine.

"You were?" Sweven gave me a lazy onceover. Again, I found her indifference to me enchanting. "Honestly, one would think you'd be searching for more important things, like your spine."

"Maybe I'll find your manners while I'm at it," I bit out.

"Oh, I don't know about that. You don't have a good track record for finding things. My G-spot can attest."

That was plainly a lie. I could find her G-spot if it was in a lineup with five fucking others, and she darn well knew it.

"Devon, do you know this gem?" James pointed at her with his glass of bubbly like she was a painting he was thinking of buying.

I wanted to punch him to the ground and then keep going until he reached the depths of hell. "She is so funny!"

"Marvelous," I said gravely. "And yes, I know her well."

"Not well enough, apparently." Belle took out her phone from her purse, determined to let me know she was more disinterested than embarrassed about the scene I was making.

"Well enough to impregnate her with my baby." I turned to James, nailing him with a frosty look. "You make whatever you want of it."

"You're pregnant?" James's eyes dropped to her midriff.

His skin went pale. His eyes flared. Perhaps he thought he hit the jackpot with wife number two.

Belle shrugged, rolling the entire thing off her back. "We both want a child. It's not like we're together."

"We *do* live together." I let loose a wolfish grin.

She patted my arm like a concerned aunt. "Only because you begged."

"Begged? No. But I did use an unorthodox way of persuasion."

"You talk a real big game, honey. You do know people have sex all the time and it doesn't end with marriage, or babies, or even, ya' know, a phone call?"

"Try to reduce what we have as much as you wish, but the facts speak for themselves. You are carrying my child, living under my roof, and getting nailed by me on a weekly basis."

This was the part where James Davidson excused himself and pretended he noticed someone across the room.

I stayed with Sweven, who stared at me like she was going to have my balls for breakfast tomorrow.

"What the fuck, dude?"

"The fuck is you're flirting with one of the worst charlatans in the business in front of my eyes, and I cannot risk his subpar intelligence and awful backward logic near my child. What if he becomes her stepdad?"

I was well aware I sounded like a terrible hypocrite.

Belle's blue eyes widened, more in anger than shock. "Are you kidding me now?"

"Not now, but maybe later. There's not much humor in our situation."

"You're *marrying* someone else!" She punched me in the chest. Hard.

We were beginning to draw the wrong sort of attention.

Unfortunately for Belle, she had finally met her match. I did not much care what people thought of me. Most were so dazzled by my titles and accent, they'd let me get away with murder.

"I'd still let you warm my bed, if you play your cards right." I knew this was going to drive her bonkers.

It did. She slapped my face now. *Hard*. I did not react.

"Take me somewhere private so I can bite your head off properly," she commanded.

I pressed my hand against the small of her back and ushered her to a mezzanine library in the corner of the room. It was a small space, painted wall-to-wall with an elaborate black sky dotted with stars that made you feel like you were in outer space.

A cluster of businessmen lounged there, talking idly as they sipped their drinks.

"Out!" I barked.

They scurried away like the hares had when my father had unleashed his hound dogs. People in this city knew I made a good friend and a terrible enemy.

I pinned Sweven to one of the walls, my eyes dropping to her luscious lips.

She had nowhere to move. Nowhere to go.

"Here," I hissed seductively to her lips. "Bite my head off. I'll even unbuckle to make life easy for you."

She groaned, pushing me away. "You're about to marry someone else, so get the hell away from me before I grab your balls and make sure the child I'm carrying is *the only one* you'll have."

I chuckled sardonically, palming her cheek. She slapped my hand away.

"You're frightened, aren't you? That I'd put a ring on her finger." I was flattered, though I still couldn't understand why she was so darn stubborn and cold.

"Actually, I couldn't care less. I'm just letting you know I'm no one's side piece." She made a move to duck under my arm, but I moved quickly, blocking her way to the door.

"Who fucked you up like this?" I seethed, demanding to know.

I held her arms, not wanting to let go but unsure how to get to her either.

"I'm trying my fucking hardest, but always reach the same dead end. You want the cock, the banter, the conversation, but not the feelings. When I give the feelings to someone else, you lose it. So let me ask you again—*Who. Did. This. To. You*?" I shook with rage. I was going to kill the wanker. End him. "Who made you so utterly incapable of having a healthy relationship with a man?"

"None of your business!" She spat in my face. I didn't even bother wiping the saliva off. She tried escaping again. I blocked her—*again*.

"Not so fast. Tell me what I need to do to get through to you."

I was completely out of my depth.

We were both fighting for control over a situation neither of us had power in.

She tilted her chin up, a sly grin gracing her Aphrodite features.

"There's nothing you can do or say to make me see you as more than what you are. A spoiled little rich boy who ran away from home, but never really escaped the golden cage. You finally found the one thing you cannot have—me—and if it kills you… Well, then *die*."

I slammed my palms against the wall, boxing her between them.

I was so frustrated I was on the verge of destroying the room. Ripping it apart.

And where the fuck did my champagne glass go, anyway?

"You're impossible!" I roared.

"You're an asshole." She yawned right into my face.

"I regret the day I offered you this arrangement. At least, before this, I had a bit of respect and sympathy toward you."

"I don't need either from you." Emmabelle pushed me away, her tone businesslike. "You think you're *so* much better than your family, don't you? Just because you work for a living doesn't make you a martyr. Don't wait up for me at home. I'll be sleeping at Pers' tonight."

"Why on bloody earth would you do that?"

"So you can have a little room to finally nail your precious new girlfriend!" she boomed. Emmabelle gave me the finger as she dashed outside, the hem of her dress flipping about her delicate ankles.

I chased her. *Of course* I chased her. At this point, I was unable of making one rational decision when it came to this woman.

But I was no longer enamored by her ability to throw me off balance. Now, all I felt was disgust and disappointment toward both of us.

I was too old for this shite.

Emmabelle stopped momentarily. Turned around. Opened her mouth again.

"You've been enjoying your precious Louisa like you don't share a roof with the future mother of your child. Well, if you're happy to screw around, I'm going to find myself some entertainment too, and there's nothing you can do about it. Come close to me again tonight, and I'll break your nose."

With another *whoosh* of her skirts, she was off.

I stopped.

For the first, bloody time, I came to the conclusion that chasing Emmabelle Penrose may not be the right, or constructive, or *fun* thing for me to do.

It was just me and the vast, dark room. I regulated my breaths and looked around.

Life was a lonely business, even if you were never completely alone.

This was why people fell into love.

Love, it seemed, was a brilliant distraction from the fact that everything was temporary and nothing quite mattered like we thought it did.

It was only after I stood there for an entire minute when I realized something puzzling.

I was inside a small, closed, confined room all by myself, and I didn't have a panic attack.

Love has some strange ways indeed, I thought, sauntering out of the room leisurely, plucking another glass of champagne from a tray.

Better to not find out what they are.

Twenty-Two

Devon

SWEVEN SUCCESSFULLY AVOIDED ME THE REST OF THE EVENING. She fluttered between clusters of people like a butterfly, all husky laughter and white, pointy teeth.

I did my own rounds among clients and associates, pretending I wasn't half-dead on the inside. Time seemed to melt like a Salvador Dali painting, and each tick of the watch on my wrist brought me an inch closer to turning around and walking away.

From my commitments.

Responsibilities.

From everything I had built and used as a wall against what was waiting for me in England.

At some point during the evening, Persephone slipped her arm through mine and tugged me from a particularly mind-numbing discussion about suspenders.

"Hey there, bud." Her lavender gown hovered along the marble floor.

She was delicate as an eggshell, pale as the midnight moon. Sweet and placid, a far cry from her fire engine older sister; I could see why she suited Cillian, who was cold and callous everywhere. She brought his temperature up, while he cooled down her warmth. Yin and Yang.

But Belle and I weren't complementary to one another. She was fire, and I was concrete. We did not mix well. I was sturdy, and even, and stable, while she thrived in chaos.

"How are the kids?" I asked Persephone blandly, already bored with the conversation.

What I'd do to talk to Sweven about peculiar animals just about now.

"They're very well, but I doubt that's what you want to talk about." She gave me a lopsided grin and dragged me to the center of a human circle, consisting of Aisling, Sailor, and herself.

I complied, mainly because between getting my head bitten off by a pack of women and talking about suspenders, I'd die at the hands of the women any day of the bloody week.

I looked between all three of them.

"Looks like I'm the victim of some sort of intervention," I drawled, cocking an eyebrow.

"Sharp as always, Mr. Whitehall," Sailor said, swinging back whiskey like it was water. *Definitely her father's daughter.*

She was the only woman at the ball to wear a suit. She pulled it off fantastically. "We want to talk to you about something."

That something was Louisa, I was certain.

I folded my arms over my chest, waiting for more.

"We wanted to know what you're going to do to ensure Belle is safe and sound. After all, we betrayed her confidence by telling you about that man in Boston Common. Now we want to know that our decision was justified." Aisling pinned me with a look.

They wanted to talk about *that*?

"Belle lives with me now, and I put Simon in charge of her. I'm monitoring her as best I can without putting an ankle GPS SCRAM on her."

"Is an ankle monitor totally out of the question?" Sailor asked with the utmost sincerity.

"Yes, unless I want to lose a limb or two," I deadpanned.

"I'm sure Simon's great, but he's only with her when she's at the club. I still think you should ask for Sam's help," Aisling insisted.

"When I broached the subject of Sam with Belle, she said she had it under control and didn't want his interference," I pointed out smartly. "Going against her wishes would mean an early grave for me. How did you feel when Cillian sent Sam's men after you?" I swiveled to Persephone, who turned salmon-pink, her gaze shifting to her feet.

"Not good," she admitted. "But I got over it, eventually."

"Luckily for your bastard husband, you're as agreeable as a peach. Your sister, however, I think we can all agree is more of an under ripe grapefruit."

Aisling frowned. "Belle is hotheaded, but sometimes you have to do things for a person, even when they don't think they need it."

"Spoken like a true tyrant. The apple doesn't fall far from the tree."

Sweven was unattainable, unreachable, and unreasonable.

And I had to keep her alive.

Yay fucking me.

"If only we had an idea who it could be." Sailor tapped her temple, thinking.

"She thinks it's that arsehole she fired a while back," I offered.

"Frank?" Persephone scrunched her nose.

I shrugged, even though I remembered his name. Of course I did. Any man in my position would.

"That makes sense. He's the only loose end I can think of." Sailor rubbed at her chin.

There was a brief silence, which I decided to fill with a question of my own.

"Has she told you anything about our situation?"

"What situation?" Persephone asked alertly. "I hope you're treating her well."

"Bitch, please," Sailor snorted. "If anyone is getting unfair treatment there, it's him."

"She's been moody," I said vaguely.

"Don't worry, it's not because you're marrying someone else." Sailor looked highly amused, tucking one hand into the front pockets of her cigar pants.

So they *did* know about Louisa.

Belle didn't hide it from them. She simply didn't care enough to expand on the matter.

"Do you honestly believe she'd be fine with me marrying someone else?"

I sounded like a teenybopper asking her BFF whether she had a chance with Justin Bieber or not.

Whenever I intended to look for my spine and Belle's manners, I should take a moment to find my masculinity too.

"She'd be fine if you marry five women. Simultaneously," Sailor said firmly. "Belle doesn't do relationships. Or morals, for that matter."

"She's never been in love," Persephone said with a longing sigh. "Never wanted to settle down with anyone."

"People change," I said half-heartedly.

"Not this person," Aisling uttered aloud my gravest suspicion.

"If you're waiting for her to profess her love to you and you're holding off on a wedding because of it, don't." Aisling put a hand on my shoulder, offering me an apologetic smile. "Belle Penrose only has enough love for herself, her baby, and her family."

Twenty-Three

Belle

Fourteen Years Old.

WINTER COMES AND GOES. THERE'S A BIT OF A BUZZ AROUND me. I win a few local competitions and even have a small article written about me in the local paper for breaking the county record, which Dad hangs on our fridge because apparently, being embarrassing is his main side hustle.

In March, Coach Locken's wife, Brenda, gives birth to a healthy baby boy. By then, we're doing the whole woods routine twice a week. He eats me out, then we kiss, then he jerks off before giving me a ride to school. One time, on his birthday, he convinced me to lick the sticky white juice from his fingers like they were lollipops. He took three pictures. I cried all night after he'd taken them. I still think about the fact they're somewhere on his phone, and I want to throw up every time I remember it.

When we do it at his office—rarely—I take note that the photo of Brenda, which has been there before, is missing from his desk. He also takes off his wedding ring, but only when we practice alone in the woods.

Coach tells me that they split a few months ago. Brenda didn't want *him to touch her anymore after getting pregnant and said mean things about his job. Like how he doesn't make enough money and stuff.*

Coach says he wishes I were his girlfriend. That he could take me out to the movies, or to a nice restaurant, or just to hang out.

Honestly, I'm starting to think maybe this Brenda chick doesn't deserve Steve (I'm not allowed to call him that when we're not alone). Anyway, it makes me feel a lot less bad about our affair.

But then Brenda gives birth and everything changes.

Coach misses three days in a row. The third day he is MIA. In the cafeteria, two lunch duty teachers gush about how Brenda gave birth at a local hospital—which why would she, if she went back to living with her momma all the way down in New Jersey?

"Did you see the baby? So sweet. He looks exactly like his daddy," Miss Warski coos, stabbing her yogurt with a plastic spoon.

"Yeah, Steve sent the pictures to everyone in the group, remember? And get this. He got his wife the best push present—a brand-new car."

"A Kia Rio, right?"

"Yes. I'm looking into buying one too ..."

His wife?

Push present?

I thought they weren't together anymore.

On the brink of divorce.

I spend the rest of the day in a haze, forcing myself not to text him.

Ross sneaks out and buys me a bottle of Gatorade. He doesn't ask why I'm upset. Why my eyes are red and my face is ashen.

More than heartbroken, though, I feel great shame.

I've been made a fool by this man, whom I put my trust in.

Something breaks in me that day.

Something I don't know if I can ever fix.

Twenty-Four

Devon

BELLE MADE GOOD ON HER PROMISE NOT TO RETURN HOME that night.

Which made me, in turn, call Louisa on my way to work the next morning.

Lou was staying at the Four Seasons, spending her days shopping and hoping I would get my head out of my arse.

The good news for her was that my head was inching away from said arse little by little.

Louisa answered on the first ring, sounding breathless.

"Hello? Devon?"

"Is this a bad time?" I rounded a street corner in my Bentley, looking for parking on the street. Underground parking seemed like a ridiculous idea. People had no business going under the ground when they were still alive.

"Absolutely not, it's a perfect time."

I heard the soft thud of a towel being dropped and the whine of a door opening as a fitness trainer in the background instructed, "Now back to downward dog position …"

"Hi. Hey. Hello." Louisa laughed a little at her own awkwardness. I slipped into a parking space on the street and reversed.

"Is everything all right?" she asked.

It was about to be.

It was time to choose a person who chose me.

"I was wondering if you'd like to have dinner tonight."

"Sure. Should I book reservations for us?" Louisa asked sweetly. "There's an amazing Italian restaurant on Salem Street that I've been wanting to try, although I'm happy to cater to any of your diet restrictions."

My father's words haunted me.

Love marriages are for the great unwashed masses. People born to follow society's thankless rules. You shall not desire your wife, Devon. Her purpose is to serve you, sire children, and look lovely.

There was a point to be made. The Whitehall family had existed for so many years, had so many traditions. Who was he to dictate the end of that line? I would not allow the man to rob me out of my rightful inheritance.

"No." I exited the car and galloped toward the front door of my office. "I was thinking we could dine in your hotel room. I have a few matters to discuss with you."

"Is everything okay?" she asked, worried.

"Yes." I took the stairs up to my office. "Everything's perfect. I just had an epiphany of sorts."

"I like epiphanies."

You're going to love this one.

"Devon ..." she hesitated.

I pushed the glass door to my office open. Joanne was already waiting with printouts of my daily agenda and a fresh cup of coffee. I plucked them from her hand.

"Yes, Lou?"

"You haven't called me Lou in a long time. Not for decades."

Another pause.

"Should I ... should I wear my finest silks?"

I could practically hear Louisa biting down on her lower lip.

I took a sip of my coffee, smiling grimly.

"Better yet, darling, don't wear anything under your dress at all."

My mother called me several times that day, skirting around the subject of Louisa without actually talking about her.

She asked about Emmabelle, if we still lived together. When I said we were, she sounded considerably less cheery.

"If Louisa and I are to have a future, the baby and Emmabelle would be a big part of my life," I said curtly.

"But you wouldn't move back to England," Mum responded. "She'd chain you to Boston forever."

"I love Boston." I truly did. "It's my home now."

Whitehall Court Castle had never been more than walls full of bad memories.

During my lunch break, I went and picked a 1.50 carat cushion-cut engagement ring from Tiffany & Co.

When I got back to the office, I instructed Joanne to purchase a large bouquet of flowers and spare no expense on the task.

"You finally gonna woo that Penrose girl, my lord, sir?" Joanne couldn't help but blurt out from behind her computer screen, munching on a celery stick that signified her fifth attempt at Weight Watchers that month. "It's high time. A child should have a stable home, you know. A mother and a father. That's how it was done when I was growing up, Your Highness."

Joanne insisted on referring to me royally, even though she had no idea what to call me. She also thought the flowers were for Emmabelle. Why shouldn't she? She had booked Sweven's weekly OB-GYN appointments and sent cabs with me in them to pick up Belle.

"It's not the Penrose girl," I said shortly, blazing into my office.

Joanne darted up and followed me, her short legs moving with force I hadn't seen from her since she had to take half a day off when her daughter went into labor.

"What do you mean it's not the Penrose girl?" she demanded.

I settled behind my desk, powering up my laptop. "Not that it's any of your business, but I'm courting another woman."

"Courting another … Devon, is that how you folks do it in England? Because here, bigamy is illegal."

Devon? Whatever happened to His Royal Highness lord sir?

"Belle and I aren't married." I waved her away.

"Only because you haven't asked!" she boomed.

"She is uninterested."

It was easier to admit this to a sixty-year-old woman with five kids and seven grandchildren who thought Ferrero Rocher was the height of sophistication than to do so in the ears of my mates and their wives.

"*Make* her interested."

I chuckled darkly. "I tried, trust me." In my own way, at least.

"If she wasn't interested, she wouldn't have let you put a baby in her, honey. Of course she's interested. You just need to give her a little push. If you go out with someone else, you're going to kill any chance you have with the girl, even if the relationship falls apart. And it *will* fall apart."

"Louisa is an absolute gem. Lovely, well-kept and extremely stylish."

"Those are good traits for a couch, my lord. Not a woman."

"In a wife, too."

I was being purposefully difficult. For some reason, I deeply wanted to catch shite for what I was about to do and knew Joanne would give it to me straight.

Heaven knows I deserved being yelled at.

Two splotches of red colored her cheeks, and she reared her head back as if I'd physically struck her.

"Wait a minute." Jo held up a hand. "Did you just say … *wife*?"

"Yes."

"But … you love Emmabelle."

"Gawd, you Americans do love to throw this word around a lot." I took out a rollie from a tin and tucked it into my mouth. "I, at the very most, want her companionship. But she is unavailable to me. I need to move on."

"If you marry someone else, Your Highness, I'm afraid I'll have to quit."

"On what grounds?"

"Well … that you're a turd and a half."

Hearing Joanne use blasphemy to describe me—or anyone else in the universe, for that matter—cemented the fact that I was, indeed, a flaming piece of shite.

I couldn't help but laugh. "Get those flowers ready and go back to work, Joanne. And if you want to quit, leave a resignation letter on my desk."

She turned around and stomped away, muttering under her breath.

For the rest of the day, she did not try to engage me in small talk whenever I left my office, nor attack me with new pictures of her grandchildren, nor give me a snack she'd packed especially for me from home—usually in the form of a healthy peanut butter and granola cookie.

At six o'clock, when I exited my office, a large bouquet with white roses, peonies, and ranunculus waited on her desk with a note.

Mr. Whitehall,

You're about to lose everything for nothing. Congratulations!
P.S. Consider this my official resignation letter. I quit.

—J

Throwing the note in the bin, I grabbed the flowers and headed downstairs.

My phone began ringing in my front pocket with an incoming call. *Mum.*

It was outrageously late in England. Or extremely early, depending how you looked at it.

I picked it up on a whim, knowing that I shouldn't.

"What now?" I growled.

"Devvie!" she cried in delight. "Sorry. I won't take a lot of your time. I would love to throw an engagement party for you. The spring is a lovely time for celebration. Is there any way you could take a weekend off and hop on a plane with Lou?"

It didn't sit well with me. The fact that Ursula naturally assumed Louisa and I were already engaged.

Additionally, the thought of being in a closed space with the Butchart brothers and a few dozen more stuck-up royals made me want to seek asylum on another planet.

"Work is hectic right now."

"You only get married once," she argued.

"Not necessarily in the twenty-first century."

"I hope it's not about that dreadful woman again. If she gets into trouble, it's on her, not on you."

That dreadful woman had a name, and frankly, my mother didn't deserve to utter it out loud. But something struck me.

No. Don't go there. There is simply no way.

"Why would she get into trouble?" I asked, throwing open the driver's door to my Bentley before slipping inside. I put the phone on speaker and tossed it to the central console. "What do you know?"

What if she was the one who was harassing Sweven?

She had all the discriminatory characteristics: a motive, a grudge, and an end game.

She knew where I lived, which meant that she knew where Belle lived.

And whatever information she was missing could be filled in by a private investigator.

But was she really capable of such a thing?

"I know nothing," my mother gasped, trying to sound offended. "I just said it because you told me she was a stripper. They tend to get into hot water. Your life choices say a lot about you. Why, what are you insinuating?"

"What are you *hiding*?" I countered.

"I'm not hiding anything. But I know you, and you are a caregiver by nature. I don't want you to give up on things because of her."

"I'm starting to think you know more than you let on."

This made her blow out a sharp breath.

"You're becoming extremely paranoid. I'm worried about you. You're losing it. Coming back home would do you good. Please think about it."

Dinner was, as expected, perfect.

The setting, the room, the meal, and the woman. All five stars.

Louisa sat across from me in the grand suite she was housed in, clad in a black evening dress, flawless for the occasion.

We dined on roasted lobster with red potatoes.

The french doors of her balcony were open, the spring breeze wafting inside carrying with it the scent of blossom.

It reminded me of Europe. Of lazy summer breaks on the shore in the South of France.

Of unprocessed meats and cheese so smelly it would make our eyes water, and bronzed skin, and chateaus I'd get lost in.

And I realized I missed home.

To a point where it started to hurt.

"You know, I tried to move on from you. I even succeeded, for a little while," Louisa admitted, running the pad of her finger over the rim of her wine glass. "Frederick was an incredible man. He taught me how to believe, a power I didn't think I had anymore. I used to walk around with this godawful sense of failure. After all, my entire purpose in this life was to marry you, and I'd managed to somehow scare you away."

"Lou," I groaned, feeling terrible, because in a sense, she was still doing just that. Trying to win me.

"No, wait. I want to finish." She shook her head. "When I met him, he spent an entire year just peeling away my insecurities, layer after layer, to try and find out who I was. It was hard … and it was a long process. He had no idea what made me the way I was. Why my wounds had refused to close. But he was patient and sweet."

I fractured the lobster with the cracker, feeling kinship to the dead animal. And for Frederick, who sounded like a good man, who deserved better.

And also a weird sense of revelation. Frederick had the ability and endurance to stick around for Lou when she was impenetrable to him—why couldn't I do so with Emmabelle?

"At first, when I was with him, I had dreams about you coming back and me flaunting my new relationship. My perfect man. But after a while, I stopped thinking about you. He was enough. Actually …" she hesitated. "He wasn't just enough. He was everything. And it hurt so bad to lose him. At that point, I realized I might be cursed." Louisa smiled, propping her chin on her knuckles.

I looked into her eyes and saw sorrow. So much sorrow. Here we were, about to become engaged to be married, and we were still pining for other people.

The only difference was, the person I wanted was still alive.

And Louisa saw me as a replacement. A consolation prize.

"You're not the only one who'd been scarred by this experience, sweets. I felt terrible about what I did to you. How I left you high and dry. I vowed to never marry anyone else. Clearly, I kept that promise," I said, pushing the lobster away. I'd lost my appetite. "I never had a serious girlfriend. My relationships, like my milk, had an expiration date of less than one month. I figured if I ruined things for you, it was only fair I'd do the same for me."

She reached across the round table, taking my hands in hers.

"We have a chance now, Devvie. Let's make up for lost time. It is not too late. Nothing's stopping us."

One thing was. "I'm about to become a father."

"We can do this together. You said you'll have joint custody, right? I can move here. Ursula would prefer it if you moved back, but I'm sure we'll still get her blessing. I can help you raise the child. We can have children of our own. I bear no hostility toward Emmabelle. I simply don't think she's a good fit for you. I'll be who you need me to be, Devvie. You know that."

She was saying all the right things.

Making all the right points.

"You'll need to be good to that child," I warned, my tone turning icy. "I wanted the baby as much as Emmabelle. We had a pact."

"I'll treat this child as if it were my own."

Louisa brought my hand to her mouth, leaning her cheek against my palm.

"I promise. You know I never break my promise."

I didn't remember standing up, but at some point I did. Louisa was up on her feet too, her body flushed with mine, her mouth moving over my own.

My hands skimmed the length of her back. We were kissing.

Belle didn't want me, my family was on the verge of bankruptcy, and really, would it be so awful to have someone to grow old with? Someone who had my back?

But at the end of the day, I didn't enjoy it.

Not the kisses. Not the way her body folded around mine possessively.

I was completely soft, my cock refusing to find a logical reason for this union with Louisa appealing.

The softer I was, the more Louisa tried to coax me into arousal, kissing me harder, deeper, rawer. Cupping my cock through my slacks and squeezing teasingly, flipping her head back and forth.

Bile hit the back of my throat.

Not good.

I took a step back in order to stop it, to buy time. Maybe produce the engagement ring I'd come here with. Put it on her finger.

But I couldn't, for the fucking life of me, take the ring out of my pocket. Make the final move. Ask her the question I couldn't take back.

I don't want perfect with Louisa. I want a big, hot mess with Belle.

Meanwhile, Louisa perceived my step back as an invitation to get undressed. She slipped out of her black frock to reveal shapely legs and a well-kept body that screamed five Pilates sessions a week.

Her dark eyes traveled to my groin, her brow furrowing when she realized there was still no detectable bulge.

"Buggers. Well, what's a little hurdle—"

"Do *not* say little."

She giggled, moving toward me again, resuming our kisses.

Swallowing back the sour taste of vomit, I tried to concentrate on the task at hand.

She was a beautiful woman. No less pretty than the women I usually took to bed.

"Maybe, I can …" Louisa slipped her hand inside my briefs through my clothes and rubbed, her fingers cold and bony. The distant sound of my father's taunting laughter echoed in my ears.

"Is that okay?"

"Great," I hissed, softer than a bloody Pillsbury roll. "Fantastic."

But I felt nothing, other than great frustration as her lips moved desperately against mine. She was doing such a thorough job rubbing my cock I was surprised a genie didn't materialize from behind my zipper.

"Wait," I groaned into her mouth. I pushed her away gently. She latched against me harder.

"I'll suck your cock," she offered. Louisa dropped down to her knees, completely naked now, fumbling with the first button of my slacks.

I stepped aside, worried the engagement ring was going to slip from my pocket.

"Don't, darling." I caressed her face while simultaneously moving it away from my crotch.

It occurred to me, rather miserably, that I couldn't have sex with Louisa. No matter how much I wanted to—and I did.

I wanted to get over Emmabelle. To move on. But it wasn't happening.

"Is your stomach a bit dodgy? Must be the lobster."

She hurried to stand up, rushing to the bathroom and coming back in a crème satin robe. "Seafood can be suspect if you don't know the place."

This was the Four Seasons, not a shack on a remote island.

I gave her a doubtful smile. "I better head home."

And I'm taking my soft pig-in-a-blanket with me.

"Oh." Her face fell.

"Lou," I said gently.

"It's just that … *she'll* be there."

"Comes with the territory of her living there."

"Is it something I said?" she asked.

I thought about what she said about Frederick. About the sort of man he was. And couldn't deny her the truth.

"Yes. When you told me about Frederick, I realized I could never offer you what he made you take for granted. I need to sort through things in my head."

I slipped my hand over her waist and pulled her into me, kissing her lips.

"Take care now, Lou."

"You too, Devvie."

My head was still spinning when I got back home. My limbs heavy with the realization that I was apparently immune to all women in the world other than the one who didn't want me.

I stomped my way upstairs, cursing myself for the millionth time that week that I couldn't use the lift like a logical human being.

Once I was done detesting myself for my claustrophobia, I began despising myself for having a traitorous body. What on earth was wrong with it? In the past, I'd been able to get it up whenever the faint scent of a woman's perfume wafted through the air. *Now,* my cock decided it had principles, feelings, and morals. Did it not get the memo that it was, in fact, a COCK? The least sophisticated organ in the human body, apart from the anus.

I shoved past the entrance door to a darkened, vast living room, kicking the fencing equipment by the door aside.

If Emmabelle was out again, working until late or being entertained by a male friend, I was going to … going to …

Do bloody *nothing* about it. I had no power over her.

Hope that month of shagging her was worth it, mate. Because this is your future.

Moving across the living room, I passed by her bedroom before retiring to my own bed.

Her door was ajar. To my great embarrassment, my entire body slackened with relief when I noticed the light inside was on.

Unable to resist myself, I stopped by the sliver of space separating both of us and watched her.

She was standing in front of an imperial full-length mirror.

Her hoodie was bunched up around her chest. Her stomach was bare. She cradled it in front of her reflection, staring at it in wonder.

My eyes trekked downward, doing the same.

For the first time, it was truly and undeniably obvious that Emmabelle Penrose was pregnant.

The hard, round shape of her belly could not be mistaken. It looked magnificent. So smooth and warm and full of a baby that belonged to us.

She was showing.

I closed my eyes, pressing my head against the wooden doorframe, drawing a breath.

"You're so fucking gorgeous, sometimes I want to devour you just to make sure no one else will have you."

The words left my mouth before I could stop them.

She turned around to the sound of my voice.

The love and wonder in her expression melted, replaced by a sly smile.

"I'm surprised Louisa let you off the leash tonight. Trouble in purgatory?"

Guess it was her version of the word paradise for us.

"Stop it," I clipped.

"Stop what?" she cooed.

"Stop acting like a brat. Stop pushing me away. Stop ruining a perfectly good moment because you're so scared of men you simply must torment them if they threaten to put a crack in your perfectly constructed wall."

"All right, then." Belle let her hoodie drop over her stomach.

"No." I pushed myself off the doorframe and made my way to her, my stroll unhurried. "I want to see."

Emmabelle opened her mouth—probably to tell me to go make a baby with Louisa if I was so interested in seeing a pregnant belly—but I managed to put a finger to her mouth before the words came out.

"It's my child too."

Silently, she pulled the hoodie up to her breasts.

I stood in front of her, gazing at the wonder that was her pregnant stomach.

"Can I touch?" My voice was unrecognizable to my own ears.

"Yeah." Hers, I noticed, shook too. The air around us stood still, as if holding its breath too.

The tips of my fingers circled her stomach from both sides. It was hard as stone. We both looked down at her belly like we were waiting for something. A minute passed. Then two. Then five.

"I don't want to let go," I said.

"I don't want you to let go," she said quietly. We weren't talking about her stomach anymore.

My eyes rode up to meet her gaze through our reflection in the mirror. "Then why are you doing everything in your power to drive me away?"

She shrugged, a helpless smile on her face. "That's the way I'm wired."

"It's bullshit."

"It's still true."

"Tell me what happened to you," I demanded, for the millionth time, thinking about Frederick, the way he had peeled Louisa's layers. Was I even close to shedding the first coat? How many more to go? And what in the bloody hell happened to this woman?

Even my mates, who were by no stretch of the imagination considered good guys, never left a woman quite so broken.

She took a step forward, erasing all the space between us.

I was hard as a rock and about to rip the clothes off of this woman.

"Stop butting into my business, Devon. You've already sampled my bag of tricks. There's nothing more to see here."

"You're more than a ditzy party girl, no matter how hard you try to market yourself this way. False advertising."

"Ha," she said dryly. "You just haven't read the fine print."

A mean smirk tugged at my lips. "You're fantastic, and thorny, and worth everything you put me through."

"No!" She pushed me, her palms slamming into my chest. She was angry now, scared. I pushed a button. "I'm not. Stop saying that. I'm the bad crop. The unweddable harlot."

"You're fucking amazing," I drawled in her face, laughing lowly. "Brilliant. One of a kind. The smartest woman I know."

She pushed me again. I got harder. "I'm no good."

"No. Not good. Fucking terrific."

"I'm going to be a terrible mother."

The last sentence was said in a rush of exasperation.

She fell to her knees at my feet, her head hanging low. "Jesus. What was I thinking? I can't do this. I'm not Persy. I'm not Sailor. This is not my life."

I lowered myself to be on her eye level, scooping her face in my palms.

My pulse rabbited. Bollocks, I was going to have a heart attack, wasn't I? Well, it's been a pleasure. Literally.

"Look at me now, Sweven."

She tilted her head up, blinking back at me, her eyes shiny with unshed tears.

"I only choose the best for myself. Suits, cars, properties, restaurants. That's the way I'm wired. Trust me when I say I was not lighthearted when I chose you as the mother of my child. You're clever, independent, shrewd, creative, funny, and, so help me god, a bit of a nutter. But you are also responsible, stable, strong and levelheaded. You're going to be an amazing mother. The best to walk upon this earth."

Her chest heaved, and she looked like she was on the brink of a sob.

"What's wrong now, darling?"

"You forgot pretty," she moaned.

We both started laughing. She lost her balance, falling backward. Not wanting her to hit the carpeted floor, I pulled her with me and fell down to the carpet myself, using my body as a cushion for her. Our legs laced together.

"Sorry, darling, but you're far from pretty."

She pretended to throw a jab at my chest. I caught her wrist and gave it a soft bite.

"Gorgeous, however—"

Her lips were on mine in no time, hot and wet and demanding. Her tongue slipped through mine playfully, stroking and teasing.

I tore at her clothes, ripping her hoodie from the collar, careful not to hurt her.

Her hands were all over me. Her mouth too. I didn't want to draw a breath. To give her time to change her mind.

She was undressed before she could blink. I was still fully clothed when I propped her back against the bed base, my tongue sliding along the back of her knee, up toward her inner thigh, teasing a sensitive spot that made her entire body shiver violently.

My lips found the sweet flower between her legs, and I sucked and bit and blew on it until she came, shoving my tongue into her to feel her muscles clenching it greedily. She hissed, her eyes widening, like she remembered something. I thought it was peculiar. The way she reacted. But then she shook her head, squeezing her eyes shut. "Continue."

Moving up to kissing her belly, I pressed hot kisses on both her tits, nibbling my way up her throat, to her lips.

"Devon. Please. Fuck me."

"All in good time, Sweven."

She reached to undo my trousers. I could feel the pearl of precum gluing my cock to the cloth of my briefs.

Belle freed my cock from the confines of my clothes and mumbled into our dirty kiss, "Say that again."

"Say what?" I asked, sliding into her, there on the floor, finding her wet and ready for me.

"My nickname. Call me that."

She matched the rhythm of my thrusts.

"Sweven." I kissed her lips.

Thrust.

"Again."

"Sweven."

Thrust.

"Sweven. Sweven. Sweven."

Thrust. Thrust. Thrust.

I plastered my forehead to hers as I drove into her faster and harder.

"I'm going to come."

"Come inside me." She clawed her nails into my skin, marking me, making sure Louisa knew. "I want to feel all of you."

My grip on her tightened. Her muscles quaked as I felt my hot cum sliding into her.

We were both sweaty and spent when I rolled off of her, breathing hard and staring at the ceiling.

She was the first one to talk. "I was abused when I was a kid. To this day, nobody knows."

My whole body tensed.

I grabbed her hand instinctively, even before I turned to look at her. I waited for more.

She continued staring at the ceiling, avoiding my gaze.

When it was obvious she wasn't in the mood to share more than the bare bones, I tentatively asked, "Who was it?"

She smiled grimly. "The usual suspect."

"How long did it go for?"

"I don't remember. I was too … I don't know, deep in denial."

"Why'd you keep it a secret?" I propped up on my elbows. I knew before she even told me her family and friends weren't aware of the situation.

I thought back to her awkward conversation with her father and chanted in my head, *No way, no way, no bloody way.* Her father did not abuse her. Because if he did, I'd have to kill him, and I was not built for prison life.

"Shit, I can't believe I'm telling you." She sniffed, the first tear falling down her cheek, sliding toward her ear.

I held my breath and, for the first time in my life, prayed to God. That she wouldn't stop. That she would step out from behind those high walls she surrounded herself with, open the door, and let me in.

"I was always the tomboy, the troublemaker. I didn't want to be the cause of yet another problem. Dumb, I know, but I was tired of being the bearer of bad news. The one who always got everyone into trouble. But at the same time, confronting him meant running the risk of everyone finding out. So I just … bottled it in. For a while, I mean. And then another thing happened …" She stopped, closing her eyes again, trying to swallow the lump in her throat and failing.

Belle wasn't like other women. She was the type of girl who'd take her secrets to her grave. But this, already, was enough. It meant the world to me that she chose to tell me.

"The two men I trusted and loved the most turned their backs on me, each of them in his own way. This no-trusting, no-getting-attached vibe you're getting? That's my fuck-you to your gender, Devon. If I decide to trust again and get hurt, it'd be the end of me. This is why I keep resisting you every step of the way. Whatever you're feeling, I feel it ten times over. But it's not worth it for me. Either I kill my feelings or my feelings kill me."

I brushed a thumb over her sunshine hair, tucking it behind her ear. "Darling Sweven, what's a little death in the grand scheme of things?"

This unbearable, infuriating woman truly understood me. My quirks, my eccentric ways. Mostly, our time together was frustrating and bad. But when it was good, when the walls came down—it was the best I'd ever had.

Emmabelle turned to look at me for the first time since she started telling me her story. "Enough about me. So what made you claustrophobic, Dev? A truth for a truth. You promised to share when I gained your trust, and I think I'm there. Tell me what happened."

And so I did.

Past.

The dumbwaiter was the size of a bookcase when I was first shoved into it, at age four.

Like a baby in the womb, it was spacious enough for me to move my limbs, but still small enough that I needed to crouch.

By age ten, my legs were too long, my arms too gangly to fit into it properly.

And at fourteen, it felt like being shoved into a sardine tin with fifteen more Devons. I could barely breathe.

The trouble was, I kept on growing and the dumbwaiter stayed the exact same size. A small measly hole.

I didn't always hate it.

At first, as a wee boy, I even learned to appreciate it.

Spent my time thinking. About what I wanted to be when I grew up (fireman). And later on, about girls I liked and tricks I'd learned at fencing lessons, and what it would feel like to be a bug, or an umbrella, or a teacup.

It all went to hell one day, when I was eleven.

I'd done something particularly nasty to upset my father. Snuck into his office and stole his poker then used it as a sword to fight with a tree.

That poker was vintage and cost more than my life, my father had explained when he caught me with the thing broken in half (the tree had obviously won).

I was thrown into the dumbwaiter for the evening.

Mummy and Cecilia were away, visiting relatives up in Yorkshire. I wanted to go with them (I never wanted to stay all by myself with Papa), but Mummy said I couldn't miss an entire weekend's worth of fencing sessions with my sabreur.

"Plus, you haven't been spending enough time with Papa. A bit of bonding time for you two is just what the doctor ordered."

So there I was, in the dumbwaiter, thinking about what it must feel like to be a bottle carrying a letter at sea, or cracked pavement, or a coffee mug in a busy London café.

That should have been it.

Another night in the dumbwaiter, followed by a morning drenched with silence and frequent trips to the loo to make up for the time I had to hold it in when I was caged.

Only it wasn't.

Because on that particular day came a storm so big and so terrible, it knocked out the electricity.

My father rushed to the servants' cottages, where the power was still on, to spend the night and perhaps be entertained by one of the maids, something I knew he did when Mummy wasn't home.

He forgot one thing.

Me.

I noticed the leak in the dumbwaiter when a persistent trickle of water kept falling on my face, interrupting my sleep.

I was all mangled inside myself, pressed against all four walls. I ached to move, to stretch, to crane my neck.

When I woke up in a flurry, the water had already reached my waist.

I began banging on the door. Crying, screaming, raking my fingernails over the wooden thing to try and pry it open.

I broke my fingernails and tore my own flesh trying to get out of there.

And the worst part was, I knew I stood no chance.

My family wasn't in the house.

My father left me for dead. Deliberately or not, I didn't know, and at that point couldn't care less.

If I died, they could try for another. My father would finally have the son he always wanted. Strong and tough as nails and never scared.

The water came all the way to my neck when I heard thudding across the hallway. Footsteps.

By that time, I was almost drunk with exhaustion and already came to peace with my fate. All I wanted was for death to be quick about it.

But this gave me new hope. I banged and I screamed and I splashed, trying to draw attention to myself, swallowing water in the process.

"Devon! Devon!"

The voice was muffled by the water. My head was going under, but I could still hear it.

Finally, the dumbwaiter door pushed open. Gallons of water poured out of it—and so did I.

I fell down like a brick at the legs of the person who was now my savior. The saint who gave me mercy. I choked and flailed, like a fish out of water. Relief made me pee my pants, but I didn't think anyone could tell.

Looking up, I saw Louisa.

"Lou," I choked.

My voice was so hoarse, you could hardly hear it.

"Oh, Devvie. Oh, God. We were meant to meet up, don't you remember? You never showed up at the barn, so I sent for you. But the driver didn't want to leave the car, so I asked him to drive me here. The front doors were locked, but then I remembered you told me where the spare keys were …"

She fell to her knees, pulling me into her arms. Her voice hovered over my head like a cloud as I drifted in and out of consciousness.

"I promised I would always have your back," I heard her say. "I'm so glad I got to you in time."

We hugged on the floor. I slackened against her, my body so much heavier than hers—and still, she handled my weight without complaint. Thudding came from the stairs, and in the darkened hallway loomed the shadow of my father, big and bad and imposing.

"What did you do, you stupid girl?" he growled, seething. "He was supposed to die."

Sweven was crying.

She didn't even try to hide it for a change.

Tears ran down her cheeks, some slipping into her mouth, others rolling down her neck.

"I can't believe the bastard put you through that. No wonder you ran away and refused to do what he wanted you to. Jesus. I'm sorry. I'm so sorry."

Her whole body was quaking, back and forth. "You looked death in the eye, Devon."

"Without blinking." I pressed her knuckles over my lips, relishing the privilege of touching her. "You told me what made a hole in your heart, and this is why I have one in mine. This is why I've never gotten married. Why I hadn't started a family. Something inside me knew that getting all the things I prevented Lou from having was just … wrong. I owe her my life."

"She did what any decent person would do."

"Is that so?" I asked idly. "Perhaps I haven't met many decent people in my life."

"Not wanting to be alone is not a sin."

"Then why'd you give yourself the exact same fate?" I murmured into her hand.

She drew back, making a snow angel on the carpeted floor. Pouting and struggling to keep her sniffles to a minimum, she looked half-girl, half-woman.

A pregnant vision stuck in limbo between two worlds.

Too wise for her years and too scared to fall in love.

"Look what you've done. Now I can't even hate her properly," Belle sighed. "She saved you, after all." She used that fake, exaggerated British accent she put on to hide her feelings when she was hurting.

I laughed, rolling over her, kissing her face, licking those salty tears away, my knee prying her legs open as I flicked my thumb along her nipple.

It was just like me to fall in love with the craziest woman on the planet.

Twenty-Five

Belle

Fourteen Years Old.

C OACH LOCKEN COMES BACK TO SCHOOL FOUR DAYS AFTER his son, Stephen Locken Junior, is born. His chest looks broader, his smile bigger, and I don't know why, but I swear he looks more grown-up. His sudden maturity grosses me out.

I show up to practice. There's no reason to leave a perfectly good scholarship on the table just because this guy is a grade-A asshole. But if he thinks I'm going to let him eat me out again, he is in for an unpleasant surprise—and probably a kick in the balls too.

Practice goes smoothly, considering I want to keel over and throw up every time I feel his eyes on my legs. I catch Locken trying to lock gazes with me a few times, but I avert my stare to avoid him.

When practice is over, he lets everyone go and claps my shoulder like a friendly uncle. "Penrose, come see me at my office."

"I have calc in five minutes, Coach. Can we talk here?" I ask very loudly, straightening my spine to show off my height.

Everyone stops and stares. Ross raises an eyebrow. I realize that while

I was under a teenybopper-induced haze, everybody on the team figured out there's something going on between Coach and me. My face feels hot from the inside.

For the first time, I see Coach looking lost and a little shell-shocked. He recovers quickly.

"Yeah. Sure. Here, let's sit on the bench."

We do. We sit at a respectable distance from one another, but I still feel sick. I want to punch him in the face. I hate feeling stupid, and I feel like he took advantage of me. I play with the hem of my shorts.

"Congratulations on Stephen Junior," I blurt out. "And the Kia Rio."

I can't keep the anger from my voice, and you know what? Screw it. I don't need to. He lied to me.

"Ah, so that's what it's about." He scrubs his stubble with his knuckles, looking like he hasn't slept all week. "You knew I was going to become a father, Emmabelle."

"I didn't know you're still with her." It's weird even talking about it. I feel like a grown-up in a TV show. I've only started getting regular periods three months ago, so this is a bit out there.

"I wasn't," he says urgently, and I can tell by the twitch of his hands that he wants to gather me in his arms and demand my attention, but he doesn't. "I haven't been with her for three months. Brenda giving birth in Boston was always the plan. And the week she came back ahead of her due date … well, one thing led to another and we decided to give it another chance. For Stephen."

"Did you sleep with her?" I ask. I don't know what authority I have to ask him that.

He looks away, his jaw clenching.

I snort out a humorless laugh. "Of course you slept with her."

"What was I supposed to do?" he asks through gritted teeth. "It's not like my girlfriend puts out."

His girlfriend. That's what I was now. Even though I thought I'd feel good about it, all I felt was dull regret. How could I have been so stupid? To start this with him?

"I'm not your girlfriend. I'm not even sure I'm your harrier. But what I definitely *am* is out of here." I stand up.

"Penrose," he whisper-barks. "Sit your ass down. We're not done yet."

I do as I'm told, but this time—and this is the real kicker—not because I want to hear his lame excuses, but because I have to. He's my coach. And now I'm starting to see the similarities between Locken and that geography teacher creeper.

"Look, this thing with me and Brenda … it's not gonna last. It's you I want. I've made that clear."

"I don't want to come between you and the mother of your child."

As I say it, I realize it's not only because I feel like a piece of flaming shit for doing what I did with him, a married man. This whole thing's just lost its shine. Days ago, in the cafeteria, as I craned my neck to listen to crumbs of information about him and his wife from the lunch duty teachers, it dawned on me that this was all a huge mistake.

What kind of man sleeps with his student?

What kind of man cheats on his pregnant wife?

Not a worthy one, that's who.

"You're not coming between anything. I want you. I love you. I haven't stopped thinking about you all week." There's a note of urgency in Coach's tone. I swing my gaze to look at him but stand up from the bench nonetheless. It probably looks weird from afar, if someone sees us. Me walking away from him and not vice versa.

His love declaration falls flat.

"I'm sorry. I don't love you back."

"I know you do."

"No, I don't." Truth is, I don't know what I feel or don't feel. I just know I'm in over my head. I have to untangle myself from the situation fast.

"This conversation is not over," he warns me, getting up after me and looking around like a thief in the night before slipping out of someone's window.

I turn my back on him and walk away, thinking, yes, it is.

Twenty-Six

Belle

T HE MAN WAS GOING TO COMPLETELY DESTROY ME, AND THERE was nothing I could do but watch him from a front-row seat.

I knew it the moment he put his hands on my stomach.

Baby Whitehall fluttered when it happened. It felt like butterflies stretching their wings for the very first time inside my belly.

The baby knew her dad had touched her for the first time and was reacting to him.

Everything happened so fast after that.

The kisses.

The love bites.

The skin-on-skin.

The *secrets*.

It felt like falling off a cliff.

Falling, falling, falling.

And still, not trying to grab onto anything to stop what was happening.

The deep end didn't feel so deep when you never wanted to get out of it.

This was why falling in love was a dangerous game.

It gave you the worst thing a girl like me could have.

Hope.

The next evening, I skipped coming home early after I finished the paperwork at Madame Mayhem. I was in a weird mood. On edge.

I didn't want to come back home just to find out Devon was still out with Miss Fancy Pants.

The alternative of Devon being home and sitting me down for a grown-up talk was equally as terrifying.

What could I say to him? Yesterday had changed nothing.

I was still me and he was still him. We still had holes in our hearts.

His family would never accept me and would go through bankruptcy if he didn't marry Louisa.

And me? I was still the same girl who closed her eyes to dream and instead saw Mr. Locken.

Instead of going home, I met with Aisling, Sailor, and Persephone at the latter's mansion for an evening of fried clam plates and beers.

Sticking to soda was hard but necessary. Pregnancy brought with it disgust of numerous things—coffee, red meat, and most types of fish. But I still longed for a glass of wine every now and again.

"Well? What kind of symptoms are you having during your pregnancy?" Sailor knocked down her drink like an Irish … well … *sailor.* "When I was pregnant with Rooney, my hoo-ha turned purple. It was horrible." She paused. "I mean, especially for Hunter. I wasn't in a position to look at it. Literally."

Persy put a hand to her mouth. "Thank you, TMI queen."

Sailor shrugged, swiping a french fry in a bowl of ketchup.

"Just kidding. He kind of liked it. It made him feel like he was having alien sex."

"I used to wet my pants. *Constantly,*" Aisling volunteered casually, popping a fried clam into her mouth. I spat my soda, peppering it all over my friends. Well, this was casual.

"Ambrose put a lot of pressure on my bladder. At first, it only happened when I coughed or sneezed. By the third trimester, all I had to do was bend over to put my socks on, and *whoops*, I peed my pants. I think I was the only pregnant woman on planet Earth who still used sanitary pads every day. Whenever I bought some at the local Walmart, the cashier looked at me weird, like, 'you know you don't need them, right?' and I wanted to scream at her that I was a doctor."

"What about you?" I turned to my perfect sister, who had two perfect pregnancies and delivered babies that were beautiful and good sleepers from day one. Persy, God bless, was incapable of imperfections.

She scrunched her nose, blushing.

"What?" Sailor demanded, grinning, a french fry hanging like a cigarette from the corner of her mouth. "Tell us, asshole!"

"Well." Persy tucked her hair behind her ear nervously. "It wasn't a symptom per se …"

All of us were now leaning toward her at the dining table, eyes wide, dying to know.

"It was just that, during both pregnancies, I was really, really horny."

"You mean you needed vitamin D every day?" Sailor arched an eyebrow.

Persy laughed. "Yeah. I wanted it … a little rough. And Cillian, well, he was torn between giving me what I wanted and making sure we didn't do anything stupid."

We all nodded, considering this.

"Now your turn," Persy giggled, throwing a french fry at me.

It felt a lot like when we were teenagers. The ease that came with being together. I knew we would always have each other. It gave me great comfort now that my feelings were all pretzeled up about Devon.

"I think my main symptom is insanity," I admitted. Munching on my corn on the cob, I knew I was going to regret later on, when I had to floss for two hours straight. "Because I think I'm … kind of starting to like Devon? I mean, for real?"

Utensils clattered. Persy dropped a piece of fried clam on the floor, making no move to pick it up, still staring at me. Sailor and Aisling looked at each other like they were contemplating whether to check my temperature or not.

Persy was the first to clear her throat, proceeding with caution. "Elaborate, please."

I told them everything. About the will, the inheritance, and the issues that came with it. About Devon's mother, and sister, and bankruptcy. I told them about his late nights with Louisa and about how I pushed him into her arms.

How I played my cards in the worst possible way.

I told them everything other than the secrets Devon and I had shared. The holes in our hearts part.

After I was done, the entire table fell silent.

Sailor seemed to recover before everyone else. She leaned back in her chair, green eyes wide, and blew out air. "Damn."

I buried my face in my hands. No good advice was ever prefaced by the word "damn."

Persy's staff began moving our plates away, making themselves invisible. For the millionth time, I wondered how my sister, who'd come from such humble beginnings, could get used to this kind of wealth.

"Any more helpful feedback?" I raised my eyebrows.

"It's just that you've never really shown interest in anyone like that before is all." Sailor looked at Aisling and Persy for help, saw that they were still processing, then added hastily, "I may or may not have told him to not even try, and just marry Louisa to spare himself the heartache. I'm sorry, Belle. When you mentioned it the other day, it seemed like you were totally fine with them tying the knot."

I wanted to throw up, but smiled faintly.

I needed to get up and leave. Maybe call Devon on my way home. He'd come, even if he was with Louisa. That was the kind of man he was.

Aisling rubbed her temple, her thick, dark eyebrows drawn together. "This is wrong. This is all wrong. You know you have to fight for him, right?"

Easy for her to say. For all her sweetness, Aisling was vicious when it came to love. She fought tooth and nail to win her husband after pining for him for years.

"And ruin his family's life?" I let my head fall to the table.

"His sister and mother are not your problem," Sailor said flatly.

"Plus, he'll be ruining his own life and Louisa's if he marries her while he is in love with you," Persy finally chimed in.

We were interrupted by the staff again. This time, they brought dessert and tea. Custard, lemon merengue, and fat pieces of nougat.

We waited until they were gone before we spoke again.

"Are you crazy?" I whisper-shouted, sticking my spoon deep into the custard. "He's not in love with me."

"This is amazing," Aisling murmured around her own spoon, pointing at the custard. "And in my humble opinion, as the person with the highest IQ in the room, he is in love with you."

"*Super* humble." Sailor popped a piece of nougat into her mouth. "But I actually agree. You have to give him the chance to prove himself, Belle. If he knew how you felt, he wouldn't even pay Louisa any attention."

"I don't know what kind of relationship they have." I helped myself to a lemon merengue.

Okay. Maybe I *did* have a pregnancy symptom in the form of wanting to eat anything that wasn't nailed to the floor.

"Time to ask," Sailor said.

"The thing about men is…" Persy sipped her tea, a faraway expression painted on her face, "…sometimes they require a little push to realize that what they need and what they want is in front of them and can be found in the same woman."

"Amen to that." Aisling lifted her teacup in the air, making a toast.

"I'm not like you guys." I shook my head. "I don't have the ability to make someone else happy. As soon as I become vulnerable to them, it's game over. I do something horrible and try to push them away. So I can't promise him all the things you've given to your husbands. The family, the children, the … you know … unconditional love and shit."

I could tell from the looks on my friends' and sister's faces that I did not manage to make my point across with tact or finesse.

"Is that all we're good for? Making our so-called men happy?" Sailor asked with a humorless smile on her face. "I'm only a former Olympic archer and the owner of one of the biggest food blogs in the country. What do *I* know about running a business or having a life outside of marriage?"

She was, indeed, all those things. But she had also married into a wealthy family and had come from one, so she had nothing to prove to anyone.

"And I'm just a doctor." Aisling took another sip of her tea. "Definitely not as earth-shatteringly important or influential as you."

Persephone, who didn't have a day job, was the only silent one, so I made a point of turning toward her to say, "Sorry, I didn't mean it like that."

"Like what?" She sat back, looking perfectly composed and unaffected. "Oh, I may not work nine to five anymore, but I throw fund-raiser events that raise millions of dollars for kids with needs, women's shelters, and animals who've been abused. I feel incredibly fulfilled and don't need anyone's permission to call myself a feminist."

Okay, maybe they all had a point.

"A woman is a woman." Persy put a hand on my shoulder, and I wondered since when had the roles reversed? She'd become the wise and worldly one, and I the one in dire need of advice.

"A woman is a wonder. We are programmed to do and be everything we want to be. Don't sell yourself short. Whatever Devon saw in you is still somewhere inside. Look for it hard enough, and you'll find it," Persy added.

Could I really salvage what I had with Devon?

The Whitehalls wanted me out of the picture. And Louisa was going to be a royal pain, pardon the pun.

But other than them, what else stood between me and Devon?

Nothing. Or rather no one—other than one person.

Myself.

I left Persephone's house, driving on autopilot back to Devon's apartment, which was in the same Back Bay neighborhood.

Drumming my fingers over my leg and thinking about my conversation with the girls, I took a right on Beacon Street, onto Commonwealth Avenue, then continued up to Arlington Street.

When I stopped at a red traffic light, a motorcycle cut through the line of traffic out of nowhere. The rider put himself between me and a Buick in front of me, blocking my line of vision. His face was hidden by a black helmet, and he wore a black leather jacket.

I let out a scream, my right leg hovering over the accelerator, wanting to run the human shit stain over before he pointed a gun at me.

But the guy took something out of the front pocket of his jeans—a note—and slammed it over my windshield.

The text was printed in *Times New Roman*.

LEAVE BOSTON BEFORE I KILL YOU.
THIS IS YOUR LAST WARNING.

That was it.

I was going to fucking murder somebody.

I threw my car into park in the middle of traffic, grabbed the gun from my purse, and pushed my door open.

Helmet Guy shook his head, roared his engine, and drove off before my hand touched the sleeve of his leather jacket.

Tearing the piece of paper from my windshield and pocketing it, I promised myself, whoever it was—I was going to make them suffer.

When I got back home, Devon was there.

He looked like he'd been there for a while, freshly showered and wearing designer sweatpants and a white V-neck.

I didn't immediately tell him about what happened.

He seemed happy and eager to spend time with me.

Besides, I was going to handle it. The police were out of the question—they were useless, and after the reluctant response I'd gotten from them when I filed a complaint, I wasn't planning to go there again. But I *was* going to visit Sam Brennan tomorrow at his apartment and tell him he was going to offer me his services, whether he wanted to or not, or I would tell on him to his wife.

Even the shaky experience I went through this evening wasn't enough to throw me off balance. Usually, an encounter like that meant I had a couple of weeks at least of radio silence from whoever wanted to scare me.

"Hello to my favorite person in the entire world," Devon greeted me warmly. I melted into a puddle of hormones and leaned into him before he crouched down to kiss my belly through my hot-pink blouse.

"Oh. You meant *her*," I murmured.

He stood up to his full, impressive height, giving me a wink. "And hello to the woman who carries her."

"So we are now in agreement that it's a girl." I kicked off my heels. Pregnancy was great, but that didn't mean I was going to start becoming best buddies with Lululemon and—God help us all—Crocs.

"I'm normally in agreement with you," he said easily.

I made my way to the kitchen, filled myself a tall glass of tap water, and drank it in big gulps, shoving the biker to a corner of my mind, determined not to let the encounter ruin the evening for me.

"I'm glad you're not with your girlfriend tonight," I commented.

Oops. Never mind. I ruined the evening all by myself.

Why couldn't I just say "I'm glad you're not with Louisa" like a normal human being? Poor Devon. Even if we were going to end up together, he was going to grow to hate me.

"I think I'm looking at her."

Hmm … *what*?

He sauntered toward me, undeterred. My heart kicked up again, now for an entirely different reason. To be someone's girlfriend—*Devon's* girlfriend—was a reality I'd never considered for myself.

I had to admit, I didn't hate the sound of it.

He took the glass from my hand and put it behind me on the marble counter before gathering my hands in his. A zap went through me. It felt so good, so right, I wanted to crawl out of my own body and run away somewhere where I'd be safe from him.

"Tell me yesterday was a mistake," he ordered, not asked. "Tell me a million times it shouldn't have happened, and I still wouldn't believe you."

I swallowed hard, staring at the floor. Being vulnerable killed me, but I had to do it. "It wasn't."

"Was that so hard?" he enquired softly.

"Yes," I admitted flatly.

He laughed. A low, sexy rumble that came from his chest.

"A weird animal anecdote to soothe your mind?" he suggested, still holding my hands in his.

"Please."

"Platypuses look like they have hot water bottles glued to their faces. You know, the ones our grandmothers like to shove under the blankets in the winter to keep warm?"

I cackled, unable to stop myself. Quaking shoulders and all.

"Speaking of unfortunate faces, the saiga antelope looks like it has a half-mast uncircumcised penis attached to its face."

"Now, what do you have against uncircumcised penises, Miss Penrose? I happen to be the proud owner of one." He jerked me into his hard body, and I giggled some more.

"Nothing, Mr. Whitehall. Nothing at all."

His lips met mine, and the space between us was reduced to nothing.

I clung onto him. His mouth smelled of spearmint and ice. Mine tasted of lemon merengue, and custard, and french fries.

He stripped me fast, and I did the same, and for the first time in years, he was completely naked in front of me, in the kitchen.

"I dreamed about seeing you like this again for a long time." Another admission fell from my lips.

"There wasn't one moment from the first time I saw you when I didn't want to see you naked, Sweven."

I took a step back, appreciating his physique.

"You're beautiful," I told him.

"You're crushing my heart," he answered.

And then we were on the floor, making love.

When we finished, spent and satisfied, he dragged me to the couch, where he nestled me between his arms. I was draped across his body like a blanket.

I liked it.

"Want to watch something?" he murmured into my hair, turning on the TV.

"Like what?"

"What do you like to watch?"

"Money being handed to me or my bartenders, to be honest."

"Take your foot off the gas, love. You've made it in life."

"Hmm." I gave it some genuine thought. "Usually, at home, when I have a minute, I watch the trashiest thing my TV has to offer. Like, *Too Hot To Handle*, *The Circle*, *Toddlers and Tiaras*. If there's even the slightest chance I could be educated or provoked to form an opinion about something, I bail. What about you?"

I felt his chest shake with laughter over my back.

He was warm everywhere. Delicious.

"I mainly watch BBC News, the Sport channel. Sometimes *Top Gear*."

"You're so British."

"Yes, madame."

"Why are you here if you still love and miss home so much?"

I turned my head to look at him. His eyes crinkled as he looked down at me, playing with locks of my hair.

"I don't know," he said honestly, and my heart sank. "Now that my father is no longer alive, I suppose I could go back, if it wasn't for the fact I now have a child to raise in America."

"So you were going to move back?"

"No." But I knew that no, I'd said it a hundred times when I actually meant yes.

"Dev..."

"I don't want to be anywhere else. Now let's watch something that might cause you to think a little. How does that sound?"

"Horrible," I admitted.

He laughed some more. "Good. Show me I'm worth it. Suffer a little with me."

We settled for something in between BBC News and my shows.

A panel game show called *Have I Got News For You.*

Presumably it was supposed to be funny. The crowd—and Devon—definitely laughed.

But to me it was just a reminder that he didn't really belong here with me. That I would be doing him a huge favor if I set him free and let him live his life with Louisa.

Plus, I couldn't stress that enough—there was *no* way I was not messing this shit up.

"I'm still being followed."

My admission came out of nowhere.

Devon's chest hardened beneath me. I could feel his pulse quickening between our bodies.

I closed my eyes and continued. "A motorcycle cut me off in traffic today and slammed a note on my windshield. It said I should leave Boston. It was my last warning. The weird thing is..." I took a breath, "...I get two different sets of threats. One claims they want to kill me and the other tells me to run away. It's almost like there are two forces who want me gone, but not for the same reason. People that have nothing to do with each other."

"Two?" he repeated, his voice cold and contemplative.

"Two."

"*Fuck.*"

It was a knowing fuck. Or at least it sounded like it. But how could that be? How could he have any idea who was after me?

Devon stood up, shoving his legs into his briefs with violent force. "We're calling the police right now."

A bitter laugh clogged my throat. I wanted to tell him I'd been there, done that, and nothing came of it.

But the tone he took with me—so haughty, so patronizing—reminded me why men, like children, should be seen and not heard.

"You can't tell me what to do." I jumped to my feet, pacing to the kitchen.

Baby Whitehall kicked up a storm inside me, letting me know that she was just as scared and angry as I was.

Devon chuckled sardonically. "I can and I fucking am. You're going to file a complaint at the police station, I'll come there with you, and also, you're officially on maternity leave from Madame Mayhem."

His words did not bode well with my no-controlling-men rule.

I let out a shrill laugh, diverting back to old habits, old lines, old, old, *old* dialogue of a woman who just couldn't let go of the past. "Oh, Devon. You are so cute when you think you have power over me."

"This is not about me and my power. It's about your safety. You're going to the police." The look in his eyes broke me to pieces. I could swear he was about to cry. Cry from frustration because he couldn't get through to me.

Now's a good time to just stop.

Take a deep breath.

Tell him you already went to the police, that it hadn't worked.

Maybe you can find a solution together.

But then I thought about Mr. Locken, promising me he was going to get me a scholarship to UCLA. Telling me how much he cared.

And Dad. I thought about him too.

Somehow that reminder hurt most of all.

"Am I?" I plucked a cereal box from the counter and poured half of its contents into a bowl. "Guess we'll just have to see about that."

He turned around and stalked toward his home office. Soon after, I heard the door slam shut.

"I can't deal with her anymore!" he roared from behind it.

The cereal box slipped from between my fingers, its contents pouring on the floor.

I plastered my forehead to the cool counter and closed my eyes.

Almost.

You almost managed to prevail.

But you didn't.

Twenty-Seven

Belle

Fourteen Years Old.

D AD BUYS A BASEBALL BAT TO SHOO THE BOYS AWAY.
 "It's a good strategy." He elbows me over casserole and soda
at dinnertime, winking. "You two are getting so tall. You're not
kids anymore. I need an efficient weapon to chase all the boys away. What
do you think, Persy? Can I take them all down?"

She giggles, pressing her finger to a crumb and nibbling on it. "You
can do anything, Dad."

"What about you, Belly-Belle? Think your old man's still got it?"

I poke the green bean casserole with my fork, trying to muster a smile.

My fifteenth birthday is coming up, and I don't know how to tell Dad
the only so-called boy I have anything with is a thirty-year-old father who
is married and doesn't seem to get the hint that we're over.

It's been three weeks since Coach came back to work. He's tried to
corner me almost every day. I always dodge him, but it's getting harder
and harder. The thing is, I can't tell anyone. Maybe if he wasn't married
… if everyone wasn't fawning all over his baby, which his wife brought to

school the other day in her new blue car. She pushed Stephen in a little stroller and stopped for everyone to coo over him. And then when Coach saw her there, he looked very flustered—almost apologetic—but had still kissed her on the lips before tucking her in the teacher's lounge.

A story about a coach and a student getting busy together is shameful enough, but when you become a homewrecker too? No thanks.

"Don't hold your breath, Dad," I say, finally. "I'm not into the whole dating scene."

"You will be, at some point," Dad sighs regretfully.

My mother piles more casserole on his plate, laughing. "Leave her alone, honey. Maybe she's not ready yet."

I'm starting to think I'll never be ready.

The next day, Coach Locken is in a sour mood. He makes mistakes. Yells at us during practice. Makes us do a hundred push-ups because he says we were late, even though we weren't.

Practice is excruciating. My knee is killing me, but I dare not complain, because I don't want his hands anywhere near me, so I push through, even when I can barely walk it hurts so bad.

"Penrose, see me in my office in five," he barks when we're done. I squirt water into my mouth, eyeing him with open resentment.

"Can't, Coach. I need to pick up my baby sister from the library."

Not exactly a lie, although Persy is used to waiting for me.

"She'll wait." He storms off to his office.

With a groan, I follow him. I have to lock my jaw not to scream from pain because of my knee. My muscles are strained. I haven't had one of his massages in weeks. When we walk into his room, he locks the door again.

This time, I feel nothing but dread. I'm on the defensive. My senses are on high alert.

"Sit down," he instructs.

I do. He leans on his desk, folding his arms over his chest. I look the other way. I'm not going to cry, no matter what.

He puts a hand on my thigh. My eyes jerk up, meeting his.

"Don't," I hiss.

"Or what?" He lifts his eyebrows. "We both know you can't tell anyone

what we did. I'm a married man. That makes you a little slut. No one'll believe you, Emmabelle. It's going to be your word against mine, and I've worked at this school ever since I graduated from college and am well loved and respected. Just get over your little petty drama and accept that this is the way things are going to be. I'm going to have to stick with Brenda for a little while longer."

"Stay with her for eternity." I jump to my feet and try hard not to wince when my knee almost collapses into itself from the strain. "It has nothing to do with me. I'm done."

"That's where you're wrong." His fingers lace around my arm.

I pull away, but he tugs me back with force. He is going to leave a bruise… and I don't think he cares.

Panic climbs up my throat. This is getting out of control. I need an out. I rack my brain for something to say that will make him leave me alone.

"I have a boyfriend," I blurt out.

He gives me a pitiful look, cocking his head sideways. "Please don't insult my intelligence. We both know Ross Kendrick is gay."

"It's not Ross!" I protest. "It's someone else. He's in college. He'll kick your ass if you get close to me."

"Oh yeah?"

"Yeah!"

"What's his name?"

My eyes wildly scan the bookshelf behind his shoulder. Run Like the Wind *by Jeff Perkins stands out.*

"Jeff," I say, finding my voice. "His name is Jeff and we're in love. And you know what else? He's a football player and huge. He can kick your ass if you as much as try to touch me!"

I whirl, trying to make an escape to the door before he asks more questions about Jeff, but he catches the back of my hoodie and pulls me into a headlock, his lips finding the shell of my ear.

"Well, tell Jeff to back off, because you already have a boyfriend."

I don't cry. But I don't try to fight my way out of his embrace either. I'm too scared he'll kill me, right here and now.

"Now tell me, Emmabelle, did he fuck you?"

I know I should say no. Poking the bear is not a great idea. But I can't help it. I think I'll always be wired to fight back.

"Yeah," I say. "He did. A few times. It was great."

Steve releases me unexpectedly, and I scramble to the door, unlocking it with shaky fingers and shooting out of there like an arrow.

Close call, *I think. But even hours after the incident, I still can't breathe.*

Because I know there's more coming.

Twenty-Eight

Devon

SHE WASN'T GOING TO THE POLICE.

I was certain of that more than I was certain the sun would rise tomorrow in the east. Astronomy was full of unfathomable things.

Sweven, however, was as predictable as a Swiss clock.

Even if *she* thought she would go to the police tonight, she was going to wake up tomorrow morning and rebel against every notion that she should be careful or timid or scared.

I didn't feel remotely bad about betraying her confidence when I called Sam as soon as she fell asleep, lighting up a much-needed rollie on the balcony of my bedroom overlooking the skyline of Boston. I pressed my elbows against the bannisters, letting my head drop between my shoulders on a sigh.

"It's eleven o'clock at night," Sam greeted in his signature lackluster mannerism.

"You're still up," I said dryly.

"You didn't know that."

"I know everything."

"Good point," Sam said solemnly. "What do you want?"

"I need to hire you for something."

That gave him pause. I was the only man in my social circle who did not hire Sam Brennan and his staff on retainer.

I kept my hands—like my professional reputation—squeaky clean.

But Emmabelle was about to change that.

She was about to change a lot of things.

I heard Sam sucking on his electronic cigarette. "Oh how the mighty have fallen."

"We all fall in the same way." The fresh air swirled my blond hair, whipping at my face. The cold tinge on my cheeks reminded me what I wished I could forget. That I actually cried a few minutes ago. Or, rather, shed three, full tears.

"And the fall always involves a woman," Sam concluded.

"Although, it should be said, for a while there, I thought all I'd been dealing with was a stumble."

He chuckled softly, and I could envision him shaking his head as he took another drag of his fake ciggy.

"How can I help?" he asked finally.

"Emmabelle is being followed."

"Ash told me something along those lines," Sam offered nonchalantly. "Do you have any suspects?"

"A bitter ex-employee. A woman who is hell-bent on marrying me…" I took a deep breath, my jaw ticking in annoyance, "…and my mother."

Luckily, Sam wasn't one for snarky comments.

"She's been trying to reach me," Sam said. "Emmabelle. I didn't take her calls."

"Why not?" I felt my blood boiling with rage.

"Exercise in humility." I heard him toss the cigarette onto his desk, growing tired and frustrated of the unconvincing replacement. "I wanted to see if she'd turn to Ash or you for help. It would do her good to be a little less prideful."

"She didn't ask me to call you. I'm going rogue on her arse. In fact, I specifically don't want you to contact her."

"All right. I'll email you a questionnaire. You'll have to fill it out completely."

"I need this employee Frank's address as soon as possible," I said.

"You'll get it," Sam said confidently. "But, Devon?"

"Yeah?"

"I ain't cheap."

"I *ain't* poor." It positively killed me to use the word ain't.

"You might be, after putting me on retainer for a month or two."

"You don't need two months to solve this riddle. Plus, you are helping me keep the mother of my child safe. There's no price tag for that."

I hung up, letting out a quick, angry breath.

I looked around the universe, which, in turn, closed in on me.

That was the thing about fearing confined places; sometimes, when it got bad, your mere existence was enough to send you hyperventilating.

Just like sometimes, in order to save an angel, you had to make a deal with the devil.

I was on the threshold of Frank's house the next day, a few minutes shy of noon.

Frank lived in Dorchester. His house had a rickety front porch, dilapidated roof, and a door with bullet holes in it.

Nothing quite said *welcome home* like full metal jacket-shaped holes in a door.

I knocked, brushing my knuckles clean over my tweed jacket.

Sweven didn't know it yet, but the minute she left the house today— whenever that would be—she was going to have two of Sam's men following her.

Since Sam found out Frank's address overnight, I had to admit begrudgingly (but only to myself) that he wasn't terrible at his job. Although I still reserved the right to dislike him on the simple basis that he was, in fact, a cunt.

Although I wasn't well versed in liaising with men who'd tried to get their ex-employers killed, I felt an odd sense of accomplishment.

I was taking care of the situation now. I never fancied myself anyone's knight in Prada armor, but here we were.

The door whined open, and a screen door flapped right behind it.

A spotty teenaged girl with ratty-looking hair and a huge pregnant belly stood in front of me, barefoot, wearing a military camouflage tunic and holed black leggings. She flinched when she saw me, taking a step back.

"Frank ain't here." She began closing the door in my face.

I sent an arm out, pushing it back open with a smile.

"How do you know it is Frank I'm looking for?"

She hugged the edge of the door, peering back at me with wild eyes.

"Figured you're some type of big shot police officer or whatnot. Only two kinda' people come to visit Frank—criminals and policemen. And you don't look like a criminal to me."

A lovely endorsement if ever I heard one.

The girl wasn't wrong, which meant she, at the very least, had two brain cells to rub together. Hopefully she was bright enough to recognize an opportunity when one knocked on her door.

As if confirming my suspicion, a loud growl came from her pregnant belly. She winced, running a hand over her greasy roots.

"Is that all?" She was about to close the door again.

"Are you hungry?" I dipped my chin down to try and catch her gaze but to no avail. Whoever Frank was, he'd trained her well to keep away from strangers.

She shook her head.

"Because I can take care of that," I said kindly.

"I don't need no charity."

"My girlfriend is pregnant too. She is growing our child inside of her. I would hate to think she goes without food. For me, it's not charity. It's a necessity."

She folded her lips on top of each other. I could tell she was at a breaking point.

She was hungry. So hungry. Her legs were two toothpicks.

The living room behind her looked like it had been trashed by every single squatter on the East Coast in the last decade.

"Who are you? What do you want?" she asked finally.

The fact that she didn't slam the door in my face was an encouraging sign.

She knew I could give her relief, an immediate remedy for her situation.

I got her attention, and for now, that was enough.

"I'm looking for your boyfriend. I suspect he is planning to do a very bad thing."

"Got no idea where he is. He's been gone for a whole week now. Wouldn't even pick up my calls. That doesn't surprise me, though." She snorted.

"Oh?" I elevated an eyebrow. Not passing judgment was rule number one in trying to get information from someone. "Is that a common occurrence with Frank? Him causing trouble?"

"Frank's yet to meet any type of trouble he doesn't like. What are you, anyway? You're too well-dressed to be a cop."

"I'm a lawyer." I took a step forward, into the hallway, and could now smell the unmistakable stench of weed, mildew, rotted food, and apathy. "Would you say he is capable of violence?"

"Sure." She shrugged again, another rumble coming from her belly. "He's gotten into plenty of fights before."

"What about murder?"

"Who did you say you were again?" She narrowed her eyes at me, taking a step back.

She wasn't going to talk unprompted. It was time to cut the bullshit.

"What's your name?" I asked.

Many people thought lawyers were combative, aggressive people. Some—unprofessional ones—were. But most were even tempered. I killed people with kindness whenever possible. I didn't have to flaunt my power. I carried it effortlessly.

"I ... um ..." She looked around her, as if there was

something—someone—who could stand in her way of accepting the help I was offering her.

Behind me, chained dogs barked in someone's back yard, trying to jump the fence. A baby cried in the distance.

"D-donna," she stuttered. "My name is Donna."

"Do you have a surname, Donna?" I took out the checkbook and a Montblanc pen from my inner pocket.

"What do you mean?" She swayed from foot to foot, ogling me openly now. Like once she hopped through the mental barrier of looking at me, she couldn't stop.

"A last name." I smiled.

"Oh. Yeah. Hammond. Donna Hammond."

"I'm writing you a check for two thousand dollars, trusting you to buy food with it, Donna." I scribbled as I spoke, my eyes still holding hers.

She seemed mesmerized, and it depressed me, how different her baby's life was going to be from ours.

How my baby would never have to think about where the next meal was going to come from, or have to deal with an untreated medical situation because we couldn't afford the bill that came with it.

I ripped the check and handed it to her. Before she plucked it from between my fingers, I raised my arm in the air, stopping her from taking it.

"There's a catch."

"I knew it," she huffed, baring her teeth. "What is it?"

"I'll give you this check. No questions asked. *But*," I drawled, "I will give you a check for ten thousand dollars *and* secure you a spot at a women's shelter if you do two things."

She looked behind my shoulders frantically, licking her lips. "Okay. But with a condom. I don't want no diseases."

Was that what she thought I had in mind? Some of my loafers were older than her, for crying out loud.

"It's not sex I want from you, Donna. I want you to give me any information about your boyfriend's whereabouts. Call me as soon as you hear from him." I produced a business card, handing it to her. "And I want you to promise me that you are packing your bags and leaving this apartment. I'll send someone over who'll take you to a women's shelter."

"Deal," she said.

I handed her the check. She took it with trembling fingers, looking up at me again.

"But what if I never hear from him again? He's not taking my calls. Will you cancel the check?"

I shook my head. "Not if you keep your end of the bargain and leave him for good."

"I will. I am," she corrected herself. "He screwed me over. I'm not going to forgive him for what he did to me and my baby."

I tucked the checkbook back into my pocket, giving her a wry smile. Even if Belle wasn't safe from Frank, his ex-girlfriend now was, and that was something too.

♛

On the way back to my office, I called Sam. He picked up on the first ring.

"If this is about Frank, I'm still trying to find him. He slipped under the radar."

I choked up the steering wheel. I did not like to be in a point of disadvantage, but right now, that was exactly where I was.

"Are you looking into Louisa and my mother too?"

"Yes." I heard Sam clicking away on his laptop. "And I can't yet rule them out. There's a lot of money anchored to that goddamn will you're ignoring, and all of it's tied to assets and valuables. I can see your mother's incentive."

"What about Louisa?"

"Ah, that bag of fucking English Delights," Sam spat out. "Yeah, she is still an option too. It appears that her family is not half as wealthy as they claim to be. I pulled some reports from the private Swiss account they're using. Whatever they have in HSBC in Britain, both private and business accounts, is not enough to maintain their lifestyle for the next five years. So I can see why Butchart is being pressured to marry you. She needs to save her and her brothers' skin. The cash pool is dwindling fast."

"Well, that's a shite show."

"Word, Nancy Drew."

"How the fuck did it get this far?" I wondered aloud.

For two decades, I'd been careful to stay out of trouble, and now it seemed like trouble found me every step of the way.

"Well, let's see. You had unfinished business across the pond, as you Brits like to call it, the woman you're with is a goddamn menace and shouldn't be left to her own devices, and on top of all this, you seem to have a golden cock because everyone wants it."

"My cock only wants Emmabelle," I said grumpily. "Isn't that sad?"

"Fucking tragic."

"Promise me one thing," I said.

"No," Sam answered flatly. I went ahead anyway.

"That nothing happens to Belle."

There was silence on the other line. I slowed my Bentley and came to a stop in front of a traffic light. Finally, he spoke.

"Nothing'll happen to Emmabelle. You have my word."

Twenty-Nine

Belle

Fifteen Years Old.

I END UP SPENDING SUMMER BREAK IN SOUTHIE.

Mom and Dad are bummed that I haven't gone to a training camp. Even more so that I don't want to go back to cross-country next year. They'll survive.

Persephone and Sailor are blossoming into little women. It's nice to watch, even if I've never felt more uncomfortable in my bones than I do now. Ross, now fifteen, experienced his first sloppy kiss. With a guy named Rain who was vacationing with his family on the Cape at the same time Ross was there with his family. They exchanged numbers, but when Ross got home and called, he realized a number was missing. He's been crying and laughing about it for days now.

Me, I made it my mission to turn myself into a chameleon. I start putting on makeup and experimenting with my hair and clothes. Anything to make myself more comfortable in my skin. The good thing about this whole year is that my knee is no longer suffering. It still hurts but it doesn't feel like death anymore.

I walk back from Ross' place. Jokes aside, he's been pretty bummed about the whole Rain thing. I wish I could tell him things could be much worse as far as first kisses go. But I know he's going to freak out if I mention Coach, and honestly, it doesn't even matter at this point. It's done. Over.

I bob my head to the sound of "Hate to Say I Told You So" by The Hives, trying to lighten my own mood. Maybe I'll ask Persy and Sailor if they want to catch a movie or something. Get all the sugar rush from the soda and eat buttered popcorn.

I take the shortcut to our apartment through an alleyway, when a blue car pulls up and blocks my way to the other side. Its blueness hits me in the gut immediately.

Brenda?

I rip my headphones from my ears, turn around, and start running without finding out. I hear a car door open and slam shut behind me. My knee slows me down, but I'm still fast as hell. All I need is to get to Main Street and then it's done. There's nothing she can do to me.

But then I feel a hand grab onto my throat, and I'm being dragged back into the alleyway, kicking and screaming. I can tell it's not Brenda. Brenda wouldn't be faster than me. And her palms wouldn't feel so rough.

"Hello, little liar. Where's Jeff? I've been keeping an eye on you all summer and noticed you haven't met a single boy. Even with your slutty new look."

His voice makes me want to throw up. I roar savagely, throwing fists everywhere.

He cups my mouth to shut me up. I feel Coach's fingers behind the small of my back as he unbuckles himself. Tugs my mini skirt up.

No, no, no. no.

"Now, now. You can go and fuck whoever you want after I'm done with you, but I'm going to pop that sweet cherry. Let me just grab a condom."

I find fresh wrath in me when I hear the word condom. I manage to turn around and claw my nails into his eyes. Momentarily free, I scream for help again. With his vision blurred, he pounces on me, tackling me to the ground. His first blow lands on my jaw and stuns me into silence, even when the rest of my body still struggles to break free.

"Fine, never mind about the condom. Bitch." He spits on my face.

I continue fighting, even when I know I've lost the war.

When all my soldiers are dead, and my horses are gone, and my land is swollen, thick with blood.

I keep fighting when he breaks me.

When he takes me.

When there's nothing left to fight for.

I keep fighting, because that's the only way I know how to survive.

Belle

The morning after my argument with Devon, I padded barefoot to his bed to apologize, but at six-thirty, he wasn't there.

I brushed my teeth, slipped into a white mini-dress that highlighted my calves, and ate a piece of avocado toast. Afterwards, I drove to a different police station from the one I previously went to, and, the good girl that I was, filed another complaint, this time with a policewoman who seemed much more competent and much more freaked out about it, which oddly made me feel better.

By noon, my schedule was clear and my ass was bored. I knew Sam Brennan, whom I was planning to corner and demand he take me on as a client, wasn't going to be in Badlands before eight in the evening, so I still had time to burn.

I stopped by Madame Mayhem to go over a few files and check on the staff. Devon didn't want me to go there, but I had my gun, Krav Maga skills, and Simon.

As much as I hated to admit it, having a bodyguard the size of a politician's ego wasn't such a bad thing.

I showed up at the back office of my own club, armed with my laptop and a smile.

"Honey, I'm home!" I announced to Ross, whose eyes bulged out of their sockets on impact. He rushed to me, shaking his head and fist simultaneously.

"Holy Cody Simpson's abs on a poster! What're you doing here?"

"Working?"

"Under these circumstances?" He cradled my belly—the belly in which a person was now fluttering and flipping and doing all kinds of amazing things, especially at night—and gasped.

"Yeah. You expect me to just drop my responsibilities and dip?"

"I'm expecting you to look out for your wellbeing as well as your child's!"

"I'm just going to do a couple hours of spreadsheets."

"Bitch, you're not an accountant. The world's not going to collapse into itself if you don't check on the Belgian beer supply today. And, sorry to break it to you, we're doing swimmingly without you."

Simon appeared out of nowhere, as if by magic, the minute my voice carried from the backroom.

To say he didn't look happy to see me was the understatement of the century.

"You're here." Simon stopped at the door, disappointment rolling from his body in waves.

"Hello to you too, Si!" I smiled broadly.

"Mind if I work alongside you in your office?" he asked me but looked at Ross, as if to say, *I'm knocking down her door if she refuses.*

I waved him off with a smile. "Sure, whatever makes you and your uptight boss happy."

"You're your own greatest health hazard. I'm on the verge of quitting." Ross slapped the back of his hand to his forehead before stomping off back to the bar to unload a shipment of alcohol. "Oh, and I'm telling your beau!"

I settled in front of my desk and popped my laptop open. "Go ahead, traitor!"

Ross popped his head back through my door, grinning like a loon. "So he *is* your beau. Girl … *so* jealous!"

I was putting a real dent in my workload, securing an out-of-state burlesque act that was visiting from Louisiana for the summer and negotiating a contract with a new liquor distributor, when there was a knock
on my office door.

Rolling back in my chair, I stretched. "Thank God. I could use a
distraction. Maybe it's food. Do you think it's food, Si?"

Simon, who sat a few feet away from me, dutifully pretending to
do some filing even though there was very little to be filed in my office,
stood up from his spot on the floor and dusted off his jeans. He motioned me with his hand to stay seated, heading for the door.

"Has anyone ever told you you're anal-retentive, Si? You could use
some loosening up."

Baby Whitehall fluttered in agreement inside my belly, and I cradled it for a moment.

"Yeah, fair point, Baby Whitehall. I know. Mommy's not perfect
either. But you have to admit at least I come close."

"There's a woman here to see you," Simon said tersely, blocking my
line of vision of who it was with his Robocop shoulders.

"My, my, my, a visitor." I laced my fingers together. "Is it Pers or
Sailor? Ash is at work, so it can't be her. Either way, they aren't allowed
in unless they come bearing edible gifts."

"I think you should pass on this meeting. It's not a social call."
Simon's face was so tight, I thought he was going to explode.

"Who is it?"

"Miss Penrose …"

Why did he still insist on Miss Penrose when I called him Si? Why
couldn't he be less uptight? Where the heck did Devon find this guy
anyway?

"Who. Is. It?" I repeated, getting sick and tired of men telling me
what to do.

Simon took a deep breath, throwing his head back in exasperation. "Louisa Butchart."

"Let her in and leave." My voice was ice cold.

"But—"

"Do it, Si. Before I kick you out of my establishment. You know I can."

Furthermore, he knew I *would*.

We stared at each other for a beat. Heaving out a sigh, he stalked out of my office. I could see his head peeking in the hallway, though, staying close by.

Louisa waltzed in, stylishly emaciated in an Alexander McQueen pleated coat dress.

I wasn't intimidated. Just pissed off she kept showing up like a fart stain on underwear every time I tried pushing her out of my mind.

"Louisa! What a delightful surprise. Lost your way to Chanel?" I put on my best fuck-you smile.

"Oh, Emmabelle, I do love your dress. What is it exactly? Victoria's Secret *shag-me-in-the-dark*?" she drawled, perching her bony ass on the edge of the seat.

Her vintage Hermes told me she meant business. Nobody had any business carrying a 250k bag unless they were willing to show what was inside it was equally as impressive.

"To what do I owe this visit?" I purred, cutting straight to the chase.

"I think we both know the answer to that question, so why don't we skip the part where I insult your intelligence and you waste my time?"

"Sounds good." I curled my hair around one finger playfully. "So you're still holding out hope you can get your claws on my boyfriend?"

I had no idea why I decided to call him that in front of her, but it felt right. The title. The weight of it. Besides, Devon called me his girlfriend the other day, so surely I wasn't completely off base. Even if I was pretty sure he currently wanted to murder me.

"Girlfriend?" she huffed. "Devvie's family will never accept you. In fact, there will *be* no family to accept you after this is all done and dealt with. Devon might seem tough and unrelenting when it comes to his mother, but trust me, he spent half his lifetime trying to cater to her every whim. Family is everything. If you care for him, you would not deprive him of his. One baby is not enough to replace all he'd be losing."

This woman had some ovaries on her—balls implied that women didn't have courage, an idea I rejected promptly. After all, it wasn't men who found themselves pushing a watermelon-sized human out of their pee pee hole.

Draping my hand on my chest, I feigned shock.

"I didn't realize I was destroying his life. Please allow me to remedy the situation immediately by moving to a tropical country and changing my name so he can't find me."

The words—you guessed it—were spoken in a fake English accent.

"Don't play dumb. We both know his relationship with you is the only thing in the way of our marriage," Louisa bit out impatiently.

"So?" I yawned. "We're both consenting grown-ups. And I don't know if you noticed, but we're kind of in the middle of taking a huge step together."

"The *step* means nothing in your situation. You're not getting married. You don't love him, I do. He means nothing to you."

This time, each of her words cut into me like shards of glass, because I realized they weren't true.

Still, I couldn't confess my feelings to Devon, let alone this she-devil.

"What's your point?" I drummed on the back of my laptop, rolling my eyes.

"Let him go. Tell him you don't want anything to do with him. Open the path for him to go back to his family, to his sister, to me. This is his destiny. It's what he was born for."

"He was born to make his own decisions."

"No, maybe *you* were. A commoner, with no legacy or responsibilities. Devon was made for greater stuff."

Outrage propelled me from my seat. I threw my hands up in the air for good measure.

"You want me to tell him to screw off so you can marry him? Give me one goddamn reason why I should."

"Very well. I'll give you one million of them."

Louisa slammed her bag between us on my desk with a thud and took out a pre-written check.

I had to blink rapidly to see if the numbers were right. Yup. Sure were. One million dollars, paid to the order of Emmabelle Petra Penrose.

I twisted my thumb ring without touching the check, which was now sitting on the desk between us. I ran my teeth over my lower lip.

My rage was replaced with worry and trepidation.

How did she know my middle name?

How long had she been gunning for me to leave Boston?

And didn't all of this feel just a little too … *familiar*? Like maybe Frank wasn't the only source of the threats toward me.

I tried to think about it pragmatically. To do what was best for me and the baby.

Devon *was* a risk. I felt all kinds of things toward him. Things I had no business feeling. If he married Louisa, I wouldn't have to worry about him anymore. I'd never touch a married man again, dead or alive. The problem would be solved.

And while we were speaking about the pros of taking the money, I would be set for life. I could keep Madame Mayhem and still take a huge step back. Provide security for myself without having to jump through hoops, carry a weapon, and beg Sam Brennan to pick up my calls.

I could put Ross in charge of the club, which I was growing tired of anyway—being raunchy and shocking was a full-time job, it seemed— and find another venture.

Maybe a high-fashion store. Or an interior design company.

Then there were the cons.

And many of those too.

First and foremost, I didn't want Louisa to win.

She was strong-arming me, and I didn't respond well to bullying.

The second thing was it wasn't fair to Devon.

It wasn't my place to decide for him who he'd marry or not marry.

Ultimately, though, there was one deal breaker—Louisa and Ursula could both be behind the threats against me, and by taking this deal, I could protect my child.

I just had to play my cards right and ensure that neither my baby nor Devon would get the short end of the stick in this situation.

Picking up the check, I threw it in front of Louisa's face with a smile.

Time to play hardball.

"Sorry, no dice, princess. Dev and I have a contract in place. I already agreed he'll be a part of the baby's life and share custody with me. I intend to keep my word."

"Oh, Devvie," Louisa clipped, massaging her temples. "You had to go for the one whore with the heart of gold ..."

"I'm not a whore," I hissed. "But I can recognize a bitch when I see one."

"He'll be in the baby's life." She pushed the check toward me again. "I give you my word. We both know I can't stop him from doing that. But he'd still be married to me."

"Dandy. Then what are you asking me for exactly?" I asked.

"Dump him," Louisa said quietly. "I'll do the rest. But please, just ... just cut it off with him. I know women like you. You don't have a future with him. You don't take him seriously. Your intentions aren't pure—"

"And yours are?" I cut into her words.

She screwed up her face in distaste.

"He is about to lose everything his family has worked centuries for."

Arguing with her on this topic was pointless. Devon had admitted as much to me himself.

At the end of the day, Devon and I weren't a good fit. No one would be a good fit for me.

"I'll take the money and leave him, but I'm not pushing him away from the baby's life, and I'm not moving out of Boston."

It amazed me, just how much I hated myself in that moment.

How I turned out to be as bad as the people who scarred me.

The Mr. Lockens of the world. Without virtue, morals, or direction.

"Fine. Fine. That's good enough for me. When will you do it?" Louisa asked.

Numbly, I pocketed the check in my purse under my desk. I felt like I was having an out-of-body experience. Like it wasn't me who was sitting in front of this woman now.

It's for the best.

He would hurt you.

Every other man you put your trust in has.

"Today."

"Good. Then I'll be sure to be on standby when he seeks my comfort."

She stood up, clapping her hands together once. "Ursula is going to be very happy with the news."

"Oh, I'm sure." I was about to keel over and throw up.

"You're doing the right thing," she assured me.

Nodding faintly, I pointed at the door. I could barely breathe, let alone talk.

Louisa walked away, closed the door behind her, and left me with the weight of my decision, knowing full well it was going to crush my soul to oblivion.

Thirty

Belle

HE WASN'T GOING TO LET ME LEAVE.

I knew that much for a fact.

For all his niceness—and Devon Whitehall was a good and true gentleman—he didn't react well to bullshit, and he and I both knew that I was serving him a healthy dose of messiness neither of us deserved.

So I took the coward's way out. I wrote him a note.

I told myself that it was fine. I would sit and talk to him face-to-face. I just needed some time to digest everything. Besides, it was better if I didn't stay in Boston, now that I suspected two different forces of trying to drive me away.

Devon would be fine. He always was. Strong and sun-washed and golden. With his title, sharp intellect, and lazy, surly drawl, he'd be fine.

Shit, I was making the biggest mistake of my life, and I was doing it for my daughter. Keeping her safe was most important.

So this was what it felt like to love a person.

Even before I knew her. Even before she was out there in the world.

I decided to handwrite Devon a letter. I wanted something personal and not too brief to break the news to him.

After all, he'd been nothing but good to me.

It took me four hours to write something I didn't completely detest.

Dear Devon,

Thank you for your hospitality and for dealing with my brand of bullshit, which, let's admit it, is too much for 99.99% of the human race.

The thing is, I don't think living together is doing either of us any good. I make you miserable, and you make me uncomfortable.

The feelings you stir in me leave me raw and scared.

As for you, I know last night you were on the verge of punching a hole through your bedroom wall, all because of me.

I know things are kind of rocky, but please know that I filed a complaint today and that the police are working on it. I promise to carry my weapon at all times, and to stay safe, but I can't do this anymore.

I'm afraid if we keep having a relationship, the stress is going to get to the baby, and I have to put her before anything else. Before you. Before me.

I'm so happy to do this journey with you and request that we remain friends.

With that being said, I'll be taking a step back and will try to look inside myself to find the grace and trust you deserve to be treated with.

Lots of love,

Belle.

P.S.
You should marry Louisa. She loves you.

Thirty-One

Belle

Fifteen Years Old.

T ENTH GRADE STARTS WITH BANGS.
Not to be confused with a bang.
Ross, of course, is behind the idea.

"Bangs really suit you. I just love your hair. It's fantastic to work with. I need to straighten my own bangs every morning," Ross moans.

We made a deal—I'll give both of us bangs if he agrees to go to Krav Maga classes with me. We go three times a week. The instructors are tired of our faces. But I no longer leave my fate in the hands of men I don't know.

I watch for Coach Locken in the hallways, in my classes, in the cafeteria. I'm never going to let him do that to me again, and revenge will come.

I've seen enough documentaries and watched enough news cycles to know that handing him over to the authorities won't do any good. I need to take the law into my own hands. Because whether he gets away with what he's done or not, my life will still be fucked forever.

I refuse to be that girl who messed with her coach. Who let him eat her out for months, and then oops, got scared and told Mommy and Daddy when he took her virginity. No. Screw that. I'm a girl with a plan.

Coach Locken stays away from me.

One month follows the other, and I almost start breathing again.

Then one Saturday morning, bright and early, when Mom's making pancakes downstairs, Dad reads the paper and Persephone is on the phone with Sailor, something happens.

It's weird that it happens, because everything else about this Saturday is so ordinary. So mundane. The scent of pancakes wafts under the cracks of the bathroom. So does Persephone's laughter as she and Sailor discuss how obnoxiously romantic both our parents are (Sailor is, unfortunately, also the spawn of two people who really need to stop pawing one another in public).

I get a text from Locken.

I'm going to do it again if you tell.
Be warned.

Consider me warned.

I'm about to throw up.

But I think I know why he feels confident in telling me this—he knows the authorities are a piece of crap. The school board would never believe me. The local police station is full of his schoolmates—people he drinks beer with—and Southie is just not a place where you go to the police. You take care of shit on your own.

I pee in the toilet. Feel like I stopped peeing—my bladder is empty, I know, because I've been peeing fifteen years straight, every day, multiple times a day, without fail—but for some reason, I keep dripping. The cramping in my stomach is bad. Like my gut is constricting against something it wants to purge out.

I look down, between my legs, and frown. A gush of blood comes out. I blink into the toilet bowl, spreading my thighs apart, and I see a clump of … something.

Oh God.

Oh God.

Oh God.

I bend over forward and throw up right there on the tiles. I'm shaking. No. It can't be. I reach above my head for a towel hanging on a rack and stuff it into my mouth to muffle my cries. I squirm on the floor and scream into the towel.

Crying, crying, crying.

I was pregnant.

The bastard got me pregnant.

Of course he did.

But … why did I lose the baby?

I calculate back and realize the pregnancy was five weeks long. I'd fallen during the last week of summer break. But still. How? Why? How come?

This is the moment I realize I am not myself anymore.

That maybe I'll never truly be myself, because I didn't have time to figure out who I was.

This is when I think my faith in humanity will never be restored.

That things cannot possibly get any worse.

And then they do.

Thirty-Two

Devon

I WAS GOING TO FUCKING KILL SOMEONE, AND IT WASN'T GOING to be Emmabelle Penrose, even though she was the woman who most deserved my wrath.

Crumpling the handwritten letter, I slam-dunked it into the bin, scooped my keys from the kitchen island, and charged toward the door.

I took the stairs two at a time, almost toppling over on my way to the Bentley.

My first stop was Sweven's still-paid-for rented flat. The matchbox-sized hellhole from which I rescued her like a flea-ridden puppy.

I banged on the door until my fists were red and sore. No one answered.

"Open the door, Emmabelle. I know you're there!"

One of her neighbors shuffled outside their apartment, clad in a Big Lebowski robe, a joint dangling from the side of his mouth.

"You're wasting your time, man. She hasn't lived here in a few months. Moved in with her rich boyfriend." The neighbor puffed on his spliff, cocking his head to the side. "Come to think of it, he looked a lot like you."

She hadn't come back home.

My next destination was Persephone and Cillian's place.

I tried calling Belle the entire journey. She did not pick up.

Not one to be deterred by her lack of availability, I left her voicemails left and right while trudging along the painfully slow traffic of Boston during rush hour.

"Hello, darling, it's your boyfriend. The one you just left with a fucking note. Yes, the same one whose baby you're carrying. If you think we aren't going to talk about it, you're gravely mistaken. Oh, and by the way, whatever happened to the fact that people are trying to KILL YOU? Ring me back. Kisses. Dev."

And then:

"Sweven. Hope your evening is going better than mine. Where are you? Also, if this is you telling me in a roundabout way Louisa's presence is bothering you, may I suggest hiring a life or speech coach to help you with your communication skills? Call me back."

And finally:

"Emmabelle fucking Penrose. Pick up the bloody phone!"

Things escalated from there.

I arrived at Persy and Cillian's place, using the lion's head brass knocker so hard it dislocated and dropped onto the floor. My girlfriend's (yes, she was still that) sister informed me, rather regretfully, that her sister was not there.

"Are you saying this because you're hiding the bloody wench, or because she's really not here?" I stood on her threshold, panting like a dog.

"My wife said her sister's not here." Cillian appeared behind Persephone at the door, draping a protective arm over her shoulder. "Are you calling her a liar?"

"No, but I'm calling you an insufferable wanker." I'd lost all form of etiquette and manners, resorting to hostility. "So I have a good reason to think someone might be hiding something. They're close. They'd cover for each other."

"Actually..." Persy squared her shoulders, looking rather haughty, "...I would like to know where she is too. I worry about her. She might not take the threats against her seriously, but I do."

"Ask Sailor and Aisling," I instructed her, but I was already pacing back to my car, making my way to Sailor. "Let me know if you hear anything."

"Will do," she called from her spot at the door.

Sweven wasn't at Sailor Fitzpatrick's house either. She wasn't at Aisling Brennan's place. She wasn't at Madame Mayhem. She wasn't *anywhere*.

It was as if a sinkhole swallowed her.

I called Brennan. After all, I paid him to have her followed, the boyfriend of the year that I was. When he didn't pick up, I decided to pay him a visit. For what I was paying him, Emmabelle should not only be safe but also warm, cozy, and getting regular pedicures and three meals a day.

Bursting into the gambling room at Badlands, I flipped over a poker table. Sam was arranging a game with two senators and a business mogul. The chips fell on the floor with a clank.

He looked up.

"What the fuck?"

"The fuck is you fucked me over. I'm paying you a retainer to keep tabs on my girlfriend. Newsflash: it's been a second since I hired you, and I have no bloody clue where she is."

Sam ushered me to his back office. We rushed through a busy, narrow corridor, passing men who wanted desperately to stop and chat with us. I swatted them away like they were flies.

"Would you shut your trap? I have a goddamn reputation to uphold."

"Where's Emmabelle?" I bit out. We got to his office and I slammed the door behind us then proceeded to trash the place. I tossed his couch over, tore at a Roman curtain, and punched a hole in a portrait of Troy Brennan—an offense which was likely punishable with death by stoning.

"I've been calling and calling your arse. It went straight to voicemail."

"Was busy buttering up Dumb and Dumber," Sam said shortly, producing his phone from his back pocket and punching in a number. "Let me call my guys and check."

The good news was they answered him immediately.

The bad news was that, well, THEY LOST HER.

"What do you mean they *lost* her?" My voice rose, and I found myself yanking his Apple screen from his desk and crashing it against the wall. "She is not a fucking thought thread. A subplot in a book. A pair of sunglasses. One does not simply *lose* a thirty-year-old woman."

"She tricked them," Sam said, lightly stunned by the revelation. His eyes were wide, his mouth slightly agape. I gathered it didn't happen to him often.

"She must've realized they were following her and tricked them."

"She's a smart woman," I seethed. God, couldn't she be just a little less perceptive?

Sam scowled. "You were the genius who didn't want to tell her I was putting surveillance on her. In my entire career, no one I followed has ever managed to slip under the radar."

"Thanks for the fun fucking fact." I grabbed the collar of his shirt and jerked him toward me so our noses were crushed together. "Find my girlfriend by the end of tonight or I will personally ensure you and the DA who is covering for your arse are both dragged through court for the rest of your miserable lives to account for every crime you've committed over the last two decades."

I stalked out of his club and went to the only person I knew may have some information—Louisa.

Louisa waited for me in a tiny crème and black lace bodysuit, complete with a corset that made her waist as nonexistent as my need to screw her.

"Hello, darling. Good to see you."

She sidestepped from the door to allow me to walk in. As soon as I closed it behind us, I pinned her with a look that said a fuck fest wasn't in the cards for us.

Know your audience, lass.

"Put something on."

"Like what?" she asked, blinking slowly.

"A fucking raincoat if you wish. Do I look like a bloody stylist?" I grabbed something I suspected was a robe lying on a back of a chair and threw it at her. She wrapped it around herself quickly, drawing in a breath.

"What's the matter?" She made her way to the wet bar to pour us some drinks.

"What did you do?"

Surprisingly, I sounded fine. Wry. Businesslike. Not like I was about to commit capital murder.

"What do you mean?" She stepped toward me with two glasses of whiskey, handing me one. I didn't acknowledge the gesture nor the drink.

"What did you do?" I repeated.

"Devvie, stop being so weird, for heaven's sake."

She took a step back.

I took a step forward.

I had no idea what I was doing, and I didn't want to find out.

Sweven brought out emotions in me I didn't care to explore.

I'd always been calculated. Calm. Full of confidence.

I was not any of those things right now.

"What. Did. You. Do?" I took both glasses form her hands, putting them aside on a credenza, crowding her against the wall. We were inches from each other.

The air was charged with menace, violence. She could feel it.

Louisa wilted slightly and finally asked, "How much do you know?"

"Enough to know it reeks of your involvement."

She stuck her chin up. "What I did may have been unethical, but it certainly wasn't illegal."

"Wasn't illegal?" Yup. I was roaring in her face now. Her hair flew back from the impact. "There are people after her! She is on the run!"

"People *after* her?" Louisa wore an expression of genuine surprise. "I did no such thing. I'd never send anyone to go after a woman, let alone a pregnant one. It goes against everything I believe."

I gave her an aren't-you-a-saint look.

She elevated her eyebrows, in a way that said, *quote me on this, motherfucker.*

I decided to strike her off the list of suspects. *For now.* Frank and my mother kept my hands full, as it was.

"You did something," I maintained.

"A small something," she countered. "Really small. Teeny-tiny, actually."

"What did you do?"

"Devvie …"

"Now."

"It was your mother's idea." She dug her fingernails into her fists, looking unbearably embarrassed, her cheek turned in my direction. She couldn't meet my gaze.

"What did you do?" I asked for the millionth time.

"I can't tell you. You'll hate me."

"Too late. Already there. Now, for the last time, before I make you regret the day you were born—what happened between this morning and this evening to inspire my girlfriend to leave me?"

All the air was sucked from the room in the moment before her confession.

"I paid her."

It was out in the open now. The admission.

And once it was out, Louisa proceeded, gingerly throwing another crumb of information.

"It's Ursula, Devvie. She was relentless. Completely unhinged. Time is ticking. She got nervous … gutted, really … and …" She shook her head frantically, reaching for my face. I threw her hands away.

"And?"

"And she wrote her a one-million-dollar check."

"Fucking hell."

"And Emmabelle *took* it," Louisa added desperately, her small fists balling around the fabric of my dress shirt. "She took the check, Devon. What does it say about her? She doesn't love you. Doesn't need you. Doesn't see you. I ache for you every day."

She spoke the words to my shirt, unable to look at me when she said them.

"You're my first and last thought. You're always in the back of my mind. Loving you is like breathing. It's compulsive. Let me love you. Please. Just give me a chance, and I'll be everything you need me to be."

"You can't be everything I need you to be." I stepped backward, letting her stumble a little before gaining her composure. "Because you're not the woman I love."

Her eyes were big and full of tears. I walked over to a small dining table, picked up her phone, and handed it over to her.

"Now you're going to call and tell your pilot that's on standby that you will be leaving tonight. Go back to England. You will never set foot in Boston again. Not as long as I'm alive. And if you ever come back—"

I paused, thinking about it. Louisa's face was now marred with makeup and tears. A concoction that gave her a slightly comical look, like she was a long-lost Cradle of Filth member.

It didn't feel good or right, crushing her like that, but I had no choice. "Darling," I gathered her arms in mine, my voice dropping to a whisper. "I'm never going to marry you. Not in this lifetime and not the next. With or without Emmabelle in the picture, I'm an all or nothing kind of bloke. With her, I want it all. With you ..." I let her complete the sentence in her head, before adding, "If you try to tamper with my relationship with my girlfriend—and she is still my girlfriend, make no mistake about it, even if she doesn't know it yet—I will ensure your family and legacy are both destroyed. I will ensure everyone knows Byron has demolished a historical church so he can place his side piece within a stone's throw of his countryside estate. The money he paid Parliament Member Don Dainty under the table to promote favorable tax laws would be revealed, and let us not forget your dear brother Benedict has a particular taste for underage girls. Your family is corrupted through the nose, and I am willing to unveil every piece of wrongdoing it has done over the years if you don't give me your word here and now that you are going to stop this."

All this dirt, courtesy of Sam Brennan and his detective work. Maybe he was worth some of his fee after all.

I could tell it sank in this time around.

That it hit her real and hard. In the same place it hit me, the day I knew my father didn't love me. Although now, it seemed like my entire family didn't love me.

Mum had betrayed me too.

Outwardly, nothing changed. Louisa was still the same Louisa. Willowy and delicate, a perfect, stainless feather in the wind. But her eyes turned from glossy to dull. Her mouth became rigid. The twinkle behind her irises was gone.

"Answer me with words," I said softly, using my hand to gently pry her jaw open. The words fell from between her lips like they were on the tip of them, just waiting to be said.

"I understand you never want to see me again, Devon."

And to my surprise, behind those words, there were cinders, still hot from where the flame had once been.

She was angry. Defiant.

She would rise from the ashes, I hoped, and find someone else.

I turned around and made my way to the airport.

I had a plane to catch.

On the way, I called Emmabelle a few more times, dropping more messages that would make any serial killer proud.

"*You're bloody crazy if you think I'm giving you up. You were mine from the moment I set my eyes on you. When you weren't even aware of my existence. When I came to serve your sister with a draconic agreement she shouldn't have signed.*"

And then:

"*The night we got in bed together for the first time, at Cillian's cabin, was the night I first contemplated breaking my pact with myself to never marry a woman. I refuse to lose the only woman who is worth breaking my word over.*"

As well as:

"*Goddammit, I love you.*"

As I zipped through neighborhoods, and skyscrapers, and lives that weren't mine, I pondered something Louisa had told me before I left her.

It was true that Belle didn't love me.

After all—she took the check.

But I loved her, and maybe that was enough.

Thirty-Three

Belle

Fifteen Years Old.

I'M KISSING SIXTEEN.
And that's the only thing I'm kissing.
My life is blissfully, disgustingly boring.

I don't date. I don't socialize with anyone other than my sister, Sailor, and Ross, but I talk a big talk, and I sure as hell show the world that all is fine with Emmabelle Penrose. That I am an invincible, happy-go-lucky girl.

And sometimes, on good days, I can even believe my own bullshit for a moment or two.

Coach Locken, however, is not doing so hot.

His wife, Brenda, is pregnant again, even though little Stephen is, what, a little over one year old? That, in itself, is hardly bad news to grown-ups.

But the fact that he's been having an affair with one of the teachers is.

Miss Parnell is my twenty-two-year-old substitute teacher—and his newest girlfriend.

The showdown at the front gate last week was legendary. Even I couldn't help but get riled up and excited.

Brenda pulled up at the curb, little Stephen still napping in the backseat. She cornered sweet Miss Parnell, bitch-slapping her in front of the entire school. Poor Miss Parnell didn't stand a chance. She just started crying. Her sobs became more violent, louder when Brenda screamed, "Did you know he got me knocked up again? Did you know? And did he tell you we broke up while I was pregnant with Stevie? Because that piece of shit scumbag sent me to my mom's saying he needed to get the house exterminated and disinfected before the baby arrived. He drove down to Jersey every goddamn weekend to get some of this ass."

Wow. Brenda wasn't the sweet woman I saw in the engagement picture at all. All the same, it made me feel easier, lighter about what I was about to do to Coach Locken. I didn't forgive and didn't forget. I was just biding my time, putting more weeks and months in the calendar between us so that when the time came, I wasn't going to be a suspect.

Now I'm walking home from school, feeling marginally better about life. For one thing, Locken got the boot after that showdown and is no longer working at my school, which is great. For another, my last two classes have been canceled, so I'm dipping early for an afternoon of breaded fried Ravioli (the frozen Trader Joe's kind), and Ricki Lake reruns. Or as some like to call it: heaven.

Persy isn't due to come home for two more hours, Dad's at work (isn't he always?), and Mom finally agreed to go to therapy and deal with her dark spells, so she is all the way across the city and won't be back until evening.

I unlock the front door to our apartment, happy in the knowledge that Coach Locken is miserable, wherever he is right now in the world. I toe my sneakers off, let my backpack slip from my shoulders by the door, and pad barefoot across the living room. I'm going to deal with the ravioli in a second. First, I'm going to pee. I still hate going into the bathroom to pee. It's like I have PTSD and expect to have a miscarriage again, even though I know I'm not pregnant. But no matter how time passes… how my life seems to look like it turned a corner… I cannot help but hate Locken *for what he did to me. For what he did to my body. In my mind, this happened because of the way he took me. It was so violent, so frantic… I'm sure he caused some kind of damage.*

I pass by my parents' bedroom and notice the door is ajar. Not shocking, considering this house is always a mess and we don't have a closed-doors or open-doors policy in place. I stroll by it when I hear a soft moan that makes me stop dead in my tracks.

Oh shit. They're here.

They're here and they're having sex.

This is worse than I thought. Their love knows no bounds. Someone kill me.

I turn around, intending to tiptoe back to the kitchen and maybe pee in the sink so I don't have to listen to this crap and get scarred any further, when I hear my father's voice.

"Oh, Sophia."

Sophia? Who the fuck is Sophia?

My mom's name is Caroline.

What in the shit?

I huddle back to the ajar door, peering through the crack, blinking the image into focus.

My dad is lying on the bed, and on top of him, with her back to me, is a woman who is definitely not my mother. Long red hair. Slender figure. Freckles on her shoulders. She is riding him.

Dad is cheating on Mom.

The perfect fairy tale I grew up believing is all a lie.

All men are cheaters.

All men are untrustworthy.

All men are trash.

I pad back to the front door and slip out of the apartment, taking the stairs three at a time up to the roof of the building.

I don't jump, but not because I don't want to.

Only because I have an unfinished grudge to tend to.

And Dad? I'll never forgive him.

Thirty-Four

Belle

I WAS BEING FOLLOWED.

I could tell I was being followed when I looked through my rearview mirror and noticed the same incognito black sedan zipping out of Boston, gliding onto the highway, staying the same four-car gap from me no matter how many lanes I switched.

Not knowing who it was—Frank? Louisa? Devon's Mom? The devil himself?—I decided to escape it.

Today seemed like a bad day to die and get buried in the woods.

I lane-hopped for a while, feeling sweat coating my forehead as I tried to think of a game plan. How was I getting rid of this strange car?

And then it hit me.

I popped my blinker to make a right into one of the small towns bracketing greater Boston and waited patiently in a line of cars. My stalker did the same. When the light turned green, I made a terrible (and I do mean freaking awful) traffic offense and continued straight ahead, not taking the right, and speeding into a busy intersection. Cars slammed their brakes, horns blared at me angrily, but when I looked back, I saw that the black sedan was way behind, trapped inside a sea of vehicles in a traffic jam from hell.

I drove and drove and drove some more, not sure where I'd end up.

And somehow, already knowing where I was going to go.

All at the same time.

For the first time since I'd turned eighteen, I was living with my parents again.

I couldn't kid myself anymore. Staying in Boston at this point was a death wish. Might as well stick an *I'm With Stupid* sign on my forehead pointing at my brain.

Several people wanted me dead. And I just signed my soul away to the devil in stilettos.

It was time to lay low until I came up with a game plan.

My parents lived in the place where sex appeal went to die, also known as Wellesley, Massachusetts.

A few years ago, my parents announced excitedly that they'd saved up enough money to fulfill their long-time dream of becoming boring retirees, moved from Southie and bought a sage green colonial house with a matching roof, a swinging chair on the front porch, and red shutters.

Persy and I called it the Gingerbread House, but only one of us was excited to come here each Christmas and play the happy family charade.

"Oh, Belly-Belle, I'm so happy you're with us again, even if the circumstances are less than ideal." Mom poked her head through the backyard's double doors, offering me an apologetic smile.

Perched on the lip of the pool they were so proud of, I dipped my feet in the water, wiggling my toes.

"Already told you, Mom, everything's fine."

"Nothing's fine if you can't afford your apartment anymore."

She walked out to the patio carrying a bowl of watermelon peppered with fresh feta cheese and mint.

Placing it on the edge of the pool beside me, she ran her hand over the yellow Lycra of my bathing suit, her fingers halting at my swollen belly.

"I moved in because I need a change of pace, not because I can't afford rent." I selected a beautifully cut piece of watermelon—square and sharp angled—and popped it into my mouth. It was ice cold. "Everyone I know and their mother begged me to step away from Madame Mayhem. They think working on my feet all day is bad for the baby."

Mom didn't know that there were people after me.

She didn't know about the letters.

She didn't know I'd lived the last few weeks with Devon.

She didn't know *anything*.

I did this to protect her.

Making her worry was futile, almost cruel.

And something else lurked behind my decision to share with her the bare minimum of my pregnancy circumstances. I suspected she wouldn't understand.

Honestly, I wasn't entirely sure *I* understood everything that'd happened to me recently.

"Are you sure everything's okay?" She began untangling my golden locks from my earring, like she used to do when I was a kid. "You've been here for a couple days now and still haven't told us why exactly."

"Can't a girl just chill with her folks?"

"I don't remember a time when you didn't go out at night since you were sixteen."

Well, Mom, I did a lot to try and distract myself from my reality at that age.

But then, I was a clubber six months ago too. I'd distracted myself for fourteen years before Devon stepped into my life and forced me to stay still and take a good look at what my life had become.

I pushed another watermelon chunk between my lips, watching her black-eyed Susans across the pool, their stems like necks craning to look up at the sun, the petals glinting under the sun's rays.

"Come with me to the farmer's market. You'll meet all my new bridge friends," Mom suggested.

"Holy shit, Mom, you're really selling this to me," I deadpanned, hands tucked under my butt.

"Come on, Belly-Belle. I can see something's on your mind."

"You can?" I frowned at my toes. "How?"

"A mother can always tell."

Was I going to know when my baby felt something once they were born without any telltale signs? Would my gut scream at me that something was wrong? Could I pick up on the vibes, like fumes from fire, before the earth beneath her feet scorched?

"Yes," my mother said as if reading my mind. She rested her hand on my back. I wanted to fold into a fetal position and cry in her lap. The last few months caught up with me all at once, and now I was exhausted.

More than I was afraid of those who were after me, and more than I was angry at myself for taking Louisa's deal, I missed Devon.

Missed him so much I couldn't bring myself to turn on my phone for the past couple days and check if I had any messages from him.

I missed his gruff, elegant laugh and the way his dark blond eyebrows moved animatedly when he talked.

I missed his kisses and the crinkles around his eyes when he grinned mischievously and the way he called the guy who worked at the convenience store under his apartment the newsagent, like he was a BBC anchor and not a dudebro who sold overpriced milk and cigarettes.

In short, I missed him.

Too much to trust myself to go back to Boston.

Too much to *breathe*.

Mom reached and gathered me to her chest, dropping a kiss on my head. "Yes, you will know when something is eating at your child, and I hope they will tell you what it is that's eating them so maybe you can help. As it happens, I raised two fiercely independent girls. You, more than your sister. You were always such a spitfire. You helped Persephone before I could get to her—with school, with homework, with her social life. You've already been a parent in some ways. You're going to be a wonderful mother, Belly-Belle, and you are going to realize the most depressing secret of all."

"Hmm?" I asked, nuzzling into her shirt.

"You're only as happy as your least happy child."

She dropped another kiss on my head.

"Confide in me, Belle."

"I can handle it, Mom."

She pulled away from me, holding my shoulders, her eyes boring into mine.

"Then do, honey. Don't run from whatever *it* is. Face it head-on. Because whatever happens, it's not just you who you have to think about now."

I pressed my hand against my stomach.

Baby Whitehall kicked in response.

I got you, girl.

Twenty minutes after my mother went to the farmer's market to meet with her bridge friends (my youth shriveled into itself just *thinking* about it), I picked up the empty watermelon bowl and pushed the screen door open, slipping back inside. The house was blistering hot since the air conditioner died a few days before and had yet to be repaired. There was a gaping, sewer-sized hole at the back of the house, waiting to be fixed.

The place felt strange to me still. Even though it was not chrono-logically new, it seemed that way. It had yet to shape itself around its occupants and was bare of memories, nostalgia, and those home scents that transported you back to your childhood.

I rinsed the bowl, thinking about what Mom had said. Dealing with my problems.

The last couple days brought me clarity.

I didn't want a million dollars. I wanted Devon.

And I was tired of running away from whoever was after me. I *needed* Devon to help me with that.

Yes, I finally realized I needed help. I couldn't do this on my own. And strangely enough, it didn't feel too terrible admitting that to myself. Maybe I *was* growing up from the girl Mr. Locken had left to bleed out all those years ago.

The front door opened and shut, and the house filled with my dad's whistles.

John Penrose could whistle any song that came out between 1967 and 2000 from start to finish. He was good at it too. When Persy and I were young, we'd play name that tune. Sometimes I let her win. But not often.

"Honeys, I'm home!"

He appeared in the kitchen, tall and broad and still kind of handsome—in a more wrinkled less defined Harrison Ford kind of way. He dropped canvas bags full of lemons on the counter next to me, grinning at me ear to ear.

"Hello, sunshine."

He pressed a kiss to my forehead, hiked his belt up what was beginning to look like a dad bod more than a father figure belly, and swung the fridge door open, on the hunt for his evening beer. "Where's your momma?"

"Out." I leaned against the counter, drying my hands with a towel. I didn't tell him where she went. To this day, I withheld information about my mother from my father, trying to make her appear more mysterious and alluring. There was little point to this exercise. She was an open book to him—always honest, straightforward, and available.

She was all the things I didn't want to be. He never questioned her love for him.

Dad closed the fridge, popping open his Bud Light, settling against the opposite counter.

"What's up, kiddo? How's that baby growing?" He took a pull of his beer.

Fix it, Mom's voice urged in my head.

Here went nothing and its best friend nada.

"You cheated on Mom."

The words came out so mundane, so plain, I'd laugh at how easy it was to say them. The smile on my father's face remained intact.

"'xcuse me?"

"You cheated on Mom," I repeated, suddenly feeling my pulse everywhere. My neck, my wrists, behind my eyelids, in my toes. "Don't try to deny it. I saw you."

"You *saw* me?" Dad put his beer down on the counter, folding his arms across his chest, ankles crossed. "When and where, if I may ask? We don't exactly hang in the same circles."

He sounded amused more than he was worried, but there was no trace of aggression in his voice.

"In yours and Mom's bed. A lady with dark red hair. I mean, I say a lady, but what I really mean is a skank. Back in Southie."

And just like that, the blood drained from his face.

He looked pale. Grave. *Scared.*

"Emmabelle," he breathed. "That was ..."

"Fifteen years ago," I finished for him. "Yeah."

"How ...?"

"Came home early from school and walked in on you. I didn't tell you because I was scared. But I saw her on top of you. I heard you whisper her name. And I never forgot. So tell me, Dad, how's *Sophia* doing these days?"

Sophia.

The woman I was sure I saw in supermarkets and parks and on the escalators at Target. The harlot who ruined my parents' marriage without my mom even knowing about it. Some nights, as I'd lain awake in my bed, I thought I could murder her. Other nights I wondered what made her the way she was. What made her seek pleasure with an unavailable man.

"I ..." He looked around him now, seeming lost all of a sudden, like we'd just been transported back to the room where it happened. "I don't know. I haven't been in touch with her in years. *Years.*"

He reached behind him to grab the counter and knocked his beer down on the floor. The glass bottle broke, yellow-white liquid running like a golden river between us.

"How many years?" I asked.

"Fifteen!"

"Don't lie to me, John."

"Ten." He closed his eyes, swallowing hard. "I haven't seen her in ten years."

He'd been with her until I was twenty-one.

This wasn't a fling. It was an affair. Of course it was. He wouldn't have brought his fling over to his house.

"Why?" I asked.

I wanted to know what was missing in his life. Mom was gorgeous, loyal, and sweet. Persy and I were good kids. Sure, we had stuff, everyone had stuff—money issues, Mom losing her sister to cancer, those sorts of things. *Life* things. Things we went through together.

"Why did I cheat on your mother?" He looked perplexed.

"Yes. I want to know."

Neither of us made a move to clean up the mess on the floor.

He rubbed the back of his neck, pushing off the counter and starting to pace back and forth. I followed him with my gaze.

"Look, it wasn't so easy back then, okay? From the moment your momma quit her job to take care of you two and your Aunt Tilda, may she rest in peace, I wasn't just the breadwinner—I was the sole provider of the family. And there were medical bills and a fridge to fill, mouths to feed, insurance and a mortgage to pay. Persy had ballet classes, and you had track. Things added up, and I just …" He stopped, flinging his arms helplessly in the air. "I was sinking. Going under. Deep. Your mother didn't want to touch me. I felt too guilty to even ask. She was watching her sister disappear, little by little. I felt like an employee of the household more than the man of it. And then came Sophia."

"I'm guessing there's a pun there," I muttered sarcastically.

He ignored my barb. "Sophia and I worked in the same office building. At first we took lunches together. It was innocent."

"I'm sure." I smiled, surprised to find out I was as bitter as I'd be if it'd happened to me. If it were Devon.

Devon is not yours. Devon is getting married to another woman, probably in the next few months. Apologize profusely and tear the check into tiny pieces or move on with your life.

"She was going through a messy divorce," Dad explained.

"Cordial divorces are hard to come by," I quipped. "And the fact you did it in Mom's bed. Ballsy. There's a pun there too, by the way."

"Emmabelle," he chided softly. "Believe it or not, I did it there because a part of me wanted to get caught. Give me a chance to speak."

Begrudgingly, I pursed my lips, allowing him to go on.

"I was there for her, and she was there for me. She was a mess. I was falling apart. Throughout all this, your mother and I had drifted apart, until I could no longer remember what it felt like to be her partner, her lover. But it was complicated. I still loved your mom. I wanted to believe I'd get her back, eventually. Our love was just on hold."

What in the ever-loving fuck was this man talking about? Love wasn't something you could put a pin in and get back to later. It wasn't a goddamn follow-up email you could schedule in advance.

"The timeline suggests otherwise." I attempted a sardonic smile. Auntie Tilda died in my early teens. Dad broke up with Sophia when I was twenty.

"Life has a way of setting the pace," he admitted. Bending to pick up the large pieces of glass from the floor, he looked at them like he wanted to stab his own neck.

"I wish I were so forgiving to myself about my actions," I mumbled.

"I'm not forgiving to myself. I've hated myself for a long time. I tried to break up with Sophia numerous times after your aunt passed away. And sometimes, I even succeeded. But she always came back. And sometimes I let her in, whenever your mother and I had issues."

"You're a sack of shit." The words coming out of my mouth stunned me. Not because they didn't make guest appearances every now and then (profanity and I were close friends) but because they'd never been directed at a family member before. Family was something sacred. Until now.

"I was," he agreed. "But finally, nine years into the affair, I managed to escape her. I quit my job. I changed the locks on our house. I told her if she got anywhere near your mother or tried to tell her, I'd make her life miserable."

"Nice."

He threw the glass into the trash can under the sink, poking at the rest of it with his boot.

"If you knew all this time, why didn't you tell your mother?"

"What makes you think I didn't?"

"She'd have killed me." Dad popped his upper body into the pantry and returned with a mop to clean up the beer, his eyes clinging to my face the entire time. "Then left me. Not in that order."

I let out a huff. "As if."

"What do you mean?" He started mopping.

"Mom never would have left you. That's why I didn't tell her," I bit out, my voice carried by emotions like they were the wind. Gaining altitude, becoming a storm.

The reason I didn't tell her all these years wasn't altruistic. It's not because I wanted to protect her.

I was worried she'd stay, and I wouldn't be able to look her in the eye.

That I would be so deeply disappointed in her, so upset with her decision, it would affect our relationship.

By not trusting her decision, I robbed her of the ability to make one.

"Yes, she would." Dad stopped mopping, pressing his forehead to the tip of the mop stick. He closed his eyes. "She would have walked away. She was tempted to do it regardless of my infidelity."

His head sloped forward, his shoulders sagging, and then ... then he started crying.

Lowering himself on the floor in front of me.

His knees sank into the golden river of beer.

My dad never cried.

Not when my aunt died, or when my grandparents passed away, or even when he watched Persephone walk down the aisle, ushered by the brother of the groom, because Dad had had leg surgery and couldn't walk.

He wasn't a crier. *We* weren't criers. Yet here he was weeping.

"I'm sorry, Belly-Belle. I'm so sorry. I've never been sorrier for a thing in my life. I cannot even imagine what it felt like for you to find out that way."

"It was terrible."

But, oddly, maybe not as terrible as seeing him like this.

I mean, a part of me still hated him for the distorted picture of partnership he'd ingrained in me, but he was also the person who took care of us.

Who bought me everything I wanted—within his ability—and helped pay off my student debt.

He was one of my investors when I opened Madame Mayhem, and he once punched a man in the face for propositioning me while we were all vacationing on the Cape.

He never locked me in dumbwaiters or was abusive or neglectful.

He fucked up, but he never intended to fuck *me* up.

"If it makes you feel any better, I couldn't eat, I couldn't sleep, I couldn't even function for a very long time after Sophia and I ended things. And, after a couple of years, I told your mother."

"Wait, Mom knows?" I grabbed the hem of his plaid shirt and hoisted him up so we were at eye level. His eyes were puffy with tears, bloodshot. "But you said she'd have left you if I told her."

"She *did* leave me."

"She never told me."

"Do you tell her everything?" He caught my gaze meaningfully, arching an eyebrow.

Fair point.

He rubbed his knuckles against his cheek. "She kicked me out of the house shortly after you graduated college. By then, you and Persy were out of the house. I think she waited until you both left because she didn't want to traumatize you. I rented an apartment two blocks down for eight months, trying to win her back."

"Go Mom," I mumbled. "I hope she got some."

"She had a two-month affair with a yoga instructor at the local YMCA. After we got back together, I got so mad just driving past the YMCA, I vowed to move us away from that entire zip code to escape that memory."

"*This* is why you moved to the 'burbs?"

He nodded.

"Why'd she take you back?" I realized I was still holding his shirt, but that did not deter me from clutching harder.

"Something very inconvenient happened to her."

"What?"

"She remembered she was in love with me, and by being away from me, she was punishing not only me but herself too."

I let go of his shirt, staggering back.

My yearning for Devon welled inside me. Wasn't that what I was doing? Punishing both of us because I couldn't handle the prospect of being in love? Of putting my trust in someone else?

My parents' relationship was far from perfect. It was littered with disloyalties, bad years, and other people.

But. It. Still. Worked.

"I hope that in time, you'll forgive me," Dad said. "But just in case you don't, let me assure you, Belly-Belle—I will never forgive myself."

I needed time to think.

"Thanks for the talk. I'm going to go ahead now and scream into my pillow for a while," I announced, grabbing a bag of chocolate-covered pretzels from the pantry on my way up to the guestroom.

I was still wearing my canary-yellow swimsuit.

I stopped by the stairway, holding the railings for dear life as I twisted my head back to look at him. He was still standing in the same spot in the open-plan kitchen.

"One more question." I cleared my throat.

"Yes?"

"What was so wrong with Sophia?" I bit out. "Why was she so fucked up?"

"She couldn't have any children," he said gravely. "That was what was wrong with her. That's why her husband left her. He married another woman three months later and went and fathered three sons."

Poor Sophia gave up on love too.

And in the end, she lost.

Maybe that's what losing was, giving up on love.

Thirty-Five

Belle

Eighteen Years Old.

*I*T'S A WEIRD THING, OBSESSION.

Sometimes it's fantastic.

Sometimes it's horrible.

Take artists, for instance. They're obsessed with their work, aren't they? The Rolling Stones, The Beatles, Spielberg.

They work their butts off to ensure every note, every word in a script, every shot is perfect. That takes obsession.

Then there are other obsessions.

Take me, for instance. I cruised through my teenage years harboring a dark, horrible secret. My cross-country coach sexually abused me then raped me. I ended up having a miscarriage because of all the stress and trauma he put me through.

See, now this *obsession is not so good.*

I've spent the last three years plotting my revenge, and the day has finally arrived.

I've been keeping tabs on Steve Locken throughout the years.

He moved away from Boston to Rhode Island to start fresh. Brenda left him shortly before she gave birth to their second son, Marshall. Brenda is back in New Jersey now and is married to a guy named Pete. They have a daughter together. She seems happy. Or as happy as one can be after what her ex put her through.

I know Locken doesn't see his sons often. That he started working at a local school in Rhode Island, and that he has a girlfriend named Yamima.

And I know that he is still sexually abusing young girls.

This is what obsessive people do. They dig and dig and dig. Until their fingernails are gone and their flesh is raw.

I sniff around. Get into the social media sites of some of the girls on his team.

They post about him.

They share pictures of him.

They have secret groups about him.

One even bragged to her friends that she jerked him off after assembly one day, in broad daylight, they were so horny for each other.

In other words: my conscience is clear. Steve Locken doesn't deserve to live.

This is where it gets a little dicey. I've never killed a person before. But I spent the last three years of my life going to Krav Maga classes three times a week, and I take my dad's Glock 22 to the woods, where I shoot tin cans lined up on logs. Massachusetts has crazy gun laws, but my dad used to work in law enforcement before he got his office job.

The Glock sits in my purse right now as I drive down to Rhode Island.

It's a nice summer day. Only days before I head off to college. I know Yamima, Steve's girlfriend, is out of town at a conference. She's a realtor and while at the conference, she is sharing a room with her colleague, Brad, who is dumb enough to elude to this on his Facebook profile.

What comes around goes around.

Steve is alone at home. He drinks two beers every night in front of the sports channel. I've watched him carefully all summer break, hiding behind the bushes of his beautifully restored craftsman house after telling my parents I was pulling double shifts at a burger shack to save for college.

Steve has no cameras installed anywhere around the house. One day, I overheard him telling Yamima that all of those cameras are connected to the internet, and he doesn't want anyone hijacking tapes of what's going on in his house.

Steve gets up every morning at five-forty-five and is out the door for an eight mile run by six.

So today, when he slips out, I slither in. When his garage door rolls shut, after he leaves the neighborhood in his car on the way to the trail where he runs, I sneak in. I open each Corona Premium bottle in his garage fridge and pour crushed Ambiens and a little rat poison into them, screwing a bottle capper I brought with me to make them appear new and turning them upside down.

When I get to Steve's suburban neighborhood again, it's almost midnight.

I round the craftsman house, trudging through the thick bushes circling his pool. I can see him through the double glass doors of his living room, passed out, from the drinks and the Ambien. I carefully pick at the lock of the door, my gloves and balaclava intact, watching him intently, in case he wakes up.

He doesn't.

I push the door open and head straight to him. He is sprawled on a maroon couch, a football game rerun playing in front of him. I snap a glove off and place an index finger under his nose. Feel the heavy breeze of his breathing.

Not dead yet. Shame.

I'm not going to use the gun if I don't have to. Too messy, and I don't want to get in trouble. Instead, I'm going to make it look like an accident.

Steve always said that a bad attitude was like a flat tire. One can't get super far before changing it. So I put my big girl pants on, think about it from all angles, and come up with a plan.

I squat down, picking up Steve's head. It is heavy and hard in my hands. Of course I want to do it like in the movies. Tie him to a chair and throw our past between us. Spit in his face and punch him. Make him cry, and beg, and piss his pants, all while swaggering off in five-inch stilettos.

But I cannot afford to get caught. Not when I'm trying to piece my life back together. I may never forgive men for being men—that ship has sailed. I will never marry, never fall in love, never give another person with a dick a chance—but I can still carry on.

With his head firmly in my hands, I angle his body to a slumped position and calculate what it'd look like if he accidentally fell on the glass coffee table in front of him. The next few minutes is a lot of me moving his limp body back and forth on the couch and turning the coffee table slightly to ensure his head meets its sharp edge.

Then I walk behind the sofa, grab Steve by the shoulders, and hurl his body forward with force. His head smashes on the edge of the coffee table.

Glass shatters.

His face is all cut up, but I can't see it, because he is lying there facedown.

There's blood everywhere.

So much blood.

He still doesn't move, not even a flinch, and I suspect he wasn't aware of dying, he was so deeply unconscious. My heart twists in disappointment, so I tell myself that even if he didn't know he paid for what he did, at least he won't be able to do it to anyone else.

"Goodbye, bastard. Hope Satan gets you."

I slide out unnoticed and make my way back to Boston.

To my new life.

To the new me.

Thirty-Six

Devon

"MR. WHITEHALL, YOUR VEHICLE AWAITS."

I fell into the backseat of the eye-catching vehicle and continued barking at Sam Brennan during our transatlantic phone call.

"You said Simon came highly recommended." I was aware I sounded one, accusatory ... two, clipped ... and three, utterly deranged. "He is a fucking joke, period. Where was he when Belle got attacked? When she was followed?"

I felt like a helicopter mother trying to convince an AP teacher why *her* Mary-Sue should get the scholar award this year. My complete transformation, from a man of leisure and pragmatist to this hysterical, illogical, blubbering mess, was not lost on me.

The young driver settled in the driver's seat of the Rolls Royce Phantom. Mum loved to parade it around whenever she thought the paparazzi were nearby. I wagered she thought the paparazzi were definitely looking for me. She had no idea I'd come here to verbally bash her back and forth on the floor a-la Hulk and deliver some very bad news to her.

She thought I'd arrive bearing an engagement announcement.

"He was exactly where he was supposed to be," Sam countered

efficiently. "In Madame Mayhem, the only jurisdiction he was allowed to cover under your contract. Did you want him to *stalk* her?"

Yes.

"No," I scoffed, flicking invisible dirt from under my fingernail. The driver crawled from Heathrow Airport into the unbearable London traffic. I loved my capital city, but it had to be said—everything west of Hammersmith should've been trimmed away from London limits and duly given to Slough as a gift.

"But he was conveniently absent each time she got into trouble."

"He was doing the fucking filing to find excuses to be near her! This is a highly trained former CIA agent." Sam's fist crashed into an object on the other end of the line, shattering it to pieces.

I pulled my phone away from my ear and scowled at it. I had recently (and by recently, I mean in the past ten minutes) decided I was no longer a smoker. There was simply no justification to engage in such a harmful habit. My unborn child deserved more than an increased chance at developing asthma and a house that smelled like a strip club.

"At any rate," I said coolly, "I want to know where she is right now. What do your men have for me? Make it good."

"She's at her parents'."

"And …?"

"And she's safe."

"She hates her dad," I mumbled, a fact that wasn't intended for his ears. I was worried. Not about Belle being unhappy with the situation—the little wench deserved a bit of trouble after what she'd put me through—but for her father's safety.

"Daddy issues, huh?" Sam chuckled darkly. "Couldn't have seen that from miles away."

"Bugger off."

"Not sure what it means, but right back at you, *mate*," he volleyed with an unfortunate, yet bizarrely accurate Australian accent.

"Wrong nationality, wanker. Make sure she doesn't leave their sight this time," I warned. "Heads will roll if they lose her again."

"Whose heads?"

"Yours, for starters."

"Is that a threat?" he asked.

"No," I said calmly. "It's a promise. Boston may fear you, Brennan, but I don't. Keep my missus safe or bear my wrath."

There was a beat of silence, in which I supposed Sam considered whether he wanted to go to war or simply bow out of the argument.

"Look, she doesn't seem to be venturing outside their house very often," he said finally. "I think having people on the house at this point is excessive. Almost counterproductive. Because as it stands only a handful of people know where she is. If there's surveillance on her ass, it may draw more attention."

This surprised me. Belle was the kind of thrill-seeking woman to arrange a public orgy in the Vatican. And I couldn't imagine her parents' house offered many attractions. Nonetheless, it was good news.

I was going to deal with her as soon as I got back to Boston, which should be within the next twenty-four hours.

"Fine. No surveillance."

"Hallelujah."

"It was terrible doing business with you."

He hung up on my arse. *Wanker*.

I sat back in the leather seat and drummed my knee, taking London in as it zipped past my window. The congenital grayness, the oldness of a city which had braved wars, plagues, fires, terrorism, and even Boris Johnson as mayor (this is not a political statement; I simply found the man entirely too eccentric to be anything other than a party clown).

I thought about how I'd left Louisa in Boston. Her tear-clogged throat, red eyes, and wilted posture. How I was never going to see her again, apologize to her again, explain myself again—and how I was completely fine with no longer hating myself for a decision I'd made when I was eighteen.

I wasn't fair to her.

But then my father wasn't fair to *me*.

I'd spent my entire adult life trying to repent for what I did to her by depriving myself of things. It was time to let go.

Show me a person with no wrongdoing in their past and I'll show you a liar.

"Sir …" The young man behind the wheel caught my eye through the rearview mirror.

I turned my face to him, arching a brow.

"May I ask you something?"

He had an old-school, cockney accent. The kind I'd only heard in movies.

"Go ahead."

"How's Boston in comparison to home?"

I thought about the weather—better.

The underground system—the T wasn't even half as reliable as the tube.

The people—both were brash and held high, no-bullshit standards.

Culturally, London was superior.

Culinary-wise, Boston was better.

But at the end of the day, none of that mattered.

"Boston is home to me," I heard myself say. "But London will always be my mistress."

And it was right there and then that I realized home was where Emmabelle Penrose was, and that I was in love with the maddening, infuriating, terribly unpredictable woman. That, in fact, Sweven had been more than a conquest, a game, something I wanted for myself simply because I knew I couldn't have it. She was the pinnacle. The end game. The *one*.

And even if she didn't know any of that.

She had to know that I loved her.

I had to tell her.

I suppose you could say I paid a surprise visit to my mother, not because she hadn't been expecting me—she had—but because I falsely indicated to her that I intended on making a pit stop in Surrey to visit an old friend.

Anyone who knew me was also aware I hadn't kept in touch with anyone from my previous life. Mum didn't quite know me, so she bought into the story.

Worse still, I didn't really know *her* anymore.

But I was about to get a glimpse of the real her.

I'd walk into Whitehall Court Castle unannounced and see what things looked like when they weren't putting on a show for me.

I slapped the grand double doors open. Two frantic servants were at my heel, trying to physically stop me from entering the manor.

"Please, sir! She isn't expecting you!"

"Mr. Whitehall, I beg you!"

"My mansion, my business." I breezed in, my loafers clicking on the golden marble into the main drawing room. The beams above my head closed in on me like trees in a forest.

"Devon!" Mum cried out, darting up from the 19th century Victorian French settee, a flute of champagne in her hand. I stopped dead at the entrance, taking the scene in front of me in.

Hustling and bustling around her, servants were removing a Rembrandt van Rijn painting and expensive furniture from the room, item by item, to make it appear bare and scanty. Cecilia was perched in front of the winged piano, looking like a woman who not only wasn't on suicide watch, but would happily commit murder *herself* if it threatened to bite into her leisure time. She wore a Prada dress—from this season—and next to her was the so-called bane of her existence, Drew, who seemed content playing with the locks of her blond hair before I walked into the scene.

"Devon?" I asked with a mocking expression. As I made my way to Mum, she put her champagne aside and was now pushing servants out of the room, shoveling them out into the vast hallway to cover for her indiscretions. She wanted me to think the house was empty, crumbling. That she was a step away from an empty fridge, she was so poor. "Whatever happened to *Devvie*?"

When the last of the servants were out the door, Mum threw herself at me, hugging me with a sob. "It's so good to see you. We weren't expecting you until dinnertime. Is your friend in Surrey all right?"

"My friend in Surrey does not exist, so it is hard to tell," I drawled. Shrugging off her touch and sauntering toward the regency bar cart, I poured myself a generous glass of brandy.

"It's not what it looks like." It was Cece's turn to stand up from the piano and rush toward me, her face flushed. She twisted the hem of her dress in her fists. "I mean, yes, it is what it looks like, in a way, I suppose, but we didn't want you to think our struggle is not real. We needed to give you a push."

I threw the brandy down my throat, pointing at my sister with the empty glass. "Are you suicidal?" I asked, pointblank.

She winced visibly. "I … umm … no."

"Have you ever been?"

She squirmed. "I had moments when I was depressed—"

"Welcome to life. It's a pile of shite. That's not what I asked."

"No," she admitted finally.

I swung my gaze from her to her husband, who was scrambling up from the piano seat, wobbling over to us, still wearing silk pajamas that did no favors for his thighs. These were the people I'd worried about for the past two decades. The ones I'd been sending checks and letters to. The folks I'd agonized over.

"Drew, can I call you Drew?" I asked with a winning smile.

"Well, I—"

"Never mind. I was being polite. I am going to call you whatever the fuck I want to call you. Are you good to my sister, arsehole?"

"I-I think so." He shifted uncomfortably from one foot to the other, looking around, as if this was a test with a definite answer and he hadn't prepared for it.

"Have you ever held a job?"

"I was a business consultant for a nonprofit organization after I finished uni."

"Did you know anyone on the board?"

He winced. "Does my dad count?"

I don't know, is the Queen English?

"Do you have a health issue keeping you from working?"

"My stomach gets very upset when I'm nervous."

"Very well. Work your way to a paycheck, and you'll have no reason to be nervous."

Next, I turned to look at my mother. By her cloudy expression, she gathered there were no happy announcements coming her way nor confetti and venue-shopping in her immediate future.

"You're not struggling," I said.

"I will, if you don't marry Louisa."

"Sell the valuables you own."

"The family treasures?" Her eyes widened.

"Family treasures are supposed to be the relationships, laughter, and support you get from one another. Not paintings and statues. I suggest you start looking for a profitable job or at the very least find out if you could go on the dole, because there is no way in hell I am marrying a woman who isn't Emmabelle Penrose."

I was already cocked and loaded, ready to fight her over sending people to threaten Sweven. By the power of deduction, I wagered there was no way at least some of the things that happened to her weren't by my mother's order.

"Please, I cannot even hear her name!" Mum covered her ears, shaking her head. "That woman ruined everything. *Everything.*"

"Is that why you sent people after her?" I leaned against the wall, one hand tucked inside my front pocket.

"Excuse me?" She slapped a hand against her chest.

"You heard what I said."

We held each other's stare. Neither of us blinked. She spoke, still staring at me. "Cece, Drew, leave."

They scurried away like rats abandoning ship. I cocked my head sideways, scanning the woman who brought me into this world who stopped caring about me when I didn't shape my life around her vision of her own dreams. I wondered when, exactly, I'd become nothing but a tool for her. In my teens? College years? As a full adult?

"Who did you hire?" I asked frostily.

"Stop being dramatic, Devvie." She tried laughing it off, picking up the champagne glass from the tray next to her, twisting it about. "It wasn't like that."

"How was it, then?"

"I, well … I suppose I did hire a man. His name is Rick. He said he collects debts and such. He has a few soldiers around Boston running errands for him. I just wanted him to scare her off, not harm her, god forbid. She is still carrying my grandchild, you know. I care about those things!"

She cared about her first grandchild like I cared about preserving the life and dignity of treehopper bugs in Turkmenistan.

"Get him on the phone right now. I want to talk to him."

"He won't talk to me." She threw her hands in the air, walking over to the settee she'd occupied minutes ago. Taking out a thin cigarette from her purse, she lit up. "He stopped taking my calls. I've tried everything. Last time we spoke, he said someone got involved in the case. Some common Irish name. Said he doesn't need to deal with this guy. I haven't heard from him since."

Sam Brennan.

"Is he still on the case?" I asked.

"No."

"Give me his details, just in case."

I was going to give them to Sam and ensure Rick knew the next time he got close to Emmabelle, he was going to leave the situation in a body bag.

Mum rolled her eyes, sticking her cigarette into her mouth and scribbling something on a side table by the settee. She tore the paper from a notepad and handed it over to me.

"There. Happy now?"

"No. So he followed her?"

"Sent other people to do it a handful of times. One of them she confronted in quite an uncouth manner to be honest."

"And sent her letters?"

Mummy frowned, taking another drag of her cigarette, folding her arms over her chest. "No. I didn't ask him for that, and highly doubt he took such a liberty."

That meant there was someone else after Sweven, just like I suspected. A second someone.

Frank.

I needed to wrap this up and get back home.

"When did Rick start going after her?"

I wanted to know when it all began. Mum gave me a guilty look.

"Well ..."

"Well?"

"Before she got pregnant," Mum admitted, her shoulders sagging as she puffed on her fag. "After your father passed away, I used Rick to try and see if there were any obstacles that might prevent you from marrying Louisa. He said you were all over this Penrose woman. So we tried to push her out of the picture."

"Real classy."

"Are we going to talk about what's going to happen to me and your sister now that you've officially decided to fail us?" She huffed. "Because this thing with Emmabelle wasn't unprovoked. You must see my point of view. You're about to flush the family's fortune down the drain to make a point about your father."

"No, I'm about to flush the family's fortune down the drain because it comes attached with a stipulation no one should agree to. And also because I'm in love with someone else and refuse to sacrifice my own happiness so you and Cece can drive fancy cars and take monthly vacations in The Maldives."

"Devon, be reasonable!" She snuffed the cigarette out, smoke still escaping her lips as she rushed toward me. She seemed to be trying tough love and groveling simultaneously, which made for quite the odd conversation. "You're burning down a legacy! All you'll be left with is the title."

"I don't care much for the title either," I drawled.

"How dare you!" She slammed her fists against my chest. "You're irrational and vindictive."

"I've tried being reasonable. But there is no reasoning with you people. You're on your own, Ursula. If you want money, go earn it, or better yet, find a sorry sod who is willing to marry you. And on that note, here's a fair warning: if you try to harm the mother of my child ever again, I'm going to end you. I mean that literally. I will end your life as you know it. Spread this message to Cece and Drew too. Oh, and my love, of course." Manners were manners, after all.

"You can't do this to us." She fell to her knees, hugging my ankles. The waterworks started. I stared down at the back of her head with a mixture of annoyance and disgust. "Please, Devon. Please. Marry then divorce Louisa. Just for a bit … I … I … I won't be able to survive! I simply won't."

I shook her touch off of me, stepping away from her embrace.

"If you don't, it's none of my business."

"You know …" She looked up, her eyes shining with madness, anger, and desperation. They were so big, so manic I thought they were going to pop out of their sockets. "I knew. That time when he locked you in the dumbwaiter and cut the electricity off so the pumps wouldn't work … we were both in on that."

Revulsion creeped over my skin.

My mother knew my father had tried to kill me all those years ago, and she was in on the plan.

Our entire relationship, as I knew it, was a lie. She never cared for me. She had simply bided her time because she knew my father would die one day and wanted to be on my good side when she asked me to marry Louisa.

I smiled coldly, stepping away from her. "Consider the will unfulfilled. You're poor now, Mother. Although, really, you have been poor your entire life. Money means nothing in the grand scheme of things when you don't have any integrity. Spare us both the trouble and embarrassment and don't call me anymore. From now on, I won't pick up."

Thirty-Seven

Belle

I FELT LIKE A RARE BIRD. AN EXPLOSION OF COLORS, HIGH HEELS, and outrageous bling as I dragged my faux-crocodile suitcase behind me, slinking into my parents' suburban house. I could feel the neighbors' stares heating the nape of my back through their Roman blinds and sensitive shutters.

I was sure there were plenty of things for a thirty-year-old former party animal to do in the suburbs of Boston.

Unfortunately, I had no idea what they were.

Not that it mattered. I couldn't exactly dance my sorrows away at a roof party, drink to a point of distraction (what a buzzkill you are, Baby Whitehall), or even treat myself to a shopping spree that ended in the same way all shopping sprees should end—munching on an order of Wetzel's Pretzels cheese dog bites while trying to balance one hundred and fifty shopping bags, their handles digging into the flesh of my forearms.

Wellesley was not known for its shopping malls and cultural landmarks.

Or for anything, really, other than being close to Boston.

But what depressed me the most was that I didn't even *want* to snort lines of coke with rock stars in public restrooms or sing "Like a Virgin" in a karaoke bar while my friends toppled over with gusto, because I was anything but. I wanted lame, weird things. Like snuggling next to Devon on his freaking eight-thousand-dollar couch (of course I Google shopped it. What am I, an amateur?).

I wanted to watch his boring, four-hour long documentaries about sustainable plastic bags and killer slugs.

I was curled into myself on the guestroom bed when my dad knocked on my door. Mom was out—she was now a part of the Ladies Who Lunch committee. The irony, of course, was that the ladies didn't lunch at all. They munched on dressing-free salads and discussed grave topics, like The Dukans or the Zone diet.

Guessed he wanted to see if we were still on talking terms.

Were we?

"Belly-Belle," he sing-songed. "I'm off to go fishing. How 'bout you join your old man? Can't go wrong with fresh air and sweetened iced tea."

"Pass," I murmured into my pillow.

"Oh c'mon, kiddo." I admired his ability to pretend yesterday didn't happen and at the same time suck up to me *because* of yesterday.

"I'm busy today."

"You don't look busy to me."

"You know nothing about my life, Dad."

"I know everything about your life, Belly-Belle. I know about your club, about your dates, about your friends, about your fears. I know, for instance, that you are miserable right now, and it can't just be about me. You went a lifetime pretending it didn't happen. Something's eatin' you up. Let me help."

Thing was he couldn't help.

No one could help the lost cause that was Emmabelle Penrose.

The vixen who didn't care so much about sex after all, but about intimacy. I wanted to know what it felt like to belong to someone. But not just anyone. To a devilish, blue-eyed rake.

"Ugh, why are you so obsessed with me," I moaned, forcing myself off the bed and dragging my feet along the floor. I wrestled into a pair of daisy dukes, leaving them unbuttoned because of Baby Whitehall, and threw on a baggy, ruffled white top. I didn't look ready for fishing anything that wasn't compliments about my killer legs, but here we were.

The drive to Lake Waban passed in silence, punctuated by Dad asking questions about Devon, work, and Persy. I answered with the enthusiasm of a woman facing death row—and just as much liveliness. Once we arrived, he rented a boat, hurled all of his fishing gear into it, and rowed to the middle of the lake.

On the boat, I complained about my early maternity leave from Madame Mayhem. Dad told me that work was a distraction from life and that life wasn't a distraction from work, and that I had my priorities all wrong. It sounded like a botched inspirational quote by John Lennon, but he was trying so hard I didn't scold him for it.

"And besides, we need to meet this Devon guy." Dad flipped his ball cap backward, trying to make me laugh, to no avail.

"Why?" I scrunched my nose. "We're not together."

"You will be." Dad spun the fishing reel, tugging at it while something in the water flipped about, trying to escape.

I huffed, watching as he pulled the fish out—a silver-scaled, helpless looking thing. Dad grabbed a fillet knife, cutting the fish's throat and letting it bleed into the water. The fish stopped flapping, succumbing to its destiny. Dad swathed the fish in a plastic wrap and threw it into an ice-filled container.

"How do you know?" I asked.

He raised his eyebrows. "To fish?"

"No, that Devon and I will end up together." I shifted uncomfortably on the other side of the boat.

"Oh. I just do."

"That's not an answer."

"Of course it is, honey." He smiled at me lovingly, handing me over the fillet knife and a pack of alcohol wipes to clean it. "And it's a good one too."

About an hour into our fishing session, we bumped into one of

Dad's new friends from town. *Literally*. Our boat kissed his while he accidentally drifted in our direction. Dad immediately reached for me, making sure I didn't slip or get hurt. Then he laughed, his eyes lighting up.

"Hey, Bryan."

"John! I thought I'd seen you out here."

"Weather's too nice to pass up. Have you met my daughter?" The pride in Dad's voice was tangible, sending frissons of pleasure down my spine.

"Can't say I have. Ma'am." Bryan tipped his straw hat down.

There was an introduction, followed by thirty minutes of fishing talk. I yawned, glancing around us. I understood that some people enjoyed nature and its peacefulness. Personally, I couldn't live anywhere where the air wasn't polluted and the crime wasn't at least a little bit out of control.

I decided to finally turn my phone on and check my messages. I hadn't done that in days, though I used my parents' landline to call Persy, Ash, and Sailor.

I scrolled through my phone when a message popped on my screen. It was fresh from twenty minutes ago.

Devon: Where are you?

It was time to face the music. Well, the screaming, really.

Belle: Fishing.

Devon: FISHING?

Belle: Yes.

Devon: Is this code for something?

Belle: Get your mind out of the gutter.

Devon: Hey, you were the one to put it in there in the first place.

Devon: You have a lot to answer for, young lady.

Belle: Ugh. Call me young again. Someone just called me ma'am.

Devon: Give me his details. I'll handle him.

Devon: Where are you fishing?

My eyes dragged up from the screen, and I looked around me. Was the middle of nowhere a sufficient reply?

Belle: Doesn't matter. I'll come meet you. We need to talk.

I was going to tell him that I'd made a terrible mistake, that I was sorry, that I was an idiot (there was a good chance I was going to say that *twice*), that I received—and promptly burned—the check Louisa had given me, and please, please, *pleasepleaseplease* could he take me back.

I'd learned my lesson. Dad scarred me, and Mr. Locken gutted me, but apparently, I still had a beating heart behind the heavy layers of façade. And that heart belonged to him.

Devon: Don't come.

Belle: ...?

But he never replied.

Don't come.

No explanation, no nothing.

So *of course* I was going.

I was going just to spite him! The bastard. I was going there right now. Well, maybe I'd put on something a little more dignified than a pair of daisy dukes I couldn't button and a shirt that screamed *I just spent the last few days with my best friends, Easy Cheese and Dancing with the Stars.*

"Dad, I have to go."

Dad and Bryan conducted a short but meaningful conversation using their eyebrows alone, perplexed that someone would want to do *anything* other than sit idly in the middle of a huge blob of water and wait for fish to bite their baits.

"Okay, honey. Let me wrap this up."

"No, I'll go alone."

"Are you sure?" he asked.

There was no point in him joining me. I was changing my clothes and heading straight to Boston to demand Devon Whitehall allow me to come back to him and love me.

"Positive."

"All right. You can take the car. Bryan'll give me a ride home."

"Awesome. What a great guy." Not super great, since he called me ma'am, but not the worst either, I guess.

Dad rowed back to shore, tucked me into the driver's seat and kissed my hair. "Stay safe, kiddo."

I bolted back to my parents' house. On my way there, I assured myself that everything would be okay. I would go straight to Devon and have my gun on me at all times. I would remain safe and maybe broach the subject of us moving somewhere else, where half the population wasn't trying to kill me.

When I got back to my parents', the first thing I did after double-locking the door was toss my bag on a side table. I removed items of clothing as I made my way up to the guestroom, already deciding I was going to wear the emerald green mini dress that made my eyes— and tits—pop.

Padding barefoot across the wooden floor, I stopped when I reached the threshold of the guestroom.

There was someone sitting on the edge of my bed.

I jumped backward, resisting the urge to yelp and draw attention. *Frank.*

Turning back on my heel, I raced down the stairway, heading back to the landing to fetch the gun inside my bag. He grabbed me around my shoulders and pulled me back. My feet were up in the air. My back slammed against his chest. He wrapped an arm around my neck in a chokehold and squeezed, cutting off my air supply. My fingers dug into his arm, clawing to get him to let go. I tried to scream, but all my mouth produced was a low, pained hiss.

Baby Whitehall, I thought frantically. *I have to save my baby.*

Putting my Krav Maga lessons to good use, I reached behind to try and get ahold of his opposite arm, but he was quicker, gathering my hands and squeezing them together behind my back.

"I don't think so. You ruined my life. It's high time I ruin yours."

His breath skated over the side of my neck. It reeked of tobacco and sugary soda. I tried to sink my teeth into his arm, but he pulled back quickly, readjusting his grip on my neck with one arm and cradling my pregnant belly in the other.

"Shhh." His teeth grazed the shell of my ear. "Don't make me do something I'll regret."

And then I felt it.

The cold, sharp metal grazing the bottom of my belly.

I froze like a statue. Closed my eyes, the air rattling in my lungs.

He was going to give me a premature C-section if I didn't do as he said.

Baby Whitehall fluttered in my belly excitedly, awake and aware of the commotion.

I'm sorry, Baby Whitehall. I'm so, so, so sorry.

"Are you going to be a good girl?" Frank's breath fanned against the side of my neck.

I nodded, the bitter taste of bile exploding in my mouth. My mother wasn't due to be home for another two hours, and Dad could spend the entire day at the lake. Persy wouldn't drop by without letting us know first.

I was officially, completely, and royally screwed.

"Now we're talking." Frank shoved me forward, making me stumble down the first stair. We went down the stairs silently, my knees bumping together with fear. He sat me down in front of the fireplace, grabbed a roll of heavy-duty tape from the back of his jeans, and taped my wrists and feet so I was immobile on the couch. He ripped the shirt off of my body, the fabric slicing through my skin, leaving red marks in its wake. I was wearing nothing but my underwear and bra.

"Stay here." He wiggled his index finger in my face then proceeded to stomp around the house, barricading the doors. He didn't have to do more than push a few chairs against the front and backyard doors.

Dad had a the-enemy-is-upon-us mentality and made the house World War proof.

I knew there was no way in and no way out of this place without dismantling him first.

Frank tossed the keys I'd used to double-lock the door into his pocket, moving toward one of the windows, rapping it with his knuckles.

"Triple-glazed." He whistled, raising his eyebrows and nodding at me approvingly. "Nicely done, John Penrose. Those are expensive as fuck."

He knew my dad's name. I bet the bastard knew a lot about my life since he'd found out I was here.

I scanned my surroundings. It was time to get creative. The only way out for me was through the central air duct work. It was big enough for me to fit, but I'd still have to tear down the vent, which was basically impossible, since my hands and legs were bound.

Frank's eyes traveled to the same air vent I was looking at. He chuckled. "Don't even think about it. Now let's talk."

He strode to the recliner opposite from the couch I was sitting on and took a seat. By the open Dorito bags and cracked soda cans littering the coffee table, I gathered he'd made himself at home before my arrival.

If nothing else, at least now I knew who was responsible for making my life a living hell for the past few months.

I was waiting for Jesus to come to me and tell me *"Now's not your time, child,"* because all other indicators pretty much pointed to my early and tragic demise.

Ugh. Getting offed by a disgruntled ex-employee was such an embarrassing way to die.

"How can I help you, Frank?" I asked, businesslike, which was hard, considering the circumstances.

Baby Whitehall fluttered like crazy in my stomach, and I thought, with a mixture of devastation and exhilaration, how much I wanted this to continue. The flutter. The kicks. And what came after. For the first time in my life, I had something to fight for.

Two somethings.

There was Devon too. And as much as it frightened me to admit it to myself—he wasn't like the men who'd let me down. I'd traded my soul to the devil the day I had taken revenge on Coach. I'd paid for the pleasure of taking a life with my youth, with my joy, with my innocence. Lacking all three made it impossible for me to get attached to a man. But Devon Whitehall wasn't just a man. He was much more.

"You can start by telling me what the fuck I ever did to you!" Frank grabbed the knife he'd threatened me with and pointed at me from across the living room, spitting each word out. "Why'd you fire me when I had a pregnant girlfriend at home? My mom's medical bills ... you know, she passed away two weeks before you fired me. I took a week off. You didn't even send me a sympathy card. Nothing."

Pursing my lips, I closed my eyes and thought back to that period of time. When I wasn't working, I was partying. *Hard.* There were a string of house parties, then charity events, then a girls' Babymoon weekend in Cabo for Persy and Aisling. I'd relied on Ross to play Mommy and Daddy at Madame Mayhem and didn't much care about what was going on in other people's lives. I was busy keeping myself distracted because that was how I coped whenever memories of Mr. Locken and what I'd done to him resurfaced. I didn't care about anything or anyone other than myself.

Worst of all—I didn't remember ever hearing that Frank's mom had passed away.

"I'm sorry for your loss." I tried to sound calm, but my words stumbled over one another. "I really am. But, Frank, I didn't know about your mother, or your girlfriend. Certainly not about your debt. I have a minimum of thirty employees on my payroll at any given time. All I knew was that you copped a feel and harassed one of the burlesque girls."

"That's what she said." He sent his knife crashing against the coffee table between us. The blade kissed the glass, and the thing shattered inward noisily. "You went and told every local reporter I tried to rape her. I couldn't get a job. Not even a temp one. Not even washing the dishes! You humiliated me!"

I swallowed down a yelp.

Baby Whitehall felt like fingers strumming piano keys, running from left to right then left again.

"Frank, I *saw* you," I insisted, exasperated. "Your hand was on the curve of her ass. Your other hand was shoved between her legs."

I remembered how they both reacted when I walked in on the scene. How she was in tears. How he was in shock.

"I wasn't harassing her." Frank darted up from the beige chaise, grabbing a soda can and smashing it against the wall. Orange liquid splashed across it like an abstract painting, dripping onto the floor. I wanted to believe one of the neighbors might hear the commotion and call for help but knew that the houses were too far apart for that to happen. Damn middle-class suburbia.

"We were having an affair. Christine and I were having an affair. I was fingering her when you walked in on us, and she got scared, because she knew you were a no-bullshit kind of boss and also because it was known around the club that my girlfriend was pregnant. She didn't want to look like a homewrecker or a slut, even though, for the record, she was both, so she made up that story that I harassed her!"

I deeply resented his characterization of Christine, even though I didn't agree with her behavior. It took two to tango, and no one forced this asshole to have an affair with her. Of course, this was hardly the time to retaliate by sending truth bombs his way.

"I didn't know all that." I hated how small my voice was.

"Yeah, well, that's because you never bothered giving half a shit about anything that wasn't your club, your parties, your clothes, and your one-night stands. Christine went after me. She knew I had access to Ross' calendar and schedule. I messed with it, giving her better hours and shifts when he wasn't looking." He picked up his knife from the ocean of broken glass in the middle of the living room, wiping it on the side of his jeans.

I moved uncomfortably on the couch. The duct tape was digging into my wrists, and I wanted to stretch my legs.

"Look, Frank, I'm sorry if—"

"I'm not done!" he roared, getting in my face. His cheeks were flushed, his eyes dancing with madness. "I lost everything. My girlfriend found out—of course she did. I got fired publicly, after all, and no one would hire me. Every time we left the house, a reporter or a photographer loitered nearby, because everyone likes a train-wreck story of a guy with a pregnant teenage girlfriend who harassed a burlesque girl and got his ass kicked by the manager of a club for it. My girlfriend didn't leave, but she wouldn't fucking let that shit go. Christine, the bitch, left the burlesque show and moved back to Cincinnati to marry some old fuck. He's about to be in for a surprise when he realizes the baby she's cooking for him belongs to me. And me? I got hooked on fentanyl. Because, you know, why the hell not?" He cackled tonelessly.

Oh boy.

"If you'd have told me—"

"You'd have done nothing," he barked, and I knew it was the truth. "You hate men. Everyone knows that. Everyone!"

I wanted to throw up. All this time, I was partly responsible for his girlfriend's condition. I remembered seeing her at *buybuy Baby*. How distressed she looked.

He began kicking things around as he spoke, determined to inflict as much destruction on me and mine. "Things got really bad at home. After a while, I just up and left. Like my daddy did before I was born. I couldn't deal with it. And now there's this cycle, you see. That you created. My son is going to come into this world with nothing while your kid is going to come into this world with everything. And why? Because you have a pretty face? A tight ass? Because your sister married some rich guy and now you two are prancing around like millionaires all day?"

I knew where this was going, and I didn't like it. Not one bit.

"You were the one who went after me. But … but who was that man who came to Madame Mayhem to threaten me?"

"My stepdad." Frank shrugged. "Did me a solid. Good guy, huh?"

"And the man at Boston Common?"

"Boston Common?" He frowned. "Ain't nobody went for you there."

My head was spinning. There were a few people after me. Frank was on a roll, though, and wasn't exactly in the mood to answer any more of my questions.

"Well, I'm here to tell you if my baby is not going to have a future—and I certainly can't give him a future…" his blade found my heart, moving down my skin toward my belly as he crouched down before me, "…then yours is not going to have one either."

"Frank, please—"

The knife halted on my belly.

He smiled as he poked the blade into it, breaking the skin.

And that was when one of the living room walls came crashing down.

Devon

I arrived at the Penrose parents' suburban house to find Belle's father's truck parked out front. Though it wasn't necessarily in my plans to try and win Mr. Penrose over by explaining that my mother had sent people to threaten his daughter and that I may or may not had planned to marry someone else at one point, I was going to have to deal with him. After I informed Belle we were getting married this week and stopping this nonsense, of course.

I walked over to the door, determined, and raised my knuckles to rap the door.

Just then, a crash sounded from the inside. It sounded like glass shattering. I moved toward one of the windows, peeking inside.

Belle was sitting on the couch, mostly naked and duct taped while a Frank-looking-guy (I'd never seen the man, but again, deductive reasoning) stood above a pile of glass, a knife at his feet. I pressed my hands to the glass and roared, but they couldn't hear me. I could tell by the thickness of the glass, and by the blurry way I saw them, that it was too thick.

I rushed over to the door and tried to pick the lock, but *fuck*, it wouldn't budge. It wasn't a flimsy door either. It was one of those steel security doors Cillian had installed in his mansion the day Astor was born. I couldn't kick that shit down if I had The Rock's quads.

Frantically, I rounded the house, trying to find a way to break in. I tilted my head and looked up to see if the windows on the second floor were open or maybe not triple glazed. No such luck.

After a quick inspection, I realized the only way in was through the ventilation. There was only one problem: confined places and I weren't exactly good friends.

Staring at the exhaust hole on the side of the house, I reminded myself that I didn't have a choice. That it was either me dying in a space smaller than the dumbwaiter or Belle … *Fuck*, I couldn't even begin to think about what could happen to her.

Pulling my phone out of my pocket, I called 911 and explained the situation, giving them the address, then crouched into the hole and crawled right in.

It wasn't the type of air duct you saw in the movies. The square, never-ending metal labyrinth you could crawl comfortably in. It was a round, flimsy one that could only carry my weight because it was bellied between bricks, the surface uneven from every direction. It felt like skulking into someone's arsehole. I had to army-crawl on my elbows and knees, collecting dust, mold, dirt, and mites on my Cucinelli suit, which turned from navy blue to gray.

My throat was thick with dirt, and every one of my muscles felt strained and shaky. Putting myself in this position was something I never thought I'd do. But I had to. I had to save her. To help ease the pain, I squeezed my eyes shut and kept pushing. I sometimes knocked into a dead end, and maneuvered myself left, right, up, and down until I found the next curve to take what would lead me to the other side.

You're not going to die.

You're not going to die.

You're not going to die.

I pushed harder, faster, my legs cramping and my biceps hurting. After a few feet, I heard voices again. It was only then that I dared open my eyes. They stung with sweat and dust. The air-con fan looked back at me. I was only a few feet away.

The voice rose from underneath it.

"If you'd have told me—" Emmabelle tried, her voice brave and strong and everything she was that I loved so much.

"You'd have done nothing," he roared.

I pushed myself farther, wriggling like a worm toward the opening of the air duct.

"Well, I'm here to tell you if my baby is not going to have a future—and I certainly can't give him a future, then yours is not going to have one either …"

Just as he said it, I punched the air duct open, and fell right through it, bringing half the wall down with me.

I lifted myself up, even though a sharp, tear-jerking pain in my left leg told me I'd almost certainly broke it.

Frank turned around, and I used the element of surprise to pounce on him, throwing all my weight against him and reaching for his knife. Unfortunately, he had the upper hand of not needing to crawl his way into this place seconds ago. He stuck the knife in my shoulder, twisting it about. I let out a growl, pushing my fingers into his eye sockets. I had no idea what I was doing. I just knew I wasn't going to die before knowing Emmabelle was safe.

From my periphery, I could see Belle hopping her way from the couch to the kitchen awkwardly, still bound at the ankles and wrists. A line of blood ran down from under her belly button, disappearing into her panties. My mind kicked into overdrive. If something happened to that baby … *my* baby …

"Ahhh!" Frank was screaming, letting go of the knife—which was still, by the fucking way, in my shoulder—waving his arms in the air helplessly. "My eyes! My eyes!"

There was a warm pool of blood underneath us, and I knew it belonged to me. I couldn't keep it up any longer. Concentrating, I tried to scoop out one of his eyeballs, which wasn't as easy as he made it sound, since his eye sockets were pure, dense bone and I had to crack through them.

"Stop!" Frank roared. "Stop!"

But then he was the one who stopped.

In fact, he fell right on top of me, driving the knife even deeper into my shoulder as he collapsed.

There was a steak knife stuck in his back. And above him, stood Emmabelle, breathing hard.

Now, I decided, was a perfect time to succumb to unconsciousness. So that was what I did.

Thirty-Eight

Devon

I WOKE UP IN A HOSPITAL BED.

Everything hurt.

Everything, other than my shoulder, which I couldn't feel at all. I snuck a peek down at it, frowning, and saw that it was bandaged and in a sling.

My eyes wandered around the room, which seemed to be never-ending, wall-to-wall light oak cabinets and medical equipment.

Cillian stood in front of a window overlooking the parking lot, talking quietly on the phone. Hunter sat on a recliner beside him, typing on his laptop, and I could hear Sam's voice carrying in from the hallway.

My mates were here.

My family, naturally, was not.

But what really worried me was Sweven.

"Emmabelle."

That was the first word that left my mouth.

Cillian swiveled, his signature cold gaze rolling over me like an icicle.

"She's fine," he assured me. "Persephone finally managed to pry her away from your side to get some checkups done. The doctors are keeping her for observation."

"I need to see her."

"She's three rooms down." Hunter looked up from his laptop, closing it.

I stared at him point-blank and said again, "I *need* to see her."

"Okay, okay. A crazy bitch with some unsolved daddy issues coming right up," Hunter murmured, placing his laptop on the light oak wooden table and scurrying out of the room.

I closed my eyes, dropping my head back to the pillow. "Is this all my bloody American health insurance bought me? This place is one fruit bowl away from being someone's 90's-style kitchen."

"Be thankful the wood you're surrounded by isn't a coffin," Cillian clipped.

The door opened, and Sam walked in. I'd never been overtly happy to see the guy, but now I was downright disappointed. I was expecting Belle.

He closed the door after him, holding his phone. "I'm sure you'd like to know my service is no longer needed. Simon's out too. Frank's dead—thanks to the deranged woman you're in love with—and the man your mother hired, Rick Lawhon, is taken care of."

I knew taken care of was code for pining for the fjords. Brennan was an extremely prolific killer. If we ever hit an overpopulation issue in the States, I had no doubt he'd be the bloke to fix it.

"I need to see her." I decided to simply parrot myself until Belle was put in front of me, alive, well, and happily pregnant. Still, I couldn't ask either of them if the baby was okay. The question seemed too intimate, and I didn't trust myself not to bawl, no matter the answer.

"Persephone is pushing her wheelchair down the hallway now," Sam said.

Wheelchair?

"Coming through. Please make room," Persy chirped just then. Cillian hurried to open the door for her, and she walked in, pushing Sweven inside.

Emmabelle looked tired in a pale blue hospital gown. Her hands were folded in front of her. I couldn't see her stomach from that angle.

Persephone parked her at the edge of my hospital bed.

I swallowed hard, everything inside me burning.

"Everybody get out. I need to speak to Belle."

They all did.

Belle stared at me for a moment, blinking slowly, as if I was a complete stranger.

Bloody hell, I hoped she hadn't lost her memory. I had just committed a heroic act, possibly the *only* heroic act I'd ever committed—past, present, and future—and I needed her to know about it so we could stop fucking around.

"The baby …" I started then stopped. A part of me was frightened to know. I *did* see blood before I passed out at her parents'.

She leaned forward, resting her cold, clammy hand against my warm one on the bed. "She's fine."

I nodded gravely, my jaw tense so I wouldn't weep in relief, like a little girl.

"Good. And you? How are you feeling?" I asked.

"I'm also fine."

"Lovely."

Silence. I tried to twitch my fingers to put my hand on top of hers. But my entire arm and shoulder felt immobile.

"Am I paralyzed?" I asked conversationally.

"No." She smiled, her eyes shining. "But you're under the influence of painkillers, dude."

"Marvelous." I smiled tiredly.

We both laughed.

"You got into an air duct for me," Belle choked on the words. "And you're claustrophobic."

Finally, I was recognized for my greatness.

"You were in danger." I half-shrugged with my healthy shoulder. "It was a no-brainer."

This made her break down in tears. She buried her head in the linen next to my legs, her whole body quivering with sobs.

"I'm so sorry, Devon. I screwed everything up, didn't I?"

"Oh, shush, darling. Of course not." I made an effort to move my hand—and this time succeeded—stroking her hair.

For the record she absolutely *did* cock up, but I was being a gentleman about it.

"Also, what are you referring to exactly, when you say you screwed everything up?" I cleared my throat.

She looked up, wiping her tears with the back of her sleeve, sniffling. "I took a check from Louisa ..." She hiccupped.

"I know." I continued to stroke her cheek. "She told me."

"And then I left you without even explaining myself."

"Yes. Yes. I was there for the entire show, remember?" I grinned.

She stopped. Tilted her head. Frowned.

"Devon, why aren't you mad at me?" she demanded. "It is not okay for you to accept this kind of behavior. What are you, a doormat?"

"A doormat, no," I said, amused, "but I am in love with a woman who suffered severe trauma when she was a wee girl. Love has failed you many times. You were never shy about it. I was the one who pushed you out of your comfort zone."

"My comfort zone sucked." She elevated an eyebrow, looking more and more like herself. I tried hard not to laugh, tilting my head against the pillow as I studied her.

"I know, Sweven."

"I thought you'd never call me that anymore." Her eyes filled with fresh tears.

"Why?" Now I *did* laugh.

"Because I told you to marry someone else."

"I don't know how to break this to you…" I laced my fingers in hers "…but not every single thing you are going to tell me to do will be followed through dutifully."

There was contemplative silence, in which both of us realized we were lucky to be here, in this room, alive.

"I burned the check," she sniffed, finally.

"I know." I had no doubt in my mind she'd spurn taking money from Louisa, even if she had been tempted for a moment or two. Which was why I kept fighting for her, even when things were looking dreadful. "Why are you in a wheelchair?"

"Hospital policy."

"Why didn't you use the gun?" I asked out of nowhere.

She flinched. It took us both back to that scene, when Frank attacked her.

"I was too afraid I'd accidentally kill you. I didn't want to take any chances."

"That is the most romantic thing you've ever said to me."

"And also…" she drew a breath, closing her eyes "…my hands are far from clean in this department." She opened her eyes again, and she looked different this time. Complex, powerful, dangerous. A Valkyrie. I swore she stood six inches taller than me in that moment. "I know the consequences and complexities of taking a life. I didn't want to do it unless I absolutely had to." She hoisted herself up on the bed, nestling next to me. Her hard, round stomach pressed against my side. My cock immediately stood up in appreciation. She laced her arms over me, careful not to touch my shoulder, and pressed her mouth to my ear.

"Devon Whitehall, you're the most gorgeous, funny, smart, witty, bougie man on planet Earth, and I'm madly in love with you. Have been from the moment our paths crossed. And it pains me to say that I don't think any man could ever measure up to you, which is why I might as well stop fighting this."

"Bloody right." I turned to kiss her lips softly. "Sweven."

"No," she said.

I pulled away from her, frowning. "You don't know what I was about to ask."

"Yes, I do, and the answer is no. I want to ask you that. But I want to do it properly. On one knee." Belle pursed her lips.

"There are far more interesting things you can do on your knees for me, sweetheart. Permit me this indulgence."

"No can do, hottie." She leaned in to kiss my nose then gave it a mocking bite. "I love you, though."

"Love you too."

"Devon …" she hesitated. *Oh no*, I thought. I couldn't take more.

"Yes, my love?"

"Can I tell you something?"

"Of course."

"Frank is not the only person I've killed in my life. I just want to come clean, before we take the next step."

Shite. Well, if there was a body we needed to get rid of, I suppose that was just the way it was going to be. Personally, I wasn't a fan of people being killed, for any reason, but for Belle … well, I mean, what could a man do?

"I'll take care of it," I clipped.

She looked at me funnily then began to laugh. What was so funny? But then she said, "No, no. It's not recent. It happened a long time ago. It was the person who abused me."

"Your dad?" I asked confused.

Now she looked disordered. "My dad? He didn't abuse me."

"I thought you two had a weird relationship."

"Yeah. I held a grudge because he cheated on my mom."

"Oh," I said for lack of a better answer. "So, tell me about the other person."

And she did.

She told me about Mr. Locken, about her youth, about the attack, about the miscarriage, and about her revenge. At the end of it all, I gathered her into my arms and kissed her with such ferocity I thought we would both burn alive.

"Do you still love me, then?" she asked uncertainly.

"Love is a very weak word for what I feel for you, Sweven."

"Thanks for making me lose my appetite. You should start your own diet method." Sailor strode into the room followed by Persephone and Aisling, their husbands not too far behind. Suddenly, the room was full of people who'd been there for me, and just then I realized that I *did* have a family. We just weren't blood related.

"You two getting married?" Sam leaned against the foot of the bed, draping an arm over Aisling's shoulder.

"Not yet, I need to propose to him first." Belle propped her head against my shoulder, and it hurt like all the bitches on planet Earth, but obviously, I did not say a thing.

"Would you look at that. Not even married, and she already wears the pants in this relationship." Hunter jerked a thumb in her direction, laughing.

"Knowing Devon, he'll find a way to get her out of them." Cillian smiled—and for a second there looked almost human.

Everybody laughed.

This was the essence of family.

Two weeks later, I landed in England.

This time with Belle.

She was in her second trimester, the perfect time for travel—according to Doctor Bjorn, anyway.

"I don't know what's worse, my constipation or my heartburn," the love of my life waxed poetic as she slid into the Range Rover waiting for us at Heathrow. This time, I opted to drive myself around London. I preferred conducting my business without running the risk of being spotted by the tabloids.

"I'll have Joanne book an appointment with Doctor Bjorn as soon as we get back home." I kissed the side of her head, starting the car.

"Thanks."

"Are you experiencing any cravings yet? Anything you'd like?" I swerved the Range Rover into a mile-long queue to get out of the airport limits.

"Do true crime podcasts and coal count as cravings?"

"*Sweven.*"

"Chillax," she yawned, gathering her ice-blond locks into a high bun. "No weird cravings. Other than sex."

I was delighted to oblige in that department.

Belle had moved back to my flat as soon as we got discharged from the hospital, and this time there were no games between us. No crazy stalkers either, a lovely development. Unfortunately, the woman still didn't make things easy for me. Two weeks had passed since I'd almost proposed to her at the hospital, and she still hadn't popped the question. I was trying to respect her feminist values, and was also perhaps a tad nervous she'd rip my bollocks off if I asked again.

"Oh! Could you please ask Joanne to ask Doctor Bjorn if it's normal for me to have ankles the size of water bottles?"

I could tell Belle was in the mood to list all the ways Baby Whitehall had turned her body into her own Motel 6, when London caught her eye. She sucked in a breath, her pupils dilating, swallowing those azure irises. "Holy shit, Dev. This place looks like a Harry Potter set."

I looked around to see piles upon piles of stingy, never-ending council flats.

"I'll ask Joanne to book you an appointment with the optometrist while she's at it."

"Shuddup. It's *purty.*"

"I'll show you *purty* once we leave my solicitor's office in Knightsbridge."

"Actually..." she turned to look at me, grinning, "...I'm going solo for a shopping spree. Gotta hit them stores fast and hard to get all my shopping done."

"I'll only take a couple hours." I frowned.

Though Frank and Rick were out of the picture, I was still worried Emmabelle was targeted. Louisa was somewhere out there in the wild, bitter about her unaccomplished mission.

"As much as I'd *love* to listen to two old farts dividing millions of pounds between charities..." she batted her lashes theatrically as if this was a dream come true, "...I think I'm good."

I was going to meet Harry Tindall to sign over my inheritance to the charities of my choice. If the Whitehall wealth was going down the drain, I wanted to flush it to organizations that mattered to me.

"There's no one to watch over you," I argued.

She cocked an eyebrow. "Hi. Nice to meet you. Belle. Been living with myself for thirty years. *Still alive.*"

"Just barely," I scoffed.

"I'm going shopping," she cemented.

"I'm not going to crawl into any more air ducts for you," I warned but knew I was about to concede.

"What? Not even dumbwaiters?" Then, before I could answer, she patted her belly. "Don't worry, Baby Whitehall. Once this old man is out of our way, we'll be binging on fossil fuel and murder mysteries."

I let her go.

This time knowing she was going to come back.

The meeting with Harry Tindall stretched over three and a half hours.

I periodically checked my phone to ensure Belle was fine. And by 'periodically,' I mean, of course, every fifteen seconds.

It was mostly productive in a sense that I ensured the Whitehall wealth had been donated to the British Red Cross, BHF, and MacMillan Cancer Support. Were it up to Edwin Whitehall, the money would have gone straight to hunting organizations, animal testing labs, and various terror groups. The man had had less of a heart than a jellyfish, and I had no doubt of his ability to worsen the human condition, even from beyond the grave.

"This has tax relief written all over it," Tindall purred, balancing the three-ton stack of documents on his desk into one neat pile. "I hope your CPA in the States knows how to make the most out of it."

I stood up. "I'm not doing this for the money."

"I know," he said apologetically, "which is refreshing."

I headed for the door, eager to return to Emmabelle.

"Devon, wait."

Tindall stood up and wobbled to the door, grimacing, like he was about to say something he shouldn't.

I stopped at the threshold, throwing him a look. I knew he was probably less than impressed with how I chose to handle the will, and frankly, I could not give a quarter of a shite regarding the matter.

He twisted his handlebar moustache between his fingers, a villainous gesture that made me stifle a laugh.

"I just wanted you to know that, all in all, you turned out fantastically well, considering your … *upbringing*. Or lack of, really. Edwin was a dear friend, but he was also a difficult man."

"Understatement of the millennium." I patted his shoulder. "Nonetheless, I appreciate it."

"No, really." He gripped the door, stepping in front of me, blocking my way out. "For what it's worth, I'm pleased you didn't succumb to pressure. The Butcharts are … an eccentric bunch. I wouldn't tie my fate in theirs."

"One would think you'd have wanted Louisa and me to have the wedding of a decade." As a friend of my late father, I meant.

"One would be wrong," Tindall said, bowing his head modestly. "You're a marquess now, Devon. You don't need anyone to assert your title."

"Actually," I said, "I don't need the title either."

I smiled, taking one step out his door, already feeling my lungs expanding with fresh air and something else.

Something I'd never felt before.

Freedom.

Though I lamented that I would rather conduct a lengthy and passionate affair with a food processor, Emmabelle insisted we go visit my mother at Whitehall Court Castle before we left the United Kingdom.

"The last person she wants to see is me," I groaned as I drove to Kent on autopilot. I threw her a look. She was buried in green and gold

Harrods shopping bags. "Actually, the last person she wants to see is *you*," I let out a chuckle. "You're a reminder of all the things that went wrong with her plan. If you expect a hug and a spontaneous baby shower, you're in for disappointment."

"Your mom can shove it." Sweven rolled her eyes, checking her scarlet lipstick in the passenger mirror. "I want to see where you grew up."

"Even if I hate the place?"

"*Especially* because you do."

We arrived just before darkness creeped in. The green rolling hills of Kent came into view. I spotted the castle from a distance. It looked darker than I remembered, folding into itself like a shrinking violet.

Like it knew how I'd turned my back on the Whitehall name—and it was not going to forgive me.

"Damn, bro. You make the Fitzpatricks look like the assholes down the street who could afford non-domestic vacations and an in-ground pool," Belle laughed. "This is rich-rich. Like, Mommy-can-I-have-a-diamond-tiara-for-breakfast rich."

"Should I have flaunted my wealth?" I side-eyed her, cocking an eyebrow.

"Are you kidding me?" She threw her arms over my neck, kissing my cheek. Harrods bags collapsed between us, the symbol of love. "I was scared shitless of averagely rich Devon. You know how intimidated I'd have been if I knew you were employing ass-wipers and people whose entire job is to blow cold air on your tea?"

At this point, I lost the thread of the conversation. What was she on about?

I pulled the Range Rover by the front gate, killed the engine, and got out. Sweven rounded the front of the car and joined me.

It was still technically my estate. A few weeks ago, I'd planned to sign it over to my mother. Now, she'd lost that privilege too. Call me petty, but I did not appreciate how she'd sent someone to chase my girlfriend away. So the current deal was that Mum, Cecilia, and Drew were to get the fuck out of there by the end of the month. Where to, I had no idea nor desire to know.

I reached for Belle's hand when I noticed the trucks. There were three of them parked in a neat row in front of the entrance, trunks open. Young blokes in coveralls yelled at each other in Polish as they flung furniture into them.

"Devon?" My sister's voice rang from the woods. I turned to see her making her way from the thick curtain of trees, lifting her skirts in one hand. "Is that really you?"

She hurried toward me. My heart caught in my throat. Just for a second, she looked like the Cece I'd grown up with. The one I held by the legs and pretended her mass of blond curls was a broomstick, sweeping the floor with them while she giggled. I blew raspberries on her bare stomach and told her to stop farting. Taught her how to snap her fingers and whistle "Patience" by Guns N' Roses—and not just the chorus.

"Cecilia. This is my partner, Emmabelle."

Cecilia stopped dead in her tracks, measuring Belle head to toe. I saw Sweven through her eyes. A stunning, self-made woman dressed like she was ready for her Vogue cover shoot.

"Hi." Cece smiled, offering Belle her hand tentatively. Belle used it to jerk Cecilia into an embrace, hugging her tightly.

"You're beautiful," Cecilia blurted after managing to weasel her way out of Belle's hug.

"Thanks! And you're … holding a pogo stick?" Belle poked her lower lip out, her eyes widening a little.

Cecilia laughed, and I realized that she *was* holding a pogo stick. I lit up instantly. "We used to race in the woods with pogo sticks to make it more difficult," I explained. "I won every time."

"Every. Single. Time." Cecilia groaned, mock-punching my arm. "Even after he went to boarding school and I practiced daily. The minute he'd come back, he would leave me to eat dust. I wanted to do it one last time, before … well …" Cecilia turned to smile at me. There was sadness there, yes, but no anger or malice.

"Already moving?" I asked.

She nodded. "Mum can't afford to stay here. The bills are just too much. There's no reason to postpone the inevitable. She is going off to London to stay with a friend."

"What about you and Drew?"

Cece wiped sweaty locks of gold from her forehead. "Drew found a job! Could you believe it?"

"No," I said flatly.

Cece laughed. "Yes! He is starting from the ground up. An admin assistant for a private bank in Canary Wharf. Can you imagine him fetching coffee and getting people's dry cleaning?"

I couldn't, in fact, but I was glad he managed to make use of himself nonetheless.

"I signed up for uni. I think I'm going to become a vet." She smiled sheepishly.

"I'll pay," I offered. After all, Cece was not a part of Mum and Louisa's plans for Belle.

"Cheers." She reached to squeeze my arm. "But a bit of student debt didn't kill anyone last I checked, and it's time I do something on my own, don't you reckon?"

Mum decided to make her grand entrance to this odd scene just then, walking out carrying a box full of knickknacks.

"Cecilia? What on earth is all this commotion? I—"

Belle turned to look at her. The minute their eyes met, two things were clear to me:

1. They both knew who the other one was.
2. If anyone was going to kill anyone, I'd put my money on Sweven and wouldn't even consider it a high-risk investment.

"Oh." Mother put the box down and pressed her fingers on her mouth like we were both naked, standing there in her driveway.

My mother couldn't stop staring at Emmabelle's stomach. The latter, in return, rubbed it protectively, like the woman in front of her was going to try and snatch the baby away if she wasn't careful. Her belly still had a shallow, faint scar from the whole ordeal with Frank, but Belle told me she loved it even more now. The story behind her pregnancy. How precious and rare our child was.

"Belle wanted to see where I grew up before we left. I took care of the will today. Everything's done." I draped an arm over my girlfriend's shoulder.

My mother was still looking at Belle's belly with violent, hungry longing.

"I hope it's to your liking." She took a step toward the belly—and the woman it was attached to—acknowledging her for the very first time. "It's free for you to use. We're moving away. You caught us at a bit of an inconvenient time. Sorry I cannot offer you any refreshments. My kitchens are all packed."

"It's always a dud when *all* the kitchens are packed. I always leave, like, three, fully stocked. Just in case." Emmabelle offered her a feline smile, producing a lollipop from behind her ear—like a cigarette—unwrapping it and shoving it into the side of her mouth.

She was a trickster. An unexpected rainbow in a bleak, gray painting. A woman of many faces, many shapes, and many hats.

Mother swallowed her with her eyes, fascinated. "Are all American women sarcastic?"

"No, ma'am. Only the good ones."

"Your accent is so ... *lazy*."

"You should see my workout routine." Belle sucked hard on the lollipop, looking around her, like she was figuring out what she wanted to do with the place. "Oh, and yours sounds like you were born to chide small children for asking for a second helping of porridge."

That earned a snicker out of me.

"I hear you're a stripper." Mother tilted her chin up, but there was no defiance in her. Only fascination.

I took a step forward, ready to give her a verbal spanking.

Belle put her hand on mine.

"I'm not a stripper, but as someone who knows a few, I can tell you no stripper I've ever met fell behind on her bills. They usually do it to pay their way through college or to just make a quick buck. Lots of tips. Don't slam it before you try it."

My mother nodded. She was impressed despite her best efforts.

"You're different from what I imagined."

"You should've never doubted it. Your son has great taste."

Mum turned to look at me.

"I don't hate her, Devvie," she said with a good portion of resignation.

"Wish I could say the same about you, Mrs. Whitehall." Belle's voice caught her attention, and their gazes locked. "But you hurt the love of my life, and we have an open beef to settle."

"We will." Mum nodded curtly, moving in our direction almost gingerly. "First, can I touch your belly? It is oh-so-full of baby. And looking at both of you, I just know the child will be gorgeous."

"You can cop a feel, Mrs. W," Sweven warned, "but that doesn't mean you're off of my shit list."

Good god, I loved that woman.

My mother put her hands on Belle's belly and grinned up at her. "She's kicking."

"How do you know it's a she?" I asked.

"A woman knows." She pulled away, smiling at us enigmatically.

There was nothing more to say really. This wasn't a part of a reconciliation or an olive branch. It was a quiet, dignified goodbye. A goodbye that should have happened two decades ago.

My mother gathered my hands in hers, and I let her. One last time.

"I just want you to know, I do love you, Devon. In my own roundabout way."

I believed her.

But sometimes, a bit of love was simply not enough.

Thirty-Nine

Devon

"HOW COME MOST AIRLINES DON'T HAVE FIRST-CLASS seats anymore?" Emmabelle pouted next to me on the flight back home later that evening. She was munching on dried fruit.

I flipped a page in the Wall Street Journal, taking a sip of my virgin Bloody Mary, possibly the only virgin I had ever consumed. I would have gone for whiskey, but Belle was the kind of woman who insisted I sympathize with her by staying sober.

"There was hardly any difference between first and business class to begin with. Add to that the fact that business-class seats by definition count as a work expense, and you'll get why most western airlines don't want to be bothered. Why are you asking?" I glanced her way.

She shifted uncomfortably in her seat, looking left and right.

"There's not enough leg room."

I tapped my lap, folding the paper and tucking it under my arm. "Put your feet on me. Problem solved."

"No, not for that. Oh shit. Fuck. I mean … this is bullshit," she scoffed, rubbing at her forehead.

"Please continue." I sat back. "I love it when you whisper sweet nothings to me."

But she didn't. She waited until we were exactly at the halfway point between the United Kingdom and the United States. Beneath us, there was nothing but the giant, deep expanse of the Atlantic. All that kept us in the air was a tiny metal tube and faith. And suddenly, I realized exactly the analogy she was trying to make.

That marriage was about giving and taking.

About making concessions and meeting each other halfway.

"Okay. Don't hate me if I screw it up. Or if I can't get up or anything. This baby is messing with my center of gravity." Belle plucked a square velvet thing from her purse and stood up, before crouching to one knee and groaning in annoyance.

I sat up straight, every bone in my body screaming at me to pay attention.

Everyone in business class turned their sleepy gazes in our direction.

"Devon Whitehall, you're the best man I've ever met by leaps and bounds. I have been in love with you from the first moment our gazes met. I want to grow old with you, to be with you through thick and thin, to have your last name. I know I've been … difficult the past few months, but I promise I'm a changed woman. Please, would you do me the honor of becoming my husband?"

"Yes."

There was more to be said.

But for now, this one word seemed to sum it up.

People clapped from the seats beside us. One woman took a picture of the whole thing on her phone. But somehow I couldn't care less if we wound up being on the cover of a tabloid.

"Oh, Dev." Belle covered her mouth with her hands, tears welling in her eyes. "This is awesome. Now can you please help me up?"

Epilogue

Belle

"DID YOU KNOW THAT WHEN A MALE AND FEMALE anglerfish mate, they melt into each other and share bodies forever? When the anglerfish bloke finds a willing participant, he latches and fuses with her. He loses his eyes and a load of his internal organs until they share a bloodstream." Devon strokes my hand lovingly, peering at me from his seat by my hospital bed.

"Wow," I say dryly, holding my breath to stop the pain. "Sounds familiar."

I turn to Nurse Pretending She's Not There, who beams at both of us like *she's* just given birth, popping my chart back onto the edge of my bed. "I just felt another contraction, and this one was baaaaaad."

So bad I thought my stomach was about to rip in two.

"When's Doctor Bjorn coming?" Devon demanded, spurring into action. "My wife is in pain."

"Your wife is not the first woman ever to give birth," Nurse About to Get Punched notes mildly. She moves to re-fluff the pillows behind me. "Two different doctors came in for a checkup and said everything is perfectly fine. Doctor Bjorn is dealing with some light traffic. He'll be here in a few minutes. You can always opt for an epidural." She peers down at me, shrugging.

"Are you kidding me? I want this kid to know how much I suffered for her and hold it over her head for eternity."

She laughs.

I don't know why.

I am *not* kidding.

"Sweetheart, we're fine. You've still got time," Devon coos, stroking my hair out of my face. It's all nice and romantic, and yet I'm about to push an eight-pound human out of me without any drugs. I slap his hand away. "Go get me Doctor Bjorn."

"As you wish, Mrs. Whitehall." He cannot speed out of the room fast enough, and I remain with Nurse Looking at Me Like I'm Crazy.

Devon and I married each other shortly after we came back from England. It was a small, intimate ceremony in Madame Mayhem. The bridesmaids wore red lingerie and garters and couldn't say shit about it. My wedding—my rules. Sam Brennan almost punched the walls down in the room when he saw his wife ushering me across the aisle in lingerie.

Things have been really awesome between us. Almost too awesome. Sometimes I wake up in the morning and think, *Today is going to be the day I screw this up and bail on him.* Or more often than not, *Today is going to be the day that he leaves me.* That he finally understands that I'm too damaged, too broken, or simply too much.

But somehow neither of these things happen, and I finish my days in the same way: draped over my husband, sharing our stories and experiences from the day, watching TV, laughing, and unveiling piece after piece of one another.

I know there will come a day when I eventually stop worrying that he is going to break me too. That day might not be today, or even tomorrow, but it will arrive.

Devon Whitehall, after all, is the man who taught me the most important life lesson—that you can still believe.

"I got you a doctor." Devon bursts into the room now, panting. "One you know, no less."

"Is it Doctor Bjorn?" I bark, twisting in my hospital bed. "Is it just me or is the baby half-out?" Something's going on between my legs, but for obvious reasons, I'm not in a physical position to bend down and check.

"Better," Devon says, and he and Aisling appear in front of me.

My face falls. "I'm not letting this bitch see my vagina!"

But she is already walking over to the little sink and washing her hands, slapping on a pair of fresh plastic gloves. "I've seen worse."

"Oh, I don't mean that. It looks fantastic. I just don't feel like I'm ready to take our relationship to the next level," I huff.

But then there's another contraction, and I scream, and Devon and Aisling rush toward me.

"Sweven," Devon utters in pain, wiping the sweat from my brow lovingly. "I'm so sorry I put you in this position."

"You put me in twenty-seven different ones. That's why we're here," I quip.

"Still don't want my help?" Aisling elevates an eyebrow. "Because I'm happy to call another doctor."

"Doctor Lynne is here," Nurse No One Asked You volunteers unhelpfully. I don't know Doctor Lynne. And Doctor Bjorn is obviously too busy braving the Boston traffic.

"Fine!" I throw my hands in the air. "Fine. Just get this baby out of me, Ash!"

Devon snatches my hand, Aisling gets to business, and twenty minutes later—just when Doctor Bjorn enters the room full of apologies—Nicola Zara Constance Whitehall is born (and before you ask: of *course* I added Constance to make sure everyone knows she's a royal).

I am not exaggerating when I say my newborn is the prettiest I've ever seen. With smooth, pink skin, bright eyes, and the pinkest lips. She is fragile, innocent, and perfect. I want to protect her from every possible harm. I know I can't but at least for now, I can. But for later, when she grows up, all I can do is try and raise her to be as strong as her mother.

"My goodness, she looks just like her mother." Devon kisses me, then Nicola, then hugs Aisling close.

With my beautiful baby in my arms, and my friends and family waiting outside, I know one thing—everything will not be okay.

Because it's already perfect.

Devon

Six Months Later.

I donate Whitehall Court Castle to the English Heritage Foundation. It becomes a museum. A part of me—an extremely miniscule part of me—is sad that I'm giving up the marquess title. That I will not be in England to ensure Nicola inherits some sort of title. But most of me is glad I am out of this place I could never truly call home.

Nicola is growing at a fast pace. Currently, she is sporting a shock of white curls that look suspiciously like Ramen noodles. She tries to sink her gums into anything she can get her chubby hands on and is a complete delight.

Emmabelle got back to work a month ago. She appointed Ross the official manager of Madame Mayhem and is now focusing on her latest venture. She opened a nonprofit organization for women and men who have been sexually assaulted, providing therapy and help with finding work and getting back on their feet.

Her new secretary, actually—the person to replace Simon and do all the filing and administrative work—is Donna Hammond, Frank's ex-girlfriend. She has a baby boy now. His name is Thomas and sometimes, when he and Nicola are in the same room, they stare at each other with wide, wait-you're-a-tiny-human-too expressions.

Now I'm picking up my wife from her parents'. Nicola naps blissfully in the back of my Bentley. I catch my father-in-law watering the plants on the front porch and roll the passenger window down.

"Hey, John, would you tell Belle I'm outside?"

He looks up from the flowers, smiles, and nods. Dumping the hose on the grass, he walks into the house and comes back with my wife.

Their arms are laced together, and he opens the passenger seat for her and kisses her on the temple before taking a step back.

"Drive safely," he instructs, peeking at Nicola in the back seat, smiling. "She is growing so fast."

"Don't they all," Belle murmurs.

"I love you, Belly-Belle."

"Love you, Daddy."

Belle and I drive to Logan International Airport. The entire journey, my stomach is in knots.

"It's going to be fine," Belle assures me, rubbing at my thigh.

"I know. It's just been a while."

"She's still your family," my wife points out.

I know that too.

When we reach the airport and unbuckle Nicola from her car seat and put her in the carrier strapped onto Belle, my wife automatically heads toward the stairway from the parking lot to the main floor.

"No." I grab her hand, squeezing. "Let's take the elevator."

She whips her head around, frowning. "You sure?"

"Positive, darling."

We wait at the appropriate gate, and even though I've put my family's woes behind me, I'm still on pins and needles. The dumbwaiter had been sealed up shortly after I took control over the estate. It helped soothe some of my anxiety over my claustrophobia, but not all of it.

When Cecilia gave me a call and asked if she could come and see Baby Nicola, I said yes. She wasn't, after all, my mother nor my father. She never tried to kill me. When I asked Belle if I should offer to pay for Cecilia's flight and accommodations, she said, "Absolutely not. Let her show you that she's changed."

And she has. Cecilia paid for everything for this trip with the money she makes working at a library near the university she goes to. She's a changed woman.

When I see my sister coming out of the terminal's gate, I rush toward her, my heart feeling lighter. She looks the same—perhaps she lost a couple pounds—but her smile is different. Genuine. Carefree.

We meet halfway, share a bone-crushing hug, and she cries into my shoulder. I let her. I know she feels it too. Orphaned. After all, when it was all done and dealt with, Ursula turned her back on her too and went to live in London with a friend.

"Thank you for giving me another chance," Cecilia murmurs into my shoulder.

"Thank you for wanting one."

I feel my wife's hand on my back, supporting me, hugging me from behind, making sure I'm never out of balance.

"Come on," Belle says softly. "Let's go make some new family memories."

So we do.

The End

Acknowledgements

The problem about a sweet goodbye is that you're never quite ready for it. The Boston Belles series has been good to me, in a sense that the relationships between the characters did not need any real prompting. They threaded together and immediately got along the minute I put them in the same room. It was a relief, but also a worry, because how do you say goodbye to people who feel so much like your family?

These characters might be fictional, but the people who helped bring them to life are very much alive. They're talented, hardworking, and deserve a round of applause.

First and foremost, I would like to thank Tijuana Turner, my PA, alpha-reader, alpha-momager, and everything in-between. And to the women around us who support me unconditionally and with fierce, burning love: Ratula Roy, Vanessa Villegas, Yamina Kirky, Marta Bor, and Sarah Plocher.

To my graphic designer, Letitia Hasser, who always absolutely nails it, and to Stacey Blake, my formatter, who sprinkles magic dust on everything she touches—thank you.

To my editors: Cate Hogan, Mara White, Max Dobson, and Sarah Plocher. I couldn't have done this without you (and I do mean all of you. It takes a village and a half).

To my agent, Kimberly Brower, for being much more than an agent. I hope you know how much appreciated you are.

I would like to thank the bloggers and the readers who supported this series and especially believed in me. You're the best and I cannot imagine my life without you.

Finally, if you could spare a few seconds to leave a brief, honest review, I would appreciate it so much.

Take care and stay tuned. This is the end, but also a beginning of a brand-new series …

L.J. Shen, xoxo

Stay connected

Join my Newsletter
http://eepurl.com/b8pSuP

Follow me on Instagram
www.instagram.com/authorljshen

Add me on Facebook
www.facebook.com/authorljshen

Also by
L.J. SHEN

Sinners of Saint:

Defy (#0.5)

Vicious (#1)

Ruckus (#2)

Scandalous (#3)

Bane (#4)

All Saints High:

Pretty Reckless (#1)

Broken Knight (#2)

Angry God (#3)

Boston Belles:

The Hunter (#1)

The Villain (#2)

The Monster (#3)

The Rake (#4)

Standalones:

Tyed

Sparrow

Blood to Dust

Midnight Blue

Dirty Headlines

In the Unlikely Event

The Kiss Thief

Playing with Fire

The Devil Wears Black

Bad Cruz

Before you leave, make sure you read a sample of my brand-new romantic comedy, *Bad Cruz*:

Bad Cruz

Prologue

Tennessee

THE IMPORTANT THING TO REMEMBER IS THAT I, TENNESSEE Lilybeth Turner, did not try to kill anyone.

Look, I'm not saying I haven't *contemplated* killing people in the past nor am I virtuous enough to declare that I would be terribly sad to learn if some people (fine, *most* people) in this town found their unfortunate, untimely demise.

But taking a person's life?

Nuh-uh.

That's something I am one-hundred percent incapable of doing.

Mentally, I mean.

Physically, I could totally take a bitch down if I put my mind to it. I'm in pretty good shape from working on my feet all day carrying twenty-pound trays full of greasy food.

Emotionally, I just couldn't live with myself if I knew I'd made someone else's heart stop beating.

And then there's the going to jail part, which I'm not super hot on either. Not that I'm spoiled or anything, but I'm a picky eater, and I've never had a roommate. Why start now?

Plus, I sort of reached my sin quota for the past three decades. Killing someone at this point would be—excuse my pun—overkill. Like I'm hogging all of the bad press Fairhope, North Carolina, has allotted its citizens.

There Messy Nessy goes again. With her out-of-wedlock baby, throat-punching tendencies, and spontaneous murders.

(I shall explain the throat-punching incident in due time. Context is crucial for that story.)

So, now that it is established that I *definitely*, certainly, unquestionably did *not* try to kill anyone, there is one thing I should make clear:

Gabriella Holland deserved to die.

One

Tennessee

THERE WAS A NINETY-NINE POINT NINE PERCENT CHANCE I was going to kill someone in this diner this sunny, unassuming afternoon.

The teenager with the yellow *Drew* hoodie, colorful braces, and stoned expression deliberately dropped his fork under the table of the red vinyl booth he occupied.

"Oops," he drawled wryly. "Clumsy me. Are you gonna pick that up or what?"

He flashed me a grin full of metal and waffle chunks. His three friends cackled in the background, elbowing each other with meaningful winks.

I stared at him blankly, wondering if I wanted to poison or strangle him. Poison, I decided, was better. Might be a coward's way to kill, but at least I wouldn't have to risk a broken nail.

My gelled, pointy, Cardi-B-style nail art was precious to me.

His neck, decidedly, was not.

"Don't you have hands?" I popped my pink gum in his face, batting my fake eyelashes, playing the part this town gave me—the airheaded bimbo with the big blond hair who was barely literate and destined to serve them burgers for eternity.

"I do, and I'd love to show you what they're capable of."

His friends howled, some of them rolling into a coughing fit, clapping and enjoying the show. I felt Jerry, my boss, glaring at me from across the counter while wiping it furiously with a dishcloth approximately the same age as me.

His gaze told me not to "accidentally" spit my gum into their fountain soda (Tim Trapp had it coming; he'd insinuated I should become a hooker to put my son through college). Apparently, we couldn't afford the legal fees nor the problematic reputation.

Jerry was the owner of Jerry & Sons. The only problem with this wonderful name was that there were no sons.

I mean, there *were*.

They were alive and everything. They were just lazy and burned their unearned paychecks on women, gambling, alcohol, and pyramid schemes. Exactly in that order.

I knew, because they were supposed to work shifts here, and yet, most of the time, it was just me.

"Gotta problem, Turner?" Jerry chewed on tobacco. The leaves gave his teeth a strange hue of urine-yellow. He eyed me meaningfully from across the counter.

Dang it.

I needed to bite the bullet and just do it.

But I *hated* horny teenagers who only came in to check what was under my dress.

Jerry's waitresses (or me—I was the only waitress here) wore pretty skimpy dresses because Jerry said it got them (again, me) better tips. It did not. Needless to say, wearing the uniform was a must. White and pink striped and shorter than a bull's fuse.

Since I was pretty tall for a woman, half my butt was on full display whenever I bent down in this outfit. I could always squat, but then I ran the risk of showing something even more demure than my tuchus.

"Well?" Yellow-hoodied boy slammed his fist against the table, making utensils clatter and plates full of hot, fluffy waffles fly an inch in the air. "Am I going to have to repeat myself? We all know why you're wearing that dress and it ain't because you like the breeze."

Jerry & Sons was the kind of small-town diner you saw in the movies and thought to yourself, *There's no way a crap-hole like this truly exists.*

Checkered black-and-white linoleum flooring that had seen better days—probably in the eighteenth century. Tattered red vinyl booths. A jukebox that randomly coughed up "All Summer Long" by Kid Rock, entirely unprovoked.

And Jerry's claim to fame—a wall laden with pictures of him hugging celebrities who'd made a pit stop in our town (namely, two professional baseball players who got lost driving into Winston-Salem and a backup dancer for Madonna who *did* come here intentionally, but only to say goodbye to her dying grandmother, and looked every inch of a woman who had just said goodbye to a loved one).

The food was questionable at best and dangerous at worst, depending on whether our cook, Coulter, was in the mood to wash the veggies and poultry (together) before preparing them. He was truly a great guy, but I'd rather eat crushed glass than anything his hands touched.

Still, the place was full to the brim with teens sucking on milkshakes, ladies enjoying their refreshments after a shopping spree on Main Street, and families grabbing an early dinner.

What Jerry & Sons lacked in style and taste, it made up for by simply existing; it was one of the very few eateries around.

Fairhope was a town so small you could only find it with a microscope, a map, and a lot of effort. Your-worst-ex's-dick small. And a real time capsule too.

It had one K-8 school, one supermarket, one gas station, and one church. Everyone knew everyone. No secret was safe from the gossip gang of elderly women who played bridge every day, led by Mrs. Underwood.

And *everybody* knew I was the screwup.

The town's black sheep.

The harlot, the reckless woman, the jezebel.

That was the main irony about Fairhope—it was not fair and offered no hope.

From the corner of my eye, I spotted Cruz Costello occupying a booth with his girlfriend of the month, Gabriella Holland. Gabby (she hated when people called her that, which was why I did it sometimes, although only in my head) had approximately six miles of legs, each the width of a toothpick, the complexion of a newborn baby, and arguably the same intellectual abilities.

Her waist-length, shiny black hair made her look like a long-lost Kardashian (Kabriella, anyone?), and she was equally high maintenance, making outrageous changes to the dishes she ordered.

For instance, the triple-sized, Elvis-style beef burger with extra cheese fries became a free-range, reduced-fat organic veggie burger, no bun, no fries, with extra arugula leaves and no dressing.

If you ask me, no thigh gap in the world was worth eating like a hamster. But Coulter still went along with all of her demands, because she always whined if her plate had a smear of oil by the time she was done with her food.

"Just give it up, Messy Nessy. Pick up my fork and we can all move on," the teenager hissed in the background, snapping me out of my reverie.

Heat flamed my cheeks.

While Cruz had his back to me, Gabriella watched me intently like the rest of the diner, waiting to see how this situation was going to play out. I shot another peek at Jerry before sighing, deciding it was not worth getting fired over, and crouched down to pick up the fork from the floor.

Two things happened simultaneously.

The first thing was I felt the douchebag's fingers pinch my butt cheek.

The second was I saw the flash of a phone camera behind me as someone took a picture.

I turned around, swatting his hand away, my eyes burning like I'd just opened them in a pool full of chlorine.

"What in the hell?" I roared.

The kid looked me straight in the eye, chewing on the straw of his milkshake with a vicious grin.

"I heard the stories about you, Messy Nessy. You like to slip under the bleachers with boys, don't ya? I can take you back to the scene of the crime, if you feel nostalgic."

I was about to lose my temper, job, and freedom and *really* kill the kid when he was saved by the (Southern) belle.

"Waitress? *Yoo-hoo*, can I get some help here?" Gabriella waved her arm in the air, giving her extra shiny hair a casual flip.

I pointed at that kid. "I hope you choke on your straw."

"I hope *you* choke on *my* straw."

"That's probably about accurate for size, I'm guessing."

"*Turner!*" Jerry barked, suddenly paying attention to this interaction.

"All right, all right," I muttered.

My only consolation was that with a face and pickup lines like those, *Drew* hoodie kid was bound to stay a virgin deep into his thirties.

Still, it sucked that I had to keep this job to be able to provide for Bear. Finding a job in Fairhope was no easy feat, especially with my reputation. Secretly, though, I'd always wanted to save up enough to study something I liked and find something else.

I stomped my way toward Gabriella and Cruz's booth, too angry to feel the usual anxiety that accompanied dealing with the town's golden boy.

Cruz Costello was—and always would be—Fairhope's favorite son.

When we were in middle school, he'd written a letter to the president, so eloquent, so hopeful, so *touching*, that he and his family were invited to the Thanksgiving ceremony at the White House.

In high school, Cruz was the quarterback who'd led Fairhope High to the state finals—the *only* time the school had ever gotten that far.

He was the only Fairhope resident to ever attend an Ivy League school.

The Great Hope of Fairhope (Yup. I went there with the puns. Deal with it).

The one who helped Diana Hudgens give birth in her *truck* on a stormy Christmas Eve and earned a picture in the local newspaper, holding the crying baby with a smile, blood dripping along his muscular forearms.

It didn't help that upon graduation from college, Cruz had followed in his retired father's footsteps and become the town's beloved family physician.

He was, for all appearances, holier than the water Jesus walked upon, more virtuous than Mother Teresa, and, perhaps most maddening of all, hotter than Ryan Gosling.

In. Drive.

Tall, lean, loose-limbed, and in possession of cheekbones that, frankly, should be outlawed.

He even had a pornstache he was unaware made him extra sexy. There wasn't a woman within the town's limit who didn't want to see her juices on that 'stache.

Even his attire of a blind senior CPA, consisting of khaki pants, pristine white socks, and polo shirts, couldn't take away from the fact that the man was ride-able to a fault.

Luckily—and I use that term loosely because there was nothing lucky about my life—I was so appalled by Cruz's general existence that I was pretty much immune to his allure.

I stopped at their table, leaning a hip against the worn-out booth and popping my gum extra loudly to hide the nervous hiccup from being touched by that kid. Whenever the occasional urge to speak up for myself rose, I remembered my job prospects in this town were slimmer than Gabby's waist. Raising a thirteen-year-old wasn't cheap, and besides, moving back in with my parents was not feasible. I did not get along with Momma Turner.

"Top of the mornin' to you. How can I help Fairhope's Bold and Beautiful?"

Gabriella scrunched her button nose in distaste. She wore casual skinny jeans, an expensive white cashmere shawl, and understated jewelry, giving her the chic appearance of effortlessness (and possibly French).

"How are you, Nessy?" she asked without moving her lips much.

"Well, Gabriella, every morning I wake up on the wrong side of capitalism, I'm pretty sure my car's about to die, and my back's not getting any younger. So all in all, pretty good, thanks for asking. Yourself?"

"I just got a big contract with a cosmetic company that will probably gain my blog a lot of traction, so really good."

"Wonderful!" I cooed, doing my best not to notice Cruz.

Gabriella did that thing where she posted pictures and videos of herself on Instagram, trying out new products, making you believe you could look like her if you used them too.

She dragged her plate across the table like there was a dead rat on it.

"Look, I don't want to be that person, but I don't think my turkey burger is … you know …"

"Cooked?" I curved an eyebrow. *Or turkey …*

"*Organic,*" she whispered, shifting uncomfortably.

I had a Sherlock on my hands.

Did she think she was at The Ivy? She should be happy her lettuce was washed and that the bun didn't come from a can.

"It's probably not," I agreed.

Her eyebrows slammed together. "Well, I specifically asked for organic."

"And I specifically asked for a winning lottery ticket and a hot date with Benicio del Toro. Looks like we're both having a bad day, hon." I popped my gum again.

Cruz was quiet as he usually was when I was around. The elephant in the room was that Gabriella Holland was my baby sister Trinity's best friend. And my sweet baby sister was engaged to Wyatt, Cruz's older brother.

Sounds super *Jerry Springer*? Why, I think so too.

Which meant that, technically, I had to play nice with both of these uppity gassholes. But while Cruz made a deliberate effort not to acknowledge my existence in any way, I was perfectly happy to show him what I thought about *him.*

"Do you think that kind of attitude will help you get a tip?" Gabriella asked incredulously, folding her arms over her chest. Some best friend to my sister she was, treating me like I was a dry horse turd on the bottom of her stiletto shoe.

"I don't think I should be given attitude over a diner burger's origin story," I supplied.

"Maybe if you were nicer and more conscientious, your poor son could have more opportunities."

Yup. She went there. She actually mentioned Bear.

A bullet of anger pierced my gut.

"Well, if you were just a little bit prettier, maybe you wouldn't have come in third on Miss America."

I smiled sweetly.

Clearly, I was willing to go *there* too.

Gabriella's eyes watered and her chin wrinkled and danced like Jell-O as she fumed.

"I would like to speak to management!" she cried out.

"Oh, you mean the big boss?" I asked. "The one in charge of this entire culinary empire?" I made a show of moving half an inch to turn to Jerry. "Management! Table three wants to speak to you."

Jerry rounded the counter, spitting his tobacco into a nearby trash can, already looking alert while I turned back to the happy couple.

"Anything else I can do for y'all?" My silky smile was as big and fake as Gabriella's breasts. "Maybe offer you some complimentary white truffle oil while you wait? Perhaps some foie gras?" I made sure to pronounce the 's', to keep that uneducated bimbo label alive.

I definitely wasn't doing myself any favors. But dang, getting sexually harassed by a kid my son's age and patronized by my baby sister's friend just about hurled me to the breaking point.

"Yes, actually. I can't believe Trinity—"

Gabriella's scathing remark was cut off when a choking sound came from booth number five, the one occupied by Grabby McHandson himself.

"Oh my gosh!"

"Jesus! No!"

"He's choking! He is choking on the straw!"

Karma must've heard my prayers and decided to intervene, because the guy who'd pinched my ass was now lying on the floor, clutching his neck, his eyes wide and red as he kicked his legs about, trying to breathe.

The whole diner was in a frenzy. People ran back and forth, chairs toppled, women screeched. Someone called 911. Another suggested we flip him on his stomach. And one of his friends was recording the entire thing on his phone, as if we needed more reason not to put our trust in Gen Z.

And there he was.

Dr. Cruz Costello, running in slow-mo to the kid, his sandy hair swooshing about like a *Baywatch* montage.

He performed the Heimlich maneuver on my assailant and made him cough out the piece of straw he was choking on, saving the day once again.

The jukebox, on cue, started belting out Kid Rock's "All Summer Long."

It wasn't like I genuinely wanted the kid to die.

Being a *gasshole* was not a sin punishable by death. But the fact that the entire diner glossed over the overt sexual assault I'd been subjected to was jarring, if not completely depressing.

And then there was the fact that Cruz Costello was standing there, tall and muscular and alive, bathing in the compliments everyone around us showered upon him.

"...saved the boy's life! How can we ever thank you? You are an asset to Fairhope, Dr. Costello!"

"...told your mother when you were three that you were going to become someone important, and whaddaya know? I was right again."

"My daughter is coming back from college next year. You sure you're set on Gabriella, sugar? I'd love for you to meet her."

I leaned against the counter, narrowing my eyes at the scene.

One of the teenager's friends called his mother, who was going to pick him up. Jerry tried to calm everyone down by announcing everyone would be getting complimentary ice cream, and Gabby clung onto her boyfriend's arm like she'd been surgically glued to it, fussing in his ear, urinating all over her territory.

Cruz tried to pay Jerry, but Jerry shook his head exaggeratedly.

"Your money's no good here, Dr. Costello."

Luckily for Dr. Costello, his money was good and welcome in *my* pocket. I pushed off the counter and strutted toward him, stretching my open palm up.

"I'm ready for my tip now."

Gabriella's mouth fell open.

Something mean was about to come out of it—the fact that my sister and she were best friends, that we were both going to be Trinity's bridesmaids in less than two months, didn't matter.

Today had reinforced the notion I was fair game in Fairhope, and everyone had the agency, the *God-given* right, to be mean to me. But Cruz stopped her, patting her flat ass with a lazy, lopsided grin.

He knew I loathed his golden boy act.

"Go on and wait in the car, honey."

"But Cruuuuuuz." Gabby stomped her foot, dragging his name out with a pout.

"I'll handle it," he assured her.

"Fine. But don't be too nice," she sulked, catching the car keys he threw into her hands, and sauntered out of the diner.

Cruz and I stood in front of each other. Two cowboys waiting to draw their weapons.

"Aren't I going to get a thank you?"

His whiskey-soaked voice stirred something warm and sticky and unwelcome behind my ribcage. He had that Justin Hartley kind of body you just wanted to feel pressed against you.

"For what?" I mused. "Being alive, being a doctor, or being a royal pain?"

"Saving that kid."

"That *kid* pinched my butt and took a picture of my panties."

"I didn't know that," he said evenly.

I believed him, but so what? My hackles were so high up, I couldn't even see past them.

"Tip me or get gone," I huffed.

"You want a tip?" he asked tonelessly, his dark-blue eyes narrowing on my face. "Here's one: get some better manners. Pronto."

"Sorry." I pouted, making a show of examining my nails. "Fortune-cookie advice is not a currency I accept at present. Cash or Venmo work, though."

"You don't actually expect a tip after your argument with Gabriella, do you?" He looked a little concerned for me. Like maybe on top of being a bimbo, I also possessed the IQ of a peanut butter sandwich. Sans the jelly.

"I do, actually. She knows we don't carry organic meat—or arugula. Why does she keep asking?"

If he was going to tell me the customer was always right, I was going to add him to my ever-growing list of people to murder. Actually, he was already in the top ten for every time he'd run into me at social gatherings and pretended I didn't exist.

"*Why* don't you give her a straight answer?" he quipped back. For a moment—for a small, teeny, tiny fraction of a moment—I could swear his good ol' boy mask cracked a little, annoyance seeping through it.

"*Why* don't you mind your own business?"

I noticed his eyes dropped to my lips when I said that.

I was aware I had enough makeup on my face to sculpt another life-size figure of myself and way too much pink lipstick for anyone's liking. But Cruz being Cruz, he never said anything mean or demeaning about anyone. Not even me.

I could see the nostrils of his straight Roman nose flare as he drew in a calming breath and tilted his chin up.

"Very well, Tennessee." That was the other thing. Everybody called me Messy Nessy. He was the only one to call me by my given name, and it always felt like punishment. "I'll mind my own business. Let's start now, shall we? Did you book our tickets for the cruise yet?"

Ah, yes.

Since my parents were paying for Trinity and Wyatt's wedding, the Costellos—Cruz's parents—had decided to invite both families to a pre-wedding cruise so we could all get to know each other better.

Because the Costellos were frequent cruisers, they used their loyalty points to book Trinity and Wyatt the honeymoon stateroom and two-bed staterooms for themselves and my parents.

My son Bear all but begged to room with my parents, who were going to have a private Jacuzzi and in-suite candy bar. Since it was his first ever vacation, I relented.

But that meant Cruz and I still needed to book rooms for ourselves, and since Cruz had a "real job" and I had so much free time (my mother's words, not mine), I was tasked with finding us rooms for the cruise.

"I'm working on it."

"I hadn't realized it took such effort to book tickets."

I patted my stiff, heavily-sprayed blond mane.

"Maybe for you it's easy. But us feather-headed people take a long time to do things. Where do I book these tickets anyway? The internet, yes?" I cocked my head. "It's that thing on the computer? With all the little words and kitty videos?"

His blade-sharp jaw ticked.

Just once.

But once was enough to spark unabashed joy. It was a well-known fact that *nothing* threw Cruz Costello off-balance.

"Book those tickets, Tennessee."

"Yes, sir. Will you be needing the double bed or just the queen?"

"Are you asking if I'm bringing Gabriella along?"

"Or any other almost-underage woman of your choice."

That wasn't completely fair, or the most extreme age gap amongst the dating pool.

Gabby was Trinity's age, twenty-five, and Trinity was marrying Wyatt, Cruz's older brother.

Cruz dipped his hand into the front pocket of his khaki pants. He wore casual exasperatingly well.

"Try not to mess things up when you book it, will you?"

Now that made my mask of indifference slip and shatter on the floor. Being the one who always messed up in this town might be the way I'd been pigeonholed, but in my opinion, I hadn't earned it.

"I'm perfectly capable of booking two cruise tickets."

"I'll believe it when I see it."

"You know," I mused, twirling a lock of blond hair that spilled from my unfashionable updo, "you're not even half as nice as people think you are."

"Been saving all this venom specially for you." He tilted his ball cap down like a cowboy. "Any parting words, Tennessee? I have a date waiting in my car."

Right, right, right.

His shiny Audi Q8 to go with his shiny girlfriend and his shiny life.

To that question, I answered with my middle finger, taking advantage of the fact everyone around us was talking animatedly about what happened to Straw Choker to notice.

It wasn't my most elegant answer, but it sure was the most satisfying one by a mile.

Made in the USA
Coppell, TX
17 February 2022